Advance

"*Reason to Kill* is the kind of traditional mystery I'm constantly on the lookout for but can rarely find: smart, funny, and plotted to the nth degree. Throw in an endearing, older protagonist like Amos Parisman, and your formula for the perfect read is complete"

— GAR ANTHONY HAYWOOD, author of
Good Man Gone Bad and more Aaron Gunner mysteries

"*Reason to Kill* is a twisty, classic Hollywood murder mystery with a detective who really knows his way around."

— THOMAS PERRY, *New York Times*–bestselling
author of *Metzger's Dog* and many more novels

Praise for the
Amos Parisman Mysteries

"Delightful.... Mr. Weinberger writes as his hero detects, at a measured and thoughtful pace. Most of the book's violence takes place offstage, leaving the detective to ponder and ruminate in contemplative fashion. And Amos himself proves pleasant company: a gruff mensch whose avowed atheism is balanced by a humanism that sees him tenderly caring at home for his dementia-prone wife. 'Everybody matters,' he says at one point, and as we follow his quest to find out what happened to Rabbi Ezra, we know he means it."

— TOM NOLAN, *Wall Street Journal*

"As with most good detective stories, the real pleasure here is in watching the gumshoe at work.... Sheer fun."

— *Booklist*

"Pure entertainment... As characters go, Parisman is as no-nonsense as Philip Marlowe or Sam Spade, but unlike those classic detectives, there's a bit more heart and nuance to our central character."

— *San Francisco Chronicle*

"The ill-assorted pair provide an entertaining tour of LA while they track down a killer with a surprising motive.... Worthy of an encore."

— *Kirkus Reviews*

"While the mystery is intriguing, the thoughtful, retired Jewish PI is the draw for this debut mystery. As he and his wife age, he deals with her onset of dementia with love and patience, that patience being a part of his nature as an inquisitive PI."

— *Library Journal*

"I loved *An Old Man's Game*. Amos Parisman must return!"
— CARA BLACK, *New York Times*–bestselling author of *Three Hours in Paris* and the Aimée Leduc mysteries

"Andy Weinberger has done something extraordinary with his first novel: he's written a truly great detective novel that is fresh and original but already feels like a classic. In the tradition of Walter Mosley, Raymond Chandler, and Sue Grafton, semi-retired private eye Amos Parisman roams LA's seedy and not-so-seedy neighborhoods in pursuit of justice. I don't want another Amos Parisman novel—I want a dozen more!"

— AMY STEWART, author of *Miss Kopp Just Won't Quit* and more Kopp Sisters novels

REASON
TO
KILL

An Amos Parisman Mystery

ANDY WEINBERGER

PROSPECT
·PARK·
BOOKS

Published by Prospect Park Books
2359 Lincoln Avenue
Altadena, California 91001
www.prospectparkbooks.com

Distributed by Consortium Book Sales & Distribution
www.cbsd.com

Library of Congress Cataloging-in-Publication Data
Names: Weinberger, Andy, author.
Title: Reason to kill : an Amos Parisman mystery / Andy Weinberger.
Description: Altadena, California : Prospect Park Books, [2020] | Series:
    Amos Parisman mysteries
Identifiers: LCCN 2020012655 (print) | LCCN 2020012656 (ebook) |
    ISBN 9781945551864 (paperback) | ISBN 9781945551956 (hardcover) |
    ISBN 9781945551871 (epub)
Subjects: GSAFD: Mystery fiction.
Classification: LCC PS3623.E4324234 R43 2020 (print) | LCC PS3623.
    E4324234 (ebook) | DDC 813/.6--dc23
LC record available at https://lccn.loc.gov/2020012655
LC ebook record available at https://lccn.loc.gov/2020012656

Cover illustration by George Townley
Cover design by Mimi Bark

For Lilla

A bisl zun, a bisl regn,
a ruik ort dem kop tsu legn.
Abi gezunt, ken men gliklekh zayn.

A bit of sun, a bit of rain,
a quiet place to lay your head.
As long as you're well,
you can be happy.

— "Abi Gezunt" ("As Long as You're Well")

Chapter 1

MY PHONE JINGLES just as I push the down button inside the elevator. I fumble around and reach into my pocket. Too late. Whomever it was hung up. Just as well, I think. Par for the course, really. I've been meaning to move out of Park La Brea for a long time now, probably as long as we've lived here. Funny how some things just never happen. I'm not complaining, it's too late for that, but the truth is you fall into a situation. You sign a lease. You know damn well it's not what you want, but it's comfortable enough, or at least bearable. You tell yourself over and over again you hate it—and you do—still, it's familiar. You don't have to think about it. That counts for more than you'll ever know. You give an automatic wave to the guards at the front gate. You've made peace with the sour smell in the elevator. You have stopped noticing the gray walls and dingy light fixtures. Every week you see the same sullen janitor, Guillermo, standing there hunched over his bucket, mopping up near the metal mailboxes. And okay, he's never said one goddamn word to you all these years. Still, you think you share a bond. Fellow inmates, that's who we are. Right, amigo? Prisoners in the same twelve-story art deco sanitarium.

The elevator halts at the fourth floor. A short white-haired lady hobbles on. She smooths down her skirt. She reaches over to tap the button for the mezzanine, and as she does my phone rings again. Before I can get it out of my pocket, it dies a second time. "Fuck!" I say under my breath. The old woman glares at me. "I didn't mean it," I tell her.

"Why'd you say it, then?"

"Look," I say, "leave me alone. I've had a hard day."

"It's only 11 a.m., young man."

"I've been up all night," I lie.

"Is that my problem?" she says. She points her gnarly finger in my face. "Don't say 'fuck' anymore, okay? It's rude."

I shrug. I don't like her, but she's entitled to her narrow-minded opinion, I figure. Only, everyone in this place has an opinion, that's the trouble.

Loretta and I settled here because it was cheap, but not so cheap as to be dangerous. Not like South Central or Boyle Heights. And because it was close to our jobs. And maybe as an afterthought, because it had Jews in the neighborhood. Neither one of us gives a fig about religion, you understand. My wife and I have always accepted all sorts, but being around people like yourself, *landsmen*, people who secretly enjoy eating *chozzerai* and can tell a decent joke, well, it was inviting, I guess.

Back then there was no fancy Grove shopping center. No Whole Foods. No Trader Joe's. There was the CBS lot and Canter's Delicatessen and an actual farmers' market where they sold broccoli and chicken and heirloom tomatoes. Real food straight off the truck. That was before the days of packaged candy and personalized license plates for kids. And people came from all over to be on television quiz shows and to eat. Loretta grew up in Northern California; at first this was strange to her. But I knew it because I graduated from Hollywood High, which isn't that far away, and because my cousin Shelly had an apartment just off Fairfax. This was our turf, or his turf, anyway.

Now I'm on the mezzanine. It's a bright, sunny September day. There's a breeze blowing in from the Pacific and they say it might rain later on, but I still have time to take my walk. This is what I do these days—walk. Loretta and I used to do it together before she got sick. Now it's just me. Me and twenty million other people. They all walk faster than I do, and lots of them run. They've got their fancy Italian track shoes on and their headbands, and have that determined look in their eyes that says they've only got another two miles to go and by God they're going to get there. I wish them luck. Sometimes when they sprint by me, I think I must be the oldest person in LA. Oh well, Parisman. The race isn't always to the swift, is it?

I head east on Third and turn onto Detroit, which is mostly large two-story Spanish houses that have been cut up into studio apartments. The crisp wind makes my cheeks turn red, and I have to be careful and keep my eyes on the ground because the pavement can suddenly crack or jut up, especially when it's too close to tree roots. I've stumbled a few times.

When I get to the corner of Sixth, my cell phone starts jingling in my pocket. I don't recognize the number, but so few people call me these days, I'd be a damn fool to ignore it.

"Parisman here."

"Mr. Parisman," a gravelly voice says, "you don't know me, but—"

"No," I say, "you're right. Who are you? Did you call before?"

"I tried."

"Well, next time try harder, okay?"

"I'll do that," says the voice. "Anyway, the reason I called. Your name was given to me by a Detective Marlborough. He's retired now. I believe he worked in Culver City."

"Marlborough, yeah. I knew him. Sweet kid. We haven't talked in a couple years, though."

"Yes, well," the voice continues, "Detective Marlborough thought you'd be the perfect man for the job I have in mind."

I stop and adjust the collar of my leather jacket. If I stand still much longer I'm going to come home with a cold. Loretta won't like that. "Okay. So who are you again? You never said."

"The name is Bleistiff," he says. "Pincus Bleistiff. Most people call me Pinky. It's easier to remember. Detective Marlborough said an awful lot of good things about you."

"That's terrific. You tell him the check's in the mail, okay? Meanwhile, what can I do for you?"

There's a pause. "I don't think I should discuss it over the phone. It's a little bit sensitive. But I'll make it worth your while, I promise. Maybe we could meet somewhere. Is that possible?"

"We could do that."

"Because it'd be much better, I mean, I'd feel more comfortable if we sat down face-to-face, got to know one another. Maybe have a cup of coffee somewhere. That'd be my preference. Are you free right now?"

Am I free? Hell, I've been free for months. Ever since I worked that Diamant case. The one where the shul on La Brea hired me to double-check what really happened when their famous rabbi dropped dead eating soup at Canter's. Free is a euphemism in my book. Free is what you are when you don't want to retire yet but nobody's beating a path to your doorbell. It's a terrible thing to be free like that; it's like you already have one foot in the grave, and if you're not careful, well. "Free? Sure, I'm free. You want to have coffee? I'm out walking right now, but I could meet you. I'm about a mile from Canter's. It's on Fairfax, by Beverly. Wanna meet me there? You know where that is?"

"Of course," he says. "I've lived here a long time."

"Good," I tell him. "But it'll take me maybe a half hour. I'll be at the bakery section right by the door. I have a weakness for their rugelach."

"Sure," says Pinky Bleistiff. "But how will I know you?"

"Easy," I say. "I'll be the oldest guy there. Without my Dodgers cap on I have gray hair. It hasn't been combed in a while. You'll probably think I need a haircut. Oh, and I'll be wearing my old bomber jacket from World War II."

"You were in World War II?"

"The jacket. Not me."

"Okay," he says, "fine. See you in half an hour or so."

I turn around and start hiking in the other direction. I don't know what this nudnik wants from me. And I don't trust him already. Something smarmy there in his voice. This is not about a job, no, he wants a donation, probably, for some *farkakte* cause. He's a salesman. I should plant a tree in Israel. Come on, I'll tell him. Israel's a tiny country. How many goddamn trees do they need? He won't know what to say when I put it to him that way. It may not stop him, though. He'll buy me a doughnut and a cup of coffee and I'll end up telling him everything I know. What kind of deal is that? On the other hand, he mentioned Marlborough. That counts.

The last time Denny and I worked together it had to do with a well-dressed corpse they found in an alley behind a gay bar on La Cienega. The body belonged to a pharmaceutical salesman from Denver named Norman Hearst. Marlborough, who was not naturally inclined toward homosexuals, thought the bar owner might possibly have had a hand in it. They took him downtown, chatted with him, and somehow, after the first hour, my name came up. He told them I could vouch for him. Which wasn't so surprising, really. The owner's name was Simon Goldblatt. We went to Hebrew school together. I knew him pretty well; he was a sweet pimply guy back then, and even if his voice cracked, he was never shy about chanting the blessings over the Torah.

Simon hired me a few days later to help clear his reputation. What I found out was it was way too dark inside his establishment. You could barely see the menu, let alone a stranger's face. None of the regulars noticed Norman Hearst enter or exit. And it turned out Hearst had been a happily married man, at least until the week he left Denver. His wife swore up and down that he was straight. His kids did, too. Someone had come along and emptied the cash out of his wallet, but what he was doing in the alley in the first place, God only knows. And that's where we left it. The good news is, Denny and I became friends, so I guess you could say it wasn't a total loss.

It takes a good twenty-five minutes to reach Fairfax. There are three tourist buses parked along the curb near the Farmers Market and people are milling around outside, waiting to get a table at Du-par's. A homeless woman with a cane and a cardboard sign is hobbling back and forth at the intersection and chanting incoherently to herself. She's got on a long gray overcoat, or maybe it's some kind of bathrobe. Rhinestone cowboy boots on her feet. A smile on her face. All the pedestrians studiously ignore her, I notice, but she's not crazy. She only moves forward when the light turns green, and then she stands there on the opposite corner, chanting and praying until it changes again. Her cardboard sign doesn't say she's hungry. It doesn't say her children have been taken away from her. It doesn't say she has nowhere to sleep tonight. It simply says, *Jesus wants you to love me.*

He's waiting for me at the bakery counter. Pacing back and forth with his pudgy hands behind his back. I appreciate that, somebody who gets to an appointment before I do. At first glance he reminds me of my best friend Maury's dad, Al. Al was a gambler. He played the ponies at Hollywood Park. He played poker. He bet on dog races and boxing matches. Basically, anything that moved. Sometimes he won, but mostly he lost. Which was sad, for a whole bunch of reasons. Maury was a smart kid. He probably could have gone to Harvard on the money Al left behind at the track. That was Al, just couldn't stop himself. This guy, he has the same intense, go-for-broke look in his eye. He's got on a black sport coat with three silver buttons and black slacks. The sport coat is bigger than he is. I'm thinking he got it off the sale rack at Ross. Salt-and-pepper hair, a black dress shirt and a white bow tie. Even with his shoes on, if he's over five feet tall, I'd be surprised.

I tap him on the shoulder. "You must be Pinky."

He smiles. "Mr. Parisman. Look at you. You're not the oldest guy here. Come on, let's get a table, huh?"

There's a small line of patrons ahead of us, but it moves fast. Doris, who's been here a thousand years, recognizes me. She pulls two large plastic menus from the stack and leads us to an empty booth in the rear. "Will this be okay, Amos?"

"This'll be fine, Doris. Can you send some coffee our way? We'll order more later on."

Pinky folds his hands in front of him and waits for the coffees to arrive before he opens up. Then, as soon as the waiter walks away he says, "I'm glad you could find the time, Mr. Parisman. You know, short notice and all." He pours some half-and-half into his cup, stirs it around, then tears open two sugar packets and dumps them in, too.

I sip mine black. "So what's the story, Mr. Bleistiff?"

"Please, it's Pinky."

"Whatever."

"The story. Okay. I'm in the music business."

I raise my eyebrows. "Musician? Really? I have to tell you, you don't look like any musician I've ever met. What do you play?"

"I don't play anything," he says. "Chopsticks now and then on the piano." He passes me a business card, which I pay no attention to. "I manage a few local bands. Some of them are getting some buzz right now. Maybe you've heard of Fever Pitch? Or Eros in Amber?"

"These are rock groups?" I say. "I stopped listening to that about thirty years ago."

"I guess you could call them rock. They're more indie pop in my view."

"Since I don't know what the hell that means, I'll assume it's like rock n' roll, just for my own peace of mind." I smile at him. "So you run these groups. And what's the problem?"

"Not with those groups," he says. "They're doing the clubs. They're doing fine." He shifts himself around in the booth, then leans forward. "I take care of some other bands. I don't make as much money from them, but they're steady. Know what I mean? I run a wedding band. The Altar Boys. They do pretty well. And a klezmer group. There's always a call for a klezmer band these days. Well, not always, but sometimes. Bar mitzvahs.

Anniversaries. All the Jewish holidays, of course. I figured it'd be a gold mine."

"And it's not?"

All at once he gets this sad expression on his face. "Well, it might be. Only, it seems like one by one they're disappearing."

"Who's disappearing?"

"Band members. Last year when I took them on, there were eight people. Seven guys and Risa Barsky, the lady singer. You ever hear of her?"

I shake my head. "Sorry."

"She's something," he continues. "Anyway, seven guys and a torch. That's the band. They call themselves Dark Dreidel. Actually, that's what I named them. A clarinet. Two violins. A trombone. An accordion. A guitar. Oh, and a drummer."

"You can't do without a drummer." I say this tongue in cheek, of course. I could leap in right about now, tell him that I'd been in bands back in the day, not klezmer bands, but so what? And we always had a drummer, but the drummer was usually the odd man out. What do you call a guy who hangs around with a bunch of musicians? A drummer. Some jokes are harder to forget than others.

When I say this, though, his mood gets even darker. "That's part of the trouble," he says. "The drummer has gone missing. And now two more are nowhere to be found."

"What do you mean, Pinky, when you say *missing?* I'm guessing it's more serious than they just didn't show up for rehearsal, right?"

"Well, that's how it started," he says. "The drummer, Dave Markowitz, didn't come over one night."

"Drums are a lot to schlep around," I say. "In my experience, bands have their rehearsal at the drummer's house, just to avoid that kind of thing."

He shakes his head like I don't get it. "They'd rehearse at my house. I have a whole set. They have a big separate room downstairs. Used to be a den."

"Okay, so Markowitz is a no-show."

He gives me a look like I don't understand how serious this is. "Maybe he's missing, maybe not. Markowitz doesn't matter. We could always find another drummer," he says. "But then the next week Art Kaplan isn't there. He's the lead violin."

"You gotta have a violin," I say.

"We have one left," he says, "but Jim, he isn't—" He pauses, and I can kind of see his brain spinning around in his head, weighing one word against another, trying to be fair—"Jim doesn't quite get what it's all about." He pauses again, takes a tentative sip of his coffee. "He can read the charts, he can do the fills okay, sometimes he even does a lead or two, but he doesn't feel it in his bones. He can't seem to let go. Not like the rest of them."

"Are you trying to say he's not Jewish?"

"I didn't say that. But he's not. There aren't many Jews named Callahan. In any case, he's only ever gonna be second fiddle in that band, no matter what."

"Who's the third one to go missing?"

"Risa Barsky. I could maybe get along without the other two. At least I could pull in another decent violinist. And drummers, well, you know. But Risa was the heart of the band."

He looks at me. There are actual tears welling up in his eyes. "People came from all over the San Fernando Valley to see her. What am I going to do?"

I scratch my head. "Gee, I dunno. To be honest, this really doesn't sound like my cup of tea. You want me to find them? Maybe they haven't gone anywhere. Have you tried picking up the phone and calling them?"

"Believe me, I've called."

"And you get no answer?"

He shakes his head.

"So why don't you just call the cops?"

At that moment our waiter appears. He's a bald, burly guy in his mid-thirties with shifty brown eyes and tattoos on

both of his bare arms. There's a dragon on one and a lizard on
the other. Something about him makes me nervous. I can't tell
whether he's growing a beard or he just forgot to shave for three
days. Also, I don't recognize him, and I eat here often enough,
I figure I know all the waiters. "Good afternoon, gentlemen," he
says, "so what will it be?"

Pinky seems distraught. He hasn't even looked at the menu.
After listening to him, I'm not sure he feels like eating much of
anything, but we're here, aren't we? And that's what people do at
Canter's, hungry or not.

"Maybe the matzo ball soup," Pinky says.

"Don't eat the soup," I say.

"No?"

"No, that's what killed the rabbi. He was in that booth over
there. Ate the soup. Big mistake, know what I mean?"

"So what, then?"

"He'll have a hot pastrami and coleslaw," I say. Pinky doesn't
bat an eye at this. "Me, I want a tuna melt on rye. And some ice
water, okay? Ice water for both of us. You forgot that. When did
you start working here? First thing you do, you always serve
ice water."

"Right," says the waiter, rolling his eyes as he disappears.

I turn to Pinky. "I didn't mean to—"

"No, no, it was fine. I was actually going to order that anyway. You read my mind, Parisman."

The food arrives. We eat, or rather, I eat. With Pinky, it's more
like a high school dissection. He peels off the sliced rye and
leaves it untouched to the side, then he takes his fork and pushes the hot pastrami and coleslaw around on his plate. Mostly he tells me about Risa Barsky. How beautiful she looks in a
black silk dress. How when she belts out a ballad in Yiddish, her
brown eyes glisten, and the audience is silent, transfixed. Old

people especially.

I take a big bite of my tuna melt and brush a few errant crumbs away from my chin. "You sound like you're in love with her," I say.

"Do I?" he says. "It's that obvious, huh?"

"Naw, just the tone of your voice is all. I could be wrong. Sounds like love, though."

"I love music," he says resolutely. "I love success. And I learned a long time ago how to put the two together. He lowers his fork and grins broadly. He's got a small fortune of gold fillings in his mouth. "Marlborough was right about you," he says. "You're a good detective."

"Good listener, maybe."

"So maybe you'll listen to me now when I ask you to find Risa and bring her back. It's more important than love, Parisman. Believe me, I need her if this band is going to go anywhere."

"How do you know she didn't disappear on purpose? Have you been to her house?"

"I called her a dozen times since Saturday. Just a machine. I emailed her. Nothing. And yes, I finally went over to her place in person yesterday."

"Where's she live?"

"Van Nuys. Just off Sherman Way. She has an apartment." He scribbles the address down on his napkin, passes it over to me.

"And?"

"I rang the bell. No answer. I even talked to the lady next door. She said she hadn't seen her in days."

"But still you didn't bother to call the police? About any of these people?" My head wags dismissively. "I have to tell you, Pinky, the old detective in me is beginning to wonder."

He holds up his hands. "All right," he says. "All right, here's what I'll do. You look for them. Give it a few days. And if they don't show up for rehearsal next week, I promise I'll call the cops. Is that a deal?"

"You don't think any crime has been committed, then. Is that what I'm hearing?"

"I don't know what to think," he says. "It could be something bad has happened, sure. Someone could have kidnapped them or killed them all. But I doubt it."

"Do you now? And why's that?"

He shrugs. I know I'm supposed to understand what people mean when they shrug, but I don't. A yawn I get. A shrug could be anything. "Musicians," he says, "aren't like the rest of us, are they?"

"I don't know," I say. "You tell me."

"I'm telling you they're not. I've been around this kind of thing for years. They come and they go. Some are wonderful, talented kids, don't get me wrong. You watch what they do with a sax or a guitar, and I swear to God they'll make you weep. But they don't know the practical side of anything. Their heads are stuck in the clouds. *Luftmenschen*, most of them. I've always had trouble figuring them out."

"Maybe you're in the wrong business, Pinky."

"Maybe you're right. But I still have to get to the bottom of this."

"Tell the truth, Pinky. The drummer and the fiddle player are replaceable. That's what it seems like you're saying."

"I'm not so worried about them, no. And they're old enough to take care of themselves. I just wish they'd think about the band."

"But what I'm saying is, if you want me to find them all, it'll cost you more, understand?"

He works his lips together. "Find Risa, okay? Please, that's all I ask."

I hand him my business card and tell him my fee for one missing person. I've raised the rate significantly over the years. This isn't due to the fact that I've gotten any better but because it's gotten harder and, in some respects, with all the guns and drugs out on the street, more dangerous. He doesn't bat an eye.

I tell him I'm an old man and I move a little slower than the action heroes on television nowadays. I'm no Superman, I tell him. I can't fly off a roof, although once somebody tried to push me to do just that. He says he doesn't care. Besides, he doesn't watch television. Gives him a headache.

Our waiter with the tattoos returns and lays a check down on the table. Pinky grabs it one step ahead of me. "My treat," he says.

We stand up and shake hands. He has small soft hands, like a twelve-year-old girl. Or, I dunno, maybe he's just one of those guys who rubs a lot of lotion on them. "I'll do what I can," I say.

He nods, tugs at his chin, then takes a pen and scribbles something onto the back of his business card and hands it to me. "This is my private cell," he says. "I don't give this out, understand? But you'll never get anywhere if you go through the regular number."

"Soon as I learn something," I say, "I'll give you a call."

"Deal." His eyes search mine, suddenly unsure. Or maybe he's perpetually unsure. "We have a deal, huh?"

"I'll do what I can," I repeat. I slip his card into my old leather wallet. "You'll be the first to know."

Chapter 2

I LIKE TO KNOW who I'm working for. Some guy comes along out of the blue with a big crazy story, a *leinga meisa* that makes no sense, well, it's always a good idea to check it out. I flip open my Rolodex at home and find the old phone number for Denny Marlborough, which is no longer in service. Then I call Maxine in personnel; she's been at the LAPD forever. She calls me honey. I like to think that's because she's sweet on me, but the truth is I'm not special: She calls damn near everyone honey. Wait a minute, honey, I'm going to put you on hold and I'll be right back. "Detective Marlborough," she informs me when she returns, "has moved on to greener pastures."

"He quit?"

"Last September. We still have his employment file, of course. Thank God for bureaucracy, I say."

"Tell me, Maxine, does that file of yours give any clues as to where I might find him?"

"More than a clue," she says. "He's got his new business card stapled right here, in case we ever need to reach him. He started his own home security service. Calls it Stop, Look & Listen. Remember they used to say that to us all the time when we were growing up."

"I remember it well, Maxine."

She reads me all the pertinent information. He has a plant in El Segundo where they manufacture electronic kits to stop home burglaries and unwanted intruders. I think about driving down there, but the last time I was in El Segundo it left a bad taste in my mouth. When I was a kid, it was just a lot of oil wells. Then when they built LAX, it became home to Douglas

Aircraft and Hughes and Northrop. Better, but still nothing much to get excited about. El Segundo was where you went on your way to somewhere else. I call him instead, and his secretary, a young man named Corbett or Corbin—I couldn't tell which—puts me through. We chat about old times for a while, what I'm up to these days, why he left the LAPD, then I ask him about Pincus Bleistiff.

"Oh yeah," he says, "we talked about installing a system at his house. That was last year, I guess. In the end he changed his mind. I think he thought we were trying to gouge him."

"That what he said?"

"No. It was all very cordial."

"But were you?"

"No," he says, "it was a fair price. Just more than he wanted to pay."

"Okay," I say. "That was then. So now he calls you looking for a detective?"

"Actually," Marlborough says, "he wanted to hire me to find that singer of his. I told him I don't do that, turned him down. That's when I mentioned your name."

"Thanks," I say. I don't think I'm being sarcastic, but my voice has betrayed me so many times in the past, that's what he must have heard.

"You could turn him down, too, Amos," he says after a lengthy silence. "I mean, if it's not that interesting. I just figured at your age, you might get a kick out of it."

"A check is more what I'm looking for, Denny. A kick I don't need."

"So you took him up on his offer, then."

"You bet."

"Well, if his house on Mulholland is any indication, he's got money to burn. I'd charge him the going rate, whatever it is. No discounts for senior citizens."

"Not to worry," I say. Then I tell him thanks again. And this time I mean it.

The next morning, after I get Loretta her oatmeal and set her down in front of *The Today Show* to settle her until Carmen arrives to take over the caregiving, I go into my office to think things over. I call it my office; it's really just a spare bedroom with a foldout couch, but since we haven't had overnight guests since my cousin Shelly slept there once when he got drunk and his first wife threw him out, I've taken to calling it my office. There's a small oak desk I got at a synagogue rummage sale. That's where my laptop sits, along with the Rolodex and a yellow legal pad and a jelly jar full of pens and pencils and paper clips. Also one of those art deco lamps, just a reproduction, really, but to the untrained eye it lends an air of sophistication.

There's one other venerable object—a six-inch framed black-and-white photo of a kid. His name's Enrique Avila. He's staring into the camera from an alley behind his house. A little boy with a thick mop of dark, uncombed hair and a goofy grin. He's got his whole life in front of him. Once upon a time he lived in Alhambra. His family was poor. Neither of his parents spoke much English, and he didn't stand out in the classroom. He never raised his hand, his teacher told me; he was a nice boy, a well-mannered boy, but that was the main thing she remembered about him. And then he disappeared one day on the way home from school. Just vanished into the warm June air. There were no witnesses, no clues, no ransom notes, nothing. He was eight years old. I've been looking for him, it must be going on forty years now.

I type in Pincus Bleistiff on my computer. He's not hard to find, and if you believe the internet, he is who he says he is—a music promoter. There were a number of bands in the sixties that he was affiliated with and a few record albums he somehow had a hand in. I hadn't heard of these groups, or maybe I did know them at the time, but hey, it was the sixties. My life then was so full of distractions—sex, drugs, Vietnam—I'm just lucky I came through it all in one piece. Other interesting facts that pop up: Pinky was married once. No mention of the former Mrs. Bleistiff, but he has two grown children—a son, Joshua, who lives in Israel, and Julie, who is married and makes her home in Santa Monica. There is no mention of the house on Mulholland Drive, the one Denny was going to trick out with electronic devices. I meditate on that neighborhood for a moment. Chances are he's sitting on a fortune. Either that or he's up to his eyeballs in debt.

Loretta's calling me from the living room. She wants me to change the channel. This has become a problem lately. She gets bored with the relentlessly happy talk, or she hates the blouse the weather girl is wearing this morning, or the commercials for certain women's skin products annoy her because she's tried them before and it's all a hoax, whatever. I've shown her at least a dozen times how to work the remote, but she can't get it straight. That's what she says. Or maybe it's none of those things, I think. Maybe she's scared and won't admit it. Maybe she's getting older and misses my company. Or not even me. Just another living human being.

"What's wrong with the channel you got?" I say now through the open door. "How many years you been watching *The Today Show*? You want me to tell you?"

There's no response. I sigh, push myself slowly out of the chair I'm in, and wander back. She's shaking her head. Her finger points accusingly at the screen. "What's wrong with those people?" she says. "Don't they know how sad the whole world is? Don't they read the newspaper? What's so funny?"

I grab a seat beside her, throw my arm around her shoulder, and give her a squeeze. "That's when you need comedy the most," I say, "when the whole world is going to hell."

She looks at me and sniffs. "You don't understand," she mumbles. "I want to see something else."

"Fine." I pick up the remote and roam around until I find a stout, earnest, middle-aged woman wearing a white apron and chopping leeks. "Big, green beautiful leeks," she says. "Just perfect for our *potage de bonne femme*."

"Here, you like this any better?"

"Much," Loretta says with satisfaction. "I used to cook, you know. You liked the way I cooked. Once upon a time."

I get up from the couch. "I'm going back to where I came from," I tell her. "You let me know if she starts cracking jokes about food."

In my office again I shut the door quietly behind me. I sit down at the desk, close my eyes, and cup my head in my hands. Carmen should be here any minute. Carmen is a lifesaver. She'll take Loretta out for a walk, or maybe they'll go shopping for cheap clothes at Ross and then pretty soon it'll be afternoon, and before you know it, evening. It's been like this for a while. Minute to minute. Hour to hour. I don't try to analyze Loretta anymore. You do what you can, of course. This pill, that pill. I stopped arguing with the doctors long ago. Whatever they give her helps, but the truth is, I don't have much faith left in modern medicine. Maybe that was another thing that died in Vietnam, I don't know. When you see your best friend collapse in front of you, when you see how fast a grown man can bleed and bleed and bleed in the tall spiky grass no matter what you stuff in his chest to stop it or what drugs the medic pumps up his arm or how loud you scream into the radio for the chopper to come, come, come now, come take him away goddammit—once you see that, it doesn't matter, once you see his eyes roll like gray marbles back into his head, something just snaps inside of you and your buddies grab you and pull you off and you bite your lip and you lie there in the cool grass and you forget everything you were taught to believe.

I hear the front door click open and close, followed by Carmen's sweet, "*Buenos dias, señora.*" The problem with the television is forgotten, and the two of them murmur affectionately like little birds on a wire. Lorerra loves me, okay. But she needs Carmen's voice and strong, caring arms in a way I can't possibly compete with. When Carmen walks in, that's when I start to relax. That's when I know the rest of Loretta's day will go off smoothly, without a hitch.

Two skinny Asian teenagers on skateboards are laughing and racing around the lot at Park La Brea outside our tower. Both of them wear identical blue hoodies and white shorts. Both of them forgot to put on socks to go with their high-top sneakers. Both of them need to be in school. I watch them fly by me and shake my head. This younger generation, I mutter to myself. Then, before I turn the key in my Honda Civic and head north on the Hollywood Freeway toward Van Nuys, I decide to call my old friend, Lieutenant Malloy. We go way back. He's on the homicide desk now, but I haven't talked to him in a while and I figure he probably wouldn't mind doing a little missing persons research for me. The LAPD has all those fancy new computers, after all. Why not put them to use?

He answers on the third ring. "You busy?" I say.

"I'm always busy, Amos. The city never sleeps, you know."

"Yeah, so I heard." I tell him about my meeting with Pinky Bleistiff and how he's missing his lead singer.

"Maybe she found a better gig," he offers.

"No," I tell him, "it's not like that."

Malloy is slightly younger than me. He relocated to California a million years ago from the frozen streets of Chicago. Once he saw the blue Pacific, he realized he'd died and gone to heaven, and he never bothered looking back. For an Irish Catholic who once walked a beat and cracked heads with his trusty nightstick, he's an exceedingly thoughtful man, which may be why we're close. *You shoulda been a philosopher*, I'm always telling him. *Or a priest.* That makes him laugh.

"Why didn't he just call the police?" Malloy says. "If he thinks something's gone haywire, I mean—what the hell— that's what you do, right?"

"I asked him that myself, Bill."

"And?"

"And he kind of danced around it. I think he's in love with her. He as much as said so, in fact."

"Okay, so it's romantic."

"Right," I say. "And when you put it in that light, well, then, maybe she's not missing exactly—maybe it's something else, maybe she's just trying as best she can to disentangle herself from seeing him anymore."

"Did you suggest that to him?"

"I—no. I didn't say that. I couldn't. I didn't want to break his heart."

"So you're going to politely take his money instead? That doesn't sound like something Amos Parisman would do."

"Ordinarily, I wouldn't. But Risa Barsky's not the only one. There's a drummer and fiddle player in the same band. Also vanished."

Malloy is silent for a moment. Three musicians kicks it up to a new level of concern, I figure. "Okay," he says finally. "Give me their names and anything else you got. I'll send it downstairs and get back to you."

"Thanks, Lieutenant. I owe you a lunch."

"You still owe me a lunch from the last time I helped you," he says and hangs up.

I fiddle with my radio dial while I cruise over to Van Nuys. Mariachi fades into basketball, which fades into rock n' roll, which fades mercifully into Jesus. Help me, Jesus. I decide there's nothing worth listening to finally and turn it off. By then I'm on the freeway, which isn't too bad this time of day, and I'm feeling lucky because I've slipped between the morning rush hour and the next one that supposedly starts up about two o'clock. That's what they say, but the truth is, it doesn't matter. If you live long

enough in LA you know damn well there's nothing to be done.
Too many people, too many things that can go wrong. You're
always under the thumb of the traffic god. I once drove to the
dry cleaner's on Santa Monica Boulevard, just a mile away—it
took an hour, I swear.

Risa Barsky lives in a three-story tan stucco apartment
building sandwiched between a series of similar ones. They
all have names like Vista del Sol and Rancho Sereno. Hers is
called Plata y Oro. The colors vary, but it's pretty much the
same bunch of pastel boxes all the way down the block. The
sameness, in fact, reminds me of the slipshod apartments they
used to crank out in the old gray Soviet Union. Only this is
California. These places aren't gray; they won't collapse in the
snow; the pipes won't break or be stolen by the tenants. That's
not how it works here in paradise. Each unit has a tiny balcony
of its own, big enough to park a bicycle or maybe a small barbecue grill. There are also newly planted magnolia trees on the
apron up and down the avenue. In twenty years, if the drought
doesn't kill them, they'll be spectacular. In twenty years, this
will be a venerable neighborhood, worth millions. Not now,
however. At the moment the street feels bored and barren and
so sunny you have to squint to see where you're going.

Except for yours truly, there is no one on the sidewalk. I
adjust the brim of my Dodger cap and step inside the foyer.
There's no art on the walls, but the air-conditioning makes me
feel right at home. Next to the elevator, management has placed
a round black table with a tall glass vase in the center full of red
and white roses. No water in the vase, but then you don't need
water if the roses are plastic, now do you?

Her number is B16. I ride the elevator up to the second floor
and wander down the industrial-carpeted hallway. The door to
B14 is slightly ajar, and I hear a young woman singing softly to
herself in Spanish. I stop at B16, ring the buzzer. No answer. I
wait ten seconds, try it again. No luck. Then I go back to B14
and knock. The singing stops, and a young, dark-haired woman

opens the door slightly and leans against it. I feel some kind of tension coming off her; it's like the door is all she has and she's coiled in back of it, ready to slam it in my face.

"Yes?"

"I'm looking for your next-door neighbor," I say. "Risa Barsky? You know her?"

I put a breezy smile on my lips as I say this. Take my hat off like a gentleman. Do what I can to make a good impression. You don't have to worry, I almost say to her. I'm not a rapist or an ex-husband. It's not that kind of thing. We stare at each other in silence. What must I look like to her? I wonder. A strange old white guy who forgot to shave this morning, knocking on her door, asking impertinent questions. Maybe she doesn't get out much. Maybe the walls of this apartment in Van Nuys are her whole world. I see her hand gradually relax around the door-frame. Whatever she was afraid of now subsides. She looks at me cautiously.

"She hasn't been here in a couple of weeks," she says. "How do you know her? You a friend? She owe you money?"

"No," I say. I chuckle, and it comes out sounding like a cough. "No, not at all. We've never met. But I like the way she sings. My grandson, Elijah, is having a bar mitzvah in June, and I thought maybe we could work something out." This is a bald-face lie, obviously. But as lies go, it's pretty harmless. I've told far bigger ones in my time. And it's good enough. I *could* be searching for someone to sing at Elijah's bar mitzvah, if only I had such a grandson and his name was Elijah. In this business you say what you have to sometimes if you want to hear what you need.

The woman, who I guess is a Latina, in her mid-twenties, with long dark ringlets of hair, squirms a little, and for the first time I notice she has a small child hiding behind her skirt. "I don't know what a bar mitzvah is, but Risa is in some kind of band."

"Right. So my question is, do you know where I can find her? It could be worth money to her."

"I don't know where she goes every day. We just moved here three months ago. You should ask Lola in B26." She points to her left. "They are good friends."

"Lola. B26," I say. "Thanks."

She closes the door, and I hear her saying something in Spanish to her child. It sounds soft and soothing, but then Spanish is a beautiful language and almost everything I've ever heard in Spanish sounds soothing, even when someone's telling you to go to hell.

I wander down the hall, stop at B26, brace myself, and press the buzzer. A shuffling noise comes from inside, followed by the sharp click of two deadbolt locks extricating themselves in the door. Then all at once, there she is. Lola gives me the once-over.

"Oh hi," I say. I smile. She's what my dad used to call an original or, sometimes, a pistol. A stout, feisty woman in her fifties. Her cheeks are powdered and her lips are painted red. Horn-rimmed glasses dangle from around her neck, and she's wearing a lavender velour tracksuit and tennis shoes, but her hair is in curlers and I'd be willing to bet you a dollar she's not about to go for her daily run.

"Hello there, handsome," she says. "What can I do for you, young man?" Maybe it's my Dodger cap, I think, that confused her. I take it off.

"I haven't been a young man for a long time," I say. "Handsome, okay, I'll give you that."

She grins. "All right, you win. You're neither. But still, you're here, so you must want something. Nobody knocks on Lola's door unless they want something."

I hold out my hand for her to shake. She stares at it, and I shove it back in my pocket. "The name is Parisman. Your neighbor told me you might be able to tell me where to find Risa Barsky."

"I might. I might know a lot of things. But why should I tell you?" She folds her arms resolutely in front of her. She's not suspicious or scared, exactly, not like the other woman with the

child, but I can see I'm not going to get very far without giving
her a few hard facts.

"As you must know already, Risa's in a band," I say. "What
you may not know is that she hasn't shown up for rehearsals in
a couple weeks."

"Oh no?"

"Not only that," I say, "she doesn't answer her phone or return messages or emails. Some people are starting to worry. It's
like she's on the other side of the moon."

"You a cop?" Lola asks. Her eyes narrow.

I frown. "Would it make any difference if I were?"

"No, not much," she says. "I've just never had any use for
cops. They didn't show up the one goddamn time I needed
them. You pay for their services, right? You'd think they'd
show up."

"I can't argue with you there," I say. Then I reach into my
wallet, pull out one of my little blue business cards, and hand it
to her. "I've been paid to find her. My client cares about her. He's
hoping she's all right, but he's anxious, you know. It's keeping
him awake at night. Like I say, she hasn't shown up in a while.
That's not normal."

Lola looks hard at my card. There's not much printed on
it—just my name and address and phone number and what I
do for a living now and then. Finally she lowers it, then heaves
a sigh.

"Who's your client?"

"I can't tell you that," I say. "Some people probably would.
Some people would say anything to get you to help. That's not
me. Not how I work. But you wouldn't know him anyway."

"Fair enough," she says.

"Tell me, Lola. Is there a manager around? Somebody with
a passkey? I'd love to take a real quick peek inside her apartment. Just to be sure she wasn't tied up in the bathtub or something like that."

"Is that what you think?"

"I don't know what to think. She doesn't answer her phone. She doesn't come to the door. Maybe she hasn't gone anywhere. Maybe she's in a coma, maybe she's still alive, maybe she's hurt, but if—God forbid—she's lying there dead on the floor, well, you're going to smell it pretty soon."

Lola looks at me sternly. "You wait here, buster. I'll be right back." Something in her manner has changed. The door slams in my face. Then, before I can speculate on what the hell's going on, she's back again and she's marching me double time like a drill sergeant down the hall toward B16. "You're a damn good talker," she says. "And I don't do this for anybody, you understand? Not ordinarily, I mean. Not unless I believe them." She halts at the door and produces a large gold key chain with a rabbit's foot attached. "Risa gave me this, just in case." She puts the key in the lock and twists. It opens. "Go on in, Mr. Detective. You look around. But you don't touch anything, and you have exactly five minutes. That's all. And remember—I'm keeping my eye on you."

I nod. "You're very kind, Lola. I appreciate it." I step gingerly into the darkened living room, which, with the blinds drawn, probably looks and feels like every other living room in this apartment complex. Then Lola switches on the lights behind me, and the first thing that comes to my attention is how messy everything is.

"Oh my God," Lola whispers. Everything is overturned. Pillows that should be propped up neatly on the couch are strewn on the floor. A large campaign poster of Barack Obama is hanging askew over the mantel, and a bundle of sheet music is scattered on the rug. In the kitchen, the three wood-veneer cabinet drawers have been yanked out, and someone has tossed all the silverware into the sink. I press my lips together and move quickly and quietly from room to room, with Lola right on my tail. No sign of Risa Barsky.

In the bedroom I pause and turn around. Like everything else, it's a jumble. The nightstand has been upended. There's a scrapbook lying on its side and a handful of fashion magazines she was apparently reading. There's also a small torn black-and-white photo staring up at me next to the bed. I bend down to check it out. It looks as though there were two people in it once upon a time, but the person on the right is gone, or maybe ripped to shreds. Now it's just a portrait of a young, dark-eyed, voluptuous woman in a tight sweater. I pick it up.

"Mind if I hang on to this for a while?" I ask Lola.

"Yes, I do," Lola says. "It's Risa's. Leave it the hell alone. Didn't I tell you not to touch anything?"

I show her the picture. "You recognize this woman?"

"No," she says, "but that doesn't matter. It's not yours. It belongs right where you found it."

"Okay, okay, you win." I nod and drop the picture, which floats back down to the carpet.

The bed is unmade, though the left side is neat and tidy while the right indicates there was once a living, breathing person there. "Does she own a suitcase?" I ask.

"Every woman in the world owns a suitcase," Lola says contemptuously. "You never know when it's time to move."

"So where would Risa keep hers, do you guess?"

She points with her head. "That closet, probably. On the rack above her clothes. I saw it in there, if I remember."

Risa Barsky has a long foldout closet with twin wooden doors. I pry them open cautiously and check out the overhead rack. Nothing. Some skirts and pants and blouses down below, but at least half the hangers are bare. "Looks like she left in a hurry," I say.

We walk back toward the front door. Lola taps me forcefully on the shoulder. She's staring hard now; this brief tour of her neighbor's has upset her. "Okay," she says, "I let you in. Now you owe me. Tell me what you think."

I shrug. "What do I think? Well, that should be pretty plain, right? I think she's in trouble. Somebody—some man—wants something she has. A woman would never do this. So a man. Maybe he's an old lover, maybe he's still fuming about how it ended and he wants to get back at her. Scare her half to death. I can't think of a better way to do that than to walk right in and tear up the place, can you?"

Lola shakes her head. "I guess not," she says.

"And then later that day she came home from wherever she works. She looked around and got the message. She's not stupid. She probably knew who he was, what he was capable of. That he might come back. She needed to protect herself, so she packed her bag and left."

"She's had a lot of boyfriends," Lola admits. "But how would he get in without breaking down the door?"

"Maybe she gave him a key in a weak moment. Or maybe he stole her key and made a duplicate without telling her. You're right, though," I say. "He just walked in the door."

We head back toward B26. Lola asks me if I'd like to come in, have a cup of coffee, talk. "Why not?" I say.

Her apartment is much warmer and more orderly. Everything is in its place, but she's obviously been here a very long time, long enough to invest it with her own personality. When she sets her glasses on her nose from a certain angle, she looks a little bit like an owl. She must have embraced this years ago, I figure, because there seem to be lots of owl tchotchkes everywhere you turn. Owl paintings. Owl throw rugs. Owl salt and pepper shakers. She has a thing about owls. She sits me down at the Formica table in the kitchen nook and presently I'm nursing a mug of black French roast. Lola sits across from me with her own cup warming her hands.

"When was the last time you saw her, Lola?"

"I'm not good with time," she says. "Four or five days ago? A week?"

"And how did she seem to you then? What did you talk about? She say anything? Was she scared?"

She shakes her head. "No, but I'm scared," she says. "Should we call the police?"

"I thought you didn't care for the police."

"I know, I know. But this isn't about me. Risa's a friend. And like you said, she's in trouble. She moved to this complex about a year ago. I was still married then, barely. She helped me get through my divorce."

"That's what friends are for. Maybe *you* should call the police, Lola. I'm thinking about doing it myself."

"All right," she says. "I will. And while I'm at it, I'm going downstairs to check her mailbox, too." She holds up a smaller bronze key attached to the gold chain with the rabbit's foot. "Risa left me a copy, just in case she was ever on the road with a band, you know. I haven't been too good about checking it, though."

"She gets a lot of mail?"

"I don't know. The usual. Magazines, bills, requests for donations. She's a big donor to political causes. Well, maybe not a big donor. But a regular one."

When we finish our coffee, Lola and I ride the elevator down to the ground floor where there's a large bank of mailboxes. She opens Risa's, pulls everything out, and hands it to me. There's a Wells Fargo statement. Also a phone bill and a heating bill and one from a dentist named Samuel Wong in Culver City. A *New Yorker* that's a week old, a plea for money from Planned Parenthood, and a glossy invitation to a new Vietnamese nail salon coming soon to Sherman Oaks. At the bottom of the pile is a small powder-blue envelope from Pincus Bleistiff. It's dated seven days earlier.

"So how much does she trust you?" I ask Lola.

"What do you mean? We're best friends. Best fucking friends in the world. She trusts me with everything."

"What I mean is, seeing as how she's missing and may be in trouble, do you think she'd mind if you took it upon yourself to look at her mail?"

"Isn't that against the law?"

I sigh. She's a long way from being a child; surely she gets where I'm going. "A lot of things are against the law, Lola, but sometimes, if you have to, if it's your best fucking friend, you do it anyway, you know what I mean?"

"Yeah. Yeah, I know."

She stares at me and folds her arms, but she doesn't say anything more, and I take her rumpled brow and prolonged silence as a form of consent. With my thumb I pry open Pinky's letter and read it aloud.

Dear Risa, we missed you the last few times. I'm writing you an old-fashioned letter tonight because I'm at my wits' end. You don't answer your phone or email and we have to have a resolution to this or the band simply can't go on. I hope you know how important you are to us. If there's something wrong, if any one of us said something that offended you, please, please tell me. I'm here to help. Love, Pinky

"Do you know this fellow—this Pincus Bleistiff?" I ask, trying not to sound too disingenuous.

Lola shakes her head. "Sounds like one of her musician buddies. There were a lot of guitar players and guys with saxophones trooping in and out of her place. Sometimes she slept with them. Sometimes they slept on the couch. That was one area of her life I never got involved in. I like to get out on the dance floor now and then, but I'm not very musical."

I open the Wells Fargo statement. There's nothing there to write home about. The phone bill gives me more hope. Seems like she made a ton of calls last month to one particular number. I pull out my notepad and jot it down. "All right, fine," I say. "You weren't very musical. But who was her last boyfriend?"

Lola kind of winces. "The last boyfriend? Or the last one I can name? Which?"

"Is there a difference?"

"Like I say, people trooped in and out of her place at all hours."

"Think, Lola."

"Okay, I don't know where he stood in the lineup, but the

last man she seemed to be sweet on was a guy named Ray Ballo."

"And what can you tell me about him?"

"He was much younger than her, in his mid-twenties. Tall, skinny, long dark hair. Cute, but he could stand to wash his hair more often, if you ask me. Blue jeans and cowboy boots, that's all he ever wore. He played bass in a country-western group, I think, but I could be wrong about that."

"Ray Ballo." I write his name down on my pad. "What'd she say about him?"

"Hell," she says, "I don't know. It was just girl talk. He was a gentleman. He brought her flowers one time, I remember that. That meant something to her. Made him special. And she liked his brown eyes, she said, oh, and the way he treated her in bed. Very slow. Very formal."

"She talked about how he was in bed?"

"We're best friends, remember?"

After I say goodbye to Lola, I cruise the neighborhood a while. Van Nuys is in the exact middle of nowhere. It always has been. When I was a kid in the olden days, if you lived in LA, you prayed that your parents wouldn't move to Van Nuys. It was a guaranteed death sentence. Death by boredom. But that was then. Now, three million more people have moved in, and there are hardly any houses or apartments for rent. It's close enough to downtown that it doesn't matter. They'll gladly crawl along on the freeway, they'll live large chunks of their lives in their cars if they have to. And they don't care how ticky-tacky or ugly it is, they're just looking for that one-bedroom that doesn't cost them more than their college degree. Welcome to Van Nuys.

Chapter 3

I STOP ALONG Sherman Way and grab a cheeseburger at a retro coffee shop called Dinah's. When you push through the glass doors, the first thing you notice is how clean and perfect everything is. Frank Sinatra is crooning on the jukebox, the polished linoleum floor is all black-and-white squares, and there's a slavish exactitude to the leatherette booths, all of which make me think this place isn't as ancient as it would seem; in fact, it probably opened just last Tuesday. The waitress wears tight blue designer jeans and running shoes. Her thick black hair is tied up in a ponytail. She looks Vietnamese or Thai. She might be twenty years old; she might also be twelve. She talks very fast and offers only the briefest of smiles as she takes my order. Coffee, cheeseburger, fries, no problem. Then she's gone. I glance around at the other clientele, then pull out my cell phone and call my old buddy, Omar Villasenor.

Omar dropped out of the Police Academy last week, which made me sad at first because I pulled a lot of strings to help get him in there. He said he wanted to make something of his life. I could understand that. His teenage years growing up in Boyle Heights weren't much to crow about. He could have easily landed in prison, but luck intervened. Omar says it was me who intervened, that I saved him from the cops at the Hollenbeck Station, that they would have happily nailed him to the wall forever on whatever phony-baloney charge they could find. Some of that's true, I guess; the Hollenbeck boys had a certain reputation. But that was a long time ago, and now he's like my younger brother. When he joined the academy, I was so excited, I went out to Crosshairs in Torrance and bought him a pistol.

A Glock just like my own, except his is a fifth-generation and mine is from the Pleistocene. Of course, when he quit, the first thing he wanted to do was give it back, said he didn't deserve it, but I wouldn't hear of it. Keep it, I told him. I know you; you'll need it someday. So it's a mutual admiration society we've got going—my age and occasional wisdom, his brute strength and native intuition. Plus the gun.

The phone rings four times. "You awake?" I say when he finally answers.

"Are you kidding me? I've been up for hours, man," he says, though the slow, meandering way this comes out of his mouth makes me doubt it.

"Good. Glad to hear it. I've got a new case, Omar. Now that school's out, I thought you might be interested."

"School's definitely out, yeah," he says. "I wasn't too good standing at attention and taking orders."

"You know something, amigo, my father used to say there are only two kinds of people in the world: the ones who need a paycheck and those who want to be their own boss. If you're one kind, you can't be the other. That's just how it is."

"I guess," Omar says. He doesn't seem all that sorry with his decision. It is what it is. "So now I know."

The coffee arrives, along with two tiny plastic complimentary containers of half-and-half. I put them aside, drink it black. I tell Omar I haven't gotten paid yet, but not to worry. I give him the limited information I have about my meeting with Pincus Bleistiff, about the other two musicians who are no-shows, then move on to my brief tour of Risa Barsky's ransacked apartment.

"Sounds like an ex-boyfriend," is Omar's first comment. "She's lucky she wasn't home when he knocked on the door."

"Yeah, only now she's missing in action and we've gotta find her."

"Hey, where I come from, that's guaranteed employment," he says.

"I'm glad you care about this stuff, Omar."

"I care. I care plenty, man."

Neither one of us talks for a while. Then Omar clears his throat. "I bet she's crashing with one of her girlfriends somewhere," he says. "Either that or her current guy. At the end of the day, it's all about protection."

"Okay," I say, "I'll buy that. But that's not going to last. Sooner or later, she either has to make peace with her intruder or disappear altogether. And the rent is coming due for that apartment. She's in a bind, wherever she is."

I drop Ray Ballo's name as someone Omar might want to check into. That the next-door neighbor said he played bass in a country band. That he was maybe thirty years old, tall, dark, good-looking. I leave out the part about how sweet and formal he was in bed.

My cheeseburger and fries land in front of me. There's also a sprig of parsley and a thin pathetic trio of orange slices curled along the side. Is this how they decorated food back in the fifties? Really? I tilt my neck at the waitress. I nod, I smile appreciatively.

"Anything else?" she asks. Another quick smile. Omar's yammering in my ear. Long ago I recognized that a man, especially this man, just can't do two things at once—not with one behind—not unless he's half-assed, as my cousin Shelly would say. Anyway, before I can open my mouth, she's gone, and whatever Omar said vanished into one of the dark alleys of my mind.

"Today's Tuesday," I say. "Why don't you see if you can turn up Ray Ballo by Thursday afternoon. That enough time?"

"Sure, sure," Omar says. "It's not that big a town. There are only—what—five hundred clubs in Los Angeles that would hire a country western band on any night. And that's assuming, of course, they aren't on tour."

"You're funny," I say. "But I bet you find him anyway."

"I'll do what I can, amigo. Give me a call Thursday. But not until after three, okay? I have to take Lourdes to her doctor. She doesn't drive yet."

"Will do."

I finish my cheeseburger. The fries have grown cold and don't sit too well in my stomach. I end up leaving most of them on the plate, along with the three limp orange slices. The truth is, I shouldn't eat that kind of grease at my age. Not if I want to live forever, and who doesn't?

When I get home, Loretta is playing some kind of strange card game with Carmen at the kitchen table. Carmen is losing, or maybe she's just pretending to lose. "You are so lucky, chica," she says, shaking her head as she folds the cards and adds up numbers on a yellow legal pad. "Beginner's luck. *Ay, Dios mío!*" Loretta is giggling. "What's the score now?" she wants to know. "Tell me the score!"

In the solitude of my office with the door closed, I commune with Enrique Avila's framed photo for a while. I run my fingers over his face. I touch his black, thick, unkempt hair, his high-top sneakers. I study the sunlight in the alley, guess what time the picture was taken. It's been so many years. His parents have passed away and his kid sister has a family of her own near the airport, last I heard. She's moved on; I haven't yet. Somehow, in spite of all the evidence to the contrary, a small stubborn part of me is convinced that he's still out there and still alive.

I put in a call to Lieutenant Malloy. It's probably too soon for him to have dug up anything yet, but I'm compulsive. When she was in her right mind, Loretta used to say I was relentless, which was not a compliment where she came from. I can tell by the way he answers the phone that he's had a rough day. "Make it short, Amos. I've got a murder-suicide in Boys Town and a string of burglaries in Hancock Park."

"Don't let me interrupt, Bill. But I just came back from Van Nuys and I thought you might be a little more interested in my missing person case if you looked at the inside of her apartment."

"Oh yeah? What's so interesting?"

"Well, for one thing, someone came through and trashed the place."

"Was she among the trash?"

"Fortunately not," I say. "And her suitcase is gone, too. There's definitely something wrong with this picture."

"She's scared," he says. "Someone's trying to scare her. I dunno, maybe he's trying to kill her, but I doubt it. So now she's on the run. Can't say I haven't seen this movie before."

"Right. Me, too. You haven't had a chance to track down the other musicians yet, have you?"

There's a muffled silence over the phone, like he's busy talking to someone else. Then he comes back on the line. "No, no, not yet. Like I say, there are a few other things on my plate at the moment. I'll get back to you, okay?"

"Sure, Bill, sure."

The thing about Malloy, one of the best things, in fact, is that he's true blue. He will definitely call me back. It may be two weeks, it may not be until after midnight, but I know when he says something, he means it. In the bureaucratic bowels of the LAPD, that counts for a lot. I couldn't get far without him.

An hour later, Carmen brings Loretta into the bedroom, helps her slip into her white frilly nightgown, and tucks her in. Then she returns to the living room, flicks off all but the essential lights, and puts on her sweater. While she's clearing the table and hunting around for where she left her purse, I emerge from my office. I pull out several twenties and hand them to her. "You do such good work," I tell her. I want to hug this woman. "You make Loretta smile."

"She is a wonderful person," Carmen says. "A special person in my life. I am blessed. I think about her, you know, even when I am working at one of my other jobs. She is often like a child, but then there are always some times in the day when she lets me see the way she used to be." She shakes her head slowly. "I can't explain. But it must be hard for you, señor."

"It is what it is, Carmen. Thank you." I hold open the door for her and watch her retreat down the carpeted hall toward the elevator.

Two hours later, I'm in my pajamas and about to turn in when my cell phone rings. It must be Malloy, I think. I pick it up, and a woman's voice comes on the line.

"Mr. Parisman?"

"That's me."

"It's Lola. Lola Emery. You know, Risa's neighbor?"

"Oh yes, of course. What can I do for you, Lola?"

There's a pause. "You left me your business card and—"

"Is there something you forgot to tell me, Lola?"

"No, not exactly," she says. "But I thought you ought to know. Risa was just here a few minutes ago. She came back for some clothes and cosmetics and a few other things. Threw them in a shopping bag. I heard some noise, so I went out and spoke with her."

"Did you tell her people are worried about her?"

"I did. I mean, not in those words, but I told her you'd been around."

"Did she tell you where she was staying? Or what she was doing? Did she know who ransacked her apartment?"

"No, yes, I don't know. She was only here for a few minutes. She said she couldn't stay, that it might not be safe. There was someone in a car downstairs waiting, I think. It was all very fast."

"Well, at least she's alive," I say. "That's good news. How'd she look?"

"What do you mean?"

"I don't know. You tell me."

"She looked—she looked fine. Scared but fine. Beautiful. What can I say? She was in a hurry."

"Did you get a glimpse of the car she drove off in?"

"I heard it, that's all. She ran down the stairs. By the time I got back to my place and looked out the window, it was gone."

"Well, thanks, Lola. If she comes back again, will you do me a big favor?"

"Sure, what's that?"

"Give her my card. Have her get in touch."

Chapter 4

THE NEXT MORNING, on my way out the door, I stop at my mailbox. Still no check from Bleistiff, but I'm not discouraged. The way the mail works, someone told me once, the only reason you get anything at all, is that in the end it's easier to just deliver it instead of dumping it down a manhole. And that was a guy who worked for the United States Post Office.

I climb into my ancient blue Honda Civic, and with the brown paper shopping bag they gave me at Peet's I spend a few minutes scooping up the dental floss, the Post-it notes, the dry-cleaning receipts, the old gum wrappers, and other debris scattered around on the floor and on the passenger seat. I'm a tidy fellow at home, but somehow here in the car I let myself go. Don't know why this always happens, but it does. Every month or so I poke my head in, frown, and vow it will never happen again.

There's a parking space in front of my local pharmacy on Third, which is a minor miracle. The store is air-conditioned, and some kind of plaintive electronic Mexican music is being piped in, not quite loud enough to hear but not soft enough to ignore, either. I go all the way to the rear where they're filling prescriptions. There's a tall, gorgeous Ethiopian clerk in a powder-blue smock standing behind the counter. I ask her if they have that brand-new drug that's supposed to help with memory loss. "You know what I'm talking about?" I ask. "The one on television?"

Last time we met with Dr. Ali, he mentioned it, thought it might do Loretta some good. You could give it a try, he said. No promises, of course. The medical profession in general, and Dr.

Ali in particular, have long ago backed away from that kind of blanket assurance. They mean well, but beyond a certain point it's just a guessing game; they're shooting in the dark. My friend smiles broadly. She has such beautiful white teeth, I think. Beautiful cheekbones and astonishing deep green eyes. In the olden days, when I was single, a woman like this could lead me into trouble, or out of it, for that matter. I wouldn't care. Now she leads me down the aisle, past the aspirin and the allergy sprays and the sleeping remedies, right to it.

"It's very expensive," she says with concern, scanning the label, "but even so, we can't keep it on the shelf. I think it's made from jellyfish. Something like that." She's just being honest, not trying to sell me. If anything, it's a warning. I know that, which only makes me want to buy it all the more.

Traffic is light along La Brea. A stiff breeze has been blowing all night and now it's one of those magnificent crystal-clear days ad men used to write about when they sold plots of Los Angeles to the world. I turn west on Beverly. It's the middle of the week. The sushi bars are closed until later, as is the boutique ice cream parlor and L.A. Eyeworks. A gaggle of tourists in baggy shorts and sweatshirts has started queuing up outside the cyclone fence at CBS. Me, I've never cared enough about television to want to sit in an audience, let alone stand in line for hours for the privilege. Otherwise it's quiet. I count just half a dozen Orthodox Jews on their way to shul with their beards and black suits and Borsalino hats, and to my happy surprise, there's not a single homeless body lying on the sidewalk. *Things are looking up, Parisman.*

I make a right at Crescent Heights which turns into Laurel Canyon at Sunset. Soon I'm climbing a long, winding hillside framed in shadows. Scrub oak and eucalyptus on either side. Famous people used to live in the remote corners of this place, and maybe some still do. Just not the famous people I know anymore. That's the problem. You get older. Certain celebrities you resonated with—we called them stars back then—certain comedians make you laugh when you're a kid, certain actors you always go to see. They're your family, your tribe. You collect them, one by one. Then, after a while, you stop. You say that's it, what's the point? But other people—younger people—they're coming along, too, and they don't know your kin. They have their own favorites. Singers and comics and stars you never heard of. And pretty soon there's this great chasm between the generations. Nothing you can do. If I say Milton Berle or Jackie Gleason to Omar, for instance, he'll just look at me.

At the top of Laurel Canyon is Mulholland Drive, a spectacular road with views of Hollywood and beyond. Weekend nights, we'd come up here as teenagers in our parents' Plymouths and Oldsmobiles. It seemed remote from the city back then, and more to the point, it was a great place to fool around in the back seat with girls. None of us knew exactly what we were doing. We wanted: That was obvious. We wanted so much, it hurt. But I can't say how much we really achieved on those dates. Of course, you could always brag. You could walk into chemistry class Monday morning and say anything you liked— no one would know. No one would ever call you a liar. I took a bunch of charming ladies up there. I always had high hopes, and what I recall now is that, though I tried my best, I rarely hit the ball out of the park. It was a different time, maybe. Toni Funicello told me once—after I had worked my way painstakingly through two layers of her clothing, plus a girdle—that she wanted to, she really did, but she just couldn't. She was a good Catholic girl, she said; she was saving herself for her wedding night. Anyway.

Pincus Bleistiff's home is not too hard to find. Like most places around here, it's a mini fortress. I have to halt at the wrought-iron gate. I lean out of my car window and press a red call button that activates a plastic box fitted onto a post by the driver's side. I don't recognize the voice that answers, but it doesn't matter because the gate slowly swings open and I proceed down a one-lane cobblestone path, past a cluster of wild oaks toward the main house. It's a two-story affair with re-inforced stone set back behind a well-trimmed, very green lawn. Kind of like a castle, but minus the moat and the turrets and those tiny cutout places where archers used to crouch. That's my first impression, anyway. The slate roof is pea green and way steeper than it needs to be for Southern California. A good roof for Norway, I think. That's one explanation. Or maybe the architect thought we were due for another Ice Age, I dunno. The front door is made of solid oak. It's painted dark blue and has a big black metal knob in the shape of a bear claw. Which adds still another layer of unease. That's my second impression. It's like I'm caught in the middle of *Hansel and Gretel* and *Little Red Riding Hood*—all those dark Teutonic fairy tales that used to keep me up at night.

Bleistiff swings open the door, sees who it is, smiles. "Paris-man!" he says. He grabs my hand, pumps it. He's wearing gray jeans and a lavender T-shirt that's one size too big for him. Across the chest, in gold block letters, it reads *Hydrogen is in the air.*

I look at it. "What are you trying to say, Pinky?"

"It's a joke," he says. "Hydrogen *is* in the air."

"Right."

"But the minute you point that out," he says, "some people—people who don't read, don't think, don't know anything—they get nervous. Trust me. I've seen it happen a thousand times in my life. You want to mess with someone's mind, you know what you do? Just tell the truth."

"You pack a lot into one line," I say. "But yeah, okay, I get it."

"I thought you would."

He puts his arm around me and we go inside. He's got a large cushy living room with a bay window that looks out over Hollywood. Two plum-colored couches on opposite sides with spotlights streaming down from the ceiling. Lots of fluffy throw pillows and other chairs and small tables scattered around. It could hold two dozen people, easy. There's a white baby grand piano facing the windows and a young woman working it over diligently with a dust cloth. I spot another one who looks just like her, maybe it's her mother, stouter, shorter, in sweatpants and sneakers, standing in the kitchen looking on. She's holding a plastic bucket and a mop.

I point to the piano. "I thought you don't play any instruments."

"Oh that? No, I don't. I bought that at an estate sale years ago. Someone said it belonged to Liberace. That he practiced on it. No proof, of course. What I was told."

He points out some of the other rooms, including the practice room downstairs. There's a full drum kit and music stands, another piano, anything a musician could want. Then we go back up to the living room. He offers me coffee and I shake my head. "I just came by to chat about the case," I say.

"Hey, that's great," he says. "Because I have some news, too. Last night Dark Dreidel had a practice and guess who showed up? Markowitz, the drummer, and Art Kaplan, my lead fiddle."

"So they're not missing after all," I say. "That mean you're reducing my fee?"

"No," he says. "Of course not."

"So where'd they disappear to?"

"The drummer said he was stuck in jail in San Diego. Held incommunicado. Between you and me, I don't believe him. I bet it was Tijuana. He could have called from San Diego, wouldn't you say? Even from jail. In America, you always get a call, right? Don't they let you call?"

"Maybe, yeah. In America. But maybe he just didn't call you."

"Yeah, well, he should have. He has a little drinking problem. I guess it got away from him. I'm thinking about finding a replacement. We can't have a *shicker* like that in the band. That won't work."

"And Kaplan?"

"Kaplan? Kaplan was just a mix-up. His mother had a

stroke and died in Brooklyn. Nobody expected it. He rushed back home to be with her, which I understand. But then there was the funeral. That took some time. He told his roommate to let us know."

"And?"

"And that guy's a flake. The roommate. He dropped the ball."

"So that leaves Risa Barsky," I say. "Which is what I came here to talk to you about."

"You found her?" He leans forward. His eyes are fixed on mine. "Is she okay?"

"Haven't found her yet, but as of last night, she was alive and well." Then I tell him a little bit about my encounter with Lola Emery, how she let me walk through Risa's battered apartment. "Clearly," I say, "somebody's out there who doesn't like her."

Pinky shakes his head. "I don't get it," he says. "Everyone loves Risa. Everyone. She walks in, the whole room lights up. You know what I'm saying?"

"Maybe an old boyfriend didn't have the same opinion," I offer. "You know anyone she dated?"

He shakes his head again. "She hasn't been in California very long. A year or so. And we never talk about that stuff. Just, you know, music gigs. Like I say, everybody liked her."

He rises slowly from the couch, goes to a nearby desk, and returns with some small glossy black-and-white headshots of Risa. "I forgot to give you these," he says. "They're from a few years back. From when she was working the clubs in New York. She's put on a little weight since then. We were going to make a record and—"

"Thanks."

"And well, maybe they'll do you some good."

He hands them over to me. There are six photos in all; I glance at them one by one, then tuck them into my jacket pocket.

"Here's the thing, Pinky. This isn't just a missing person case anymore. I'm happy to keep hunting for her, but now that somebody's out there threatening her, or at least scaring her half to death, well, the cops are going to be involved. At least the Van Nuys cops. There's probably no way around that."

"I understand," he says. The mention of police has darkened his mood. He checks his wristwatch and makes a slight grimace, like he just remembered an appointment he has with a federal prosecutor. He walks me to the door. He reminds me of what he said the other day at Canter's. That he'd promised to call the cops if it wasn't resolved. "But now Markowitz and Kaplan are back, right? So we're getting somewhere. And they can play without her for now. They're pros."

"I'm sure they can," I say.

His arm moves tentatively to my shoulder. He leaves it there for a few seconds. It's a tiny gesture, so tiny and harmless it almost didn't happen, except it did. I'm not offended, but it does make me wonder. Maybe he's thinking I'm as overwhelmed as he is inside, or maybe everything is naturally personal in his world, or maybe he's one of those touchy-feely Hollywood guys who's been around so long he doesn't know any other way to express himself.

"I just want her to be safe," he mumbles. "That's the long and short of it, Parisman. Really, that's my only interest. You want to call the cops, you go ahead."

I don't tell him about my conversations with Lieutenant Malloy. I tell him I'll keep on it and get back to him as soon as I learn anything else. I settle into my car and turn the key. And I'm halfway down the cobblestone driveway when I realize that I completely forgot to ask whether or not he mailed my check.

By the time I get down from Laurel Canyon, my stomach is telling me I'm hungry. I stop at an organic cafeteria on Sunset near Cahuenga. It's right across the street from the mom-and-pop bank I used to go to before they got big and forgot who their customers were. The cafeteria has a line out the door, but it moves quickly. It's full of twentysomethings lost in their cell phones, which doesn't surprise me since that's what most of LA looks like. Everyone is friendly, or distracted, or both at once somehow. I check out the handwritten overhead food menu. I've been here before. It's a place where they specialize in hummus and couscous and tahini and fresh-squeezed lime drinks infused with ginger and a few other mysterious ingredients. I play it safe with the hummus platter, a small Greek salad, and a large iced tea. This is how I'm trying to eat these days, or rather this is how Dr. Flynn would like me to eat. He's also told me a dozen times that he'd prefer it if I chose some safer line of work, too, but that's not going to happen.

I eat half the salad and about a third of the hummus platter before I lose interest altogether. Then I call Lieutenant Malloy. He seems in a better frame of mind. Maybe he's had lunch. Yeah, maybe that's it.

"You can forget about two of the missing musicians, Bill. I'll bet that's a load off your head."

"Which two?"

"The drummer and the fiddle player. They both turned up for rehearsal. The drummer claims he was locked up in San Diego but my client thinks it was Tijuana."

"Locked up where? For what?"

"Locked up? Where—I don't know, probably a county facility. For what? Try drunk and disorderly. David Markowitz."

"That should be easy to track down," he says. "And the fiddle player? What jail was he in?"

"Went to Brooklyn for his mom's funeral, apparently. But forget about him. The problem—and it's a real one—is Risa Barsky, the singer. I went through her apartment."

"Yeah, I know," he says. "Somebody trashed it. You told me already."

"Sorry, I'm an old man, an *alte katchke*. I repeat things. You will, too, someday."

He ignores my little jab. "And still no sign of her, huh?" he asks. "Nothing?"

"Well, not nothing. Looks like she came back after it happened, grabbed a few schmattes, and left. The neighbor saw her come back last night for five minutes to collect a few more things, but she didn't stick around the second time, either. What do you think?"

Malloy doesn't speak for a while. "I think you should call the Van Nuys Police, let them handle it. Not my bailiwick, is it?"

"No, it's not. But that's not what I mean, Bill."

He clears his throat. "No, of course not. You want me to tell you what I think, which you're hoping comports with what you think. Okay, so here's our working hypothesis: Risa What's-her-name is a beautiful, talented singer. Everything would be coming up roses for her except for one little detail. She has terrible taste in men. She is drawn—kind of like the proverbial moth to the flame, if you get my drift. She may not even be aware of it, but she finds strong, jealous, even violent men, irresistible. And if you ask me, she just found one."

"All that came to you just because someone broke into her apartment and trashed it? That's impressive, Lieutenant. You deserve a raise."

"I'm just giving you the obvious scenario, Amos. What any rookie cop from Van Nuys would come up with. No more, no less."

"Does that mean you don't think that's what's happening?"

"It could be. Whoever got in had a key. He—and I'm fairly sure it was a he—didn't have to climb a ladder or jimmy open a door, so she knew him well enough to let him have a key. To me, that says, boyfriend or father or brother. Someone close. And unless her father or her brother have mental health issues, well, I would toss them out of the mix."

"I don't know, Bill. You're right, it comports with my thinking, but now that I hear it coming out of your mouth, well, it's just another theory."

"Right. And you never want to get too comfortable with your own ideas," he says, "even if they make perfect sense. Criminology 101."

He tells me again that he'll look into the true whereabouts of Markowitz and Kaplan to see if their stories are on the up-and-up. I ask him if he could also run a check on Pincus Bleistiff as well. "I'd like to know who I'm dealing with," I tell him. "Just as a precaution."

"He's like you, right—a member of the tribe? And you don't trust him?"

"Sure, sure, I trust him. I even like him. He's funny. But he still hasn't paid me what he owes me."

Chapter 5

THE NEXT AFTERNOON a woman named Cynthia from Malloy's office calls. Well, actually, she doesn't say she's from Malloy's office. I don't recognize the phone number, so she could be calling from Mars. All she says is that she has some information that a Mr. William Malloy asked her to pass along. He also asked that I please be very discreet with what she's about to tell me. Hey, discretion is my middle name, I say. That's swell, she answers. That was a joke, I say. Ha, ha, she goes. Though she doesn't come right out and declare it, there's something in her voice and manner that shouts Texas at me. Or maybe it's just that she seems way too chirpy and polite for the job she's in, and I wonder how many months she'll last in a severely buttoned-down labyrinth like the LAPD. They pull in all kinds of people to work there, I suppose, and if they pass the lie detector test and all the other psychological hoops they put them through, hell, what can you do? But even so, Cynthia is an odd bird.

David P. Markowitz, she says, was incarcerated in a cell in Tijuana over the weekend and charged with public intoxication. This is nothing to be concerned about, however. The good news, she tells me, is that he has paid his debt to society, and according to the Mexican authorities has now been released on his own recognizance. She also thinks I'd be interested to know that someone named Arthur J. Kaplan took an 11:05 p.m. United Airlines flight to John F. Kennedy three nights earlier, and that last night someone with that name departed John F. Kennedy for LAX. We assume it's the same individual, she says, but you ought to bear in mind that there is a whole heap of

Kaplans in the phone book. That's probably so, I say. As to Pincus Bleistiff, she continues, he has no criminal past, although, you know, nobody's perfect and maybe there were a few vehicular violations over the last forty years. She thought these might have been expunged from his record, but if I would like her to dig a little deeper and tell me what they were, she would be happy to double-check with Mr. Malloy and see what he says.

"No, that's okay," I tell her. "You've been a big help, Cynthia. Please give my regards to the lieutenant. Er, I mean Bill."

"I certainly will," she says. "Oh, and by the way, I couldn't help but notice that the first two gentlemen you inquired about, Mr. Markowitz and Mr. Kaplan, are members of a band here in town. They're called Dark Dreidel. Strange name, right? That's what I thought, too. Well, it turns out that a dreidel is a little top—you spin it—and Jews, I guess, play some kind of gambling game with them during Hanukkah."

"Really?" I say. "How very peculiar."

And then before she hangs up, she gives me the dates and places the band will be playing this month, just in case I'd like to see what they sound like.

I jot them down on a yellow legal pad in front of the phone, along with the name CYNTHIA in big block letters.

Omar has a serious date with Lourdes the night I want to go check out the band, so I end up sitting alone in a corner, nursing a cardboard cup of scalding hot and barely drinkable coffee at a white-linen-table at the Jewish Community Center on Olympic. I've been here before, it seems to me, although it doesn't matter, and it could easily have been a dozen other places like this. I glance around at all the shiny faces. Tonight's event is Simcha Torah, the annual celebration of the Torah, and even though it's early, the bright lights are bearing down overhead, and the social hall is already starting to feel crowded. A few gray old men in ill-fitting suits are bending over, setting up metal folding chairs around the perimeter, and ladies of a certain age are toting trays of gefilte fish and challah and cheap red wine in little plastic shot glasses to some prearranged locations. Near the entrance there's a table with store-bought cookies and fruit for the kids, some of whom have already started to zero in on it. The wine disappears behind a golden curtain, which is a good thing, in my opinion. Because you'd have to drink several bottles' worth to do any damage, and it's so tasteless, who the hell would want to? The room is full of happy families with young cherubic children wandering around under their parents' watchful eyes. I notice several hand-knit, multicolored yarmulkes and a few dazzling and irreverent prayer shawls that would have caused my grandparents from the Old Country to frown. That was then, I think; this is now. There is a parquet dance floor in front of a slightly raised stage, and six aging musicians in black vests and Greek sailor hats are tuning up and arranging their charts. There's also an elegant, rakish woman with hollow eyes in her fifties. She's wearing a long flowery dress and darts around very quickly, like a hummingbird. I watch her operate for a few minutes. She seems to know almost everybody. One by one she's pulling her lady friends and their reluctant husbands off to the side, organizing them into straight lines and showing them the basics of Israeli dance, which is not that hard, but still you have to have some idea which foot goes where. I can't tell if she is being paid to do this, but she is very determined and focused, almost militant in her commands. She doesn't want to overlook anyone who might be willing to try their hand as soon as the music begins.

Which it does, with a sudden crash and roll from Dave Markowitz on the drums. The dance instructor looks up. Her face says it all: No, no, no, she wasn't ready yet, this is not the way it was supposed to happen. But, apparently, she is the only one feeling that way. The audience applauds, the well-formed lines dissolve, and all at once people are dancing—or not dancing, but giving themselves up to wild, untutored movement of arms and legs. It's a fast tune they're playing—an upbeat version of "Oy Mame, Bin Ich Far Lieb" ("Oh Mama, Am I in Love"). Which is something the Barry Sisters made famous when my parents were courting. I close my eyes and listen. Whatever it's called, I heard it a million times growing up. It's in the blood.

They follow this with a slower, more mournful piece where the violins take charge, then a medley of *freylachs*—zippy dance stuff from Romania and Bulgaria and Poland that leaves the audience in one big collective pool of sweat. There's nobody who doesn't respond to a *freylach*. I find myself tapping my foot to each one. I probably couldn't give you a single title, but if I hum a few bars I'm suddenly ten years old again in my parents' living room, and it all comes roaring back to me.

An hour later the rabbi takes the mic and shepherds the crowd toward the tables laden with food and wine on the far side of the room. The band members sit back in their chairs. They're all perspiring. Someone has brought them bottled water from the fridge. Somebody else mumbles something about a cigarette, and five of them stand up and head slowly toward the open metal doors on the side. Only Art Kaplan remains seated with his violin. Which is fine with me. He's the one I wanted to talk to, anyway.

"You guys are pretty tight," I say as I approach and offer my hand.

He nods.

"I mean, a lot of those tunes could use a singer. They've all got lyrics, right? A shame you don't have someone who could belt them out in Yiddish."

"You wanna sit in with us?"

"No thanks," I say. "I'm just a critic. And whoever built a monument to a critic, right? Nobody."

"Actually," he says, "we do have a singer. Only she—she just couldn't be here tonight."

"She any good?"

His shoulders go up and down. "She's all right, I guess. Not the best torch I've ever played behind, but I'm not complaining, far from it. We've been lucky to get as many gigs as we have."

"I hear you," I tell him. "I used to be a musician myself. We did standards mostly. Cole Porter. Sonny Rollins. Monk. I can't tell you how many bars I dragged my sorry ass out of at 3 a.m. Had to stop when I got married. Get a real job, that's what my wife said."

"I know what you mean," says Kaplan. "But this klezmer stuff is pretty specialized. And LA's a good town. If you get yourself a good manager you can work three, four nights a week. Bar mitzvahs, weddings, all the Jewish holidays...."

"Except Yom Kippur," I say. "Not much to cheer about then."

"Okay, forget Yom Kippur. But you get my point."

"So when's your crooner coming back? I'd like to catch the whole group in action."

Kaplan pulls out a rag from his back pocket and starts wiping down his violin. "That's a good question. The truth is, she's kind of vanished."

"Vanished? Really? As in nobody knows where she is?"

"Nobody I know, brother." He leans in closer. His voice drops. "And between you and me, I'd be just as happy if she didn't return. We were a good solid crew before she came along, and she doesn't add that much. Okay, she's prettier than anyone on this stage, but how much is that really worth, I ask you?"

"Why'd you let her join, then?"

Kaplan frowns. "I'm not in charge of this band, buddy. Our manager is. He gets the gigs, he pays us, and he's the one who told us to. What are you going to do? She auditioned. Afterward a couple of guys made some noise, said she really wasn't up to snuff."

"And?"

"And nothing came of it. Pinky—that's our manager—he told us point-blank, she's in the band. We can take it or leave it."

"So you're telling me I shouldn't make a special trip to see you guys again when she's in front of the mic?"

Just then the metal doors open and the other five musicians start filing back in.

"No," Kaplan says with a tinge of sadness. "I'm not saying that at all. She's a nice kid. She's beautiful. She's like—she's like the cherry on top of the hot fudge sundae. You gotta have it, don't you? Otherwise it's not a sundae."

I nod and return to my lonely linen table in the corner. There's still some coffee in my cardboard cup, but it turned cold long before.

Most of the following week I spend at Loretta's bedside on the third floor at Cedars-Sinai. I thought it was some kind of urinary tract infection at first, but then I discovered that she flushed all her prescriptions down the toilet one afternoon and had just been pretending to take them after that. Which worked all right until one afternoon when she passed out in the living room.

"I know you don't like to take that stuff, honey," I whisper to her while she's lying there sleeping with a saline drip in her arm and the soft autumn sun filtering in through the blinds. "But you don't want to end up here, do you? That's what those drugs are for. To keep you out of here." I'm whispering because there's another woman in the bed next to hers watching television; her name is Alice, she has blond frizzy hair, and the one and only time she spoke to me I found out she's a makeup artist at Disney and she's recovering from a burst appendix.

They keep Loretta for three days and nights, until they think she's stabilized. Then she belongs to Carmen and me. Sometime during all that I see an article in the *Times* about how cowboy music is catching fire in Russia and the Ukraine. That's when I remember to call Omar back and ask him what he's learned.

"I thought I liked all kinds of songs" is the first thing he says. "But you know what? It's not so. I really hate country-western. It's the same goddamn story over and over and over. Not only that, it's the same three fucking chords."

"I'm guessing you've been to a lot of bars, Omar."

"You're damn right I have. I've lost count. But I did find your boy, I think. Raymond Ballo, also known as Ray Ballo, also known on Facebook as Pretty Boy Ballo. He's in a band called Tumbleweed."

"You've seen him?"

"No, not yet. But they have a regular Saturday gig at a joint in Tarzana. I figured we should go together. You know what you want to ask him, and I'd kind of like to tag along, just in case things get rowdy."

"What makes you think that, Omar?"

"Just a feeling. Like you said, I've been to a lot of bars lately."

We go together. I pick him up at his home in Boyle Heights. I'm dressed down for the evening—blue jeans and my old leather bomber jacket. I debate whether or not to keep my Dodger cap on. Depending on your viewpoint, it could be dorky or it could fit right into the landscape. On the plus side, it covers my gray hair, and in a poorly lit club I could pass for twenty years younger. Omar, who's wearing black pants and a black felt jacket, says to keep it on, so that's what I do.

The place Ray Ballo appears at is called Jingles. It's on Tarzana Boulevard, and it has a large, garish neon sign with a pair of purple spurs blinking on and off in quick succession. The spurs are attached to two green neon boots, which feed into two provocative pink neon legs that seem to straddle the entrance. I count six gleaming Harleys in a row. A flyer outside advertises Live Girls Tuesdays and Fridays. "We just missed them," I say to Omar as we push through the door. "Damn."

Inside it's dark and woodsy. Once upon a time, I think, this place was probably organized around one simple theme—I don't know what, naked girls, cowboys, hunting; now it's just vaguely masculine. There are a few ancient stuffed animals peering down from the walls—deer and elk—and each table features menus with reproductions of wanted posters from the nineteenth century. Laminated pictures of Billy the Kid and Doc Holliday, that kind of thing. At the far end there's a small raised, unoccupied stage. Everything is there, waiting. A drum set, mics, amplifiers, monitors. Most of the crowd is lined up studiously at the bar, however, their eyes fixated on the silent Rams game being shown on four separate television screens overhead. Most of the crowd is tense and middle-aged and male. They're following the flow. They want someone to win, or at least to score. Women are few and far between. They're also watching the game, but they don't take it nearly as seriously as the men do. It's just a game, boys running around, chasing a ball. I can see it in their eyes. Meanwhile, everyone is working overtime to soothe their pent-up feelings. They're holding manhattans and margaritas. A few sturdy buckos down at the end are staring at shot glasses of something even stronger. We find an opening and ask for beer.

"What kind?" the bartender asks. He's a paunchy bald guy. He leans in close to take our order. He's got pockmarks on his cheeks and watery blue eyes and a general expression that says he's been working here too long and doesn't much like what he does.

"What Mexican beers do you have on tap?" asks Omar.

The bartender scowls. "Nothing Mexican. Coors. Bud Light. Miller. Take your pick."

"Okay, then," Omar says. "Miller."

I hold up two fingers to indicate the same. The bartender nods and goes off. It's too early to look at the dinner menu, but when he comes back, we take our beers and little white paper coasters and find a table near the stage. A few minutes later, the band members file in from a door off to the side. There are five of them. Four guys dressed in well-worn jeans and boots and silk shirts from Hollywood's finest consignment shops. The drummer, who's black, wears a Panama hat and shades. The one girl—their torch—is almost a foot shorter than the lanky men behind her. She looks about nineteen. Beautiful and sure of herself, but who isn't at that age? She's got corkscrews of way-out-of-control ash blond hair, and for tonight she has squeezed herself into a tight pink crinoline dress that doesn't quite reach her knees. Hard to tell what that's all about. "I think she's the leader," I lean in and whisper to Omar.

"I think she's the reason they call themselves Tumbleweed," he replies.

One by one they tap their microphones to make sure they're live. They tune up. A golden spotlight hits the stage and dances around until it centers itself. The singer rushes off and returns with a large clear-glass gallon tip jar, which she sets down carefully in front of her. Someone has already dropped a few dollars in to grease the pot.

A waitress arrives and we order two more beers, a couple of BLTs, and, at the last moment, a side of guacamole.

"You don't want to try the Rodeo Burger?" she asks. "That's the house special."

"No," I tell her. "We're fine. Maybe you could bring out the guacamole first, though. That'd be great."

She wanders off, and Omar stares at me. "I wouldn't have gotten guacamole in a place like this," he says. "They don't know what the fuck they're doing."

"Hey, it's on the menu," I say. "And besides, who do you think does all the cooking around here? Norwegians?"

"Good point," he says. "My people are everywhere."

Without any fanfare, then, the show starts, and the girl, who introduces herself after the first number as Phoebe, welcomes the audience. That would be me and Omar, but then, like I say, it's early. Surely the rest of the bar will migrate over and make an evening of it. I glance back hopefully at the clot of what now seems to be scruffy overweight men in motorcycle jackets. They're still drinking. In any case they aren't quite ready. The band is oblivious. As far as they're concerned, they could be playing in their living room. They run through an easy medley of Patsy Cline tunes, one after another, and they're surprisingly good at what they do; I say "surprisingly" because for all intents and purposes, it's just me and Omar following along. We're like voyeurs, clapping appreciatively at the end of each song, although, really, what kind of enthusiasm can four hands put together generate? Not much.

Even though she's young and strangely decked out, Phoebe has a nice, practiced, mellifluous voice. And more than that: She's serious. You can tell by the way she talks about herself in between tunes and what she says she's learned from the example of her hero, Patsy Cline. She has hopes and dreams that don't include working in clubs like Jingles the rest of her life. You can also tell by her demeanor—the way she closes her eyes and drifts like a passing breeze into each number. By how she wraps her fingers lovingly around the mic while the boys unpack the tune, how she waits patiently for the last note of the lead guitar to fade before she ever opens her mouth. You believe in her, I guess. That's what it's all about.

Another older couple shows up and grabs a spot closer to the stage. Then a group of five women take a table in the corner. They're all in their forties or fifties. Married probably or on their way to being divorced. All wearing tight jeans and T-shirts and running shoes, ladies' drinks jiggling in their hands. Laughing nervously, talking past each other. The table is too small for everyone. They cram in anyway, which makes them uncomfortable, which in turn makes them raise their voices. A pair of them look around to see if anyone else has noticed. I tip my Dodger cap.

Onstage, the lead guitar leans back and turns down the

volume on his amp. Their first set is coming to a close. The spot-light dims. I give Omar a twenty-dollar bill, tell him to stick it in the tip jar and see if he can persuade the bass player to come talk with us for a minute. He returns with Ray Ballo, who offers his sweaty hand. He takes the empty chair opposite me.

"You're pretty good with that thing, Ray," I tell him. "Buy you a beer?"

"Oh gee, thanks," he says. "I don't usually ever drink, at least not until we're done for the night. But ask me again in two hours."

He's a tall lanky kid in his late twenties, long dark hair that he keeps tucking restlessly behind his ears. There's an earnest-ness in his brown eyes, coupled with a sweet, genuine smile. He talks slowly and deliberately, almost like he's a farm boy and new to city ways. I can see why Risa might find him attractive.

I hand him my business card. "Actually," I say, "I have to confess I didn't come clear out to Tarzana to hear you play. Though, like I say, you've got a nice sound. I was in a couple bands once upon a time—before you were born—so I know what I'm talking about."

He looks at my card. His smile fades. "Okay," he says. "So what are you talking about, Mr. Parisman?"

"Risa Barsky."

"Oh, yeah? And what about her?"

"I've been hired to track her down. She's disappeared, did you know that?"

Now he's taken aback. He pushes a few errant hairs from his forehead. "No, I—I haven't seen Risa in—God, it's been nearly a month. We broke up. I mean, she broke up with me. I was still in love—"

I nod. "I get that, Ray. But you haven't had any contact with her in a month?"

"I called her a few times. I tried. We talked some on the phone. I thought she would come around and we could start over. She did this once before and that's what happened."

"But not this time, huh?"

"No."

"What'd she say?"

"This time? This time she said she'd given it some thought. Weighed it out. According to her, we just weren't right for each other."

"How come?" Omar asks. I glance over at him. I didn't think he was going to say anything at all tonight, but every so often he surprises me. Maybe he quit the academy too soon. Or maybe there's a tiny space in his heart where he still wants to be a cop.

"She's going to be thirty-five in another month," Ray Ballo says, "and I'm twenty-seven. We're just too far apart. We think about different things. We have different priorities. She even had a special word for it. A Yiddish word. Said it was *beshert*. You know what that means?"

"It's fated," I say, "meant to be. Or in your case, not to be. Nothing you can do about it."

"That's right," he goes. "She didn't say anything specific. Maybe she didn't want to hurt my feelings, but I've thought about it a lot and now I'm pretty sure all along she was desperate to have a child. Not so strange, really, when you put it like that."

"And you're not ready for that yet, are you, Ray?"

He lifts his hands. "At some point, sure, I guess, why not. I like kids. Kids are great. I'd like to get married, have a family. But someday, not now. You know how it is, the life of a musician."

"Wasn't Risa a musician, too? Isn't that how she paid the rent?"

"She sang in this klezmer group in Hollywood, and they got some pricey gigs now and then. Nothing very steady, though. Mostly she worked as a temp at this agency in Reseda."

"You remember the name?"

"I do. But before I tell you, who's paying you to find her? What's this whole thing all about?"

"I told you. She's missing. There are people out there who care about her."

"I care about her."

"You didn't pay me to find her, did you."

He frowns but keeps his silence "You're going to have to trust me on that stuff, Ray. My client wants to be anonymous."

"Yeah, well, how do I know you are what your card says you are?"

I give him a long stern fatherly look, the same kind of look my dear old dad gave me years ago when I told him I wanted to drop out of high school and go live in the woods like Henry David Thoreau. "Listen, Ray. Risa's neighbor gave us your name. She said you were the last boyfriend she truly cared about, that you were a real gentleman, and that if Risa were ever in trouble, she might turn to you. That's what the neighbor said."

"Terrific," he says. "Only she didn't, did she? If she's not in her apartment in Van Nuys, I don't know where she is, man. I'm sorry."

"What about her parents?" Omar asks. "Are they around?"

"I dunno. She wasn't tight with her folks. I know that much."

"You're sure about that."

"No, I just sorta figured it out. She barely mentioned them."

"So you don't know their names? Where we might find them?"

"No, man, nothing." He shakes his head and lowers his voice to what passes for a whisper. "They were like—they were difficult people—communists, intellectuals. I think they lived on the Upper West Side in New York. That was years ago. She told me once they made a shitload of money in the market and then felt bad about it. I couldn't understand that. What kind of communist plays the stock market, I wanna know? Anyway, by the time Risa came along they were back to being straight arrows. Except for her name."

"Huh?"

They named her Emma. For Emma Goldman. That's still on her birth certificate, she said. Pretty awful, if you ask me. She dropped that, naturally, the minute she landed in LA."

"I used to date Emma Goldman," I say.

"You did? Really?"

"No. Not really."

Ray Ballo studies my face, shakes his head. "How old are you, Mr. Parisman?"

"Never mind," I say. "Just give me the name of the temp agency in Reseda, will you? That may get us somewhere."

"Fishman Referrals," he says, rising out of his chair. "I hope you find her. If you do, tell her I'd like to see her again, will you? Would you do me that favor? Tell her it's not too late. I gotta—I gotta get back onstage for the next set."

Chapter 6

LORETTA IS STILL fast asleep and I'm loitering around the kitchen chatting with Carmen over coffee the next morning when the doorbell rings. I open up the door. In walks my cousin Shelly with a big brown paper sack. I haven't seen him in weeks, not that it matters. Shelly never changes. Well, he gets older and wider around the middle, but that's par for the course. He likes to dress well, and even though it's Sunday and the rest of Los Angeles is wearing sweatpants and flip-flops, Shelly's got his tasseled dark leather loafers on and a pink Ralph Lauren shirt under his powder-blue blazer. He drops the sack on the table. What brings you here? I want to know. Pastries, he says. Raspberry bear claws, among other things. He was in the neighborhood and stopped by La Brea Bakery on Sixth. He had a hankering. "And besides," he says, patting his stomach, "I couldn't possibly eat them all."

Carmen pulls the goodies out and arranges them on one of our platters. She offers him coffee.

"Well," he says, "since you asked."

We talk and eat. Loretta wanders out of the bedroom in her yellow nightgown and gives Shelly an enormous hug that lasts far too long, if you ask me, but I don't say anything. They've known each other forever, but what does she honestly remember about him? And after all this time, and all she's been through lately, are her memories accurate? Who does she think she's hugging? These are just questions; maybe in the end they don't matter. Maybe it's all right for my wife to be exceedingly fond of my cousin; Shelly has three ex-wives he's still supporting. And they're certainly not showing him the love.

At some point, I let Shelly know that I have to be shoving off. "There's a new case that's come up," I say with a shrug. "You know how it is."

He doesn't seem to take it personally. "I thought you were retired, boychick."

"Sure, I'm retired," I say, "but I'm also available. You know. Just in case."

Shelly chooses a powdered lemon bar with crumbs on it. Part of it sticks to his chin. "You're smart, Amos. No reason a guy like you can't go on doing what he loves forever, I mean, assuming you've still got your health and wits about you. *Zei gezunt* and all that."

"I'm okay. My legs haven't quit on me. I walk an hour a day, just to clear my head. You ought to try it, Shelly."

"You're not the first person to tell me that." He smiles and pops what's left of the lemon bar into his mouth and, in the same motion, wipes his chin clean.

"I don't want to be the last," I say. I slip on my sport coat and cap, grab my car keys, kiss Loretta on the forehead, and start for the door. Then I stop and look at the three of them at the kitchen table. It's like some kind of lost painting by Vermeer. The light is streaming in the window. Loretta's working on a cookie. Behind her, Carmen's stacking the dishes to go in the sink, and Shelly is leaning back contentedly in his chair, staring off into space, his coffee in front of him, hands folded like a pasha over his generous middle. "Anyway, you don't have to leave just because I do," I say.

"I wasn't about to," he says.

"That's good. Because Loretta likes your company. Carmen, too, I think. Stick around. Have some more coffee."

I sit back in my Honda for a few minutes with the engine off, wrap my fingers around the steering wheel, and take a few deep breaths. I need to clear the cobwebs out of my head, and it's always peaceful in this spot. No one ever bothers you if you're sitting there staring into space. Of course, this is LA, you don't exist without a car, it's part of your anatomy. Truth is, I just needed to get out of that apartment; I don't know why and I don't know where the hell I'm going. I'm not one of those guys who just naturally enjoys the open road. That was my dad, not me. Sundays, he'd back his Plymouth convertible out of our old cobwebbed garage on Poinsettia, take Wilshire Boulevard all the way to Pacific Coast Highway, then drive north as far as his gas tank would let him. He'd come back spent and happy, his cheeks flushed from the sun and the sea breeze, his clothes smelling of cigars, because he smoked them in the car. Never in the house because my ma forbid it. It was a different time. Or maybe he had more time on his hands than I do, I couldn't say. For me, these days, without a destination, there's no point in turning the key. I just sit there and take in the late morning sun. I drum my fingertips on the edge of the steering wheel.

There are things about this case that don't add up, little microscopic things mostly, but still. If you take all those bits that don't add up and put them together, well then, you've got a real mystery on your hands. For instance, it's already seven days into October and Risa Barsky's rent was due on the first. So maybe she's late. I don't know how the apartment manager handles things like that. Maybe she's usually late and it doesn't bother him. Maybe he's a nice guy. Or maybe he's not a nice guy. Maybe he's one of those weasels who are secretly happy she's late because he can come around now and put pressure on her to sleep with him. I knew a landlord in Berkeley who did that more than once. Then I think, maybe she's already sleeping with him and that's why she's missing.

I take out my phone and call Lola Emery. "Hi, Lola," I say. "Any further sightings of Risa Barsky?"

"No, not yet," she says. "She did get a bunch of new mail, though. I'm stacking it up for her on my kitchen table."

"Oh yeah? Anything interesting?"

"Bills, mostly. But there was a thick manila envelope from that guy on Mulholland Drive."

"Really? What's in it?"

"Hey! Damned if I know. I certainly didn't open it."

"Lola, your friend is missing. Her life may be in danger. This is no time to be a Girl Scout."

"You want me to open it? I—I'm not sure I should do that."

"You want to find her alive?"

"Well, of course I do."

"Then open the damn envelope and tell me what's in it. Look, if you're worried about the consequences with the postal authorities, just tell them I came around and opened it. Tell them it's my fault."

"It *is* your fault," she says. "And I don't like this. It's flat-out wrong. But okay, wait a minute, I'll go get the letter."

When she comes back on the line, she seems subdued. "Well, sir, I opened it."

"And?"

"And there's no letter. There's just—just a great big wad of money."

"How big, Lola?"

"I don't know. Big. A bunch of brand-new hundred-dollar bills. My goodness, let me count it."

"Fine." Money, I've discovered, acts like a magnet on people. Or not a magnet, maybe a drug. Large amounts of money have this strange, irrational energy to them. Especially if it doesn't belong to you. Just holding it in your hands can make you sweat.

"Fifteen hundred dollars," she says after a bit.

"You're right," I say. "That is a lot of cash. And no name on the envelope?"

"No, but it's the same address on Mulholland, and the same tight little handwriting. Same purple pen, even."

"You don't happen to know what Risa pays in rent, do you?"

"Same as me, I imagine. $1,250. Why?"

"And it's due on the first?"

"Right."

"And what happens if it's not paid then?"

"I think you have a grace period. A week. Ten days. I don't know, I'm never late."

"But Risa is now, isn't she?"

"I guess so. Why are you asking this?"

"No reason. Just professional curiosity. You know how it is." I tell Lola thanks, that she should stuff the money back in the envelope now and leave it on the counter. I tell her I'll be in touch and that if Risa should ever show up again to please give me a holler.

Now I know where I'm going. I turn the ignition key, and the Honda springs to life. At the end of the driveway, the sensor on the long metal gate sees me coming and slowly rolls open. Half an hour later I'm on Mulholland Drive pulling up in front of Pinky Bleistiff's. Today the gate is ajar so I'm free to drive right up to the front door. I ring the bell once, twice, three times. Finally he answers in his underwear. Well, not just his underwear. He's got a green silk kimono over it, but basically he's walking around barefoot in his underwear.

"Sorry to show up like this, Pinky. I shoulda maybe called ahead." I push past him into the living room.

"It would have been nice," he says, scratching at the fuzz on his cheek. "I mean, I could have shaved at least or thrown some clothes on. I don't like surprises. What the hell time is it, anyway?"

"Early," I say. "Eight. Nine. Something like that." He flips on a few lamps, even though the sun is beginning to filter through. The living room is lush and inviting like before, and I sit back on the couch and cross my legs. There don't seem to be any servants milling about, but this is a huge place. You'd need a small army just to tamp down the dust. Maybe they're upstairs, busy tidying up other rooms. Or maybe he gave them all Sunday morning off so they could go to church. Whatever. I don't hear any vacuum cleaners or dishwashers. Nothing. It's cool and quiet like a tomb.

"You want some coffee?" Pinky asks. "I could make us a fresh pot. I haven't had mine yet."

"Sure," I say. "You go ahead. I'll be right here waiting. We have to talk."

He disappears into the kitchen. I hear him jiggling cups and saucers. I hear water flowing from a tap. After a while he returns with two big mugs of dark steaming liquid.

"I forget what you put in it," he says. "You want cream? Half-and-half? That's what I use. I have all that stuff in the ice box."

I accept the mug he offers. "No, thanks. Black is fine."

Pinky sits opposite me in a soft leather chair. He folds his legs underneath, takes two quick sips of coffee, scratches his unshaven cheek again, smiles. "Okay, then, my friend. What shall we talk about?"

"You told me you were very fond of Risa, Pinky. Why don't you tell me a little more?"

"You woke me up for that?"

"That, and a few other things."

He makes a face. "Of course I am fond of her," he says. "She's got a great natural voice. And yes, she's a sweetheart. Everyone likes her. You'd like her, too, Parisman, if you ever get to meet her."

"Yes, but when we talked the other day at Canter's, you seemed to indicate that it was just professional interest you had in her. Nothing more than that. You wanted to keep the band together. That's why you hired me, right?"

"There's not much of a band without Risa," he says with a shrug. "I just don't see it going anywhere. Risa's critical."

"Some people in the band would disagree with you," I say.

He raises an eyebrow. "Oh yeah? Well, some people would be wrong. I've been around a long time. I know what I'm talking about."

I nod. "How old are you, Pinky? You don't mind me asking, do you?"

"Old enough," he says coyly.

"Ever been married?" I know what he's gonna say. At least I think I do. Still, it never hurts to throw your curveball once in a while. Keeps them honest.

His brow wrinkles. He takes a long, deep gulp of coffee before he answers. "Not that it matters," he says, looking me straight in the eye, "but my wife passed away seven years ago. Breast cancer."

"And you've been all alone in this great big house since then?"

He puts his coffee cup down. "Look, Parisman, I'm paying your salary. Why are you grilling me like I'm some kind of criminal?"

"I'm sorry you lost your wife, Pinky. I sympathize, really, I do. And I'm sure seven years is a long time. Some people, they lose their mate, it's practically a death sentence."

"You got that right," he says under his breath.

"But I'm just trying to understand. I need to get to the bottom of things, Pinky, and to do that, I need your help. The fact is, you haven't been all that straight with me."

"What the hell do you mean?"

I set my coffee mug down on his end table. "You told me you wanted me to find Risa Barsky. That she'd gone missing. That you were worried about her safety. But that's not exactly true, is it?"

"I was worried," he says. "Of course I was worried. I'm still worried."

"Sure, sure, but not because she was missing. She wasn't missing. How could she be? All that time you were sending her envelopes of cash. Lots and lots of cash."

"I was worried about her!" His voice goes up several octaves. "I was worried sick."

"You wanted something from her, didn't you, Pinky? Why

else would you send her that much money? Why would a man give that much money to a young, attractive woman like Risa Barsky? Any idea?"

He hangs his head. Then, after a few moments, he once again regards me intently. "I wanted her to know," he starts out. "I wanted her to realize that I'd always be there for her, I'd always be there, no matter what." He pauses, makes a fist with his right hand. Then he bites his lower lip. "Okay, wise guy, so I'll tell you. She was here with me. I thought she liked it, you know. She seemed happy, I mean. At least in the beginning. We were happy. And I was doing the best I could by her."

"You didn't actually think it would last, did you, Pinky?"

He half smiles, shakes his head derisively. "I'm seventy-five years old," he says. "When you're seventy-five, nothing lasts. You don't do a whole lot of planning. Not so much. You're grateful for each day that comes along. You know what I mean? I'm just in the here and now."

"But Risa made it so much more, didn't she?"

"I won't lie to you, Parisman. It was paradise with her here beside me. I never felt more alive. Even my Sophie never did that for me. And we were together forty-five years."

"Okay, Pinky," I say. "At least now we're on the same page. I'm guessing at some point you stopped making Risa happy."

He stares hard at me. Not quite a nod but close enough.

"You stopped making Risa happy," I say, "and she decided she wanted out. And when she fell off the radar entirely, you panicked. You wanted her back in your bed. That's when you called me. Am I right?"

"I looked for her long and hard," he admits. "I'm too old to do that kind of legwork, but I know a few people, people who'll do it for me."

"And you sent someone to her house?"

"Twice," he says. "Twice I sent Javier. She didn't answer her buzzer, so he never got past the foyer. That's how it is in places like that. If the door to the foyer's not open, you need a key."

There's a sadness in his voice—not a critique on security systems in apartment buildings so much as a general bewailing of modernity.

I finish my coffee and set the cup down. "Tell me something, Pinky. The way I look at this, you got lucky. And then your luck ran out. Didn't she talk to you before she took off? Women don't usually pick up and leave without saying goodbye."

"We talked. And you're right, women are more polite about that kind of thing."

"So, *nu*? Did you two have a fight the night before?"

"Not a fight. But she was restless, I guess. She kept walking all around. She talked about wanting to go to the movies or a club to hear some music. She was always doing that, and most of the time I went along with her."

"But not that night?"

"That night my stomach was acting up. I thought I might be getting sick, so I said no, you wanna go by yourself, that's fine. Or if you need company I'll get Javier to go along with you."

"And what happened?"

"Nothing," he says. "Nothing. She just said never mind. You don't feel well, I can watch something on TV. She's a trooper, Risa. She always makes the best of it. So I took a pill and went to bed early. When I got up the next morning, she was gone."

"She cleared all her clothes out of the closet?"

Pinky Bleistiff rubs the few errant hairs left on his head as if to smooth them into place. A fat tear glistens in his eye and tumbles slowly down his cheek. He ignores it, even as his lower lip starts to quiver. Sitting here silently in this sprawling house on Mulholland Drive, unshaven and barefoot in his green silk kimono, he's like an imposter, someone who simply doesn't belong where he is. And the crazy thing is, I find myself forgiving him. It's not your fault, I want to tell him. It's bigger than you. Blame it on Hollywood.

"She didn't bring much with her," he whispers at last, "and

I didn't notice right away. But yeah, a lot of it's gone. I thought maybe she'd gone back to work at that temp agency in Reseda. I don't know why she'd do something dumb like that. She coulda stayed here forever."

"That would have been nice, huh?"

"You ain't kidding. She wouldn't have had to lift a finger for the rest of her life."

I get up then, and we walk toward the front door. I pat him reassuringly on the shoulder. "Thanks, Pinky. It was good to talk with you. I just needed to clear the air, is all. You were very helpful."

I get in my car. He stands by the driver's side. A breeze flutters his kimono. He has pale, spindly legs, I notice.

"You'll keep looking?" he wants to know.

"I'll keep looking," I say. "We'll be in touch."

Chapter 7

TWO DAYS AFTER that, Pinky's check arrives in my mailbox. He's also included a short, folded square of lilac-colored paper—*So sorry this didn't reach you any sooner, Parisman. I thought I'd sent it, but I guess I was dreaming. Forgive me, Pincus.*

I make a mental note to share a chunk of this with Omar, then I tuck it away in my wallet.

Later in the afternoon I drive east on Sunset and end up at Echo Park. It's 1:30. Lieutenant Malloy has asked to meet me here; he didn't want to talk about it over the phone, but he thought maybe we could walk around the lake together. I said sure, why not. Malloy is fond of water, even when it's artificial. Water and conversation just naturally go hand in hand, he believes. And Los Angeles has precious little water, so here we are.

School has let out. There's a small gaggle of black-haired children in hand-me-downs, laughing and shouting in Spanish, chasing one another all over the pathway, hiding behind the rows of palm trees. A few mothers sit on park benches rocking babies in carriages or tracking their older kids' shenanigans from afar. The sun shines unrelentingly. No matter what the houses here are selling for these days, this still feels like a working-class neighborhood. It's after lunch, and the green plastic trash cans are filled to the brim and beyond with sandwich wrappers and beer bottles and Styrofoam debris. It's a feast for a pair of brazen crows. They hop all around, poking at the ground for stray beans and tortilla chips and other tiny morsels.

I spot Malloy on the other side of the pond. He has one hand in his coat pocket, the other one's holding on tight to a slim brown leather briefcase. Later on I'll remember that scene, and it will strike me as odd. Later on I'll realize that I'd never seen Malloy with a briefcase in his hand. Not that there's anything wrong with it; it's just not who he is. I don't think about it then, however. He's plodding slowly around the edge of the water. He's got a red tie on today, against a black shirt. Not his usual look, I think, which is almost always more subdued. The Lieutenant himself is subdued, however. I give him a little wave, and he nods in my direction.

"Hey, Bill."

"Hey," he says. We start to stroll together along the water's edge. A bunch of bare-chested young men in their twenties are tossing a football back and forth. It's not an organized game, but they're running, leaping. One of them makes a spectacular one-handed catch and everyone yells their approval. We watch them for a while, then move on. Malloy comments on how beautiful the water lilies are, the way they shimmer in the sunlight. Also on the fact that in the beginning this wasn't a lake at all but a reservoir. "That was before we started importing our water from up north," he says with a hint of sadness.

"I didn't know you were such a local-history buff," I say.

"I'm not," he says. "It's just a thing I found out, a thing that got stuck in my head. How it was built to be a reservoir. Not a tourist attraction. "Once you hear that, it's hard to forget."

I nod. "That's not what you wanted to talk about, is it, Bill?"

"No," he says. "Tell you the truth, I wanted to talk about Pincus Bleistiff."

"What about him?" I say. "He's a nice old guy. Kind of eccentric, but who isn't at that age? He finally sent me the first installment on the money he owes me this morning."

"Yeah, well, I don't think you're going to get too much more out of him. He's dead."

I stop in my tracks. "I just talked with him a few days back. What the hell happened?"

"That's what I was hoping you'd tell me," Malloy says. "His housekeeper came to work this morning and found him just inside the front door. Stiff as a board. Somebody emptied a whole clip into his chest."

"Jesus."

He stops, unclasps the briefcase, and offers me a manila folder. "Here, take a look at this."

There are a dozen grizzly full-color snapshots of the corpse from every angle imaginable. In the basic one, Pinky is lying flat on his back in the arched doorway of his house. The oak door is ajar; a welcoming light is pouring through behind it. His white cotton pajamas are rumpled and shredded by the bullets, and he seems to have forgotten one of his slippers on the lawn. There's a dark, crusty, reddish pool emanating from all around him. There is no obvious pain, not anymore. His eyes are bulging and his mouth is open. His arms are splayed out like he was right in the middle of telling a joke. Maybe it was a good joke, too, maybe his killer would have laughed if he let him finish. Only he never got the chance. That's what it feels like, more like an insult than a murder. If you didn't know he was dead, you might not even think he was unhappy lying there. He's staring in wonderment up at the camera. I sift through the other photos. Most of them are of the torso. It looks as if four bullets plowed through that area alone, more than enough to do the job.

"What kind of slugs were they?" I ask.

"Thirty-eights," Malloy answers. "We counted six hits. Two in the stomach, one in the lungs, one in the shoulder, and one in the right arm. It didn't matter. He was probably dead before he hit the ground, a guy like that."

"I guess so."

"Six slugs," he says. "I hadn't thought about it before. That could be significant."

"What do you mean?"

"I'm just adding things up at random," he says. "It's a habit, you know me. We did some research on Mr. Pincus Bleistiff. He was a big deal once upon a time in the music business."

"When?"

"Twenty, twenty-five years back," Malloy says. "Made a lot of careers in his day. Probably killed a few as well."

"That was a long time ago, Bill."

"I know," he says. "A long time ago. But six bullets? At that range? For a frail old man?"

Malloy is like a bricklayer. He's focused, methodical; he always builds his ideas one on top of the other, nice and plain and even. And yeah, anyone can guess where he's going but still I have to ask, just to be sure. "So are we thinking of this as revenge? Musicians—even bad ones—aren't known as murderers, not usually."

"I dunno," he says. "You tell me."

Now my mind is racing. I think about Frank Sinatra and Sam Giancana. All those people Pinky hung around with in Vegas. Or Chet Baker. How he just tumbled out of a two-story window one day in Amsterdam. "Maybe some kind of old-fashioned Mob hit? What do you think?"

He shrugs. "You have to take it all in, Amos. Let it marinate. Everything counts. Why waste a man with six bullets? Why, when you can do it with just one or two and still be pretty damn sure. Six means they didn't want there to be any doubt whatsoever."

"Yeah, or maybe it was dark. Or maybe they'd never fired a gun before in their life. Maybe they were crazy or scared shitless and couldn't tell if they hit him even once. How about that for a theory?"

"That has some appeal as well," he admits.

Malloy slides the photos carefully back into his briefcase, and we pause to watch the water geyser plume up in the middle of the lake.

"I don't know a thing about his Mob connections, Lieutenant. Like I've said before, he just hired me to find a singer he was in love with."

"And we'd like to find her now, too, Amos. Who knows

what she knows? After all, she was sleeping with him. Maybe he said something that rattled her. Maybe that's why she ran off."

I go silent then, but it doesn't take a genius to read what's going through my head. Risa Barsky ran off, but she could always change her mind, I think. She could turn around in a rage and come back in the middle of the night. She knew the gate code. I picture her there with a gun in her hands, shivering, hunched in the doorway. And yeah, something might have happened between them. Maybe Malloy had it right; it was just something he said, but I doubt it. Words alone rarely lead to murder. Women hear things, say things all the time. They're used to words. That's how they fight. So what, then? How else could an old man shove her across the line? If she was the one who pulled the trigger, it was because she was in pain. I was sure of that. Because she had been used, violated. Because she could not allow it. Because it had come to this.

Malloy rubs his hands together. He has large, strong, expressive hands, hands that could have cobbled together a spectacular career playing piano if that's the direction he'd chosen. "The sooner we pick her up and talk to her, the sooner this thing will be solved," he says. "I know that much."

We find an empty park bench. There's some cryptic gang graffiti spray-painted in black on it, but we sit anyway. I turn and squint at him. "What do you want from me, Bill? Just say it. I'm not hiding anything."

"You must have been poking into her background," he says. "In fact, I know you have. So why don't you tell me about it."

"There isn't a whole lot to tell," I say. "You could try pumping her ex-boyfriend Ray Ballo like we did. He's a decent kid. Plays bass in a band called Tumbleweed. Omar and I caught them the other night at a biker bar out in Tarzana. Except for the singer, they're not all that good, by the way."

"We're going to be interviewing lots of musicians in the next few days," Malloy nods. "I'll put him down on the list. You never know."

We pause as a trio of young women pass close by. Two of them are visibly pregnant. One girl, who has the face of an angel and can't possibly be more than eighteen, smiles at us. We smile back.

"What else can you give me?"

"You should talk to her next-door neighbor, Lola Emery. Also, I'd get a search warrant put together for Risa's apartment. Don't know if the Van Nuys cops have been there, but it's worth a try."

"What am I looking for?" he asks. "Any judge is going to inquire."

"You need help with that? Really? She's a fugitive. Maybe she left some hint about where she ran off to."

He jots down everything I say. Then he stands. I can see it in his eyes; it's time to hit the road. "What are you going to do now?" he asks.

"Now?" I say. "Now that my client is gone? I don't know, exactly. If I was still in my prime, if I had ten other cases to worry about, I guess I'd just call it quits. That's what you do, right? When the money dries up?"

"I might," he says.

"You might. But that's the difference between us, Bill. You're still on the clock. For you, it's a job. But when someone kills my client—my only client—I dunno, it feels personal. Maybe I should be more of a professional, but now I really want to get to the bottom of this. I didn't spend all that much time with him, I didn't get to know him or anything, but you know what? There was something I kinda liked about Pinky Bleistiff."

"How's that?"

I start talking with my hands. This is an old quirk, something Loretta, with her stolid Presbyterian background, has been warning me about for thirty years, always trying to get me to quit. Something I suppose I picked up from watching my father rant and rave around the dinner table. We argued at my house. Politics, baseball, books. The kind of girls I was dating. Whether he could ever forgive Henry Ford for being an anti-Semite. How could there be a God if such a creature would permit the Holocaust. No subject was off-limits. Anyway, the subject was beside the point. It's what we did. What Jews still do. "Bleistiff wasn't perfect," I say now, my hands rising and falling, shaping the air, "and he lied to me at first, but I think I understand why. He wasn't just one more instant millionaire holed up in the Hollywood Hills. He had a past. It was complicated. He came from somewhere."

"And where was that?"

"I don't know, Bill. I don't know, but I can guess. Some place he probably wasn't proud of. A dark, poor place, maybe. And he turned it around. He made something of himself. He had a story to tell."

"You didn't get to hear it, though, did you?"

"No, I didn't have enough time. It's okay, though. Now I have all the time in the world."

The next morning I settle down on my couch in the living room, prop my bare feet up on the coffee table, and put in a call to the business number on the front of Pincus Bleistiff's card, the one he said I shouldn't ever bother with. A British accent answers. She identifies herself as Victoria. I can't tell her age, but she sounds young, and she is obviously well-educated and thoughtful about how she speaks.

I give her my name and what I do for a living. She doesn't seem overly impressed. I have the feeling that nothing impresses her, in fact. Maybe money, but I'm not about to offer that. Not yet.

"Unfortunately, Mr. Bleistiff is not available at the moment," she replies. "But if you'd care to leave your number, perhaps—"

"Unfortunately," I say, dropping my tone to a more funereal

level, "that's the right word, in fact." Then I lower the boom. "Unfortunately, Mr. Bleistiff is dead, Victoria. It was quite sudden. Just the other day."

"Dead?" The shock in her voice is palpable. Now the balance is lost and forgotten; her proper little airplane has gone into a tailspin. "Dead?"

"Unfortunately," I repeat.

"I had no idea," she says quietly. "Was he—was he ill?"

"Somebody shot him," I say. Not much point glossing it over, I think. She'll find out soon enough when the newspapers get wind of it. But except for that one little sordid detail, I try to steer the rest of our conversation in a more neutral direction. "We don't know why, of course. And the police are just beginning to investigate, so I wouldn't be surprised if you heard from them before the day is out."

"Me? What do I know?"

"They'll have questions, Victoria. I wouldn't worry about it too much. But I'll tell you what. You might want to follow up with his relatives as soon as possible. Just touch base, you know. For the funeral, I mean. I heard he has a son in Israel and a daughter who lives nearby."

"Yes," she says suddenly, "yes, yes." The notion that she can be useful in this darkest hour of need is a compelling one, and she welcomes it. "Her name's Julie. She's in Santa Monica. I know how to reach her."

"That would be swell," I say. "There are lots of people who'll want to pay their respects, I imagine. Musicians he worked with. Old friends in the business. Also, if you don't mind, I'm trying to get ahold of one of Mr. Bleistiff's personal assistants—a man named Javier? You know him?"

"Javier Escovedo," she says at once. "I believe that's who you mean." She pauses a moment, then reads me his telephone number.

"Thanks so much. You've been very helpful," I say. "And I'm sorry about all this. Really I am. It's a crummy way to start your day, isn't it?"

"You can say that again," she says. I hear the equanim-ity slowly returning. She's much too young to remember, but there's a sturdiness in her genes; the way she speaks reminds me of that old British keep-calm-and-carry-on line that saw them through the Blitz. "I only met Mr. Bleistiff a few times," she says. "He would come in at Christmastime with boxes of chocolates. Always such a gentleman. But virtually everything we did was on the phone or by email. Without him around now, I can't—I can't believe I'll have a job here much longer."

I don't tell her then that I wished I needed a secretary. I don't tell her that I'd hire her in a heartbeat.

Chapter 8

JAVIER ESCOVEDO LIVES in a modest peach-colored bungalow at the end of a cul-de-sac in Eagle Rock, which is a neighborhood of modest houses sandwiched between Glendale and Pasadena. In my day it was entirely forgettable, nobody ever went there, but lately there's been a resurgence, and now there are hip restaurants and bars. Young people, many of them students at nearby Occidental College, are now claiming it as their own. I haven't checked the real estate pages lately, but if it's like everything else with a view, even a shoebox of a house like Javier's is more than Loretta and I can afford.

I'd talked with him briefly on the phone the day before to tell him what happened. I left out most of what I knew, but it didn't matter. He'd already heard the news about Bleistiff, which seemed a little strange to me at first, since the police are being so tight-lipped, but then he mentioned that Victoria had called him. "I was his personal assistant for so many years," he said. "Mr. Pinky and I were close, you know, like brothers." Only he used the Spanish, *como hermanos*. It was kind of endearing at the time when he said it. Either that or patronizing.

Then he gave me his address, and I made a date to see him the following day at 3 p.m. Which is why I'm here now in my vintage blue Honda at the curb, parked next to an unkempt rubber tree. Omar is sitting beside me. He's on edge, I know, because he's feeling squeezed: He agreed to come along in case my interview with Javier should suddenly get complicated and I needed a translator. That was nice of him. But he reminds me now for the umpteenth time that his life is not so simple anymore. He's got a girl. He thinks he's starting to fall in love, and he promised Lourdes he would take her out to an early dinner.

"Well," he says, "what are you staring at, man? What are we waiting for?" He lays his hand impulsively on the door handle.

I turn to him. Omar is a good thirty years my junior. He's taller than me, his head is shaved clean, and he's built like a bull. At first glance you might not think we have anything in common. He's an Indian; in his heart he's never really left the village in Oaxaca he was born in. Me, I grew up on the streets of Hollywood. I like to talk. He can go three days straight without saying a word. It's a different kind of energy surging through him, but still we have this silent, visceral bond. We both feel it, and neither of us can understand it. He could be my son. That's what's going through my mind.

"There's no rush," I say. "I'm studying his front door, Omar. Take a look. What do you make of it?"

"What do you mean, what do I make of it? It's a door. A brown goddamn door, with a brass goddamn doorknob. C'mon. Let's go inside and talk to him. I've got things to do."

"Look at the screen door," I say. "Just look, will you? It's torn. Somebody came along and sliced it right down the middle. What does that say to you?"

"Says he lives in a rough neighborhood, just like mine."

"That's one idea. What else?"

"Hell," he says, "in Boyle Heights, nobody even bothers with a screen door out front." He pauses then and searches my face. "All right, I give up, *pendejo*. What does it say to you?"

"It suggests," I say, "that something's out of whack. If it happened a few days ago, well, okay, maybe it means he's been too busy to fix it."

"Maybe he comes home late at night," Omar says. "Maybe he hasn't even noticed it yet."

"Maybe," I say. "I might buy that. But do you see anything amiss in the other houses around here? No, you don't. They're all neat little bungalows. Which to me says this isn't a high-crime neighborhood. I'll bet everyone here comes out on

Sunday mornings to mow their lawns and wax their cars. It's
called pride of ownership, Omar. Very commendable."

"But not Mr. Escovedo."

"Well, it looks like he might have mowed his lawn in the
last month or so. Just hasn't bothered with his screen door. I
can't help but wonder."

Omar sighs, gives me a consternated look. Maybe Indians
just don't wonder much about the meaning of torn screen doors.
Maybe screen doors don't exist in Mexico. Or maybe he's right
and I'm full of soup. We climb out of the car, then, and walk
up to the front. I yank open the screen door. There's no buzzer,
so I knock hard. A minute later Javier Escovedo appears. He's
a short, tan, sturdy fellow in his early fifties. Salt-and-pepper
hair. Even though he knew we were coming, he looks startled
and confused; it's like we woke him from a long afternoon nap.
He's wearing a wrinkled Dodger jersey and sweatpants. Blue
plastic flip-flops on his feet. Omar speaks to him in Spanish.
He squints at us, rubs his unshaven cheek, nods, and points
vaguely to the couch in his living room.

It's cool and orderly inside. Not a lot of light, and even less
air moving around, but maybe he likes it like that. Anyway, the
living room couch is comfy enough, and there's ample room for
all three of us. A bachelor's pad. All I'd need now is a bowl of
guacamole and a glass of beer, I think. Especially if I felt like
looking at the muted football game in progress on his large-
screen TV on the opposite wall. But except for a well-worn
copy of the Bible in Spanish and yesterday's *La Opinion* newspaper, the coffee table is bare; there is no beer, no guacamole,
nothing. I take another look at his disheveled state and touch
the fabric beside me with the flat of my hand. It still holds the
heat from his body. He must have been snoozing through the
football game when we arrived.

I start out with some niceties. How sorry we are about Mr.
Bleistiff. He was such a generous soul. This must be hard on
you. You've worked for him a long time, I understand.

"Twenty years," he replies. "More than twenty, maybe. I forget."

Omar asks him in Spanish where he's from, and he says something about a little village in Guerrero, the name of which I don't quite catch. Then in English he lets us know that he's a U.S. citizen now, although it's true, he crossed the border a very long time ago. "Almost before there was a border, you know." He smiles ruefully when he says this.

I want to ask him what he intends to do, now that his employer is gone. Has he thought about looking around for other work? No, of course not, it's too soon. There is still so much pain in his heart.

At first his answers are lethargic, but now he's starting to wake up, bit by bit. And the more he wakes up, the more wary he looks. Every now and then his eyes dart over to the silent football game on the television. He'd rather be watching television, I'm sure. Or napping again. Anything besides entertaining two inquisitive strangers in the afternoon.

"I wanted to speak with you, Javier, because they told me at his office that you were the one he often turned to at the end. He had maids and gardeners, I know, but you were there in his house almost every day. Is that correct?"

"Yes."

"And so you knew everyone who came and went, right?"

He nods.

"Did he have any unusual visitors in the last week? People you were unfamiliar with?"

The question seems to catch him off guard at first. He shakes his head. "No, no strangers."

"You worked for him for twenty years, you say. What did that involve?"

"I ran errands," he says. "I made arrangements, phone calls. Little things sometimes. I made sure there was always gas in his cars. A full tank, that's what he liked. It wasn't difficult, but you had to pay attention to the details."

"You weren't a part of his business, though, were you?"

"No. That he handled by himself."

"And what about his wife? Did you work for her, too?"

"Yes, of course. Sophie. I took her shopping. To the hairdresser. I carried her bags. Helped her in the kitchen. She was the love of his life."

"And I imagine, then, that you were also familiar with his recent girlfriend as well."

He looks at me steadily. "*Sí*. Very familiar."

"And what can you tell me about her?"

"Señora Barsky was not like Sophia. She was young, you know. Independent. She came. She went. They had their disagreements. But I was never involved with that."

"You must know what they fought about, though. You were there in the house, right?"

He shrugs. "Lovers quarrel about all kinds of things. I didn't listen. Honestly, I don't remember."

He heaves a deep sigh of resignation, then plants his hands down on his knees. "You know what I do remember, gentlemen, from all my days with him? Shall I tell you? It was the way Mr. Bleistiff praised me. I took care of so many things and he was grateful that I could be so...so discreet. I will never forget that. That was why he valued my service."

"Of course he did. But now he's dead, isn't he?"

He looks at me uncomprehendingly.

"Don't get me wrong, Javier. I agree with Mr. Bleistiff. Discretion is a wonderful trait. And you did your part. Only, the thing is, those days are gone."

"I did my part, yes."

"And now you don't have a job anymore. If he could speak, don't you think he'd want you to tell us the truth? If it would help find his killer?"

He goes silent then. His eyes seem to briefly close, and it's almost as if he's lost in a momentary prayer. "You believed she killed him? Is that it?"

"We need to find her," I say. "We need to talk to her. Everyone wants to talk with her. You understand."

He nods solemnly. "*Sí*," he says, "*por supuesto*." Then he asks us if we'd care for some beer. I say yes, although Omar gives me a stern look. Even though he's fond of beer, he doesn't want to socialize with this fellow. Or maybe he's just anxious to see his girlfriend. Javier gets up off the couch and disappears through the archway into the kitchen. I hear the sound of a refrigerator opening. He returns with a church key and three cold, glistening bottles of Bohemia on an orange lacquered tray.

"She was a beautiful woman," he says after a sip. "I mean, she is a beautiful woman, it's true, *pero más joven*, so much younger than him."

"He must have been in love with her."

"Oh yes. Yes, very much in love. Well, anyone would love her. But…but it was not good, you know. I understood this right away, from the first day she came here. There were problems."

"Such as?"

"He was an old man, *señores*. A lonely old man. And she did not think about the results. What might happen. She was always playing with him. Smiling, laughing. It could never work."

"Because?"

He wags his head. "I do not blame her. It is not for me to blame either one. Not really. Love is a mystery, is it not? But when a man like that falls under a woman's spell—especially someone so young and talented—he can, he will, make mistakes."

"What kind of mistakes, Javier?"

"This is just my opinion, *señores*. I've known many women, but I never married anyone. I am not an expert."

"You know what you see, though, don't you?"

He nods. "And the truth is, he should not have given her so many things. I told him so. Privately I cautioned against this. Women appreciate gifts now and then, but it is wrong to try to buy them. That's what he did. Even a rich man can lose his dignity that way."

"What did he give her?" Omar asks.

"What didn't he give her?" Javier says. His eyes grow wide. "Money. She needed money, she said. Also a car. Oh yes, and jewelry. I kept quiet about that."

"Why?"

"It was Sophie's!" he says, suddenly animated. "He offered her his poor wife's jewelry. Some of those pieces were old, but they were very valuable. I know. I helped him pick them out."

He turns again to the silent football game in progress. The men in red are chasing the men in blue across the field. For a moment he studies it intently as though what they're doing there might contain the answers to life's pressing questions.

"Someone broke into Risa's apartment in Van Nuys, apparently. Made quite a mess. Scared her."

"Yes, yes, I heard about that."

"She stayed away for a while, so I understand. But then one day she decided it might be safe enough to come back and get some clothes from her closet. You know anything about that?"

"Yes, in the first week that she was here. I helped her. That was before El Señor let her have the Jaguar."

"And you drove her there and back?"

"That's correct."

"And when was the last time you saw her?"

Javier stands up. He grabs the remote and turns off the football game. "Recently," he says. "They had some kind of fight around dinner time. It must have been the night he was killed, I believe. There was a lot of shouting in the bedroom."

"How much of that did you overhear, Javier?"

"Not much. Not enough to know what was going on. She was angry, that's all."

"You didn't hear what was said?"

"There was a great deal of swearing. Very loud swearing."

"And then?"

"And then she slammed the door and left."

We work on our beer in silence for a few moments. Omar speaks to him in rapid-fire street Spanish. My language skills are pretty good, but four years of high school can only take you so far. I catch a few words, and they seem to be largely about money; in any case the tone of their conversation tells me that the conversation has moved away from murder and missing persons and on to another plane altogether.

I stop nursing the beer bottle and glance meaningfully over at my partner. "Okay, so do you want to tell me what you said?"

"I asked him about his future. Whether he can expect any kind of financial reward from Bleistiff's company. That kind of thing."

"Yes," Javier chimes in. "And the answer is, I don't know, *señores*. Probably. I have to sit down and discuss this with them. But not until after the funeral, of course."

I stand up. Omar does, too. Javier stays put on the couch. "One last question," I say. "You said Risa slammed the door and left. I'm guessing she drove off in the Jaguar."

"That's true."

"And I'm hoping you can tell me the license number of the Jaguar."

"I can get it for you. He has all kinds of records around the house. But if you're in a hurry, I would call Victoria at Mr. Bleistiff's office. I'm sure she has it in a file cabinet somewhere. It was owned by the company."

"Thanks, Javier. You've been very helpful." I give him my business card, which he glances at and drops on the coffee table. We make for the door. Omar is two steps ahead of me and halfway down the path. I stop on the top step and turn back. Javier is watching us with a steadfast expression from behind the torn screen door. "You know, if I were you, I'd probably get this taken care of," I say, pointing to the problem. "It's not urgent, but you know how neighbors are."

"Right," he says. "I guess I hadn't noticed."

Chapter 9

SHELLY CALLS ME later that night and announces he wants to help find Risa Barsky. Well, he doesn't say he wants to help, exactly. That's not how Shelly operates. And I don't mention Risa's name, not at first, anyway, so his help—whatever it is—is of a more general type. As in, this nice, voluptuous Jewish singer has gone missing in the universe and it is therefore incumbent upon me, a fellow Jew, a *landsman*, to do whatever I can. Shelly gets this way every once in a blue moon, usually when he's trying to impress a new girlfriend. I've seen it before. A religious impulse seizes him by the throat, and he feels compelled to write a thousand-dollar check to a perfect stranger he meets in a hospital waiting room. She has cancer, he tells me. She only has a few months left. Or he gets into his shiny black Mercedes and takes his turn delivering sandwiches to folks down on skid row. Or he suddenly becomes kosher and throws out all the pork in his kitchen. It's an old pattern, and it usually lasts just until he's tricked the woman he's after into moving in with him. But then I remember that Shelly's latest girl is Simone, and she's blond and French and about as Catholic as they come. So unless they've broken up already, this isn't for her.

"What's going on, cousin?"

"What do you mean? I want to lend you a hand. Is that so strange?"

"How's Simone?"

"Simone?" he says. "Simone's got nothing to do with this. Simone's perfectly lovely. She's all curled up in our bedroom at the moment. What do you take me for? You think I'm doing this because of Simone?"

"Not unless she's promised to convert, no."

"Well, for your information, boychick, she hasn't. And I haven't asked her, either. Not yet."

"But you're planning to, right?"

"If she ever wants to get married someday—I wouldn't lie to you—that may be in the cards. It's a question, sure, but I'm not asking. And for now, you know, who the hell cares? We're in love."

"So how do you want to help me, Shelly? What can you really do?"

"I've been to my share of bar mitzvahs," he says. "I know people. People in showbiz, people who book bands, even a few decent klezmer musicians, believe it or not."

"Maybe so, but she's disappeared. She's not working at a temple or a nightclub somewhere."

"But what if one of them knows Risa Barsky? You don't think that's possible?"

"No. And anyway, the cops are already out there doing interviews. Dozens of them. They've got computers and databases full of names. Can you match their resources?"

"I can make some calls," he insists, "ask around. It's a tight community of artists, even in a big place like LA. You'd be surprised. They all look out for one another."

"That's nice to know. But I'm curious, Shelly. Why are you so interested? What's in it for you?"

"What? You think there's always an angle? Is that it?"

I pause, do a little drumbeat with the pencil I'm holding at my desk. Shelly's lived a long time. Even though he's retired from the car-leasing business where he made himself a small fortune, he's still a battler. He has a thick skin, but I don't want to hurt his feelings. On the other hand, this feels odd, intrusive even, especially for a close relation.

"There's always an angle, Shel, let's not kid ourselves."

"I'm doing this because I want to help you, boychick. That's my angle. Because you're the only blood I've got left in this fucking world. You don't think I see the pain you're going through with Loretta? I know you're living on next to nothing these days. Don't tell me you're not."

"You don't know that."

"I can guess. I'm a pretty good guesser. I know I couldn't survive on what you make."

"You have three ex-wives to support, Shelly. You're still paying off that mortgage in Bel-Air. I can see how you might think that. But honestly, I'm doing just fine. Really, man. You don't have to worry."

The tone of the conversation changes then, and I figure I must have hit a nerve or at least temporarily knocked him back on his heels. His mortgage payment is killing him, I know, and so are his ex-wives. He seems subdued; I get the distinct feeling that he wants to hang up. I tell him if he'd like to make some phone calls, sure, go right ahead, but there's no denying how lukewarm I am. As I get into my pajamas afterward, I think I shouldn't have given him such a hard time about it. What's the worst that can happen? Maybe he'll find out being a detective is a lot tougher than they make it look on television. Maybe, but I doubt it.

First thing in the morning, I pick up the phone and call Victoria at the Wilshire offices of Pincus Bleistiff. And just in case she forgot, I tell her who I am again.

"Oh yes," she says. "Mr. Parisman. I do hope you aren't bringing us more bad news today."

"No, not today," I tell her. Then I ask her if she might have a file somewhere on the old man's Jaguar.

"You know, you're the second person to ask me that," she says.

"Oh yeah?" I say. "Who was the first?"

"A Sergeant Remo from the Los Angeles Police Department.

He just called ten minutes ago. What's going on? You know him?"

"We cross paths every now and then. Did he ask you for the license number?"

"No, he already had the license from the DMV. He wanted to know where Mr. Bleistiff took it for servicing and repairs. I told him. It's down on Pico near Western."

"He didn't say why he wanted that, did he?"

"Not really. He said he knew it was an old car, and that Jaguars that age were often finicky."

"Meaning?"

"Meaning you wouldn't want to take it out for a long road trip. Not without a complete physical first." A call comes in then on another line, and Victoria puts me on hold. "I'm sorry," she says when she comes back, "I've been so busy orchestrating the funeral this afternoon at 3, I don't know which end is up."

I ask her where it's being held, and she says Hillside Memorial Park in Culver City. The one with all the movie stars. "They've delayed it twice already," she says. "Once because of the autopsy, then another day because his son was flying here from Israel. I know that's not the way they usually do things. It's all supposed to happen in twenty-four hours, right? At least that's what his daughter said. I don't get that. I mean, the poor man is dead. What's the hurry?"

In the back of my mind I weigh the pros and cons of offering Victoria a crash course in Judaism over the phone. Would it do any good? Is it my responsibility? Am I the best teacher? Do I really need to repair this small broken shard of the universe? The answer is no, no, no, and no. Still, she's asking.

"I guess it came from all those years they say we spent wandering around in the desert," I tell her. "Forty years? That's an awful long time to be outdoors. Jews just wanted the body in the ground, the quicker the better. That's the tradition."

"Oh," she says.

"I don't suppose you're too familiar with what happens

when a person stops breathing, are you? I mean, have you ever seen a corpse?"

"Not actually," she admits. "I guess I'm too young."

"Yeah, well. You have to do something with them right away. There's no two ways about it. Keep 'em on ice or bury them. And we were burying each other long before refrigerators came along."

"I suppose," she says. "I never read the Old Testament, I'm ashamed to say. Or if I did, I don't remember. High church and all that."

"I'm glad you mentioned the funeral, though," I say. "I wouldn't want to miss it."

She gives me the address, which is on Centinela Avenue in Culver City, along with the Jaguar's license number. I thank her and hang up.

Carmen lets herself in a few minutes later. She has her lemon running shoes on and she has brought along her plastic picnic basket, the one she got on sale at Target. She plans to take Loretta to Griffith Park. Loretta, we've both discovered, likes to watch the children ride the ponies there. It cheers her up, and, besides, it's good for her to get out in the sunshine, didn't her doctor say that? Yes, he did, many times. I tell her that sounds wonderful. I press an extra twenty bucks into her hand since she's driving her own car. And somewhere between my second and third cup of coffee, I also let it be known that I have a funeral to go to on the west side of town, so she shouldn't expect me until dinner.

"*Dios mío*, who has died, *señor*?"

"Just an old man I knew briefly," I say. "He was my client, but he died unexpectedly."

At the mention of death, she crosses herself and nods sagely. I debate whether to tell her anything more, then decide to just let it be. Carmen has her world, I have mine, and there's more than enough pain to go around in both.

I comb my hair, put on a tan sport coat, a fresh white shirt, and a nice, simple, light blue tie. No sense wearing my dark suit, I think; I liked Pinky well enough, but for me this is business, not grief. I leave the building extra early, because even though it's the middle of the afternoon and people are still at work, you never know when traffic will suddenly turn into a pudding. Which is what happens shortly after I take the ramp onto the Santa Monica Freeway at La Cienega. While I'm crawling along in the heat and glare, even though it's illegal, I pick up my phone and tap in a quick call to Malloy.

"So I hear we're both looking for the same Jaguar," I say.

"We are," he says, "only my boys will find it sooner than you. That I can just about guarantee."

"And what'd you learn from the people who service it down on Pico?"

He doesn't seem surprised by this question. "She took it in last week. Told them she and her boyfriend might want to take it up to Portland soon. Asked for a complete lube and oil. Also told them to check the brakes and rotate the tires if it needed it. They said two of the tires were starting to go bald, so she had them put new ones on."

"Makes sense, I guess."

"Sure it makes sense. Bleistiff was paying for it. What did she care?"

"Oh, come on, Bill. You're making her sound like a heartless gold digger."

"She's more than that," he says. "She's absolutely a gold digger. And quite possibly a killer. And now she's on the run in a '58 silver Jaguar. A convertible, no less."

"You think?"

"That's the theory at the moment. Although if I were her, I'd find something a little less conspicuous to drive."

"If she were on the run, yeah, I'd agree with you."

"You're losing me, Amos. She's clearly on the run."

"Yeah, but from who? The cops?"

"Damn right, the cops."

"If she killed Bleistiff, okay. Then it might make sense. But what if she didn't?"

"What if she didn't?" he says, incredulously. "C'mon, man."

"How can you be so sure, Bill? Somebody shot him, okay. But it's not like you've got an eyewitness."

"No," he says, "but we've got a decent motive. And a suspect who's making herself scarce right now."

"But what if she had a fight with him and just took off? Most women I know don't go looking for more trouble after that. They scream and walk out. That's what Javier Escovedo told us."

"I know," he says. "We talked with Javier an hour after you did. Sounds like they did have a giant fight. Sounds like her hair was on fire when she left. But that's all the more reason, isn't it, for her to come back and gun him down."

"This whole thing is just about anger, then? A woman scorned?"

"Don't underestimate emotions, Amos. You'd be amazed at the things some people do when they snap. That's where I think this is headed. And a few months from now, I'd bet that's what the DA will tell the jury when she takes the stand."

"DAs have been known to lie through their teeth if they have to. But it still has to add up."

"For my money," he says, "it does. They were living together. She was sponging off him. Maybe he'd finally had enough. Maybe he said something. They had a fight. She walked out, realized just how angry she was, realized she wanted to get even, drove back later that night and shot him. End of story."

"You really think a jury will believe that?"

"I believe it, Amos. There are still a few loose ends, but for the most part, it adds up, as you say. Murder in a rage."

"Oh yeah? Then tell me this: Why would she do it in his doorway?"

"What are you talking about? What difference does that make?"

"Pinky gave her the keys to his beloved Jaguar. That's how much he doted on her. Wouldn't you presume she also had a key to the front door?"

"Maybe so. Why not? Yeah, that would figure."

"So why would she stand around in the shadows and wait for him to come to the door? Why do that, when she could just as easily let herself in with a key, walk into the bedroom, and plug him in his sleep? Where's the logic there, Lieutenant?"

He doesn't answer immediately. The freeway traffic is beginning to loosen up. The Centinela exit is approaching; I hit my turn signal and slide deftly into the right-hand lane.

"You make a fair point," he says. "But there are other ways to explain that. Maybe by the time she got there, she'd cooled down some. Maybe she began thinking she could get away with it somehow. Make it look like a bungled break-in. Maybe she didn't want the finger pointing at her."

"But that sounds like someone with a long-term plan. A rational plan."

"It does, doesn't it?"

"And that's where we come to the question of the antique Jaguar. Didn't you just tell me she should have chosen something less conspicuous to drive? I couldn't agree more. No one fleeing the scene of a crime—no one in their right mind—would ever set foot in a car like that."

"People who kill people don't always think clearly afterward. They panic. They make mistakes."

"I'll give you that. And you still have to pick her up and talk to her. But I'd count to ten before labeling her anything."

"It's just a theory, Amos. It's what we have to work with. Maybe tomorrow you'll tell me something different and I'll believe you."

"I'll do what I can," I say.

There's more traffic along Centinela. Two cars have piled into
each other outside a strip mall, and one has completely flipped
over. There's chrome and glass spewed all across the road, and
no question that somebody's hurt. Three Japanese kids on bikes
are standing on a curb, pointing and taking turns speaking to
a young blond woman and her camera guy. A black-and-white
police cruiser is blocking one lane at an angle, a helicopter is
doing delicate daisy loops overhead, and the air is filled with
sirens. Even though it could have happened to me, even though
it might have happened just ten minutes ago, there's already
something abstract and disconnected about the whole scene.
You're rolling past in slow motion, and it's hard to see it as a
tragedy. I don't know the older lady in the rumpled gray skirt
lying faceup on the pavement, don't recognize the two burly
cops in sunglasses kneeling beside her. An ABC-TV minivan is
parked in front of a dentist's office, and the whole story is being
packaged for the nightly news at 6. If you're one of the unlucky
cars on the road like me, you're just part of the scenery. There's
nothing to be done.

By the time I finally turn into the cemetery and find the
cement canyon where they're entombing Pinky, the show is
practically over. I work my way through the crowd of mourners,
which isn't nearly as huge as I thought it would be for someone
like him. Eighty people, maybe, tops. The rabbi is standing next
to the casket with his arms outstretched and his palms turned
up to the heavens, mumbling in Hebrew. He's a short, nerdy
fellow: black robes, thick tortoiseshell glasses, the same kind my
former accountant used to wear, and a bad haircut. Nice little
yarmulke, though.

"I know we are living in modern times," he says. "And it is
easy—sometimes far too easy—in America to forget, to fall
away from tradition. But for those of you here who remember
your Hebrew, please look at the sheet we've given you and join

me now in reciting the Kaddish. If you don't know Hebrew, there's a transliterated version right below it. This is one of the holiest expressions of the Jewish people. Yes, it's our prayer for the dead. Yet it never once mentions the word. The Kaddish speaks instead about our life on earth, and about how we can—how we must—sanctify God's work on earth."

Then he closes his eyes and begins the chant, and I, along with six or seven others, open our mouths and the old words form themselves. *Yit'gadal v'yit'kadash sh'mei raba.*

After that, the crowd shuffles off past the canyons of neatly stacked crypts on either side to a grassy makeshift reception area at the bottom of the hill. There's a quadrangle of folding tables all covered in white linen, stainless-steel containers with finger food, and a small platoon of caterers to dish everything out. Someone even thought to bring in a trio—a clarinet, accordion, and violin—to make a little bittersweet background noise. I don't recognize the stocky woman in black on the accordion. She's also far better than the other two. They're doing a slightly syncopated version of *Oseh Shalom*, which is probably the only part of the Kaddish every Jew knows by heart. It's supposed to be sad, but today for some reason they're treating it like a bossa nova tune. Pinky would have been tickled.

The mourners who haven't left immediately in search of their cars, the ones who just came to eat, they're not music lovers. A few of them begin to talk and hug one another. Two white-haired guys about Pinky's age approach the musicians. One of them is holding a bottle of beer by the neck. The other one has a fancy woven prayer shawl wrapped around his shoulders. He nods to his drinking buddy, taps his feet appreciatively. Then he pulls out a crumpled bill, bends down, and drops it into the violinist's case.

In the center of the crowd a tanned, broad-shouldered fellow in an open pale blue shirt is getting a lot of attention. I figure it must be Pinky's son, just in from Israel. From the paper program in my hand, he's listed as Joshua Eleazar, and somewhere else in the group is probably his sister, Julie. He doesn't seem particularly grieved, but I know from experience that Israelis can be fairly cavalier about death; they've seen so much of it, after all.

I glance back at Pinky's casket. A pair of workmen in jeans and matching company logos on their baseball caps come out from the shadows and slide him gently onto a special forklift. They do this without any apparent effort, or at least this seems to be something they've done dozens of times before. The younger of them sits beside the casket and straps himself into a small padded chair attached to the forklift. Then they glance over at the rabbi, who nods. A button is pressed, the machine begins to hum, and both the worker in the chair and Pinky Bleistiff levitate in slow unison. The bodies here are stacked in fives. When the forklift reaches the fifth floor, it shudders and stops. It's then that I notice a tiny brown cloth curtain in front of the empty crypt there. The man in the chair pushes it aside. When he's sure everything is all lined up, he shoves the casket inch by inch into the cool, waiting darkness.

I shake the rabbi's hand, and as we make our way slowly toward the picnic, I thank him for a job well done.

"Are you a relative?" he asks.

"Me?" I say. "No, I was doing some work for him. But he died before I could finish."

I hand the rabbi my business card. He looks at it and wags his large owlish head from side to side, which dislodges his yarmulke. It flutters to the ground. He bends down automatically to retrieve it, gives it a little kiss, and tucks it into his pants pocket. I remember kissing my yarmulke whenever it fell off my head. It's what everyone did back then. Keeping it holy. But the gesture reminds me of all the agonizing afternoons I spent in Hebrew school not paying attention, longing to escape, longing to be home listening to records or out on the playground shooting hoops, and now as I study his bare head again it also makes me realize what a truly bad haircut he has.

"You're not with the police?" the rabbi asks.

"We collaborate," I say. "He hired me to find a klezmer singer he was in love with. Then someone shot him. I'm still looking."

"Klezmer?" the rabbi's tone immediately perks up. "I'm a big fan. But then it's in the blood, right?" He taps his chest with his fist a couple of times. "You can't help yourself."

"It's fine," I say, "but I was always more attracted to jazz."

"They're not so unrelated," the rabbi says. "We were all street musicians at one time. Oh, I know blacks like to think that jazz is theirs. They invented it—lock, stock, and barrel. Not true. We played a part. You can't deny that. Remember Benny Goodman?"

"I remember."

He gives me a self-satisfied look. This case is closed, says his face. We walk on a few more steps in silence. "Okay, so what's her name?"

"Who?"

"The one he was in love with. The girl you're looking for."

"Risa Barsky."

"Sure, sure, sure," he says at once. "I know who she is. Risa Barsky. Beautiful singer. We had her and her whole group over to our shul for a Purim party last April. What did they call themselves?" His eyes grow wide, trying to remember. "Wait, wait, I got it: Dark Dreidel, that was it. Dark Dreidel. Something cute like that." He stops briefly in his tracks. "Where'd she go?"

"That's a good question," I say. "And now the man who was paying me to track her down is dead. Which makes it even better. Or worse."

He wags his head thoughtfully again. "Quite a *tsimmes* you've gotten yourself into, young man."

"You're joking about the young man stuff, aren't you, rabbi? I mean, young man? C'mon. See this white hair?" I point to the fringe around my ears. "I could be your father."

"No, you couldn't," he says with a twinkle in his eye. "One of the hidden benefits of being a rabbi is that you are forced to learn who you really are. I'm the spitting image of my father. And my father was a particularly ugly man. People would stop him on the street sometimes just to let him know."

"I'll take that as a compliment," I say.

We walk together back toward the sanctuary, which is at the base of a small, steep, green hill, next to a vast gray parking lot. A few other mourners are milling around, chatting, embracing.

"I didn't know Pincus Bleistiff was involved with that girl," the rabbi says. "That girl, Risa, she was what? Only in her thirties, as I recall. And he—" He stops there in midsentence.

"Yeah, it was kind of a May-December romance they had going on. He'd been married a long time. I don't think he ever expected to be a widower. Most men don't."

"No, I think you're right. Men don't generally do well all by ourselves." He folds his arms in front of him. His face stiffens and he shakes his head. "I don't imagine I'd last more than a year without my wife."

I watch Joshua Bleistiff, or the man I assume to be Joshua Bleistiff, escorting a slender woman dressed in a fashionable black dress and high heels. They climb into the back of a Mercedes and head off toward the exit.

"Rabbi, just out of curiosity," I ask, "who brought you in to do the funeral today? You didn't know the family, did you?"

"No, I met the children a few minutes before it was time to begin. I just received a call from the mortuary two days ago. Had to put my sermon together on the fly. I can do it if need be. Normally, of course, a Jewish funeral would have happened sooner. But because of the circumstances, well."

"But it's not easy to get into this place, right? I mean, they're running out of room." I point back at the crypts behind us. "Storing people above ground."

"That's true," he says. "But this is LA. There's a space

shortage for everyone, dead or alive, doesn't matter."

"Okay, so who paid for the ceremony? The flowers? The crypt? Was her name Victoria? British accent?"

"Oh, I couldn't tell you that, I'm afraid. You can check with the head office. Somebody arranged for it, that's for sure. I can tell you this: Hillside doesn't bury anyone unless they have a hefty credit card to work with."

Chapter 10

IT'S STILL TWO full weeks to go before Thanksgiving, but Hollywood has jumped the gun as usual and already deployed their Christmas decorations. The elevator music has quietly changed—jazz standards and Broadway show tunes replaced by harps and vibraphones doing things like "Silver Bells" and "Away in the Manger." Fake snow and tinsel are spreading inexorably across storefront windows, and little wistful plastic cherubs are smiling down from the streetlamps. Hell, there's even a red-nosed cardboard cutout of Santa leering up at customers from behind the counter at the Power House on Highland.

I'm sitting all by myself at the bar, watching two young men who maybe just came out of the military, two young emphatically strong men with crew cuts in polo shirts, their arm muscles bulging, laughing and hurling darts at the wall. They're not that far away from the dartboard, with its red and black and green pattern of circles, but they've had more than enough to drink. Now, they're literally hitting the wall.

I've been here for twenty minutes waiting for Omar. When he finally arrives, I give him a little wave and he slides onto the stool next to mine.

"Sorry, man," he says, "parking is a bitch in this neighborhood." The bartender approaches and he orders a dark beer, or whatever you have on tap, he tells him, it doesn't matter.

I take a sip of my own beer, which is light and tasteless, but that's what I knew I could handle this late in the afternoon. "So what do you have for me?" I ask.

He shrugs. "I decided to get a little tighter with Ray Ballo, since he was the last person in the world Risa Barsky had anything in common with. I sat in on a show they were doing in Castaic. It was another biker bar, smaller than this one, but I wasn't so crazy about the clientele."

I motion with my head toward the two guys playing darts. "You meet the best people in bars, Omar, you know that."

"Yeah, right. Anyway, I sat down with him afterward and bought him a few drinks. That seemed like the way to his heart."

"And what'd he tell you?"

"He's sad, man. Depressed, I guess you'd say. He keeps thinking about Risa. Can't get her out of his head."

"He's young," I say. "He'll get over it."

Omar's beer arrives. He takes a long gulp, which empties almost half of it, wipes the moisture off his upper lip, then turns to me. "He's sad because he talked with her again. She called him up."

"Did she, now? I thought she dumped him."

"She did, she did. But she was acting all different on the phone. Crazy, according to him. Talking a mile a minute. Said she'd been thinking it through, and she realized she'd made a big mistake, maybe a whole bunch of mistakes. That she was sorry now for everything, that she never should have run off, that Pinky was all wrong for her."

"Did she happen to mention that she shot him? Was that one of her mistakes?"

"No," Omar says, "she didn't talk about that. Actually, Ray claimed he didn't even know he'd been murdered."

"Guess he doesn't read the paper," I say.

"Are you surprised?"

"No, not really."

"Okay, but I'll tell you what was interesting to me, Amos. The look on his face when we talked about Risa and Bleistiff. Ray was confused. Stunned, if you wanna know. He'd only met Pinky twice before, he said, and it just never occurred to him that they could—I mean, that they might—that they had anything at all in common. I'm kinda confused myself. Was she really in love with him?"

"Oh, I wouldn't call it love," I say. "That's a loaded word. I don't think it means much in this context. But she *was* poor. You know what that's like. Every month the landlord was probably banging on her door."

"Yeah, well, there's a simple answer when that happens," Omar says. "You go out and get yourself a job."

"Not so simple," I say. "Not if you believe you're an artist. How old is Risa? Thirty-five? That's a long time to be betting on a dream. It's not hard for me to imagine what happened."

"And what was that?"

"I think she was just worn out," I tell him. "I think she was tired, always living hand to mouth."

Omar takes another small chug of his beer and stares off into the middle distance without blinking. He's trying hard to think like me, but we're different people and it's a reach. Even after all his tumultuous years in the barrio, even after his run-ins with the legal system, the way this country works is still a mystery to him.

"I don't know," he says, shaking his big shaven head.

"You don't? Can't you see how a person in her circumstance might be tempted to let someone—anyone—take care of her? She's young and gorgeous." I point my index finger. "Well, all right, maybe not quite so young, but she still has her looks. And what's more important—she's broke."

"Yeah, so?"

"So Pinky Bleistiff comes along and she starts weighing her options. Pinky wasn't just rich, he was lonely. It's an old story."

The dart throwers have finished their game, or what passes for a game. All their darts except for one are planted firmly in the wall. They brush past us on their way out the door. Omar doesn't move a muscle. The bartender stares them down as they depart, then ambles slowly over to the wall and yanks out all the darts. He frowns, shakes his head, tucks the little feathered missiles one by one in his shirt pocket, and returns to his nice secure place behind the counter.

"So why'd she phone him, Omar? To say she was sorry?"

"No," he says. "That's what I don't get. She wanted his help. She wanted to meet him. She was scared and she was talking about running away from here, finding a new life, starting over. That kind of thing."

"Running away from what? From Pinky? From LA?"

"It wasn't clear, man."

"Okay. She wanted to run away. So where were they going to meet?"

"That never came up. Ray killed the whole idea. He didn't know anything about what had happened to Pinky. Not then, at least, and she didn't fill him in. Hell, maybe Pinky was still alive when she called. I'm not sure about that, either. She went on and on, and it was all about her fears, her needs. Talked fifteen minutes straight without taking a breath."

"He ask her where she was staying?"

"No. It wasn't with Pinky, he figured. And it sure wasn't with him. Anyway, he didn't ask."

"You said she was scared."

"Ray thought so. But she acted nuts, and he didn't like what he was hearing, he said, not after the way she treated him before. Said he felt used. Even though he loved her, there was this voice in his head that kept telling him no, no way, not again, you don't want to be dragged into whatever's going on."

"And then?"

"And then she hung up on him."

I swallow the last of my beer and slide the glass gently away from me. On the jukebox another patron, infected by the spirit, has put on Elvis Presley doing "Blue Christmas." Of course, I think, what else? The bartender looks over—did I want another?—but he can see by my expression that I'm done. I lay a crumple of bills on the counter, and we both lumber past the leering cardboard Santa toward the exit.

Outside on Highland the air has gotten cooler and the afternoon shadows have grown perceptively longer. My eyes wander across the street where there's a pawnshop, a thrift store, a psychic parlor with a large tarot card depicting Death hanging in the window, and next to that, a laundromat. Only the laundromat is open. At least, the neon lights are on. A homeless man in a pointy-hooded jacket and red high-top sneakers walks right past us, then heads toward the corner. A Druid, I think—someone straight out of the Middle Ages, anyway. He's pushing a rusty shopping cart piled high with clothes, and he's muttering rapidly to himself. It may be English, but nothing either one of us can possibly translate.

Omar tells me it seems to him that we've hit a wall with this case. "If you want to go on, I can understand," he says, "but there's no point you keeping me on the payroll. I can find other jobs. Especially now that the money's dried up."

"I'm not in this for the money, Omar."

"What then?" His gaze momentarily drifts off toward the homeless guy, who has halted abruptly in the middle of the sidewalk. He's out of earshot, but he hasn't stopped babbling, and he's forcing the oncoming pedestrians to give him a wide berth.

"Sometimes you just want to know the truth," I say. "At my stage of the game that's what gets me up in the morning. That, and a good strong cup of coffee. Am I making any sense?"

"*Estas bromeando?*" he says. "You joking?" He indicates the homeless Druid on the corner. "Maybe about as much as him." Then he shakes my hand and looks me in the eye. "It's noble what you want to do. I get that. But that's not how the world works. Not my world, anyway. I don't want to sponge off you."

"You're not."

"Yes, I am, Amos. If you have a sugar daddy—someone who's paying you, well, that's one thing. I'm happy to help."

"I know."

"But that's the only way we can ever work together. Fair is fair, right? Meanwhile, I also have to feed my girlfriend. She likes to eat now and then."

I nod, thank him for taking the time to talk to Ray Ballo, and before he turns to go home, I push five crisp twenties into his hand.

"Hey, you don't have to do that, man." He looks down at the money. It's hard to read what he's thinking. I don't know what it means to him, but I know where he comes from and that he needs it more than I ever will.

"I want to," I say. "You earned it."

He gives me one of his cryptic half-smiles, which seems to cover a wide range of ancient emotions. His hand cups my shoulder and lingers there for a second. Then he vanishes into the late afternoon.

Loretta and I have a light supper. First a green salad. Then shrimp and angel-hair pasta with olive oil. Some roasted garlic. A little parmesan. No salt for either of us. I have a cold glass of chardonnay and she has her orange juice, like the doctor ordered. I make sure she takes her pills before I bring out the coffee gelato. And half an hour after she's gone off to bed and my hands are still damp from doing the dishes, the phone rings. It's Malloy.

"We got lucky," he begins. "We found the Jag."

"Well, now, that was quick," I say. "What happened?"

"It was in a long-term parking lot at LAX. We couldn't find a ticket in it with an entry time, but the surveillance camera they had showed it coming in two days ago around 7 at night."

"That would be two days after Bleistiff was murdered."

"You got it."

"So now we think she's flown away?"

"Maybe. We're checking with the airlines. If she used her

real driver's license or a credit card, they'd be able to flag it pretty quickly. If she had cash and a fake ID, well, that's something else again."

"Of course, she could have just left it there, Bill. No law says she has to hop on a plane just because she's in the neighborhood."

"That's another idea, yeah."

"What about the car? Anything interesting inside?"

"Forensics is going over the whole thing—inside and out."

"They've got some decent prints, right?"

"Yeah," he says, "but so far, nothing else. There's no trace of blood or gunpowder residue on the car seats or the steering wheel. It's all pretty clean. No gun, for that matter. All of which I think is strange. I mean, if she snuffed him in a blind rage and drove off, you'd think she'd make at least one mistake."

"To err is human," I say quietly, and when he doesn't respond, I add, "Alexander Pope."

"Who? That's one pope I never heard of," Malloy says. "Before my time, probably."

"No," I say, "Alexander Pope, the writer. He's the guy who said it. It's a famous essay. He wasn't talking about murder but...oh, never mind."

"She's not a professional," Malloy says, refusing to be derailed. "You think she'd leave a little something behind for us, wouldn't you? But it's early."

I tell him what Omar told me about his conversation with Ray Ballo. How Risa Barsky was acting crazy when she called him up and wanted his help. How she was scared and crying and wanting to run.

"That would seem to put her on a flight out of town, then," he says.

"That would also presume she has friends or family who would take her in. Friends who wouldn't ask too many questions if she just showed up in the middle of the night."

"Yeah," he says. "That's a big if."

The next morning after breakfast, after Carmen has made Loretta comfortable on the couch and started dealing her in for a round of gin rummy, I say goodbye and let myself out the door. There's no mail in our box, so I walk out past the security guards in their funny broad-brimmed hats and down to the corner of Wilshire and Hauser. A stiff wind is blowing. I'm standing there in front of Ralphs, taking in the fresh collection of homeless folks who've spent another hard night out on the sidewalk encased in sleeping bags and filthy pillows, refusing to leave their worldly possessions, refusing even to slouch off to a quieter place. The sun rises like an old, worn nickel above the San Gabriels. A well-dressed foursome climbs out of a cab and passes them by, briefly obscuring my view. It's quite a contrast. The women are wearing high heels and sunglasses. The men are both toting briefcases. Three of them are talking on their cell phones, and the one who isn't—the woman—seems to be quietly learning Italian. That's when I pull out Pinky Bleistiff's business card. It has his office address on Wilshire. Judging by the 3000 number, I figure it must be a few miles east of here, somewhere in Koreatown. I cross the street and hop on the Number 20. It's times like these that I love being old. If you're of a certain age and ambulatory and don't mind the fumes, the truth is you can go almost anywhere in Los Angeles for thirty-five cents.

The bus leaves me off near Kingsley, and I start walking. I'm in the permanent shade of many tall glass buildings. I glance at the signs. Almost everything is in black-and-white Korean script, but what isn't seems to be all about insurance and financing. Lots of Asian faces on both sides of the street, lots of food trucks and barbecue joints. Young male office workers in white shirts and ties are standing around in small clusters, taking their cigarette breaks and staring silently at the women in short, tight skirts going by.

Bleistiff's music business is housed in one of the tall glass buildings. There's a Korean barbecue joint on the ground floor and next to that, a ramen palace. In between is a set of revolving doors that takes you to the elevators. He's on the sixteenth floor, which is shared by a lawyer (Kim), a tax accountant (Park), and a financial analyst (Lee). How they let Bleistiff into this place is a mystery to me.

I open the door, and I'm staring at a diminutive young woman in blue slacks and a white sweater seated behind a large desk. Except for a flat computer terminal, an orchid in a small porcelain vase, and a notepad beside her, the desk is entirely vacant. There are two blue metal filing cabinets to her right.

"May I help you?" she asks, rising at once. The British accent is clear and unmistakable. It's also clear and unmistakable that I've startled her, barging in like this. I'm willing to bet she hasn't had a visitor here in weeks.

"Victoria?" I say. "I'm Amos Parisman. The investigator? We talked on the phone, remember?"

"Oh sure," she says, smiling now. "Right." She resumes her place and motions me into the chair across from her, "Sit down, do sit down."

On the wall above the metal filing cabinets are faded color posters of bands and singers I've never heard of, though judging from their dorky suits and haircuts they seem to have stepped out of some fifties high school classroom en masse. The Rockets. The Four Angels. Goldie Jones. There's an obviously defunct klezmer group, the Mavens—five bebop guys in yarmulkes and tallises. They're all wailing away with their saxes and trombones around an Orthodox rabbi with a fake beard, who is cringing while he cradles a Torah in his arms. The photo is maybe meant to be some kind of political statement, I think—music and modernity against that silly old-time religion. Everything is neatly labeled, like a museum. Right above the Mavens there's a framed picture of a black trio who call themselves Two Hits and a Miss. It looks much older than the others, maybe from the

Depression or the war years. The two men look dapper, with
yellow ties and silver sport coats. One sits at the piano, the other stands with his arms around a bass. They're looking up at a
camera that must be close to the ceiling. Their teeth are pearly
white and they're grinning. Their female accomplice holds a mi-
crophone. She's seated on a stool. Her bare legs are crossed in
a provocative, come-hither manner, with one high heel barely
dangling off her foot.

"So this is Pinky's headquarters?"

"For the time being," she says. She waves her hand dismissively. "Until his son or daughter tells me to hand over the keys."

"And you think that's gonna happen?"

A little enigmatic smile. "I'm not paid to think those sorts
of things, Mr. Parisman."

"So what, then?"

"I beg your pardon?" she says.

"What do they pay you for? I mean, nobody wants to sit
around on the sixteenth floor all day and wait for the phone to
ring, do they? I'm just curious."

"There's mail," she says. "Bills. And Mr. Bleistiff still has half
a dozen bands we manage. I'm in the process of finding other
agents who might want to handle their contracts, of course, giv-
en the situation."

"That's what his children told you to do?"

She nods. "Actually, Joshua didn't have to tell me much of
anything. We both agreed that without his father, it couldn't
continue. There was no logic to it. What he did was very personal. He was a hands-on manager, I suppose you'd say. He *was*
the business."

"What about Dark Dreidel?"

She shrugs. "What about them? They're hardly a band
without Risa, are they."

"I don't know. I guess not."

"And at the moment, they don't have many gigs on the horizon. I have the name of a guy in Westwood who could possibly

manage them. He hasn't returned my messages yet, but my sense is they're just going to call it quits."

"So then the plan is just to wind things down? What about the office? What happens to the lease on this place?"

"Oh, I've already been down to the ground floor and spoken to them. They were very understanding." She points vaguely to the orchid. "That arrived yesterday morning. Lovely, isn't it?"

"Yes," I say, "very thoughtful of them."

"That's exactly what they are," she agrees, "thoughtful. And they've already got three people lined up, ready to move. Koreans, of course. It's not a problem."

"Of course." I give her a sideways glance. Victoria's a deceptively beautiful girl. She's wise beyond her years, and part of me assumes she's probably looking forward to busting out of this air-conditioned nightmare and finding a brand-new life for herself. I think again about offering her a job as my secretary, then in the very same instant I realize I have no money and no client who'll give me money, so what the hell are you doing, Parisman? Let it go, you old fool.

"Is Joshua hanging around to help you with all this? Or are you and his sister going to handle things?"

She shakes her head. "Josh flies back to Tel Aviv tomorrow morning. As for Julie? Well, she's got a young family, and to be perfectly honest, she's never been much involved in Mr. Bleistiff's world. Takes after her mum, I expect."

"So it's all up to you, then?"

"They're paying me well enough," she says evenly. "I can manage."

I stand up and get ready to leave, but before I do, I reach into my wallet and lay one of my business cards on the desk. Victoria eyes it but leaves it untouched.

"Here," I say. "Just in case you should think of anything else that could help me."

"Help you do what?"

"Help me find Risa Barsky," I say. "Actually, everyone in

town seems to be looking for her these days. They haven't said so yet, but between you and me, the cops think she's the one who did it."

"Do you?"

"Could be," I tell her. "I dunno. Maybe. It would sure be nice to talk with her, though, see what she has to say."

Then Victoria offers something up that startles me. "I met her only a couple of times," she says. "Mr. Bleistiff dropped by the office with her one evening, just as I was about to head home. She was hanging on his arm, you know, like the proverbial piece of candy." She blushes a bit. "Maybe that's cruel. Maybe I shouldn't speak of her that way. Anyway, they were both dressed to the nines. You could tell it was some kind of date they were on."

"And when was that, Victoria? You remember?"

"September? October? I didn't mark it on my calendar."

"But at least a month or two ago, is that right? Are you sure about that?"

"Perhaps. I couldn't swear to it. I'll tell you what I was sure of, though. They were in love."

"They?"

"Well, he was, for sure. And she seemed—she seemed happy enough."

I study Victoria's features as she speaks. She's a smart girl, an achiever. Her parents probably told her she could be anything she wanted in life, and like a fool she believed them. Of course she did. How can you not? Especially when you're one of those talented people who always winds up at the top of your class, always gets straight As, or whatever the equivalent is in England. Aptly named, Victoria. But she's also young. I watch the rapid way her lips move. The confidence in her perfect body. Does she even know what love is? How is that possible?

"I've been in love maybe twice," I say to her. "The first time it was with this girl I knew back in high school. Mr. Rubalcava's Spanish class. Her name was Melanie. Long dark hair like you.

I loved her so damn hard, I was too scared to even speak to her."

Victoria giggles. "Oh, I know that feeling."

"Okay, but now you've made me curious. Pinky—er, Bleistiff—and Risa were in love?"

"Absolutely," she says.

"Based on what?" I ask. "Are we talking intuition here? You only met her very briefly. Those were your words. She was in her thirties, he was twice that." I shake my head. "That's an odd couple, if you ask me."

The color rises in her cheeks. "It might not have been a match made in heaven, but they were in love," she says sharply. "I could see it in their eyes."

"Yeah, well, this is Hollywood, remember. What you see is not always what you get," I say.

"And what do you mean by that?"

I shrug. "Risa may have liked him once upon a time," I say, "but somewhere along the line things changed. Something went wrong. That's what all the evidence points to. Something scared her out of that house on Mulholland Drive. And someone pumped six slugs into Pinky Bleistiff and left him there to die." I start to make for the door.

"Yes," she says quietly, behind my back. "And all I'm saying is, it wasn't Risa."

"In your opinion," I say, turning back. "Based on meeting her once or twice. For what? Five minutes, maybe."

She stares at me. I don't know, maybe I hurt her feelings. "Goodbye, Mr. Parisman," she says crisply.

Chapter 11

THE NEXT MORNING, I get in my blue Honda and drive out to Venice to see Pete Dominic. Dominic and I were in a band together once upon a time in high school. I played guitar back then, badly, but they kept me on anyway. That was the difference between us. Dominic was the pianist, but the fact was, he could pick up any instrument and play it well. He had a whole bedroom full of trumpets and saxophones and violins, things he'd bought for next to nothing at pawnshops and flea markets. Music was his fix, he used to say. Of course, like a lot of musicians, he found other fixes along the way, which fucked him up and damn near killed him. But he never gave up on music. He had a sitar and an ocarina, I remember. At one point he even owned a theremin. All kinds of strange *chozzeraii*.

Dominic lives on the third floor of a dilapidated triplex a few blocks up from the beach. The roof leaks now and then when it rains, and the plumbing is hit or miss, but he stays there because he's just bumping along on Social Security, and this is LA, and if he sold it he'd have to move to Lancaster or Palm Desert to find anything remotely affordable. If you step out onto his rickety balcony after dinner, you can catch the sun dropping into the Pacific Ocean, though these days there's less and less to see because of all the high-rises going up around him. This is a sore subject.

"All I ever wanted when I retired was to sit on that balcony and watch the ocean," he declares. "That lasted approximately ten minutes. Then all those rich motherfuckers came along. Ruined everything, know what I mean?" He shakes his head, raises his middle finger vaguely toward the Pacific Ocean.

We're huddled around his tiny white plastic kitchenette table, where more than two people would constitute a crowd. We're drinking espresso in little ceramic cups. Chet Baker's playing on the radio, and everything's neat and clean. Not a fork out of place. This is his domain. He's been a bachelor over twenty years. He doesn't think about women anymore, although he tells me he's still sort of friends with Brigitte, his ex-wife, still sees her once in a blue moon at the farmers' market, but it's awkward now since she clearly prefers women over men. "What're you gonna do, huh?" This is a question he asks people like me; that is, anyone who comes by to see him, anyone willing to listen. It's not a conspiratorial thing, and he's not waiting for an answer, either. He knows there's no reply.

I tell him a little bit about the murder of Pinky Bleistiff. That is, I tell him I'm on this case, with next to nothing to go on. I don't give him the particulars, just who my client was, and who his girlfriend is, and how the cops are now hunting all over for her. Even though Dominic spent his whole life in the music business, I don't expect him to know Pinky's name, and he doesn't.

"LA's a big place," he says with a nod. "All kinds of music, all kinds of hustles. I've never been able to keep track." He reaches into his breast pocket for a pack of Marlboros. Taps one out and lights up, blows out the match as he exhales. He's hunched forward, wearing a tangerine-colored running suit with silver stripes down the legs. Wrinkled T-shirt underneath. Flip-flops on his feet. It's not his best look. Dominic hasn't aged nearly as well as I have, I think. He could use a shave and a proper haircut. His lips are cracked. His face is sallow, the backs of his hands have liver spots, and he exudes a general air of disappointment.

"You can't keep track," I say, "but maybe you still know somebody in the industry. Someone who might know Pinky?"

He pulls deeply on his cigarette, which causes him to cough slightly. Then he takes it out from between his lips, holds it delicately with two fingers, and studies the lengthening ash. Finally he sighs and snuffs it out in the glass soap dish in front of him. "Arthur Boewes," he says. "There are a couple of other dudes, but they're probably long gone." He coughs again, gulps down his espresso to relieve the dryness in his throat. "And I haven't talked to Artie in maybe fifteen years. He was younger than me, but he could play the game at Capitol Records. Better than I ever could, that's for sure."

"Arthur Boewes." I take out my notepad and jot it down. "How do you spell that?"

"You're asking me?"

"I was."

"Well, don't bother. But hey, I might have an old phone number for him in my Rolodex." He pries his way out from the table, then turns and looks back at me. "You know what? I'll bet I'm the only man on earth who still uses a Rolodex, what do you think, Amos?"

"I bet you're right, Dominic."

"Fuck you." He chuckles and heads off to his bedroom.

I dial the number the minute I get home. Thanks to Dominic's trusty Rolodex, Mr. Arthur Boewes is pretty easy to find. He's not at that number any longer, but the receptionist is only too glad to transfer me. I talk my way past his secretary and he answers right away. He's all tight-lipped and business at first, but when I drop Dominic's name, and explain who I am, and mention Pinky Bleistiff, his whole demeanor suddenly shifts. "I was just at his funeral," he says. There's genuine affection in his voice. "What a lovely man, Pinky. A real mensch. They don't make them like that anymore." Then, almost as an afterthought: "I only hope they catch the *mamzer* who killed him."

Sometimes it just takes a single word to change everything. My ears tingle at the sound of Yiddish. It's like I'm back sitting on the couch in my parents' living room again. "You'll forgive me," I say, "but how did a nice Jewish boy like you ever get a name like Boewes?"

The question doesn't surprise him. "It was a mistake, Mr. Parisman, what can I tell you? One of those Ellis Island goof-ups. Our family name was actually Borstein, but my grandfather had a stuttering problem. He was so nervous, he couldn't get it out. Bowsz, bowsz, bowsz. There was a long line. The inspector was in a hurry. Okay, he said. Boewes. Next."

"That's funny," I say.

"Could have been borscht," he says, dryly. "That would have been awful."

We talk for maybe forty-five minutes. He and Pinky used to collaborate on record albums, and when that ended he would run into him and his wife now and then at parties. When I ask him whether there was anyone he knew in Hollywood who might have a reason to kill Pinky, he reacts quickly. "You met him, didn't you?"

"Of course I met him. He hired me."

"So then surely you understand. Pinky Bleistiff wouldn't hurt a fly. Not only that. He was a cupcake, the kindest, sweetest man I ever met."

"A cupcake, huh? But somehow he managed to make himself a ton of money. Those two things don't usually go hand in hand."

"I'd agree with you ordinarily. But Pinky was different. Honest to God, he didn't have any enemies. Not a one. And that's saying an awful lot for the music business."

"When was the last time you got together with Pinky, Mr. Boewes?"

"I couldn't say, really. It's been a while."

"You knew his wife. You ever meet his girlfriend, Risa Barsky?"

"No," he says. "I knew he was lonely after Sophie passed away. We invited him over to our place once for Passover, but he begged off. You know how it is. It was going to be all couples, people he worked with back in the day. I guess he didn't want to be the odd man out."

The conversation moves on to other things. Whether he thinks there's still any elements of organized crime in the music industry. "No, not really," he says. "Not anymore. Not unless you count multinational corporations." Then he kind of laughs privately. I don't ask him to explain.

That evening, just as I'm about to turn in, the phone rings. It's Malloy. "We got her," he says. "Turns out she'd gone back to her old apartment. Her neighbor had her over for a cup of tea, then right after she left, she called the cops. It was pretty easy."

"And did she confess?"

"Confess?" he says. "No, no way. Claims she's innocent. Said she had a big fight with Bleistiff, told him to go fuck himself."

"Then what?"

"Then she drove off in the car he gave her."

"Which she subsequently abandoned at the airport."

"Right."

"She mention why she did that? It's hard to be without a car in LA."

"She said she was worried that Pinky would follow her. He thought he owned her. Those were her words. She's been hiding out in different motels all this time, waiting for him to forget about her once and for all. She said she wanted to throw him off the track."

"Hmm," I say. "I just talked with a guy today down at Capitol Records. He told me Pincus Bleistiff was an absolute cupcake."

"Now what's that supposed to mean?"

"That he was a nice man. A Boy Scout. Kind to homeless women and newborn puppies."

"Yeah, well, Risa Barsky has a slightly different opinion," he says.

"So did you charge her with murder, Bill? Where is she now?"

Malloy pauses, and I can almost feel his consternation. "No, Amos, that's the thing. She didn't have a gun, the car was clean as a whistle, and her story about Bleistiff, well, people get mad and break up with each other all the time, don't they? No law against that."

"You mean she's free?"

"For the time being, yeah." Malloy clears his throat. He has to be uncomfortable with this; it goes against his Irish copper's instincts, but the law is plain. "We couldn't exactly hold her on anything. I've got Jason and Remo keeping a sharp tab, though. Don't you worry, this is far from over with."

I put my bare feet up on the coffee table and readjust the phone to my ear. My watch says it's eleven o'clock, way past my bedtime. "Are you saying that for my benefit, Bill? Or your own?"

"Maybe both of us," he says. "But I thought since Bleistiff gave you good money to track her down, you'd like to know where to find her."

"I appreciate the call, Lieutenant."

An ambulance is wending its way lethargically down Third Street toward the emergency center at Cedars-Sinai. Must not be much of an emergency, I think, as I strip down to my underwear and crawl in beside Loretta. Her reading light is still on. The fashion magazine she was looking at has fallen onto the rug. She's fast asleep. Her arms are folded neatly under her breasts and her mouth is open, and when I bend down to kiss her cheek I can see the new gold crown Dr. Mardian put in last month. The siren nine floors below us doesn't bother her. Nothing bothers her, in fact, once she hits the pillows and shuts her eyes.

I lie there on my side, staring at her in the muted light of our bedroom, stroking her hair. In the tower across the way, a party has started. Arab pop tunes are pulsating between our two buildings. It's not bad music. There's a yearning there I could get into, or if I wanted to go to sleep, I could tune it out. But my mind is caught on something tonight, it's spinning around, running itself ragged like a hamster in a pet store. I could wake up tomorrow morning and tell myself this case is closed. I know that. Risa Barsky's been found. Hallelujah. End of story. And nobody's paying you to find Pinky's killer, are they. Pinky, who had no enemies at all. Pinky, the cupcake. Pinky, who was loved by everyone. Musicians, movie stars, the whole glittering Hollywood universe. Pinky, the kindest of men. Who stood in his doorway and took six slugs for no reason anyone can think of. Or was that out of love? You gotta wonder. Love, and not hate, that's what killed him? Don't go there, Parisman. No need to go crawling down into that hole. A headache like that. A thankless task.

I sigh then and flip off the rest of the lights. My eyes are wide open. So what else is new, Mr. Detective?

Chapter 12

OMAR MEETS ME at my apartment a little after 8:30. It's a gray, overcast morning. From our living room window on the ninth floor you can barely see the observatory at Griffith Park. I should have waited a while longer until the rush hour traffic cleared out, but patience has never been my forte. Early's always better than late, I say. Gives you an edge. We drive together slowly up Highland toward the Hollywood Freeway. Clusters of Orthodox Jews in dark suits and fedoras are striding purposefully down the street en route to morning prayers. They're wrapped in their prayers, oblivious to the world spooling out in front of them, indifferent to (or do they just choose not to see?) the three weary Latina cleaning women climbing down off the bus and the homeless man curled up in his orange sleeping bag in the bushes nearby. It must have rained a little in the night, not nearly enough to clean the sidewalks, but now this odd, animal fog has rolled in to put a monkey wrench into things. In LA it never takes much to change the mood. As we near the intersection at Sunset, people are suddenly walking around in thick jackets and sweaters, which wouldn't mean a goddamn thing anywhere else but here. Here it does. This place is crazy. When I was a kid, they closed the schools one time when it snowed for twenty minutes. Go figure.

Omar is still nursing the medium black coffee he picked up at Peet's on his way in. "You didn't need to call me back, Amos. I mean, don't get me wrong, I'm happy to help, and I can always use the cash, but what's the point?"

"Pincus Bleistiff was murdered, Omar. Don't you want to know why?"

"Not unless somebody pays me, no."

"He was a friend of mine."

"That's a better line. Okay, I'll give you that. Friends count. But what the hell are you talking about? You hardly knew him."

"Not true," I say, which makes me think about George Washington and his famous inability to tell a lie. That's never been my problem. I've lied on plenty of occasions. I was never a Boy Scout, but there are also times in life when sincerity is called for, and this is one of them. "He was my people, Omar. A *landsman*. A fellow traveler. You know how it is."

"Yeah, sure, I know. But that's your world, maybe. I can't afford to take things so personally."

"Sure you can. Life's personal, amigo. What else is there?"

"No," Omar says. "Not true. If I followed up on every fucking Mexican they gunned down in LA, I'd never get a night's sleep, now would I?" He swallows the last of his coffee and sets the paper cup down gently on the floorboard in front of him.

We drive on in silence. I study the freeway, see how the traffic's breaking, and consult my rearview mirror compulsively. I signal before changing lanes and make sure I stay four proper lengths behind the nearest car. I like to believe I'm a good driver. Trouble is, everyone in LA likes to believe he's a good driver, so where does that get you?

My mind keeps coming back to Pincus Bleistiff, all alone, moldering away in his crypt five stories up. Omar's right, of course. That's what I think at first. It's not practical. You can't spend every waking moment on earth crusading for justice. The clock's winding down. You're just one man, and an old one at that. You've still got a wife to take care of, not to mention that pile of pills you take every morning. Nowhere even close to practical. On the other hand, who cares? Since when was the last time anyone ever called you practical? In my family, practical meant you were boring in my family. Almost a four-letter word. You want practical, boychik, my Uncle Bobby told me more than once, go stuff your money in a mattress. At least it'll be there when you wake up. So what else should an unemployed detective do with himself?

"See, it's not like I don't get it," I tell Omar. I signal and press my foot down on the gas pedal. An eighteen-wheeler disappears in my rearview mirror. The muscles in Omar's face contract slightly. I have just my left hand on the steering wheel now. The right is busy jabbing at the air, conducting a silent symphony. "I know it doesn't make sense to you."

"Damn right," he says. "No sense at all."

"But this is something I feel." I lay my hand briefly over my heart as if to prove a point beyond words. The song is over, yeah. But the melody lingers on. "I just have to do it."

His eyes narrow, then he gives me this cold, hard, piercing look. Contempt? Is that what it is? Maybe so. All I know for sure is it's a look that comes straight out of the grit and eternal misery of the barrio. A look that says you're not just a terrible driver but a hopeless gringo. A romantic. And that's being kind.

"Actually," I say, "it's something I need to do." I hesitate a moment. I'm about to lead him into deep water, and since he's a pure-blooded Indian with an eighth-grade education and I'm a Hollywood-born Jew who doesn't believe in Torah or Talmud or God or much of anything anymore, I'm not sure he's ready. Not only that, I'm pretty sure I'm not the right one to teach him. But here we are, just the two of us zipping along on the freeway together at seventy miles an hour, testing Death. "You wanna know what's going on, Omar? What makes me tick? Okay, so I'll tell you. I have this—this little thing."

"Thing?"

"Yeah," I say. "In fact, it's more than that. It's like an obsession. That's a big thing, a tune that plays in my head all the time, something I can't stop thinking about. There are days when I wish I didn't have it. My life would be so much simpler without it, *comprendez*? The Hebrew term is *tikkun olam*."

"Which means what?"

"*Tikkun olam*?" I say with a shrug. "It's the whole ball of wax, the reason I wake up in the morning. Something I'm com-manded to do. I'm searching for oneness, I guess you'd say. Or unity, maybe. Maybe that's a better word."

"I don't know what the fuck you're talking about, man."

"You don't? Really? It's an old idea. I'm trying to repair the universe, Omar. Like Humpty Dumpty. You never heard that Mother Goose rhyme in school? Humpty Dumpty sat on a wall? Putting things back together?"

His eyes go wide. "Humpty Dumpty."

I nod. "That's what we're supposed to do. That's what Jews in particular are supposed to do."

"Hey, man, didn't you tell me you swore that stuff off? You don't pray anymore, you don't even go to church."

"I don't. Most of what passes for Judaism is nonsense. Rules. Stories. Happy talk. Like every other religion."

"So?"

"Most, but not *tikkun olam*. Not that part. Something breaks, you fix it. Putting things back together, I like that idea. That speaks to me." I glance in his direction. "And that means finding Pinky's killer."

Omar shakes his big, bald head. The gold stud in his ear glitters. "Okay, man," he says, still without any comprehension, "whatever."

Half an hour later we find ourselves squeezing into a nice, quiet parking space under an enormous spindly palm tree near Risa's apartment. It's actually the only spot on the block, but it's right across the street from her place, and my Honda fits like a glove, so I won't complain.

Even though it's early, you can feel the glare and the heat that's on its way. We cross the newly paved two-lane road and make our way up the path. I'm about to ring her buzzer when Jason comes loping out of the shadows. He's wearing a Panama hat, a gray sport coat, and a dark red silk tie, which I've never seen before. It makes me think that Malloy must be on his case, giving him grief about looking professional. Behind him I spot his pudgy pal Remo sitting on the landing to the right, sunning himself. He's still wearing his silver Air Force sunglasses, but he's taken his sport coat off, his legs are crossed, and his gun is plainly visible in his leather shoulder holster.

"Morning, Parisman. What the hell brings you here?"

"Oh, good morning, Sergeant. We're looking for Risa Barsky. You haven't seen her, have you?"

"Not since last night. She came back from the supermarket about 9. Two big bags of groceries. She's still sleeping in, I guess." Jason stands there with his hands on his hips and gives both of us the official hard-boiled cop's appraisal. I've known him since he was a rookie. He's married now and has a kid, but that hasn't softened him up as far as I can tell, and we've never managed to become more than passing acquaintances. He probably recognizes Omar from his brief stint at the Police Academy, and I'm pretty sure he genuinely hates his guts for dropping out.

"You were here last night?"

"No, no, no, we generally knock off around 4 and let the local boys take over." Jason frowns and glances over his shoulder at Remo slouched on the stairs. "This kind of stuff gets old, Amos. We need our beauty rest."

"I'm sure you do," I say. I turn back to the key pad and find her name next to B16.

"She knows you're coming?" Jason asks behind me.

"Not that it's any of your business," I say, "but, as a matter of fact, she does."

"Hey, wiseass, everything's my business."

"Oh, right. I must have forgotten." I turn away and leave him standing there, his arms akimbo. I press her buzzer. There's a moment's hesitation, then the door to the foyer clicks open. A minute later, after a short elevator ride, we're standing in front of her door.

"Gentlemen," she says. Risa Barsky looks both better than her photo and worse than I thought she would after these last few harrowing weeks. Still, it's not hard at all to see why Pinky would fall for her. There's a carelessness in the way she turns her head and smiles as she opens the door, or maybe I'm just mistaking that for a carefree spirit. She has adventure written all over her. She greets us in her nightgown, which is not see-through exactly, but it could be in the right light and certainly doesn't leave much to the imagination. It's a frilly peach-colored thing with clusters of little white stars sewn over all her most strategic locations. The makeup on her cheeks still looks okay to my untrained eye, but also looks like it was what she wore the night before. She leads us barefoot into the living room. Her long dark hair is disheveled, and I think Jason was not far wrong to guess she had been sleeping in. Two big handle bags of food from Ralphs sit on the coffee table, waiting to be unpacked, along with an empty wine glass and an open half bottle of chardonnay.

"I hope I can interest you in some coffee. It won't take long. I'm having some. And anyway, that's the way it is. I'm not coherent until I've had coffee."

"Sounds splendid," I say.

Omar grabs a red plush chair in the corner, and I follow her into the kitchen. The apartment looks more or less the same as when I visited before, courtesy of Lola Emery, except now it's neat and tidy. At least it doesn't look ransacked anymore, which is a plus.

I watch her fill the pot with cold water in the sink and measure out the coffee into a brown paper cone. She's very meticulous. Not too much, not too little. Soon the water starts to drip gently into the pot. She stares at it until the coffee's making a steady drip-drip-drip. Then she swivels around to face me and leans her hands against the counter. "You wanted to see me, Mr. Parisman? Okay, then. Here I am. Are you satisfied? Are you another kind of cop like those two goons downstairs? I don't like cops. Well, no, I don't mean that. What I mean is, I'm tired of cops. I've seen too many recently."

"They can be annoying, I hear you. I have problems with them, too. But the answer is no, I'm not a cop. I'm sure Lola told you as much."

"What, then?"

I reach into my side coat pocket and hand her my card. "I was hired to find you by Pincus Bleistiff. He was worried about you."

At the sound of his name I see her body stiffen. "That's him. The kind of thing he would do," she says without much affect. "Hire a fucking detective." She shakes her head and shivers then, as if whatever she was thinking just ran right through her like a freight train.

"But I don't understand. Why are you here now?" she says suddenly. "Aren't you—just a little bit late?"

"A little, you're right. It won't do him any good." I start to open my mouth again, then I decide no, I'll let it go, just skip the lecture about my burning need to repair the universe, which is a shame, because I'm sure she'd appreciate it far more than Omar.

"Okay, so you found me," she mumbles. "That's terrific. Mazel tov." She turns back to check on the coffee.

We share a silence then that seems as wide and dark and deep as the Amazon. It strikes me that Risa Barsky is the missing piece in this puzzle. Maybe she didn't kill Pinky that night, but she's probably the only one who can lead me to the one who did. "How long did the police interrogate you, Risa?"

"Oh, a long time. I couldn't tell you, really. Hours. They sat me down in this tiny room and took turns asking questions. They asked the same questions, over and over again. Sometimes they tried to trick me. They read my own words back to me, then they said, that was a lie, now wasn't it? And I felt like I couldn't breathe. It was more like a closet than a room. There were no windows or pictures. Nothing. Just a table and some folding chairs. Nothing to let the air in or out. It was awful. Smelled like Lysol."

She looks away, tries to rub the goose bumps off her arms. She's a smart girl. She still remembers, I hope, what we talked about on the phone. She understands we're not the cops, not trying to hound her, that all we want is to find Pinky's assassin, not frame her for something she didn't do.

"They thought you killed him, I hear."

"That's what they said. And they were so smarmy, so god-damn sure of themselves, too. 'Why don't you tell us about the murder, Miss Barsky. Take your time. We have all the time in the world if you like. We're here to help. Just tell us everything, okay? Let's start at the beginning. You killed him. No one doubts that. It's an open-and-shut case. You did it.'" She turns to me directly. Her eyes widen. "But I didn't, Mr. Parisman. See, that's the thing. I wouldn't kill Pinky. He was good to me. Why would I do that?"

The coffee pot is gurgling behind her and she turns around, pulls three cheap white ceramic cups—things she probably bought on sale long ago at Pier 1—from the overhead cupboard and lines them up in front of her.

"I'll help you with that," I say.

"I can manage," she says. She bends down, reaches into the refrigerator, and produces a cardboard container of half-and-half. "What do you put in it?"

"Black is fine," I tell her. "Same for my friend, Omar."

"I need everything in mine," she says. "Cream, sugar. Hell, I'd put some Jack Daniels in right now if I had any."

"That's a helluva way to start the morning," I say. I grab my cup and Omar's, and we wander back to the living room.

After a few quick sips, Risa seems to come miraculously to her senses. I'm not a mind reader, I can't climb inside her head, and I can't tell whether she's embarrassed all of a sudden to be lounging around with us in her underwear—she sure wasn't be-fore—but there's no doubt about it, the chemistry in the room has changed. She sets her coffee down and excuses herself. "I'll be back in a flash," she says, "okay?" She asks it like it's not a question, just something pressing she has to do. Then she darts off into the bedroom and shuts the door.

We're silent a while. Omar gives me a bemused look. "What do you make of that, boss?"

"Go easy on her, Omar. She's a lovely girl. And she's probably in shock about what's happened the last few days. You'd be, too."

"So?"

"So sometimes lovely girls don't appreciate it when grown men like you and me stare at them."

"Especially when they're half-naked, I get that."

"Like I say, go easy."

The bedroom door opens then, and Risa Barsky returns. She's in a sensible black cotton skirt with a long-sleeve white blouse, and now she's wearing silver Chinese slippers on her feet. Or are those ballet shoes? Don't ask me. She's even put on some artsy gold earrings and lipstick, all of which add to her new civilized outlook. Now she's no longer risqué; now she could be a librarian, I think, or, okay, nothing that demure, but at least a grad student. She settles back down onto the couch and crosses her legs.

"All right, then," she says. "So what would you like to know?"

"Well, for starters," I go, "what exactly did you and Pinky fight about?"

"The police asked me that," she says.

"And what did you tell them?"

"The truth. That I'd had enough. That I was suffocating in that house. I told him I was leaving, and he was trying every cheap line he could think of to get me to change my mind. I didn't want to hurt him. Like I say, he'd been good to me, but we started yelling at each other and it got pretty heated."

"You didn't love him anymore?" Omar asks.

"I never loved him," she declares. "He knew that. I moved in with him because I was scared, that's all. Someone broke in here and tore this place up. Scared the shit out of me."

"Okay," I say, "but why Pinky? What about your boyfriend? Ray Ballo? Why didn't you just move in with him?"

She rolls her eyes as if I was just another ape, as if I couldn't possibly understand what goes on in a woman's mind. Or I don't know, maybe she's just surprised that we know his name. "Ray Ballo. Ray's apartment is about the size of this coffee table," she says. "That's one reason. Also, also, we were having… some personal issues at the time."

"You want to tell me what those were?"

"No," she sniffs, "I don't particularly want to tell you anything. But maybe it makes no difference, not anymore. I thought he was seeing someone else on the side."

"You were jealous?" Omar asks.

"I was angry," she says, trying to keep an even tone. "I thought he loved me."

I nod. "All right. So you came home and you walked in and you found the apartment wrecked. And you were scared."

"I was fucking terrified."

"And you didn't want to take a chance on Ray. So you picked up the phone and you called Pinky? Is that it?"

"No. No, actually, he called me. It was a lucky coincidence, I guess. I was going to run down the hall to my neighbor's. But the phone rang and it was Pinky. He was calling to talk to me about a gig, and I told him what had happened, and he was very kind. He wanted to take care of me. He sent his man Javier over right away. Javier drove me to his place on Mulholland. What else could I do? It made sense at the time. Wouldn't you have done the same? I thought somebody was trying to kill me."

"You could have called the cops," Omar offers.

She stares at him. "Is that what you would have done? Really? Where are you from, Omar?"

"Boyle Heights," he says. "And before that, when I was a kid, Mexico."

She nods. "Boyle Heights. Not too different from my old neighborhood in Morningside Heights. Let's put it this way: I've had experiences with cops," she replies. "A long time ago they caught me smoking dope in a car with some older boys. I was fourteen, a teenager. They took my name and let me go, but the two guys in the front seat had outstanding warrants. They ended up on Rikers Island. You don't forget stuff like that."

"I get it," Omar says.

"So why would I invite them over and tell them someone's trying to kill me? You tell me."

"Any idea who?"

She shakes her head. "I'm just a singer, Mr. Parisman. I work at a temp agency whenever the gigs dry up. I'm known for my filing skills. I don't have any enemies."

"Funny, that's what everyone said about Pinky. That he didn't have any enemies, I mean."

"He was a kind man, a generous old man," she says. "But he was also a very lonely man. He needed me. I dunno, maybe he needed me too much. Said I was the love of his life. He asked me to marry him."

"Oh my. And you said?"

"I said no. No, I couldn't." She trembles a little. "I thought about it, though. For maybe a minute, you know. But it didn't feel right. I just couldn't reciprocate."

"Tell me, Risa," I say. "Are you the only one with a key to this apartment? Anyone else?"

"The manager has a master, I guess. And Lola down the hall, just in case. Oh, and I gave one to Pinky when I first arrived. He found this place for me, paid the first two months' rent. I figured it sorta belonged to him. You know what I mean?"

The coffee in my cup is growing cooler and I haven't touched it yet, but there are still things I want to find out. "Do you own a gun, Risa?"

"No. Of course not. That's a silly question."

"Why?"

"Because if I had a gun, I wouldn't need a man to protect me, now would I?"

"Not if you were willing to use it, no. But lots of folks buy a gun and never bring themselves to pull the trigger when the time comes. That's a problem."

"I don't own a gun," she says.

"Ever fire a gun?" Omar asks.

"Never."

"Okay," I say, "so tell me about the Jaguar, then. Pinky gave it to you, is that right?"

"He said I could use it whenever I liked. He never signed over a pink slip, but it was mine to use. Pretty generous, if you ask me. That's how he was."

"And the night you left, you drove off in the Jaguar?"

"That's right."

"And you left it at a long-term parking lot near LAX. Why'd you do that?"

She sighs. "Why? I wanted to vanish, that's why. I wanted to break free. My first thought was to get on a plane and go some-where—anywhere. London. Tahiti. Tokyo. I could have, too. I had my passport. I still had the jewelry he'd given me. I even had a brand-new American Express card. I never had one of those before."

"So you were all set. What stopped you, then?"

"Pinky," she says. "I knew Pinky. The way he thought about me. He wouldn't hurt me, but I knew he'd never let up. He'd hire detectives"—she points vaguely in our direction—"guys like you. That's how he lived his whole life. That's how he always got what he wanted." She pauses and gulps down her coffee. "And that's when it hit me that I could buy some time if I just left it there at the airport."

"So you came back here?" I look around, wag my head, shrug. "This ain't exactly Tahiti. You could have done a lot better somewhere else."

"Also," says Omar, "the fact that you left it there and

disappeared, well, that's what the police would call a presumption of guilt. Look at it from their point of view. They have a dead body in the Hollywood Hills and someone like you—a friend, a girlfriend, an ex-girlfriend, whatever—who's running away in a fancy car. Maybe you're stealing him blind. Maybe you're flying off to Rio, that's what they're working on. You can see how they'd have a bunch of questions."

She nods. "I know it doesn't look good. But I told them the truth. And in the end, they must have believed me because, hey, I'm not in jail, am I." She serves up a wistful smile at this. She has a lovely smile, a genuinely delightful expression that reminds me a little of a cheerleader named Cindy Bushnell whom I pined for all during my junior and senior high school years.

"They couldn't charge you with anything, Risa. That's true. But they haven't given up. You're still a person of interest. I don't think I'd say they believed you, either. Otherwise they wouldn't still be hanging around your door day and night."

The moment seems right then to stop. Of course I could always go on. I probably have another fifty questions I could put to her, but what's the point? Malloy couldn't crack her story, and he's better at this than I am. We all clamber to our feet. I ask her what her plans are now. She says she needs to think. She's not sure whether her old Subaru will still start, but she's hoping she won't have to call the Auto Club. She says that Pinky gave her some diamond bracelets. He wanted her to have them, which is very nice, but she never wears bracelets, so she's planning to take a trip soon down to the Diamond Mart near Pershing Square and see what those people will offer her. She doesn't want to have to go back to the temp agency in Reseda, not right away, at least, and without Pinky running the band, well, there are no bar mitzvahs or wedding gigs on the immediate horizon. "I'll survive," she allows as she walks us to the door, "I always have."

Chapter 13

IT DOESN'T MAKE a dime's worth of difference that you've lived somewhere for years. At some point even the largest, gaudiest castle, the most elaborate palace in the whole world, becomes—despite your best intentions—just a house. Plain old dirt. Real estate. A transaction waiting to happen. To quote my father, greed will make you a monkey in the end. Sooner or later everything turns to cash. That's what's going through my brain right now. That the home of Pincus Bleistiff on Mulholland Drive—his six capacious bedrooms and four-and-a-half baths, his tennis court and swimming pool and cactus garden, his sweeping views of Hollywood—the whole enchilada is not immune to this process. The great man was gone. Enough time had passed. Was there anyone around who was still sitting shiva? Still felt keeping their eyes closed? Their heads bowed? Anyone still weeping and wailing? Risa called him a generous old man. Okay. But he was also rich. Question was, how rich? Rich enough to murder? I don't think so, but it doesn't hurt to check off all the boxes.

It's late morning. Omar and I have just driven through Studio City and are headed up Laurel Canyon. "I like it," he says after a long silence. He looks out the window at the opulent tract homes along the road. This is not his natural turf. Too much dappled sunlight. Too many hand-planted trees and exotic shrubs. Too many high walls and security cameras. He works his tongue around the inside of his mouth the way he always does when he's thinking hard.

"Why?"

"Because it's simple," he says, "A rich guy like that, he's a target. Honey to a bear. There'll always be some *gonif* out there trying to get his hands on his wallet."

"Did I teach you that word?" I smile.

Omar gives me a look. "Let's put it this way," he says. "I understand a thief. I know why people steal. And I like a thief a whole lot better than an angry lover. Makes sense where I come from."

"It only makes sense if you're due to inherit," I say. "Nobody took his wallet that night. And anyway, he probably left everything to his kids."

"So maybe his daughter was hard up. Maybe she has a gambling problem. Maybe she couldn't afford to wait."

"Is that where you're going? Really?"

"I dunno. It's possible. Children kill their parents now and then. Even if it's not about money. Sometimes they just hate them, you know? I could get comfortable with that, too."

"Oh, c'mon, Omar. He was a feeble old man. And besides, I saw his daughter at the funeral. She looked pretty sad."

"Hey, anybody can look sad for an hour. Especially in Hollywood. It's called acting."

I shake my head. "You are such a cynic," I say. "I don't know how you manage to drag yourself out of bed in the morning. His daughter didn't kill him."

"Oh yeah, Mr. Detective? So how do you know? She has a motive, at least. Where's your proof?"

"Because. Because even if she wanted to, she didn't have to. You don't kill somebody if you don't have to."

"What if she was desperate? What if she needed the money?"

"She didn't."

"You sure?"

"I'm telling you, she didn't need the money. I mean, you're right, technically. I haven't seen her bank balance. So she could be broke, yeah. But even so, she wouldn't need a gun to solve that problem. He would have given it to her. He didn't have that much time left on earth. I knew that the moment we shook hands at Canter's. I'm sure his daughter knew it, too. All she had to do was wait."

He shrugs.

We pull into the circular gravel driveway. The iron gate is wide open. There are three late-model cars and a dented cream-colored Toyota pickup parked in the shade under a eucalyptus tree near the service area. Even though Pinky is tucked away in his crypt with all the famous Jewish comedians, someone is obviously still here, still running things. There are no bright metal lawn signs jammed in the ground yet, no indicators of what's to come, according to my wise old dad. I turn off the motor and we walk along the large flat stone path—every stone ringed like a jewel in moss—toward the massive front door.

"Look," I say. "You notice anything missing?"

"Like what?"

"Like there are no FOR SALE signs."

"You wanted to see one?"

"I kinda expected it. Pinky's been dead for weeks."

"Where you and I live," he says, "okay. But these places, these people with their maids and cooks and putting greens, who the hell knows? They're like corporations, if you ask me." His lips curl into a slight but noticeable sneer.

"They're still people, Omar. They live, they die. And when they die, they sell."

"Maybe, but not right away. A house this fucking big, you need a roomful of lawyers sometimes just to untangle things."

"Could be."

"It's just not their way, man. You know what I'm saying?" He spreads his brown, beautiful hands into an expression of helplessness. Or maybe it's just more condescension on display. He's not impressed by the rich. I think at some level they offend him. We've had this discussion many times before.

I press the buzzer. Then I turn around again and scan the

front yard a second time, try to see if there was a For Sale sign posted by the curb or near the gate that I missed. There wasn't.

The door opens. It's Javier Escovedo. His gray hair is slicked back. He's wearing a white linen sport coat and a simple blue tie. His white slacks are pressed, and his black shoes are polished so well, you'd swear they were new. He clearly didn't drive all the way here from Eagle Rock to mop the floors.

"I thought you'd be out of a job by now, Javier."

He smiles. "I thought so, too, Mr. Parisman. But after the funeral, Miss Julia called and asked me to stay on a little longer. They need someone here to supervise. That's what she said. At least until the estate is settled." The quizzical look on his face tells me that like Omar, he may also have ambivalent feelings about the rich, but for now at least, he's not complaining.

"You must be grateful," I say.

"Yes," he says, nodding. And then because he is a natural-born gentleman from an old and proud country, he extends his arm and invites us in. "Please, señores."

The living room is unchanged from when I visited before, except that the plum-colored couches have been covered in clear plastic. All the lamps are turned on, and there's a young, slender, Asian girl hard at work. I realize she's the same one who was here before, but last time she was polishing the baby grand. She's got on blue jeans and a large tan T-shirt that she's knotted artfully around her waist. She's bending over each piece of furniture with a rag; she has an aerosol can in one hand and every few seconds she sprays some lemony mist into the air. In another room, not far away, is the sound of a vacuum cleaner purring relentlessly against a carpet. Javier tells the girl to please not forget about the end tables, that everything should be spotless when they finish. Then he leads us on into the kitchen.

"Why the cleanup?" I ask. "You having a party?"

He raises an eyebrow. "There's a meeting tomorrow morning with a group of realtors," he says. "Julia wants to show them all around, ask a few questions. She doesn't know which one will do the best job."

I glance over at Omar. "So she *is* putting it on the market."

"As soon as she finds the perfect agent," Javier says. "And a price she likes."

Omar rubs his palm lightly over the black granite countertop. "I bet she'll be asking a huge sum for this place."

"Oh yes," says Javier. "And she'll get it, too. It doesn't get much better than this in Hollywood."

"And then?"

"And then I'll be out of a job, as you say." Javier allows himself a small, almost secretive, smile. "But I am not worried. I will be okay."

Another Asian woman, short and squat and much older, comes in from another door. Her hair is pulled into a bun, and she walks with a slight limp. She reminds me of those grandmas I saw a long time ago in Vietnam. How they just stood there in the sun and stared as we went by. Passive, silent, impossible to read. She has a black plastic garbage bag in her hand. She pays no attention to us as she heads straight to the huge chrome refrigerator, which is twice her size. She pries it open and starts cleaning it out, one jar at a time.

Javier, Omar, and I pull up barstools around the island in the middle of the kitchen. I tell Javier we came back because we still have a few unanswered questions. He seems surprised.

"But I thought—I mean—I was told that the police had caught Señorita Barsky."

"They did."

"So what more do you need from me? She is the one, yes?"

"They wanted to talk with her. We talked with her, too. The truth is, it doesn't look like she killed him. The cops are still on the fence about it, but that's because she had his Jaguar and had a big fight with him and ran off in the rain."

"They often had fights."

"You know what they were about?"

"Love," he says. There is a sadness in his voice. "Love and

money. Isn't that what people always fight about? He wanted to marry her, I remember. He loved her voice. He loved to hear her sing. And also she was like his first wife—of the same faith, I mean."

"That counts sometimes," I say, "for some people."

He nods. "But she was so very young, you know. Well, not so young, but compared to him. Maybe she thought about his offer, maybe she didn't like the idea of being a widow. I don't know."

Out of the corner of my eye I watch as, one by one, the woman dumps a large bunch of old limp celery, three hard-boiled eggs, a moldy slice of Brie, a shriveled tomato, a half-eaten jar of olives, and a few other unidentifiable odorous items into her garbage bag. She pulls the drawstrings on the bag, shuts the refrigerator door gently, and trudges out by the same door she entered.

"How long had it been since Pinky's wife died?" Omar asks.

"Sophie? Sophie passed away, it must have been—oh—maybe seven or eight years ago." A wistful, beatific expression comes to him. He brushes back his hair, blinks. "She was the one true love of his life."

"Seven or eight years. And all that time since, he's been alone?"

"No, no," Javier says. "There were others. Several women, in fact. But Señorita Barsky was the first one I think he was even a little bit serious about. The first one he asked to marry."

"If he was going to marry her," I say, "I'm guessing he might have wanted to put her in his will. Make it official. You know anything about that?"

"Please, I'm just the personal assistant, Mr. Parisman. I kept his cars running. Paid the gardener. I don't know anything about wills."

"So who would?"

"Those kinds of business matters were handled by people in his office. You should ask Victoria. She kept his papers, made sure the musicians signed and dated their contracts. Maybe she could help you."

"Or how about a lawyer, Javier. That's more likely. Did Pinky have one?"

"He did, yes. A man named Rupiper. They talked on the phone mostly. I never met him. But I can find you his number if you wish."

"I wish."

Javier excuses himself and vanishes down the hallway into Pinky Bleistiff's bedroom. He's gone for maybe five minutes. The vacuum cleaner in the next room stops, then starts up again, farther away this time.

When he returns, he hands me a slip of yellow paper with a phone number scrawled on it. "I'm sorry I don't have an address for you."

"That's okay, we're pretty good at putting two and two together."

"I'm sure you are," he says. There's no sarcasm in his voice; like everything else about him, it's stated as something clear and inevitable, all part of a simple truth. But still, as we settle into my car and pull slowly out of the wide gravel driveway, I can't help but wonder.

Chapter 14

MELVIN RUPIPER'S OFFICE is downtown on Olive near First, on the third floor of an old art deco building that once housed a bank, back when banks were still places that actually kept your money and people like John Dillinger made a fine, if not decent, living robbing them. It has a large revolving glass door at street level. When you grab the old brass railings and push through, you find yourself in a lobby with a thirty-foot ceiling, a vaulted cathedral dedicated not to God but to business and finance. It makes you feel small and insignificant. When your shoes touch the black-and-white tile floor, they echo. And what you notice right away is how cool and sterile and odorless everything is. That's the first thing. The second thing is an old-fashioned information kiosk made of ebony or some other extinct wood. And inside the kiosk sits a twentysomething girl with blue eyeshadow, big brown eyes, and long tight braids. She doesn't look up as I approach, maybe because she's busy thumbing through *People* magazine.

I ask about Mr. Rupiper and she points, barely lifting a finger, to her left. "It's faster, you take the elevator," she says. "Suite 309."

"Thanks," I say. "You're very kind."

That last remark makes her glance in my direction. "Say what?"

"Thanks," I say again. I go past the potted ficus plants in their lovely red ceramic containers, step inside the brass-plated elevator, press the button marked 3, stuff my hands in my pockets, and wait. Elevators are not only the safest form of transportation known to man, they're also the slowest, which may be related. The good news is, hardly anybody ever dies in an elevator. Not by accident, anyway. Someone tried to push me out of one once, but that's another story.

Rupiper's suite is at the end of a hall. I open the door and immediately come face-to-face with his secretary, a stout, bosomy, fiftyish woman in a tight white pantsuit. Her eyebrows have been plucked and painted over. Her fingernails are neat and newly pink. A small gold Jewish star hangs from her neck, and there's a needy look in her brown eyes. She has short, black, bobbed hair, kind of like the sexy way Liza Minnelli styled it in *Cabaret*, I think, but that's where the resemblance ends. The name tag on the desk reads Mirna Kravitz. She has invested heavily in perfume.

"He's not available," she says before I can even open my mouth. "Gone for the day."

"Oh dear," I say. "Is he in court?"

"Hah!" she goes. "Court! Now that's funny. You're a funny man. Melvin never goes to court. Not anymore. I've been here a long time. Let me tell you something, he's not that kind of lawyer."

I hand her my business card. She looks at it, unimpressed, puts it down. Waits for me to fill the silence.

"Okay, so what kind of lawyer is he?"

"Well," she says, "years ago he did lots of things. All over the map, you know, but mainly it was civil litigation. He went to court a lot back then."

"Meaning?"

"Meaning somebody would get run down by a kid on a Harley, or an old woman would slip and fall in a dark movie theater. Things like that."

"He liked to sue people?"

She shrugs. "Like? Not like? It was just business. Good business, too, but too much work. He wore himself out. He doesn't do that anymore. Now it's wills and probate. Steady. Predictable. Not so interesting, though, you want my humble opinion. I mean, the good news about wills? You don't have to talk to the client that much. He's usually dead." She smiles at her little joke.

I tell her I'd like to talk with Mr. Rupiper. I tell her my client's name was Pincus Bleistiff and, unfortunately, he's dead, too.

"Oh yes," she says. "Yes, I just read about him in the *Times*. Such a horrible way to end up. I think Melvin did some work for him a while back."

"Melvin—Mr. Rupiper drew up his will. That's what I understand," I say.

"Uh, I don't know that"—she consults my business card—"Mr., Mr. Parisman. I don't know that for a fact." She taps the fingers of her left hand lightly on the surface of the desk. She has beautiful, soft, manicured hands. The ring finger, I notice, is minus a wedding band. There's just a pale circular space where it used to be. "And even if I did know, I couldn't tell you. That would be confidential, now wouldn't it?"

"I suppose," I say. "Except I have it on pretty good authority that he did. I didn't come here on a whim, Mirna. The man who manages his property gave me Rupiper's name."

"Even so," she says, batting the ball back into my court, "what difference would that make?"

I lean forward and peer quietly into her trembling brown eyes. I've been in these situations before. There's always an immovable rock, it seems, standing in the way of an irresistible tide. That's life. I smile, just to let her know that I'm not an enemy. Not someone she has to be afraid of. "Well," I whisper, "the truth is, I really need to get a look at Bleistiff's will. It might make a big difference in the case I'm working on. It might even save somebody's life. You'd want to save someone's life, now wouldn't you, Mirna? You'd do what you could, right? Even if you never met her? Even if she were a total stranger?"

She hesitates, but only for a moment. "I wish I could help you, Mr. Parisman. I do. Maybe you should make an appointment with Melvin. He might be fine with letting you see it, I don't know. If he had a copy in his file, I mean."

"Pincus Bleistiff won't care," I tell her. "That's for damn sure."

She doesn't respond.

"You read the story in the *Times*. I did, too. But the reporter left out the most gruesome details."

"He did?"

"Yeah. He left out—or maybe his editor deleted—the stuff about the bullets. Bleistiff was shot six times at close range. He was an old man. Just one bullet would have probably been enough, especially with a .38. You know what I mean? Six bullets means he was butchered. Practically cut in half."

Her eyes are tearing up. She's blushing. "Oh," she says, "oh God."

"I'll tell you a little secret, Mirna. The woman they're about to charge was his girlfriend. She was a singer in a band he managed. I don't really think she killed him, the evidence is a little dicey, but it's hard to convince the cops sometimes. They're a stubborn bunch. You realize how it is with cops, right? They get these ideas stuck in their heads."

"Yes."

"But if I could see his will, that might just clear everything up."

A small tear glistens; it worms its way out of her eye and wriggles down her cheek. "I wish I could." She shakes her head. "But I can't. I don't have the authority. I—I could lose my job. Do you understand?"

"Sure," I say. "Sure, I understand."

She dabs her eyes with a Kleenex, then clears her throat, grabs the scheduler on her desk, and glances down at the dates. "You need to talk with Melvin. I can help you with that. How does next Tuesday sound?"

My hand reaches out and touches hers. "Tuesday might be too late, I'm afraid. They're watching her now. She'll be behind bars by tomorrow night." I stand up straight. "But I appreciate you listening, Mirna, honest. I'll be on my way now. I didn't mean to torpedo your afternoon. You keep my card, though, okay? If Melvin says it's fine, or—or if you should have a change of heart, you give me a call. Will you do that?"

"Yes, of course," she mumbles. "I'll do that."

We look into each other's eyes one more time before I turn and saunter down the hall. In the back of my mind I'm trying to put a name on the perfume she's wearing. She might like another bottle, is what I'm thinking. It's familiar. Didn't Loretta used to wear the same damn thing years ago? Midnight Musk? We'll Always Have Paris? Oh well. It's been too long, right? And besides, my nose is out of practice.

Outside the revolving door there's a cool afternoon breeze blowing down the street. An ambulance is wailing a couple of blocks away. The sidewalk is crowded. A hint of marijuana smoke wafts by, and I'm standing there scratching my head. I'm not sure I've softened Mirna up enough. In fact, I kinda doubt it. Maybe I should have kept working on her. She was close. If I were ten years younger, I think, maybe I could have charmed her into it. Hell, I could have asked her out on a date. I did that once a long time ago, and it worked. I got what I needed. But of course Loretta didn't go for that idea. She was furious. And we had a huge fight about it afterward. She told me it was a cheap trick. There have to be better ways to find out what you want to know, that's what she said. Also, even though there was nothing at all romantic going on, I guess it made her jealous, which I can understand. So forget about it, Parisman. You're too old, and there are other roads to Rome.

I check my watch. It's almost 4:30. I call Omar, ask him to meet me out in front of the twenty-four-hour parking lot two blocks away. He shows up forty minutes later and we walk slowly, past the jewelry stores and the pawnshops and the taquerias, back to Melvin Rupiper's office.

"What you got in mind, boss?"

"We're in a little predicament here, Omar. We need some information and the people in this building, the ones who have it"—I point vaguely toward the third floor—"well, they're just not cooperating."

"So you want me to rough them up? Is that it? Or just intimidate them?"

I chuckled. "No, no, nothing like that. Mirna's a sweet lady. A dedicated employee. But that's the bad news." I check my watch. "The good news is it's after five o'clock. She's left for the day."

"You're sure?"

"She's dedicated, I told you. But her boss isn't there, and she's got nothing to do but watch the clock. She's gone, trust me."

We push through the revolving doors into the vaulted lobby. Two chunky, middle-aged men in gray suits and a young anorexic woman in sunglasses and high heels with a black leather briefcase under her arm walk briskly past us. They're all headed for the outside. It's definitely time to go home around here. The girl who was hunkered down at the help desk is no longer in sight. Probably left like everyone else the minute the clock struck 5, I think. Amazing how much some people love their jobs. We cross to the elevator, and I press the button for the third floor.

In a few short steps we find ourselves at Suite 309. The hallway is still, and the lights are turned off beyond the clouded glass door. I try the knob. Locked, naturally.

"You stay here, amigo. Keep your eyes peeled. Let me know if we have any unannounced visitors."

"What happens if we do?"

"You run interference, okay? Step between them. Make some noise. I'll be quick." Then I pull out my handy-dandy burglar tool from my jacket. I've owned this thing a long time. It was a gift, in fact, from Jerry Vournas, a guy I went to high school with, also the same guy I helped send to prison once for a couple of smash-and-grab jobs in West Hollywood. Jerry was a sweetheart, if you can believe that. If it weren't for his little heroin problem, he'd be the perfect brother-in-law, I always thought. Funny and charming. You'd *want* your sister to marry him. Anyway, he gave this to me after he got out. Said he found it in his mother's garage. Said he became a Christian in prison and didn't want anything more to do with his old ways. Fine, I said, mazel tov.

Now I slide the device gently into the lock and jiggle it. Omar sees what I'm up to. I don't imagine he approves, but he's been down this road before. He shrugs, shakes his head, and turns his attention to the vacant hall. After a few more twists, I find the sweet spot in the lock and the door clicks open. "I'll be back," I whisper, and go in.

There's a window that's still catching a bit of sunlight, so the office isn't in total darkness. I walk past Mirna's desk and head for the metal filing cabinet. Thankfully, she's well organized. Or at least she's a devoted fan of the English alphabet. I flip through the cabinet, find the file marked Bleistiff. I slip out his last will and testament, which is the only item in the manila folder, bring it over to the Xerox machine, turn it on, and wait until it warms up. Then I copy all six pages. I slide the original back in the cabinet where I found it. Before I leave, I borrow Mirna's staple gun from her desk and clip the pages together. I fold them up and tuck them inside my jacket, turn off the Xerox, and just like that I'm out the door.

Omar is staring at me contemptuously with his arms folded. "This is why you needed me here? Really? To be your accomplice?"

"It's for a good cause," I tell him, though I doubt he'll buy that. "Remember how we always need to keep our eyes on the prize?"

He frowns. "Fuck the prize," he says.

We reach the elevator, push the down button, stand there. I glance over at him and I can see right away he's still unhappy.

"I was going to be a cop," he mumbles. "Remember? It was just a few months ago. Hell, maybe somewhere inside me I'm still a cop. Kinda."

"Which means?"

"I dunno. The cop in me feels like I ought to bust you."

"It's just a feeling, Omar. You don't have to act on it."

We drive in our separate cars back to my apartment at Park La Brea. Omar doesn't want to stick around too long; he's going to a movie with his friend, Lourdes, but he also wants to hear what's in the will. Carmen is playing dominoes with Loretta at the kitchen table. Loretta's winning, but it looks to me like Carmen's really throwing the game, just to make her happy. The kitchen smells warm and sweet; they've been busy making bread all afternoon. We go straight into my office and close the door to drown out their laughter.

The last will and testament of Pincus Bleistiff is a little short on specifics. As I expected, he leaves the house on Mulholland Drive to his children, Julia and Joshua, along with a small assortment of US stocks and Israeli bonds. In addition, while he hopes they will choose to continue it, Julia and Joshua get to dispose of his music business as they see fit. On the next to the last page he also leaves $200,000 to Javier Escobar for the loyalty he has exhibited during all his years of service. Below that item, there is a line about Risa Barsky. To Risa Barsky, for whom I have searched for years, and whom I have come to cherish beyond life itself, I leave the sum of $1,600,000. This constitutes the remainder of my personal wealth, which is secured in a municipal bond account in my name and currently managed by Morgan Stanley on South Lake Avenue in Pasadena, California.

"That should make her happy," says Omar. "I wish somebody would leave me that kind of cash."

I read the will over twice. "Why does he say that business

about searching for her for years? Doesn't that seem odd?"

"People get poetic sometimes about the one they love," Omar says. "That doesn't bug me."

"Yeah, but Javier said Pinky was stuck on Sophie. That she was everything."

"And Sophie's been gone for how long?" Omar says. "So now it's Risa. Didn't you already tell me you thought he was in love with her? What's the problem?"

"I don't know," I say, "you're probably right. But he didn't need to say he's been searching for her for years, did he? That's what jumped out at me."

"A fool in love says all kinds of things," Omar goes.

"True." I lean back in my chair, rub my eyes. "But this may be the final nail in the coffin as far as Lieutenant Malloy is concerned. He's already got her fleeing the scene of a crime. Then leaving the car at LAX, that didn't help. That could speak to her cunning. And once he hears about the dough she's about to inherit, well, there's his motive, right there in black and white. Any prosecutor worth his salt would go to town on that."

"Wait a minute. Just the other day you were telling me that that wouldn't fly with his daughter, weren't you? That just because she was going to inherit, that wasn't a reason for her to shoot him. Now you think this is enough to convict Risa?"

"Convict her? That I couldn't tell you, Omar. It's something, though. There's probably a difference—at least in the mind of a juror—between a girlfriend and a daughter. You'd have to admit that. And this may not be solid proof. But it is another brick in the wall."

"It's luck," he says. "That's all it is. She won the lottery. So what? You can't send someone to prison for that."

"You're right," I say. "It wouldn't be fair. But that doesn't mean it couldn't happen." This is America, remember. Anything's possible."

Chapter 15

THANKSGIVING CAME AND went. Loretta and I used to make a big *tsimmes* over it. Before they retired to Ecuador, we'd invite our old friends, Jack and Carol, and when my mom was still alive, we'd bring her over from her garden apartment in South Pasadena. She always made a little song and dance. She didn't want us to bother. She didn't want to get all dressed up. Nothing fit her anymore, not the way it used to. Anyway, when it came right down to it she didn't much care for the taste of turkey. Besides, you know, the tryptophan, it always put her to sleep. My mom and her whining were part of the holiday soundtrack. Shelly would usually drop by, too, with whichever wife or girlfriend he was working on at the time. Shelly was always a wild card. You were taking a chance, you never knew what his mood would be like, especially if he was in the middle of something. Come to think of it, I can't remember a time when Shelly wasn't in the middle of something. A deal gone south. An ugly divorce. More often than not, he'd be off in another room, talking on the phone with a lawyer or his bookie. That was Shelly in a nutshell. Or his latest squeeze drank too much and forgot where she was and blurted out something embarrassing at the dinner table. That happened a couple of times. Not this year, though. This year I bought a nice, plump chicken on sale at Ralphs. I got some cranberry sauce from Trader Joe's and some fresh yams down at Farmers Market. It was just Loretta and me, and she ate every bite, no complaints, smiling all the way, thankful.

The next morning, after I've emptied the dishwasher and put everything away, I go back into my office. Pincus Bleistiff's will is lying there on the desk. I pick it up. I've already read it through twice. A picture of him is starting to come into focus. Risa said he was generous, but he was also stubborn. He knew what he had, he knew what he wanted, and when it came down to playing with her hopes and fears, well, he was a pro. It was never a fair fight, I think. And really, when you consider it, what's a million six to someone who knows he might die tomorrow in his sleep? Just paper. That he'd dangle that much cash in front of her doesn't trouble me, not really. Chalk it up to another one of those ploys of his to keep her around, like the Jaguar. Maybe he even showed her the will one fine night in his bedroom. Here, I want you to read this, honey. This is what you mean to me.

That makes sense. Maybe he never stopped thinking she could be bought. But the idea that he's been searching for Risa Barsky for years still trips me up, somehow. I don't get it. Why would he say a thing like that?

I reach for my phone then and punch in Malloy's private cell.

He picks it up on the third ring. "Happy Thanksgiving," he says.

"That was yesterday, Bill. You're late."

"You didn't call me yesterday."

"I forgot."

"Yeah, well, it hurt my feelings."

I ask him how his holiday went, and he tells me it was just him and Jess and the Wallaces, of course, from next door. He doesn't like the Wallaces much. He's never said why, but I'm sure he only invites them over on account of the fact that he feels sorry for them because their teenage son drowned at Zuma Beach and they've never been the same since. Oh, and this year his niece, Lindsay, and her family, the ones who live in Thousand Oaks, drove down once again because they had tickets to Universal Studios and needed a place to stay. Pretty much the same as always, in other words. As he's talking, it comes to me that Bill Malloy is probably my closest friend in the whole world, which almost brings a little tear to my eye. It's passing strange, too, because I realize that in all the years we've known each other, I've never once been over to his house for dinner. And he's never come over here, either, except a couple of times to talk business. It's not what we do.

I ask him whether he's getting ready to arrest Risa Barsky. He says he can't really talk about that. Not yet.

"But you're working on it, right? Building a case? I mean, if I were in your shoes, I'd say she's just about the most likely suspect."

"Because?"

"Opportunity. Access. She had that. Plus the fact that she ran away and left the car at the airport. That counts. There's just one thing missing, really."

"And what might that be?"

"Motive. That's where it falls apart. He took her in. Gave her a safe place to stay. Bought her clothes, jewelry. Protected her. Women don't usually go around shooting someone who does that."

"No," he says, "you're right."

"Anyway, Omar and I were thinking it over some. We went out to the house on Mulholland again and spent some quality time with Javier Escovedo."

"The manager?"

"Yeah, I guess that's what he does. Anyway, we talked, and he mentioned that Pinky had a new will drawn up not long ago. Interesting, huh?"

"Very."

"Just what I thought, too. So like a good little gumshoe, I followed up. I went downtown, tried to convince them to let me have a peek at it, but you know how those things go."

"No, I don't," he says. "Tell me."

"I tried, Bill, but I never got past the front desk."

"Okay. Then why don't you give me the lawyer's name,"

Malloy says automatically. "People often change their minds when someone flips a badge in their face. I may be more persuasive."

So that's what I do. After I hang up, I sit there a minute and wait for the dust in my mind to settle. An ambulance is tooling its way down Third Street, probably headed for Cedars-Sinai, and though I can't hear it, I can see a police helicopter circling like a vulture in the distance. Maybe there's a drug bust going on in one of those shabby apartments down below on Gower. Or maybe there's an accident at La Brea and Melrose. There's always an accident somewhere; you can count on it. I lean out my window, take a deep breath. The sun is climbing over the soft, muted skyline of Los Angeles. Everything is always in flux in this town. The movie never ends. Nine floors below me a skinny woman in a purple sweater is walking her dog along the little grass apron, waiting for him to pee. She's coaxing him, she has a Russian accent, and she's talking to him like he was a human being and not a dog. She's talking to him like he was her friend, like the two of them belonged together. I recognize her. I've met her many times in the elevator. She's lived here forever, but we've never said more than six words to each other, and I still don't know her name.

Pinky's will is right there where I left it on my desk. Now I wonder whether I should have just kept my mouth shut. Maybe I was hasty. Maybe I just sent Risa Barsky to prison for the rest of her life.

Omar calls the next morning, says he needs to see me pronto, says it's important. We meet up at Bru. It's a brand-new coffee and pastry bar on Vermont, just south of Franklin—a narrow industrial-looking building with high ceilings, bare surfaces, and a few artificial palm trees thrown in. Omar likes it because they make seriously strong coffee. I like it because it's clean and air-conditioned and everyone is twenty-five years old and thinks the screenplay they're working on is destined for glory. Actually, that could describe most of Hollywood, I realize, as we settle into a couple of sculpted plastic art deco chairs. The place is crowded, but they're all lost in their computers or other electronic devices.

"Okay," I say. "So what's so important that you couldn't tell me over the phone?"

Omar is tense. He leans forward. "I went over to Ray Ballo's apartment an hour ago."

"Ray Ballo? How'd you even find him?"

"I looked up his band on the internet and ended up talking to Phoebe. Remember her? The singer? Anyway, she told me he'd come into some unexpected cash and just rented a new place in Burbank."

"Why did Phoebe tell you that?"

"Who knows, man. I think maybe she's sweet on him."

"Okay, that makes sense. But why did you want to see him?"

"Because I thought we missed something when we talked to him at that bar. It was a feeling I had. It was just…I can't put my finger on it, man. What can I tell you? I trust my feelings."

"They're usually right on the money, I'll give you that."

"He knew more than he was letting on. I thought maybe if we were alone together that he might be a little more—" He stops there. Sips his coffee some, licks his lips. He's looking for the right word.

"Forthcoming?" I offer.

"Yeah, forthcoming. Something like that. If that means what I think it does. I just wanted him to be straight with me."

"And was he?"

"No, man, he wasn't straight at all." His voice drops to a bare whisper. "He was dead."

"Dead?"

He raises his eyebrows. "Fuck, keep your voice down, man."

"Dead?" I whisper this time.

"Yeah, the door to his place was ajar. The TV was on pretty loud. Some kind of talk show. *Good Morning, America* maybe. He hadn't even unpacked all his stuff. Cardboard boxes everywhere. I walked in and he was just lying there on his back. Right next to the couch."

"You called the cops, I assume."

He pauses, sucks in his chest. "No, that's the thing. I didn't. That's what I wanted to talk to you about. I know I should have, Amos, but they're a difficult bunch."

"You didn't call them?"

"I should have. I get that. I should have, right away. I made a mistake, okay? Everybody makes mistakes. You remember all the trouble I had with them."

"Is that a question? Sure, I remember, sure."

Omar frowns. "I'm not such a shining citizen the way they see things. Anyway, he'd been dead for a couple hours already. I could tell. His face and hands were swelling up, changing color."

"You touch anything?"

"Nothing. Not a goddamn thing. I swear. I just saw what I saw, turned around, and left."

"Any idea how he died?"

"That's another reason I didn't want to be there when the cops showed up. He had a switchblade sticking out of his chest. Fuck, man, I don't even own a switchblade anymore. But I know what some of those guys think about Mexicans. You do, too."

"Well, well, my friend." I flash a quick, awkward smile in his direction, then just as abruptly I let it go. My fingertips start carving out a nervous drumbeat on the edge of the table. "Jesus. This is certainly not how I thought I'd be starting the day."

Omar gulps down what's left in his coffee cup. He hasn't stopped staring at me. "What are we gonna do?" he asks.

"We aren't going to do anything," I tell him sternly. "But you can't just leave it there. Somebody has to tell the police." I reach into my coat jacket and pull out my cell phone. "That would be me, I guess."

"Okay," he says. "Okay, go ahead, but leave me out of it, all right?"

"You? Who are you? I don't even know you." I hit the numbers for Lieutenant Malloy, lean the phone up to my ear, then think better of it and put it on speaker so Omar can hear.

Bill Malloy picks it up right away. "What's up?" he wants to know.

"The strangest thing, Bill. I got a call from my house. You know Carmen, the woman who takes care of Loretta? Yeah, well, this morning while Carmen was in the lady's room someone called, and even though I've told her at least a dozen times not to pick it up in those situations, just ignore it, they'll call back, you know how women are."

"What's your point, Amos?"

"My point is that Loretta answered it. And whoever it was had a message for me. Said to tell me that Ray Ballo was dead. Said I might find that intriguing. Then he hung up."

"Ray Ballo? Ray Ballo? The name's vaguely familiar. Help me out, will you? Do I know him?"

"You should, Lieutenant. Ray Ballo is Risa Barsky's boyfriend. Was, anyway."

"The one before Bleistiff?"

"Bingo," I say.

"Every man she touches seems to die," he says. He's not saying it to be funny, I know, but that's how it comes out. Then his tone turns more sober. "Have you phoned this one in to the authorities?"

"That's why I'm calling you."

He asks me for Ballo's address. I look at Omar. He scribbles it down on a paper napkin and I read it off to him. He tells me to hang on a minute. Two minutes later he comes back on the line. "Burbank PD doesn't know a fucking thing about this," he says. "They're sending a squad car out right now."

"Good."

"And I don't know what this has to do with Bleistiff," he

says, "but there's no way we can pin this on Risa Barsky, even if we wanted to. Not right now. Not directly, at least."

"Because?"

"Mainly because she hasn't left the house in three days," he says. "We've been watching her around the clock. I was thinking maybe the fear would catch up to her and she'd try to run off again."

"Didn't happen, huh?"

"No. The only time she went out was yesterday, and that was to go shopping at Vons. Bought a lot of vegetables, Remo said."

"Maybe she's a vegetarian, Bill. I could see that."

"Hitler was a vegetarian, too," he says. "That never stopped him."

Omar treats himself to another chocolate-fudge brownie, which, when combined with the two black coffees he already bolted down, renders him unable to sit still. I take out my checkbook and pass him one for three hundred dollars. "Here," I say, "you need a rest. And I appreciate what you've done. Why don't you and Lourdes buy a motel room at the beach for a few days? Walk around in the sand. Get your feet wet. Breathe the sea air. I know you're worried, but this'll all blow over soon."

"You think the cops are onto me? Is that it?"

I shrug. "I just think you need to make yourself scarce for a while. I'm sure you had nothing to do with this. But like you say, you're not a shining citizen in their opinion. You say you didn't touch anything. God, I hope not. They're going to scrub that place for any clue they can find. I also hope nobody saw you walk up to his door this morning. Don't mind me. I'm just being extra cautious, that's all. I can't afford to lose you."

Omar looks down at the check, picks it up, folds it in two, and tucks it in his shirt pocket. He's wearing a hip black short-sleeve shirt speckled all over with small white notes. He hasn't bothered to tuck it in, but that's the style these days. "Thanks, man," he says. "I owe you."

"No, you don't."

"Yes, I do."

"Go fuck yourself, Omar. I love you, man."

I drive back to Park La Brea. Marvin, the weary old guard at the gate, raises the barrier and waves me through. Inside my apartment, Carmen is baking something sweet and sugary in the oven. Loretta is bundled up in a blanket on the couch, absorbed in a soap opera. "Carmen," I say, sitting down at the kitchen table, "we need to talk."

She is the soul of decency, of course, and I don't usually involve her in my work, but there are times, times like this, in fact, when you have to make exceptions. Slowly, carefully, I explain what happened with Omar. How this morning he came upon a corpse unexpectedly. How he has had difficulty with the police in the past. That he was therefore scared. That he didn't want to go to jail. Which is why he turned to me to report the matter. "And I had to make up a little story," I tell her. "It wasn't true. It was a *mentira*. But I only did it to protect Omar. You understand, don't you? *Entiendes?*"

She nods. And that is where it ends.

Chapter 16

BEING A DETECTIVE is like no other profession in the world, and I'll tell you why. For anything else you sit around on your *tuchus* in a classroom while they teach you the theory. You read books and write papers, and the teacher marks them up in red ink. Then comes the hands-on part. That's where you realize that most of whatever you learned in the classroom was abstract bunk, stories, *leinga meisas*. That there's a difference between theory and practice, and what they want you to do now is practice. So you do.

Let's say you're looking for a normal job. You practice take-offs and landings or sawing a block of wood in half or setting a broken arm, whatever. And after a few years of doing the same damn thing over and over again, it becomes automatic, you've got it down. And one day, after they've sucked enough cash out of your bank account, you climb up on a stage and some old guy in a robe gives you a piece of paper and shakes your hand, and from then on, brother, you're golden.

Most careers are like that. But not a detective's. What I do is not 9-to-5. What I do can't be contained in a cardboard box with a ribbon around it. I'm a primitive. What keeps me alive is my animal instincts. A detective worth his salt is willing to sit in the dark forever, if need be. He knows how to wait. He doesn't let years of book learning or even experience lead him around by the nose. He has no plan. His mind is empty. It has to be. And that's because everything he was ever taught, everything he believes or wants to believe in his heart of hearts, might be entirely wrong. The future doesn't exist as far as he's concerned. He can't be sure of anything, not until the end. Not until the thief or the killer or the missing woman walks through the door. No other career is so demanding. Yeah, sure, you can spend time at the Police Academy, you can practice shooting and collecting fingerprints all you want, but it won't make you a detective. There's so much more to it. A fellow could land a plane or build a house with far less skill.

I wake up the next morning with all these notions buzzing around in my head, and I wipe the dirt out of my eyes. My throat is parched. Loretta is lying beside me, her bare arm hanging off the mattress, her head buried in a pillow. She's sleeping more and more these days, which may just be the way her disease progresses, or it may be a function of the new meds she's on, I don't know.

I get up and wander barefoot into the kitchen. Put on a fresh pot of coffee. Rescue the newspaper from outside the front entrance. We are the only people—at least the only ones on the ninth floor—who still get a paper every day. What does that suggest? Aside from old Mr. Wu, my neighbor, whom I haven't said three words to in all the years we've known each other, the rest of the folks here are strangers. Most of them are under thirty. I have no idea how they manage to pay the rent. They wheel bicycles onto the elevator each morning. They have tattoos on their arms and legs. They own small, yippy dogs. They play their music at all hours of the day and night, and different groups of them seem to move in and out of the building every few months. We meet in the elevator. We nod. We smile. That's always as far as it goes.

The *Los Angeles Times* doesn't have a single word about Ray Ballo's sudden death, which doesn't surprise me. There are probably a dozen murders each day in a town this big, and he wasn't exactly a star. After my first coffee, I decide to check in with Malloy. What the hell, I think, it's almost 8. He's an early riser.

"You ever do anything about that will?" That's the first line that comes out of my mouth.

"As a matter of fact, I did," he says. "Though that Rupiper

wasn't the easiest lawyer I've ever dealt with, I have to say. Usually, you just show 'em your badge."

"He wouldn't let you read it?"

"Oh, he let us read it. But not before I called him twice and threatened to go to a judge and get a search warrant. Then he changed his tune right away. Not that it does us much good."

"What do you mean?"

"I mean it was a straight-up, ordinary will, near as I could tell. Almost all of his estate goes to his children."

"Really?"

"He did leave a little something to the LA Jazz Foundation. They take care of aging musicians. Other than that, nothing."

"He didn't mention Risa Barsky?"

"Sorry, old man."

I pour myself a second cup of coffee. "That is so strange," I say. "And here I thought she was the love of his life."

"You're telling me," he says. "We were kind of hoping she'd be on the receiving end of his largesse. Then at least we'd have ourselves a perfectly good motive. Greed."

"Right. What about Ray Ballo? Did the Burbank cops figure anything out?"

"They're working it, but it's slow going. The neighborhood he lived in had a couple of active street gangs. The knife in his chest—he was stabbed, by the way—came from Mexico. Whoever did it ransacked the place, and his wallet was empty, so you tell me."

"Ray Ballo didn't seem like the kind who'd have much to do with gangs. He was a musician. Just a sweet guy, I thought."

"Yeah, well."

"And you don't think it's connected to what happened to Pinky?"

"Other than the fact that Risa Barsky was banging both of them at one time or another? No." There's a moment of silence. "Is this why you called me so early in the morning, Amos? Tell the truth."

"The truth?" Something snaps then. There's no other way to explain it. I stop to feel my heart beating inside my rib cage. It's like I've just tumbled down an elevator shaft. I haven't felt this way since Vietnam. "The truth is I'm a lonely old man, Bill. My wife's in the other room. She's asleep now, but she's dying. I'm not gonna lie to you. It's going to take a long, long time, I think. She's dying, and no one seems able to stop it no matter how many pills she takes and how many doctors she sees. You want to hear the truth? The truth is I don't sleep so well. I haven't slept since forever, and the only thing I've got left to grab onto, the only goddamn thing I have that keeps me from going crazy, is this case. You—you know what I mean?"

"Yeah, Amos, I know. I do. And I'm sorry."

After we hang up, I catch my breath and all at once I find myself weeping. Nothing convulsive or dramatic, just a couple of very polite tears slipping effortlessly down my cheeks. An accident, almost. I reach for a Kleenex, and just like that, the kitchen comes back into focus and everything returns to normal.

Two hours later I'm walking down the hall into Melvin Rupiper's art deco law office. The sun is shining, my hair is combed, and I'm wearing my best blue suit and a checkered silk tie that I snagged for fifty cents at a temple rummage sale. It isn't fancy exactly, but for someone like him, I figure it'll be fine. I turn the knob. "Is he in?" I ask Mirna Kravitz.

She looks up, startled to see me. She raises a cautionary finger. "Well, well, yes, he's—"

"How about you tell him I'm here, then." I lay my card down on the desk just in case she somehow forgot my name.

"Oh. Okay." She hoists herself with practiced deliberation out of her chair, adjusts her pink knit sweater. "You're actually fortunate," she says. "He had a ten o'clock, but the woman had to reschedule."

"I've always been lucky," I say.

Again with the cautionary finger. "You wait right here, Mr. Parisman. Okay? I'll let him know. Give me—give me a moment." Then she vanishes through the glass door.

The moment lasts approximately five minutes. I hear considerable murmuring on the other side of the partition, but no complete sentences, nothing coherent, anyway. Finally, Mirna emerges. "Go on in," she whispers.

Melvin Rupiper, attorney-at-law, stands up and clears his throat and nods at me as I enter the room. He is a slight, anxious man. White shirt, black tie. Rimless glasses that went out of style around the same year the Beatles broke up. He's around fifty, which isn't old in my book, but he gives off the tired aura of someone with one foot already in the grave. There's also something slightly vain about him. He's in this funny antique building downtown, and he's wearing gold cuff links. And nobody I know in LA wears cuff links anymore, unless he's going to the Oscars; also, he's got a bald spot at the top of his head, which he has tried to comb over without much success.

He has a large antique mahogany desk with a glass top. Framed pictures on the wall of his wife (I suppose) and three adorable children. Also on the desk is a clutch of small framed photographs—two children, a boy and a girl at various ages, along with the same adoring wife. In one of them the girl is seated on a couch cradling a puppy, and the boy, who is maybe nine, is standing at attention beside her in his Cub Scout uniform, his arm raised in salute. In a separate picture the wife is wearing a long-sleeve sweater and her head is tilted provocatively to the side. She's both pert and alluring at the same time. There's also a yellow legal pad, a ballpoint pen, and a black old-fashioned telephone, the kind my parents once used, complete with a cord that runs into the wall. No computer. It's as if he's deliberately chosen to live in an earlier, simpler age.

I pull out my business card. He holds it between his thumb and forefinger. "Mr. Parisman," he says. He shakes my hand perfunctorily. His hand feels cool and damp. We settle into heavy leather chairs opposite each other.

"Thanks for making time for me this morning," I start.

"Oh yes, well. We had a cancellation. You know how these things go." He crosses his legs, shifts his weight. "Would you care for some coffee? Mirna makes a wonderful cup. I don't touch coffee after 9 a.m., but that's what my clients say."

"No," I tell him, "that's not necessary. The reason I came over, the only reason I'm here today, is because of Pinky Bleistiff."

"Yes," he says. "I'm well aware. I read what happened to him in the newspaper. Terrible."

"Exactly. I barely met him before this happened."

"So Mirna said, yes."

"But a week or two before he died, Pinky hired me to track down a missing friend of his. Apparently, she meant a lot to him. I'm thinking maybe you know her—Risa Barsky."

"Risa Barsky?" Rupiper's eyes cloud over. He tilts his head. The overhead light catches his bald spot. "Barsky. No," he says, "can't say that I do."

"You put together his last will and testament, didn't you?"

"I did a great deal of work for Mr. Bleistiff. It was a while ago, however."

"Including a will?"

"A great deal of work over the years. And, not that it's any of your business, but yes, I probably did draw up a will for him, among other things. I wouldn't be surprised. Pincus and I go back a long time."

I frown. "That's great," I say, "because Lieutenant Malloy and I also go back a long time. And he's the one who told me about the will. I know it's sitting here in your file cabinet. So let's not beat around the bush anymore, shall we?"

"You're friends with Malloy?" His demeanor hasn't changed, he's still world-weary, but now at least there's a hint of apprehension.

"The best of friends. I spoke with him this morning, and

he said you wouldn't mind at all if I dropped by and had a look at it."

Rupiper blinks, runs his tongue over his lower lip. "I'm not in the habit of releasing my client's private documents to strangers who walk in off the street," he says.

"Your client is dead," I say. "Somebody pumped six bullets into him."

"That may be," he says. "But my duty now is to the heirs."

"You let Malloy read it," I say.

"When the police come calling, well, that's another matter, isn't it." He tucks his fist under his chin. "Let me ask you something, Mr. Parisman. Why do you think this document has anything at all to do with you? And the woman? This Barsky person you're looking for? How will it help you find her?"

"The cops are interested in Risa Barsky. In their mind, she's the most likely suspect. They know where she is, but they can't move in and bust her, not unless they have enough evidence. A motive, for example. You don't kill somebody without a reason, do you?"

He sits up straight. "Wait just a minute now. The police know where she is? And they're friends of yours?"

"We're close."

"So unless I'm missing something, you must also know her whereabouts."

"Oh, I know, sure."

"But just a moment ago you said you were trying to track her down."

My hands go up in mock surrender. "I lied. Nobody in your line of work ever does that, do they?"

He lets that remark slide by with a simple shrug. "I like you, Parisman. You're a bulldozer. You do whatever you have to do. You don't care."

"That's not so, Melvin. Can I call you Melvin? I care more than you'll ever understand. For example, the reason I want to see that will is because I have a feeling there's a problem with it."

"It was drawn up incorrectly?"

"Oh no. I'm sure you did an excellent job. But I happen to know it's not the only one you've got."

He blinks. "I don't—"

"You put together two wills for Pinky, didn't you? Both of them neat and clean and legal. But one was to show somebody like Lieutenant Malloy. That's what's sitting in the drawer."

"I don't know what you're talking about," he says.

"I'm talking about two wills. It's not so complicated. The first one you wrote up many years ago, after his first wife died and before he met Risa Barsky. People write new wills all the time, don't they?"

"Not so often," he says.

"Sure they do," I say. "Especially when they meet somebody special and fall in love."

"I didn't write two wills," he says quietly.

"Oh, come on, Melvin. Tell you what, here's what I'll do: I'll bet you a nickel that the will sitting in your file right now doesn't say a word about Risa Barsky." I reach my hand across the desk. "Shake?"

He eyes me impassively.

I lower my hand. "And I'll even up the ante. Another nickel says you wrote one in the last month or so. What shall we call it? Oh, I know—let's call that one the real will. What do you say, Melvin? Do we have a wager?"

He settles back in his chair and folds his arms. "Okay," he says. "Okay, let's suppose—just for the sake of argument—that you're right. Maybe I did draw up a second will. Why on earth would I try to conceal it? What's in it for me?"

"Now that—that's a damn good question." I beam at him. "You should have been a lawyer."

He seems distinctly uncomfortable now. The conversation is drifting steadily into deeper and deeper water. He purses his lips. He stares at me for a moment, then at the family photos on his desk. Then he glances up at a corner of the ceiling before he begins to speak. "So again, just hypothetically: Are you thinking there may be something in this—in this second will that's important? Something I'm trying to hide from the police? Is that where you're going?"

"Game, set, and match." I smile.

He pushes the chair back and stands. "You spoke with Lieutenant Malloy. Didn't you ask him what the will contained?"

"You bet I did."

"And?"

"And he said there was no mention of Risa Barsky. Said it was a pretty plain vanilla document, in fact."

"Then why are you here?"

I reach inside my jacket then and pull out the real will. I unfold it and lay it on his desk so he can read it. "Because this was what was in your file the other day. And the two of them are not the same, are they? I hate it when things don't match, Melvin. Don't you?"

He stares down at the document. For a minute, neither one of us says anything.

"Where did you get this?" he asks.

"Never mind. Like you said, I'm a bulldozer."

"That's the most recent will," he concedes. He's mumbling now, but I can hear him.

"Why did you switch them when you heard the cops were coming?"

"I'm no fool, Mr. Parisman. If they opened up that file and saw that Risa Barsky was due to inherit Pinky's estate, what do you think they'd do? He's worth millions."

"They'd have their motive, then."

"Exactly. And they'd arrest her."

"Maybe so. But what's wrong with that? You tell me."

His hands ball up into little fists. He taps them lightly on the desk. "What's wrong? Well, for starters, she didn't do it."

"You know that?"

"I know her. Pincus brought her here and took us out

to lunch several times. I know the whole arrangement looks strange, because of their ages, but honest to God, they were in love. They couldn't keep their hands off each other. It was genuine. You'd have to be blind not to realize."

I pick up my copy of the will, the one with Risa's name on it, fold it in half and tuck it in my jacket. "Well, I'm glad you're such a good judge of character, Melvin. Maybe you can be a witness for her at the trial."

He grimaces. We both stand at the same time.

"One last thing," I say. "I kind of get it why you wanted to keep this from the cops. But when were you planning on telling her? About the inheritance?"

"Oh, she knows," he says. "She's known for a while. I wired her a small portion of it already when she told me she was running low on funds."

"How much was that?"

"Not much. Ten thousand. All she has to do now is come down to the office, sign a few papers, and the rest of the money's hers. Pinky told her, actually. He took her out to Spago. It was her birthday. That's when he showed it to her. Some present, huh?"

"I guess. And how about the other heirs? Is his daughter okay with this?"

"Julie never read the previous will, so I don't think she'll feel cheated. Besides, that house on Mulholland is nothing to sneeze at, is it? She and that brother of hers in Israel will be just fine."

Mirna Kravitz tugs at her fingers and regards me mournfully as I pass by her cubicle on my way out. The reception room suddenly seems shabby and old and unloved, and I'd never be able to prove it, but I have the feeling that she's been there all along, leaning in and clutching her pink sweater and listening behind the door to every word we've said.

Chapter 17

"I THOUGHT I TOLD you to go to the beach," I say. I'm standing with my arms crossed on Omar's rickety wooden porch in Boyle Heights, peering in through the open door. I can't see inside. He's turned off all the lights, except for the one in the hall. Everything is shadows and cool darkness. He comes out after a while, barefoot and bare chested, just his jeans on, a Modelo Negra sweating in his hand. We sit on the old wooden swing and watch a trio of lowriders rev their engines down the avenue.

"I tried it for a day," he says. "But after a couple hours Lourdes started acting up, said she wanted to go. The ocean makes her edgy."

"Why's that?"

"Her village is in the middle of nowhere, man. And I think the water scares her. The truth is, she never learned how to swim."

"Really?"

"*De veras.* Besides, she said she had work to do. That was fine by me."

"Okay," I say. "But you need to take a vacation, man. Or at least slow down. This is stressful, what we do. A professional needs to know when to turn it off."

He takes a long, serious pull on the beer, his dark eyes straight ahead, a young man still sure of himself, who still believes he can afford not to listen. "You're right," he says.

"Anyway, I'm kinda glad you came back. There's something else you can do for me now."

"You mean, besides disappear again?"

"I just said that out of an abundance of caution. You didn't kill Ballo. And you didn't leave any prints behind, right? So let's move on."

He offers to get me a beer out of the fridge then, but I tell him no, it'll interfere with the prescriptions I'm taking.

"You don't drink nearly enough," he says, shrugging. "You should. It would calm you right down. Look at me."

Then I tell him about my meeting with Rupiper. How he tried to lie about the two wills. How I had the distinct feeling down in my gut that he wasn't being straight with me, that he knew a lot more than he was letting on.

"So what did you expect?" Omar asks.

"Not all lawyers are covered equally in slime," I tell him. "I've even met a few honest ones over the years."

"Lucky you."

"But once they start lying about little things, well, that's a sure sign something else is wrong. I can't put my finger on it, but I'd like to know more about him. How he spends his time. Where he goes. Who he sees."

"I can do that for you."

"I'll pay you, of course."

"Of course you'll pay me, *pendejo*. My time is money." Then he takes another swig of beer and laughs.

The next day, Malloy meets me for lunch at Raffi's, an upscale Armenian deli on Fountain near Crescent Heights. I don't know the people who own it, but it's obvious that cooking wasn't the only thing on their minds when they went into business. There's a quiet subtext to this place. The music is wistful, haunting, from another era. They don't want to upset you exactly, maybe just get you to think about what happened once upon a time. Think about what was and is no more. Everywhere you turn there are laminated newspaper headlines in an alphabet almost no one here can read. And right beside them are large sepia prints to remind you of the whole tragic Armenian experience: village people on cobblestone streets; women with big, toothy smiles; shoeless children; and old, unshaven men smoking cigarettes and drinking coffee in outdoor cafes—all of them now dead and gone. I feel right at home with this sort of thing, of course. Good food and bad memories, how can you go wrong?

"What's that you're eating?" Malloy asks as he pulls up a chair beside me.

"Shawarma and hummus," I tell him. "Try it, Lieutenant, you'll like it."

He rolls his eyes, scans the menu perfunctorily. "I'll stick with the tuna salad," he says. "Jess thinks I'm gaining weight."

We exchange pleasantries for a few minutes. I tell him about the experimental new drugs they're trying out on Loretta, little yellow capsules she's supposed to take morning and night to improve her recall.

"And?" he asks. "Are they working?"

I tilt my chin. "Am I a doctor?" I don't tell him that I have no faith anymore in the medical profession, that I saw too many guys I loved die in Vietnam, that I'm trying everything I can to help with Loretta, but in the back of my mind I know damn well it's a crapshoot.

He wags his head. "None of us are getting out of this alive," he says. "That's a sure thing."

When his tuna salad arrives, I reach into my pocket and pull out a sealed envelope with my purloined copy of the will. "Here," I tell him, passing it across, "here's my contribution to law and order."

"What's this?"

"Open it," I say. "Go ahead. It's what Melvin Rupiper didn't want you to see."

He reads it slowly, turning the pages, his lips moving every now and then. When he gets to the end, he looks up. "Where'd you get this?"

"Where do you think?"

"Rupiper wouldn't give this to us, why the hell would he give it to you?"

"He didn't, Bill. Let's just say I took it out of his office and he didn't complain."

"You stole it?"

"He knows I have it. We talked it over like civilized human beings. What can I say? He's a lawyer. We came to an understanding."

"You want to tell me more about that?"

"Sure. I won't lie to you. He was upset when I showed him this, very defensive. Said he'd done nothing wrong, that he was perfectly within his rights to put together a second, more current, will."

"Okay, fine. But why didn't we get a look at it? Why the charade?"

I put down my fork. "Because he knew what you'd probably do with it, Lieutenant. And so do I." I plant my finger on the document. "This could be your motive, right here. If a jury hears this stuff, you and I both know Risa Barsky goes straight to prison."

He holds up his hand. "Slow down, Amos. For sure it helps, but a prosecutor's going to want a helluva lot more than that before they press charges."

I down the last of my iced tea and raise my glass imploringly at the waitress behind the counter. Malloy takes a small bite of his sandwich, then lays it aside. "It's not her fault," he declares. "So what if Bleistiff put her in the will? Even if she knew about it beforehand, so what's that supposed to prove?"

"That she was good in bed, maybe."

"Which is no crime, last time I checked."

"Still, the lawyer wanted to protect her."

"Why?" Malloy frowns. "Don't tell me he was in love with her, too. Is that where you're heading?"

"No," I say, "no, nothing like that. But he does seem to have a soft spot for her. He only met her a couple of times, but in his humble opinion, Pinky and Risa were really in love."

"And what's that supposed to mean?"

I shrug. "I dunno, Bill. He's a hard guy to read. I guess maybe he didn't think she had it in her to do such a thing."

"Yeah, well, what he thinks is pretty fucking worthless." Malloy folds the will into neat little quarters and tucks it in the breast pocket of his jacket. "You don't mind if I keep this, do you? Evidence."

"Not at all," I say. "Why I came in the first place."

Later that afternoon, just as the sun is about to set, I'm lying on the old, lumpy secondhand couch in my office. Loretta is in the living room watching a game show with the sound turned up very loud. I don't know why she always does that; she hears better than I do. Maybe the noise of people laughing and applauding on cue reassures her.

I'm really on the fence about this case. Part of me—the romantic part—agrees with Rupiper. They could well have been head over heels in love. And why wouldn't an an old duck like Pinky leave his money to her? Hell, I'd probably do it, if I was lonely and if I had anything to spare. But then there's the matter of her running off in the Jaguar that night, and now the ugly business about Ray Ballo with a knife in his chest. But who knows? Maybe that's not related. Maybe she could somehow manage to pull a trigger in the dark, and maybe at close range she hit him six times. That's possible. But I can't quite picture her stabbing a guy as gentle as Ballo, or anyone, actually. No, that doesn't fit.

I close my eyes. And as I do, the cell phone in my hip pocket starts to vibrate. I grab it on the third ring.

"Parisman here."

"Mr. Parisman, this is Risa Barsky. I—I need your help." In

a breathless voice, she tells me that she's been talking with Pincus Bleistiff's attorney, a man named Melvin Rupiper. She says that Pinky has left her a great deal of money, which surprised her at first, but now she's worried. Terrified, really.

"And why's that?" I switch the phone around to my better ear, try my best not to act like this is old news. "Hey, you're rich. Sounds like you should be thrilled."

"Because now the police will have a good reason to arrest me," she says. "They're already camped outside my apartment. They're going to say I killed him for his money."

"They can say that. People do all kinds of things for money, Risa. It's true. That's what makes the world go round."

"Yes, but it's not true! Not at all! I didn't even know he was leaving me anything. He never said a word!" She starts sobbing then, loud, rasping sounds like someone with a rock caught in her throat.

I wait for her to stop. Somebody's lying here, I think. She didn't just learn from Rupiper about the inheritance, did she? That's not what he said. But why would Rupiper make up a story about her going to Spago with Pinky on her birthday? It doesn't add up. I wait for her to stop, and when she does, I tell her to relax. "Look, just because he left you money, that's not a reason for the DA to bring charges."

"It's—it's quite a lot of money, Mr. Parisman. And they've been following me around for weeks. I don't know why. Maybe they think I'm going to try to run away."

"Well, you tried to once before, didn't you? On the night he died? Remember?"

"That was different," she says, defensively. "I was running from Pinky. We'd had a huge fight. We were through. I—I told him I didn't want him in my life anymore."

"Yeah, well, if you say that to the police, that's probably not going to help you much. I mean, they may look at it in a different light."

"I've already told them."

We are both silent then. I can hear her breathing on the other end. "What did you really fight about, Risa? Can you tell me?"

"Maybe. Sometime, yeah. Sure, I'll tell you. But not over the phone. What I need now is your help, Mr. Parisman. Can you come to my apartment? Is that too much to ask?"

I hear laughter and wild applause probably from the living room. Someone has just given the right answer. A bell has gone off. Someone has won a hundred thousand dollars and a week's vacation in Greece, all expenses paid. "Not this moment, Risa. I'm afraid I can't just walk out the door and leave my wife. Not without someone to help her. She's been ill and—"

"Oh, I'm sorry to hear that. What about tomorrow morning, then? Can you do that?"

"Tomorrow? Sure, tomorrow would be all right. But I don't see how I can help you. I'm just a private detective. Maybe if you're worried about the police, a criminal defense lawyer would be a better investment."

"I don't know people like that," she says. She sounds defeated. "I'm not like Pinky. I don't come from his world. I'm just the singer in the band." She starts to sob then, and I tell her all right, keep calm; I'll be there first thing tomorrow.

The black-and-white cruiser parked across the street in plain sight belongs to the Van Nuys Police Department, so naturally I don't recognize the burly officer sipping his coffee behind the wheel. He gives me the standard once-over as I make my way to the apartment complex and push the buzzer next to Risa Barsky's name. I'm half expecting he will climb out of the vehicle later and jot down my license plate number once I've gone in. That's what cops like him often do, not that I care. I mean, it's still a free country, right?

In the hallway, I run into Lola Emery. Her hair is in curlers.

She's wearing a red plaid sweatshirt and floppy pants, and she's got a plastic crate of laundry in her arms. "Oh, it's you again," she says.

"I'm like a bad penny," I say. "You can't get rid of me."

She grins. "You're here to help Risa, aren't you? I wouldn't call you that."

I step aside then and let her pass by with her bulky load.

Risa's door is slightly ajar. I knock twice, and just that little force pushes it open some more.

"Come on in," she says. She's sitting forward on her couch with a nail file in her hand. It's only a little after 8:30, but she's got on neat black slacks, a white silk blouse, and high heels. Her hair is pinned up off her neck, and she's put on lipstick and mascara. She looks a lot better than I do, but then that wouldn't be too hard to do.

"You going somewhere special later on?" I ask. "Shopping? A job interview?"

"Why?" she says. "Because of this? No, not shopping. And I don't think I'll be needing a job after today. I made an appointment to go downtown to see Mr. Rupiper. He wants me to sign some papers." She waves her nail file suggestively. "And I thought—I was hoping maybe I could persuade you to come along."

"What do you need me for?"

"Protection," she says. "You saw the policeman camped out there? I haven't left this apartment in three whole days because of him."

"He's not going to bother you, Risa. He can't. You didn't do anything wrong, did you?"

"I didn't, no. I didn't kill anyone, if that's what you mean."

"Okay. Then forget about him."

She stands up, wipes her palms briefly against the sides of her legs. "I haven't had my breakfast yet. Nervous, I guess. Have you eaten, Mr. Parisman? I make a fabulous cheese omelet. That's what Ray used to tell me."

"I've eaten, thanks, but I wouldn't turn down some toast and coffee."

"And then afterward, you'll come with me?" She has a hopeful look in her eyes.

"I'd rather not," I say. "Actually, I don't think Melvin Rupiper would appreciate seeing me. Not quite so soon again."

"Again? You know him?"

"We've met."

She wrinkles her brow. "I take it that the two of you didn't get along."

"Like I say, we've met." I follow her into her tiny kitchen, and while she's whipping a pair of eggs in a ceramic dish I tell her a little bit about my encounter with Rupiper. Not what I really think of him. Just the fact that there were two wills, and hers was the latest.

"He didn't leave everything to me?" There's surprise in her voice, and even more than that underneath, fear.

"He has a son in Israel. And a daughter here. Santa Monica, I believe. You must have run into her."

"No," she says. "No, he never said a word. She briefly sets down the fork she's whipping the eggs with. "Are you saying there could be a fight over his estate? That his son and daughter might—"

"I doubt it. Like I said, your will is the latest. That's what generally counts. Besides, he's given his kids plenty, I'm sure. And now they'll split whatever that house on Mulholland goes for. It's probably worth at least as much as what he left you."

She brings out plates, and we crouch next to each other on barstools. She's got a lovely cheese omelet, I've got my buttered toast and coffee. I let her eat about half of it. Then when she gets this satisfied beam in her eye, I ask her again what she and Pinky fought about that night.

"Oh, it's—it's what I told you on the phone."

"You didn't say anything on the phone, Risa. Remember? I need specifics."

"Right," she looks straight at me for a nanosecond before averting her eyes. She bites her lower lip, then starts haltingly to speak. "Well, it…it was about 9 or 10 at night. He was getting ready to turn in. He had this…this little routine he always did, taking his pills, brushing his teeth, putting his hearing aids on the dresser. I reached for my nightgown and something just snapped inside me. I told him I couldn't do this anymore. I wanted out."

"Couldn't do what, Risa?"

She makes a you-must-be-kidding face. "Sleep with him, of course. I couldn't. Not anymore."

"You didn't love him?"

A bloodless look this time. "I told you before. I mean, I cared for him, in a way." She shudders, laughs bitterly to herself, as if remembering an experience from the past. "I was suffocating where I was. I had to get out, that's all. I had no choice."

"But why? Was it the age thing? Something physical?"

"Oh, Jesus, I don't know." She rolls her eyes. "I don't think so. Maybe. It didn't help. He was a good man, a generous man—"

"But that wasn't enough?"

"No. He was kind to me, but in the end that didn't matter. He wasn't Ray." She shakes her head. "It's funny, I started missing him right after I moved in with Pinky. I even had a dream about him one night. Does that make any sense at all? Am I crazy?"

I take a slow sip of my coffee. I watch how she holds her knife and fork, the meticulous way she's chipping away at her breakfast, and I wonder if she knows what's happened to Ray Ballo. I doubt it. A murder victim in LA is about as rare as a parking ticket. In an alternate universe I picture the unwritten headline: *Country-western bass player found dead with knife in chest. Who cares?* I glance over at the living room coffee table. There are no newspapers lying around, and it certainly didn't make the ten o'clock news.

"I talked to Ray once, and I'll give you that much, he's a

sweet guy."

"The best," she says with a nod.

"You haven't seen him lately, have you?"

"No," she mumbles. "Not for a while. It's been weeks. We're not exactly a couple anymore, you know. And I'll bet he's still mad at me. Not that I blame him." She takes her now clean plate and lays it gently in the sink, along with the frying pan and her utensils. "Mr. Parisman," she says, "you need to hear the whole story. I need your help and I haven't—I haven't been entirely truthful about this."

I stare at her and wait for what's to come. She's a beautiful woman, but I can see it in her eyes, at the moment she's wrestling with something, something big and hard and rough. It's like there's a rock in her throat.

"We fought," she says, "as I said before. And Pinky begged me to stay. He was weeping. He told me he'd give me anything I wanted. Anything. At one point he dropped down on his knees. He looked so pathetic like that, but I knew I had to be free. I started screaming at him. I called him every name I could think of. He didn't move. He just sat there on his knees, bawling like a baby. Then I ran out of the house and drove off. About halfway down Laurel Canyon I realized how stupid I was. I'd left all my clothes there."

"So you came back?"

"Yes, but not immediately. And not alone. I didn't think I could face him all alone. I needed somebody. So I went over to Ray's apartment. I woke him up and asked him to please come with me."

"What time was that?"

"I don't know, honestly. Late."

"Okay. You asked him to come help you. And he did."

"Yes," she says. "He did. Even after the shabby way I treated him. He loved me. Amazing, huh? He was still there for me."

We go back into the living room and sit together on her couch. She crosses her legs, brushes a loose hair from in front of her eyes, and tries her best to smile.

"Okay," I say. "The two of you drive back to Pinky's. Then what?"

She sighs. "I was driving the Jaguar and trying to explain to Ray how I felt about Pinky. Maybe I should have taken more time. It was complicated. Ray was kinda groggy. I didn't know whether he understood. I mean, he was half asleep and he told me he'd been out drinking with the band that night, so what he heard or whether my words meant anything to him, who can say?"

"And?"

"And then we suddenly hit a bump in the road, and the glove compartment popped open. And Ray reached in and came out holding a gun in his hand. I think he was as shocked to find it as I was. I had never looked in there before. It frightened me to see it. I mean, you don't expect a gun to come out of nowhere, do you?"

"I guess not."

"I think I yelled at him. I told him to please put it back. And he did. Then a few minutes later we pulled in at Pinky's."

"What time was that? Any idea?"

"No. Why would I? Midnight maybe. There were several lights on, I can't remember how many, at least one in the kitchen and another one in the master bedroom. I glanced over at Ray, and something about his expression told me it didn't matter that I was scared to go back in there alone. It would be a lot better if he didn't come face-to-face with Pinky. So I told him to stay put. I'd get my stuff and we'd leave."

"He was okay with that?"

"I didn't wait for him to answer, really. I just got out of the car and ran to the front door."

"Did Pinky answer it?"

"No, I don't know where Pinky was. But it didn't matter, I had a key, so I went in and walked straight into the kitchen."

"Why?"

"I needed some big plastic bags for my clothes. You know,

those black garbage bags."

"Okay. Then what?"

Then I went into the bedroom. There was nobody there. I started grabbing my clothes as fast as I could and stuffing them all into the bags. I had two bags. And I was almost done clearing out the closet when Pinky came up behind me."

"He surprised you?"

"Yes. No. He—he touched me. He put his hands on my shoulders. He tried to caress me, you know. Said he was sorry. Real sorry. Said he wanted us both to take a deep breath, maybe sit down and talk this whole crazy thing over like two sensible human beings. That we were better than this. He kept repeating that. That we shouldn't just let our emotions run wild. Well, I wasn't having any of it. I spun around, pushed him off. He fell on the carpet. I told him to leave me the fuck alone. I screamed at him, told him to go fuck himself. Then I marched out the front door, dragging the bags behind me."

"And Pinky chased you?"

"Yes. He couldn't walk so fast. He was limping. He might have hurt himself when he fell, I don't know. I heard him shouting at me from behind. But I didn't slow down. I got to the car and opened the door and threw the bags in the back. I didn't do such a good job of packing, I guess. Things fell out on the floor of the car—dresses and blouses and one black shoe. When I looked over at the passenger seat it was empty. Pinky was standing in his robe in the doorway. His hands were raised. And Ray was right in front of him pointing the gun, pointing it this way and that way and waving it around like a wild man. He acted real jittery. Maybe he was jealous. Maybe he thought I was in danger. Maybe he was trying to protect me. I—I couldn't speak. My heart was pounding. But Pinky was talking, trying to calm him down. There were some words back and forth. I don't know what they said to each other. Don't ask me. Then all at once the gun went off. Again and again and again. I swear, Mr. Parisman. I swear to God. I've never heard anything so terrible in all my life."

Chapter 18

AFTER THAT, IT TAKES a very long time before she stops shaking and choking back her tears. I don't move a muscle. My impulse is to hold her and console her, but I keep remembering that Risa Barsky isn't my wife or my lover. Or even my friend, to tell you the truth. But she is a human being. And her tears are real.

"You see—you see now why this is so difficult, don't you?"

I nod. "You haven't told this to the police, have you, Risa?"

"I haven't told anyone," she whispers. "Nobody. Except for you. I don't want to get Ray in trouble. I don't want any trouble, period."

"Okay. I understand. But what did you do next?"

"Next? You mean after he killed—?" She takes a deep breath. "Ray shoved the gun back in his jacket and we got into the car. We drove down the hill. I kept looking over at the bulge in his coat. It scared me. What if I hit another bump and it went off? Ray was trembling. He thought he was going to throw up, so I pulled over by the side of the road and let him out for a minute. It was a residential neighborhood. When he came back, he looked a little bit better. Not smiling or anything, but relieved, I guess you'd say. He told me to drive him to his apartment. That's when I noticed the gun was gone and I asked him what happened to it."

"And what did he say?"

"He said there was a trash can out in front of the house where I'd parked. He'd dropped it in there. By tomorrow night he figured it would be buried in a landfill somewhere."

"All right," I say. "So you took him to his place."

"Yes, but when we got there, I realized that the police might be looking for me. People knew—some people, anyway—that I'd been spending time at Pinky's."

"What people?"

"Javier might have still been somewhere on the grounds. And there was an old housekeeper. Yuriko. She had a tiny room of her own near the kitchen. Some nights she stayed over, if it was late or if nobody was around to take her down to the bus stop. I didn't see her, but she could have heard the shots. Who knows? And that car—the Jaguar—it felt like a noose around my neck. I had to get rid of it."

"So that's when you came up with the idea of leaving it at LAX."

"No," she says, "that was Ray's idea, actually. Let them think I'd left town. But I was too crazy to think of anything. Ray told me to drive there, and he would follow along in his car. Then he'd bring me back, either to his place or mine, whichever I wanted."

"Practical guy, that Ray. And you said you wanted to be in your old apartment in Van Nuys."

She shrugged. "I thought it would be safer—better for both of us—if we didn't see each other for a while. I could say that Pinky and I broke up, and no one would have to know about what Ray did or why." She looks at me and tears start to fill her eyes once more. "You see? Do you get it now? What I'm going through?"

My foot starts to tingle suddenly like it's going to sleep. I force myself up and shake it, then walk around until the feeling subsides. Her living room is remarkably clean, neater than the first time I came through here. "I don't know how to break this to you, Risa, but I'm trying to look at this the way the cops will. Maybe your prints aren't on the gun, maybe it was Ray Ballo who shot him, but right now you're an accessory after the fact."

"Accessory? What's that mean?"

"It means you made some unfortunate decisions. Helping

your boyfriend get away that night, for example. Letting him dump the gun in the trash can. Not reporting any of this to the cops. That's what you did, right? That makes you an accessory. It's just as bad as pulling the trigger."

"I didn't kill him! How could I know that Ray was going to do that? It happened, okay? He didn't plan it or anything. It was almost—almost an accident. I just went there for my clothes. Jesus Christ, you have to believe me!"

I fold my arms in front of me. "Well now, here's the thing: There's only one other possible witness who could back up your story. And he's got his own set of problems."

"Ray Ballo's a sweet, sweet guy," she says, reaching for the first of several Kleenex. "A decent guy. I woke him up. He was half-drunk. He thought he was doing me a favor, don't you see? It was all a giant mistake!"

"I see that," I tell her. "Like you say, sometimes there's no rhyme or reason. Things happen. And if the cops could just sit down and talk with Ray, maybe they'd understand."

"You really think so?"

"It's possible," I say. "Maybe."

She frowns. "No, they wouldn't. They'd charge him with murder. They'd do everything they could to send him to prison."

"If he were still alive, they would. Unfortunately, Ray's dead."

Later on, as I'm steering my battle-scarred Honda down the Hollywood Freeway back into the city, I try to think of other, more elegant ways I could have broken the news to Risa. I knew what would happen. It was no surprise. And I didn't intend to cause her pain. No, of course not. I meant well. I always mean well, which, as my dear old dad, Irving Parisman, *Alav Hasha-lom* (may he rest in peace), used to say, is the road to hell. And she'd been through more than enough pain already.

I frown, reach over, and fumble around with the radio dial until I finally land on a station that's playing something thumping and timeless and saccharin from my youth. I want to say it's the Beach Boys. It could be, but I'll never find out. The disc jockey doesn't even bother to talk about it, he's all snark and speed and telling jokes about his short-lived career as a beach bum. Then he cuts away to a Budweiser commercial. I ease up slightly on the gas pedal to let a little pea green Fiat squeeze into the lane ahead of me.

My heart is pounding louder than it should be, and right now I feel like I'm going nowhere in a hurry, like a hamster on a wheel. Do I tell Lieutenant Malloy? Really? And what's he going to do with the information I have? Laugh at it, I guess. No reason to believe me. Or okay, he might believe me. And then? Well, arrest her, for openers. Bring her downtown and try to make something more of what she said. He could always throw the book at her, but I doubt it somehow. I don't remember how many years you get for being an accessory after the fact, or obstructing justice. Not that it matters. A good lawyer could whittle it down, and right now she can afford a good lawyer. And she'll probably get points for saying it was all an accident, that Ballo was drunk and Pinky was sick with love. That everyone was out of their minds and that the gun literally just fell out of the glove compartment. Bad chemistry, she'll say. Bad chemistry, your honor, I swear. And maybe she'll get lucky. Maybe there's a judge in an air-conditioned courtroom in greater Los Angeles, someone who hasn't heard it all before, someone who would look down at her cherubic face and watch her weep and listen to her pain and take her at her word.

"So what are you going to do with this, Parisman?" I say out loud. And that's when I realize I'm all alone. There's nothing but the electrified golden surf coming out of the radio and the polished muscle cars effortlessly gliding past me on either side. "Well, if I were you," I say, "I'd wait."

Which is what I do. It isn't easy, but I force myself. I stay at home. I make oatmeal for Loretta. I spoon it with love into the ceramic bowls we bought in Little Tokyo. I brush her hair. I pick up the newspapers and the magazines and toss them in the chute. I even vacuum the carpet. And one week later Omar calls. He wants me to meet him down at the Starlight Motel on Sunset. Four o'clock sharp. Says he thinks I'll find it educational. *Educational* is not a word I've ever heard come out of his mouth, and he laughs when he says this. It occurs to me that Omar didn't graduate from high school in Boyle Heights, and I almost ask him what he means, but then I don't.

I get there a few minutes ahead of time and pull into a cyclone-fenced ten-dollar-all-day lot down the block. A short, squat, dark-skinned gentleman in a starched white shirt and pressed jeans and polished shoes comes out of his kiosk. He has a warm smile. He grins, takes the bill I pull from my pocket, and adds it to the considerable wad he already has in his pants. Then he tells me the lot closes at six o'clock sharp.

"I thought it was all day," I say.

"That's when the day ends, *señor*" he says. "Six." I'm about to point to his sign and argue this with him, but the truth is he doesn't give a damn about what all-day means, and, besides, we both know it's rush hour and there's nowhere else to park within a ten-mile radius so I just shrug. Fuck it, I think, and walk away.

The Starlight is located on the east side, where Sunset starts to get a little sketchy; it's been around in one form or another for as long as I can remember. They've made an attempt at remodeling in the last decade or so, it looks like, and now there's a double-decker strip of rooms, with a kidney-shaped pool and parking for guests in the back. The powder-blue neon sign in front of the office features a lone palm tree and, beckoning off in the distance, a twinkling golden star.

Omar's standing on the corner with the back of his foot propped up against a mailbox. There's a lump in his pocket, which I recognize as the mini cam I gave him long ago for surveillance jobs. He nods and I come closer. "So what do we have?"

"This is where your boy, Rupiper, spends his Wednesday and Friday afternoons," Omar says quietly without looking at me. "He's in 109 upstairs."

"I'm supposed to get excited by this?"

"Maybe you would, if you knew who he was in there with."

"Let me guess, Omar." I close my eyes, place my fingers on my forehead in mock concentration. "Could it be…a woman?"

"Actually, today it's two women, which, to tell you the truth, I wouldn't care about, you know. Each to his own and all that. But these are kids, Amos." He frowns, shakes his head. "They're carrying backpacks from school. Kids. They look like twelve-, thirteen-year-olds."

"Really? How long have they been in there?"

"Half hour maybe. Maybe more. A man can do a lot of damage to a minor in that much time, don't you think?"

"And you've seen them come here before?"

"Last week he had a couple dates with an older blonde."

"How old?" I ask. "Older than you?"

"She was thirty, forty. I dunno. The blond hair looked like she maybe bought it in a drugstore. She could be fifty, who knows. Wore very tight orange pants. Tight pants, spiked heels, that's all I remember." He pulls out the little video camera. "But it's in here if you wanna look."

"And this week it's young, underaged girls."

"They came last Wednesday. The same two."

"And you're sure they're just kids?"

Omar wags his head. "I didn't ask to see their school IDs, man. Maybe they're not twelve. Okay? Maybe they're midgets."

"But that's not what you think, is it?"

"No," he says. "I think he's sick, that's what I think."

Just then the door to Room 109 opens. Omar pulls out

his camera and points it deftly with his right hand. Two young black-haired girls wearing sneakers, hefting backpacks over their shoulders, slip out. One of them is wearing a Minnie Mouse sweatshirt. Her companion, whose dark, thick mane cascades like a waterfall down her back, stuffs what looks like bills into her front jeans pocket and they head for the stairs. When they reach ground level, they both turn and stare across the street at us. The girl who'd pocketed the money, licks her lips, mumbles something to her companion, and they quicken their pace as they head east in the lengthening shadows.

"They look to be Latinas, don't you think?" I ask Omar.

"Yeah man," he says. "The rup a little bit like the way my sister did when she was that age. Only she never got herself in trouble like these two. My mother would have killed her if she did."

We film them as they slowly get smaller and smaller in the distance, then cars intervene. They are just dots when they turn left and finally vanish altogether.

I motion to Omar. When the light turns green, we make our way through the crosswalk and climb the stairs of the Starlight Motel. I stop in front of 109, knock gently.

Rupiper coos from the other side. "Is that you again, Dolores? Did you forget something, my sweetness? Please, *por favor*, come in."

I push open the door and we step into his space. Omar points the camera right at him, lets it roll. There's a painting on the wall, spots and drizzles in the manner of Jackson Pollock, only it's obviously not Pollock, just some cheap hack they hired to knock these things out by the dozen to give these rooms some class. There's also an art deco—ish lamp on in the corner near the bathroom. Rupiper is standing there beside it, looking down at his clothes, which he's folded methodically over a nearby chair. He acts so surprised and vulnerable in his blue boxer underpants. Okay, maybe surprised is the wrong word. He's trembling and he looks scared and sad all at once. The party's over. On the king-size bed, the sheets are rumpled and the pillows strewn about. He's not wearing his glasses, they're sitting on the bedside table, but even in this skewed light he can still see enough of us to know we're not Dolores.

"Gentlemen," he says. He nods and picks up his wallet, which was lying on the bed, half offers it in our direction. "You've caught me at a—that is, you've come at a—at a very inopportune time. Well, we all make mistakes, don't we? You can put the camera down, by the way. Nothing to see. We're all human, huh?"

"Remember me, Rupiper?" I say. "Amos Parisman." I point to Omar. "And this is my associate Mr. Villasenor. He's been documenting your travels."

Rupiper's cheeks turn red. His lips start moving very rapidly. "Documenting? Is that what you call it? Yes, well, but this is—this is ridiculous. I mean, we can come to a civilized arrangement about it, now can't we? We're both reasonable men, you and I."

"I don't know about that. I'm a reasonable guy, all right, but my man here, he told me you have some—well, how shall I describe them? You have some pretty unusual tastes."

"And as I said before—"

"You like little girls, it turns out. That's what he's been telling me. Little Latina girls, especially. Like the pair of kids that just walked out. In my book, anyway, that's not normal, Rupiper. Not only that. It's illegal."

"They told me they were eighteen."

"Did they now? And before they took their pants off I'm sure you checked their drivers licenses, right?"

"I took them at their word."

"I'll bet you did."

"Please," he says again, staring at Omar with more urgency now. "Please put the camera down."

"Mr. Villasenor here is from Mexico," I say. "Did you know that? He grew up poor. Never finished high school. Had to fight every inch of the way to get where he is. Do you see where I'm coming from, Rupiper?"

"I—I'm not sure—"

"What I'm trying to say is, he's fought all his life, and now he's here in this great land of ours, and he has this bad temper sometimes. I've tried to help him, but you know how it is. He hates it when things are unfair. He gets angry, very angry, when he sees someone like you—a big, high-powered lawyer and a married man—mistreating little girls."

"Yes, yes, of course, I can see his point—"

"In fact, I'm just guessing, but Mr. Villasenor would probably like nothing better than to slice your balls off right about now, wouldn't you, Omar?"

"It would be my pleasure," Omar says calmly from behind the camera.

"Gentlemen, please—" Rupiper's voice starts to quaver now. He sits on the edge of the bed with his palms spread flat against the mattress. His eyes are glazed, searching. There's a sour stench coming off of him, as if the shock and fear I've talked him into has taken over. His words are useless here; there is nothing he can say to persuade us. A shiver runs through him, then he rises suddenly and makes a great desperate lunge for the door, but Omar is right there and with his free hand he shoves him back onto the pile of twisted sheets and pillows.

"Shall I cut him now, boss?"

"No! Please God, no!" Rupiper looks at Omar, then back to me. There are tears forming in his eyes.

"I'll tell you what, Melvin. You don't deserve this after what you just did to those kids, but like you say, I'm a reasonable man. So here's how it is: You're going to answer all my questions about Pincus Bleistiff—and I mean *all* of them. You're going to tell me the truth, the whole truth, and nothing but the truth. Are we on the same page, counselor?"

He nods.

"And if you do, well then I'll do my best to try to persuade

Omar here to leave you alone."

"Okay, fine," he says nervously. "Fine, anything you want."

"But later on, if I find out you're lying, well—"

"I wouldn't lie to you."

"I know you say that now. But that's because you're scared and you want to go home in one piece. I understand, Melvin. Just remember that we have video of those girls coming and going here. Also, footage of the cheap blonde you were with last week. The one with the tight pants? You know who I'm talking about? It's a film I'm sure your wife and kids will enjoy—"

"I wouldn't lie to you, I said!" He gazes once more at Omar. "Now will you please, for the love of God, put that thing away?"

I nod slightly and Omar lowers the camera. I fold my arms in front of me. "Good," I tell him. "I'm glad we understand one another."

If I have to, and if Omar is standing by my side, I can always play the heavy, even at my advanced age. I don't mind lying, not if it gets me somewhere. And I think I do a pretty good job of it, too. But the truth is I'm not prepared for what I find out when I put the arm on Melvin Rupiper.

"I did a lot of things for Pinky," he starts out. "We go way back. I did whatever he asked, basically."

"You mean, things related to the music business?"

"No, not that so much. Personal favors, mostly."

"Give me a for instance, why don't you."

Rupiper stares at me intently. "Look, Mr. Parisman. I know what you're after. And Pinky's dead. I liked him, he was good to me, but I have no further obligation, do I?"

"No," Omar jumps in, "not unless you want to die."

Rupiper shrugs. His old attorney's face has returned. "No, I don't. So why don't we just cut to the chase?"

"I'm waiting," I say.

Rupiper wriggles into his pants and slowly, meticulously begins to button his shirt. "The first time I saw Pinky Bleistiff was at the Troubadour in West Hollywood. Thirty years ago, it must have been, maybe more. I was just out of law school. In fact, I don't even remember if I'd passed the bar yet. I was sending out résumés, looking for a job."

"We don't need to hear about your career path," I say. "What went down with Pinky?"

"He was there to check out this new rock band," Rupiper says. "We got to talking, hit it off. He bought me a drink. When I told him I was a lawyer, that seemed to animate him. I didn't know how it came up, but at some point in the conversation he mentioned that he was trying to find a distant relative. You're a lawyer, he said, maybe you know a good detective."

"Did you?" Omar asks.

"No," Rupiper says. "I didn't know anybody. But I let him think I might. Anyway, he started telling me his life story. How his parents came over here from Hungary, but all the others— his aunts and uncles and cousins—they stayed behind. When things got ugly in the thirties, his mother wrote to them. She told them to leave, come to America, go to Palestine, but of course they wouldn't budge. They were stubborn. They thought they could ride out the bad times. They'd been through anti-Semitism before, that's what they said."

"A lot of Jews thought that," I say. "Some of my family, included."

"Exactly," Rupiper says. "But then the war started and all of a sudden it was too late. They were trapped. The letters from Europe became few and far between. They were okay until 1944. They managed, somehow. Then, somewhere along the line, their luck ran out. Pinky didn't say how it ended. He probably didn't know for sure. He just assumed one night the Nazis rolled into their neighborhood, rounded them up, shipped them off to Auschwitz."

"And they all died?"

"Most," says Rupiper, "most, but not all. Pinky'd heard a ru-
mor that he still had a cousin."

"He knew this person?"

"He had a name, that's all. And somebody told him she'd
ended up in New York after the war. It's just something he
heard. Who knows? It could be a mistake. Could be another
person with the same name. New York's a big town, I told him.
And the war's been over a long time. Yes, yes, he said. He knew
all that. But would I mind looking into it? Would I track her
down?"

"He asked you to find her? Out of the blue? A total stranger? Why?"

"I can't answer that," Rupiper says. "It sounded crazy to me,
too. I don't know for sure, maybe he was drunk. I tried to tell
him I wasn't a detective, but he was so desperate, I don't think
he really cared. He wrote me a check right there in the Troubadour. I was a young man. Young and broke. Not even sure that
I'd passed the bar. What was I gonna do, turn him down? Sure,
I said, I'll look. I'll try, anyway."

"And did you find her?"

"The name he gave me was Helen Hartman. And he had
a feeling she lived in Brooklyn. That's what he remembered.
Could have been Helene. Could have been Hartmann with two
N's. It's fairly common, right? But I checked the records and
there was someone with that name who was in a displaced persons camp near Bonn in 1946, and this person did find her way
to New York in 1951."

"So?"

"So that Helen Hartman—relative or not—unfortunately
died before I could meet her. But what I learned is—and this
will interest you—Helen Hartman married an older man, a
cab driver named Richard Barsky. And they had a daughter,
Marissa."

"Marissa. Risa Barsky? She's his second cousin?"

Rupiper nods. "Maybe. It's possible. I mean, we're shooting

in the dark here, but that's what I found out."

"And this Richard Barsky?"

"He died when Marissa was an infant."

"You're sure?"

"About the father? Yeah, I'm positive. He's buried in Flat-bush. Big Jewish cemetery there."

"Because I heard a story that her parents were communists, rich New York intellectuals. You know anything about that?"

"No, I never heard that story. That's a new one to me. But I can't say I'm surprised. Maybe you noticed Risa's pretty good at pulling rabbits out of a hat when she has to. Very creative."

"So no Upper West Side commies?"

"Not that I knew of. The truth is, when her dad died, she ended up in foster care until she turned eighteen. Then she started to make her way in Soho and Tribeca, waitressing and bartending. For a year or two she sold cosmetics at Macy's. Somewhere along the line she started singing in a band after hours with friends. Nothing big, really, just two-bit places in the Village."

"And what was Pinky's reaction to all this?" I ask. "You told him, right?"

"Of course I did. He got excited. Told me I'd made his day. He arranged to fly there by himself and take in a few of her gigs. But then he made me swear to keep it a secret."

"What was that all about? Any idea?"

Rupiper shakes his head. "He didn't go into it. Not with me, anyway. But I could tell. It was clear he didn't even want her to know he was in the audience."

"But this was a relative. A link to his past. Wouldn't he want to tell someone? What about his wife?"

"Sophie was never to know, either. Nobody else, he told me. Nobody, just you and me." He turns his empty palm over and lets it hang there. "I mean, I don't suppose it was very hard hiding something like that from Sophie. He often went to New York anyway on business. It wasn't unusual. And by the time he found out about Risa, Sophie was already preoccupied with doctors and tests. It wasn't much fun anymore for her to travel."

"Still, he kept this news from his wife."

"I thought about that," Rupiper says. "The irony is Sophie probably wouldn't care one way or the other. A lost cousin—so what? But I didn't ask any questions. That's not what he paid me for."

"And then what?" Omar asks.

"What do you mean?"

"How did Risa Barsky go from singing in clubs in New York to a klezmer band in LA? That's a long drive, no?"

"Pinky watched her for a week. Or rather, he had one of his people watching her. Then he asked another music promoter he knew there, a guy named Felix Zapruder, to approach her and tell her about this band that needed her in LA. Pinky paid Zapruder—actually I paid Zapruder with Pinky's money— some of which he pocketed and the rest he offered to Risa. It was a lot of money, and of course Risa couldn't refuse."

"So she came out here to join this band," I say. "Was there a band?"

"Pinky put one together," Rupiper says. "It wasn't that difficult. There are plenty of Jewish musicians in this town looking for a gig. He even came up with the name: Dark Dreidel. You need a catchy name in the klezmer business, he said."

Jitlada is just a hole in the wall in Hollywood, but it's close by and has some of the best Thai food around, so that's where Omar and I end up an hour later. Omar is a fan of their beer and chicken curry, and I can't resist their spicy mint noodles. They've decked out the place for Christmas. Festive, fruity-colored balls hang from the ceiling, even though there can't be more than twenty devout Christians in their whole country and the owners obviously have no fucking idea what it's all about.

That's why I love LA.

I wait until the food arrives before I ask Omar what he thought about Rupiper.

"You mean, did I think he was lying?" Omar takes a short sip of beer, smacks his lips. "No, man, I thought he was too scared of me and my camera to lie." Then he adds: "I think he wanted to lie. The lawyer in him wanted to, you know, but I believed him."

"I did, too," I say. "Which makes me wonder. Why would Pinky be so generous with a distant relative? I mean, I have a few cousins left in Chicago and New York. I haven't seen them in years, but even if I had the money, it would never occur to me to do what Pinky did with Risa. Fly her out here. Set her up in an apartment. Put her in a professional band. Does that sound right to you?"

"Maybe he takes his family more seriously than you do."

I shrug.

"Or maybe," Omar continues, "it's a way for him to make up for losing so much of his family in Hungary."

"I like that idea better. But why be so secretive about it? Why keep it from his wife? Why keep it from Risa?"

Now it's Omar's turn to shrug. "People are weird," he says. "I have a niece from Guadalajara. Nice kid. She goes to Pasadena City College and she's living with this guy who collects the *LA Times*. I mean, he has a couple of garages stacked up full of the *LA Times*. Clear to the ceiling. Is that loco or what? Hasn't it all been digitized? What's he thinking?"

"You got me there, amigo. I don't have a clue. But maybe you should have a little chat with him. You know, for your niece's sake."

Omar finishes his beer, signals the waitress for a second. "I did. He doesn't trust the new technology. That's what he said. He trusts paper. Paper's been around for hundreds of years, and it'll be here long after the internet disappears. When that day comes we'll need a record, he said. You mark my words. He was dead serious, this guy."

"Is your niece in love?" I ask. "I've heard love often clouds people's thinking."

"She wants what she wants. He's sweet to her and they seem to get along all right. He just has this one tiny crack in the mirror, you know. Just one imperfection." He swallows some more beer. "And every time I think about it—"

"Don't think about it, then," I tell him. "Just because he's crazy doesn't mean you have to be, too.

Chapter 19

IN THE MORNING I meet Lieutenant Malloy for breakfast at Du-par's in the Farmers Market. I was hoping to get together with him at Canter's, but he only ever goes to that place
reluctantly, to please me. Fact is, Canter's probably makes him
a *bissel* nervous. He's a staid, monkish fellow, really. His own
mother back in Chicago begged him to throw his lot in with
the Church, and while he thought about it, in the end he opted
for that other vaunted Irish profession. I asked why once, and
he told me it's because while he always admired the character of
Jesus, he had a tough time believing in God. Now, constabulary
duty, that's different, that's a world he understands. You don't
have to believe in God to carry a badge. Better, in fact, if you
don't. I get that. Besides, when you think about it, it's organized
like a priesthood. Rules and uniforms and regulations. An inner
logic that bends toward justice, eventually.

We get a nice, cozy spot in the corner. He grabs the inside
seat against the wall so he can keep an eye on the entrance. An
old cop's habit, he probably can't help it. We read the menu,
which hasn't changed in the last fifty years. Canter's is right
up the street, but okay. No matter how much I push him, he's
never going to feel comfortable around the noise and banter
and camaraderie of perfect strangers. I'm not even sure he gets
my jokes sometimes. It's not that he doesn't like Jews. Nobody
would ever accuse him of that. So Du-par's, then, all right.
Leatherette booths. Ham and eggs and cottage fries. No flirting
around with the waitress. *Mind your manners, Parisman.*

I pass on what Rupiper gave me about Pinky and the an-
cestral connection with Risa. And I deliberately leave out the

part about Rupiper's fascination with young girls. I wanted to talk about it, of course. But I couldn't. Before we left the motel room, Rupiper made us both a solemn promise. Said he was done with that kind of thing. No more, he said. And I believed him, not because he'd suddenly found religion but because he knew damn well we had all the film we needed to ruin his life. Also, Omar really scared the living shit out of him.

Malloy is pleased with what I have to say. "Second cousin, huh? Hmm, that's cutting it close, but I guess it's still legal here in California."

"Lots of things still legal in California. Maybe they shouldn't be."

"That's above my pay grade, Amos." He works methodically on his short stack of buttermilk pancakes. "I talked to the district attorney," he tells me. "Cimino's still working out the details, but he's decided to go ahead and press charges against Risa Barsky."

"She didn't kill him, Bill. C'mon, there's no proof."

"No proof for murder, no. But you don't get to watch someone get gunned down, then help the killer get away. That's a little too much audience participation in my book. No, they're going to tag her for accessory to murder. It shouldn't be hard. She's already admitted as much."

"So what was holding them up?"

"Nothing, really. I guess they're just trying to determine whether or not she was lying. And now that Ray Ballo's dead, the DA wants to mop up the whole mess as best he can."

"I don't know, Bill. I still think there's more to this."

"Maybe so, but this isn't the only unsolved crime on my plate, now is it. Really, you don't want to know what I'm looking at."

"Depressing, huh?"

"It doesn't make me happy, I can tell you that. But there comes a time when you just gotta move on."

"What about the gun?" I ask.

"What about it?"

"Well," I say, "she told that whole *meshugenah* story about finding the gun in the glove compartment."

"Yeah? So what?"

"So what? Well, number one, it couldn't happen. It's physically impossible. Not the way she told it."

"Fine. But I can think of lots of ways for a gun to come out of a glove compartment. Nobody on the jury's gonna care about that. What's number two?"

"Number two, the question is, what was it doing there? Did Pinky have a license to own a gun?"

Malloy looks at me, pauses, frowns, nods his head. "Yes. Yes, he did. He bought a .38 a couple years back. Registered and everything. Said on the form he wanted one for home protection. That there'd been a rash of burglaries in the neighborhood. Which is true."

"And it hasn't turned up yet?"

"No. But once it goes to court it won't matter, Amos. Pinky owned a .38. He was killed with a .38. The .38 he owned has gone missing. How many guns are floating around in this town? How many of them are .38s? And how many are registered? Will the jury care? You tell me."

"And nothing more on who did Ray Ballo? Don't you think it's odd? Don't you think these things are possibly connected?"

"Maybe. Maybe not. That's not how the DA's looking at it."

"The DA's just looking for an excuse to put Risa away."

"Nothing wrong with that, is there? She's no angel."

I finish the last bite of my scrambled eggs. "Well, will you at least do me one tiny favor, then?"

"A favor? For you?" He shrugs with contentment. The pancakes and the maple syrup must be getting to him. "Sure, okay, Amos. What do you want?"

"You know where she lives. You've got her under twenty-four-hour surveillance. She's not going anywhere. Will you give me a few more days to talk with her before you take her in? Can you wait that long?"

"Why?" he asks. "Are you on the verge of a breakthrough?"

"She trusts me. You bring her in now and book her, she'll clam right up. That'd be a shame."

"She's got more to tell us?"

"She's coming off a giant roller coaster, Bill. Up, down. One day she's singing for tips in the Village, the next thing she knows she's living on Mulholland Drive, tooling around in a Jaguar. She's been through a lot. In the last few weeks she's lost not one but two boyfriends. She's afraid of her own shadow, but for some strange reason, we get along. I don't understand it myself, but I think if I just sat down with her now and talked it over, we might just come to a whole different view of this."

"You'll probably end up being a witness," he cautions.

"That's okay, I don't mind."

"Wait," he says quietly. "You want me to wait? Okay, Amos. I can do that, I suppose. I'll talk to Cimino. You have until this Friday, 9 a.m. But that's when I'm sending Jason and Remo to Van Nuys to pick her up. Understood?"

"Fair enough. Thanks, Bill."

"Oh," he adds, "and just so you know: You're buying my breakfast."

Pinky's daughter, Julie, lives a couple of blocks north of Montana in Santa Monica. She goes by her husband's name, Collins, not because she needs to pass—there are plenty of Jews in this neck of the woods—but for the children's sake. That's what Victoria let drop when she arranged for us to meet this afternoon.

It's not an especially luxurious neighborhood, but the streets have a sense of generosity about them, as though everyone living here has arrived at some glorious juncture in their lives. The sun shines down on their endeavors. They have succeeded in whatever it is they had set out to do. If that has a calming effect, I wouldn't know. The cars parked by the curb are uniformly sleek and modern and foreign-made, and no one seems to mind the untimely heat, maybe because the beach is down the street. Jacaranda and palm trees and giant sprawling sycamores provide a modicum of shade here and there. I climb slowly out of my car and stretch. Some of the houses in this area date back to the 1920s, it seems like. They aren't that large, not by Pasadena or Bel-Air standards, but still, many of them have a Spanish flair—red-tiled roofs and arched windows. In a normal universe you might not look twice at anything here, except that this is Santa Monica, which means that the price tags on them have all gone completely mad.

Julie answers the door almost immediately.

"Thanks for having me over, Mrs. Collins."

"Oh, please, call me Julie." She leads me into the living room, which has two small black leather couches set up like an L and flanked inside by a gorgeous Persian carpet. There are tiny overhead lights sunk into the ceiling like stars. Julie Collins is slender, in her forties. She has that perpetually weary look in her eyes that many mothers have, an almost wistful expression that knows she can't turn back the clock from the path she's on and that someday this will all be a memory, something she'll be glad she did, but not now, not quite yet. She has a paperback in her hand, and she wears large tinted glasses that hang from a silver chain. It looks as though she's only managed to get through the first twenty or so pages of the book. She runs her fingers self-consciously through the mass of long, dark, curly hair that stops just below her ears.

"You'll forgive me, I was so absorbed in this book I'm reading, I actually forgot you were coming. I—I never get a chance to read." She smiles, then curls up onto one of the couches and motions me to do likewise. It's a sunny day beyond the windows and she's dressed in silver sneakers and a forest green tracksuit. Still, clothes aside and apart from chasing after her children, I don't get the feeling she's devoted to exercise.

"Can I get you anything to drink?" she says now. "This is a good day for iced tea. I have some in the fridge. That's all my husband drinks these days. Part of his new diet."

"No, no," I say, "I'm good." I plop myself into a nearby armchair. She lays the book on the carpet. I catch the title. It's something I read years ago, *Zen and the Art of Motorcycle Maintenance*.

"My youngest is napping, but I can't predict how much longer that will be. Victoria said you had some questions about my father?"

"I was working for your father before he died."

"Doing what?" she asks, without missing a beat.

"He told me one of his singers had disappeared. He gave me an ungodly amount of money to find her."

Julie doesn't register any surprise. She folds her hands into her lap. "Tell me," she asks evenly, "was my dad in love with her?"

"It looks like it," I say. "I believe he was. It may have even been mutual, too, at least for a short time."

Julie nods. "And so have you found this woman, Mr. Parisman? Or is she still on the loose?"

"Oh, I know exactly where she is."

"Then your job is done," she says.

"Well no, not quite. You see, the police are about to arrest her."

"For what?"

I don't answer immediately, and Julie looks at me with concern. She forces herself into an upright position. "Is she the one?" she asks. "She—she killed my father?"

I shrug. "Did your father own a gun, Julie?"

"He had one, I know. At least he told me he did. I never saw it. He kept it in a kitchen drawer. I must have told him a dozen times to get rid of it, but he wouldn't. He was a stubborn man, my father."

"Yes."

"Is that—is that what she used to kill him?"

"We don't know. And they'll have a hard time proving any of that. He was shot, yeah. And she may have seen the man who shot him. She might have even helped him get away. It's all up in the air. What I'm pretty sure of is, she's involved."

"Involved." Julie shakes her head, shivers slightly. "So what—what do you want from me?"

"Her name is Barsky." I pause a moment. "Risa Barsky. It's short for Marissa. She may be a distant relative of yours."

"I'm sorry," Julie says, "I don't recognize that name."

"How about Hartman, then. Helen Hartman? Does that ring a bell? Did your father ever mention someone like that? She came over from Hungary. After the war."

Julie closes her eyes for a few seconds, then opens them again. "There were lots of people in Hungary. We have old photographs, of course, but as far as I know, none of them survived."

I nod. "The same thing happened to my *mishpuchah*, too. Gone. Every single one." We're both silent for a time then, just sitting there in her splendid living room, mulling over the enormity of loss. "But still, you know what? Thank God for cameras, huh? That's what I say."

"Yes," she says. After a few more seconds she seems to snap out of it. "You want to see my family albums, Mr. Parisman? Is that why you came?"

"Maybe," I tell her. "If it's not too much trouble, yes."

She vanishes into another room, and I wander over toward the window to take in the late afternoon sunshine filtering across the back lawn. A young, stalwart lemon tree is pushing its way up in the far corner near the fence, and right in the middle there's an orange swing set anchored firmly into the ground. A child's shovel and plastic bucket sit in a tiny homemade sandbox, and a few tennis balls are strewn about, waiting perhaps for a spirited dog to fetch them. The lawn seems overdue to be mowed, but all in all it has a happy, well-lived-in look.

"Here they are," she says behind me.

There are two thin, blue albums, both framed with gold

edging. The bindings are worn, and one of them has been kept together with strips of tape. She sets them down gently on the dining room table and opens the first one.

"My father's family were pretty much the only ones to come over. There may have been a few others, but they stayed put in New York. My great-grandfather arrived in 1908, I think. Here's a picture from the Bronx. His name was Schmuel. I don't know what he did in Hungary, but here he made a living going door-to-door buying and selling old gold. That's what my dad always told me. I can't imagine."

She lets her finger rest on her ancestor's shoulder. He's a gaunt gentleman in a rumpled three-piece suit standing on a city street corner next to a lamppost. There's what seems like a hat in his hand.

"He was a dapper fellow," I say. "I like the beard and the mustache."

"Yes," she says.

I point to a smaller photo on the next page. Three boys in sailor costumes with their arms wrapped lovingly around one another, and off to the side, a girl in a ruffled dress. They're out in the country somewhere, or maybe it's a park. You can't tell. "And who are these kids?"

Julie brightens. "My great-uncles. Bernie, Mike, and Sam. The little girl there under the tree is my grandmother, Judith. I'm named for her. Yudit—that's my Hebrew name. She looks like me, don't you think?"

"Dead ringer," I say. "I don't suppose any of these folks are still around, are they?"

Julie smiles, shakes her head.

I riffle through several more pages. It's what you would expect: birthdays and bat mitzvahs. School graduations. Family dinners. Then on the next-to-last page I come to a picture that brings me up short. At first I don't know why it jumps out at me. Then I remember: It's the same snapshot I saw on Risa Barsky's carpet a month ago—the one that Lola made me leave behind, the one that was torn in two. But this one's intact. The young, comely woman in a tight sweater is staring straight into the camera, and beside her is an older, somewhat heavier man. He has a cigarette in his mouth and he's wearing a rumpled polo shirt. I get the impression that he's irritated, that he doesn't really want to stand there and have his picture taken, that this is all happening against his will. Still, they're standing close together near a window. You can't see the cigarette he's holding, but there's smoke rising above her shoulder and he seems to have his arm draped around her. "Who's this?" I ask.

Julie studies it for a moment. "Oh, that's my cousin, Magda, I believe. I never met her. She was part of that New York clan. Died when I was a baby. Cancer, they said."

"And the guy she's with?"

"I think he was her boyfriend or her husband. But don't quote me. I want to say his name was Rick. It was a long, long time ago."

I cross my arms. "What would you say, Julie, if I told you I've seen this picture before?"

"Huh?" The shock on her face is genuine.

"Well, part of it, anyway." I point to the pretty woman. "This part. The part with your cousin, Magda."

"Where?"

"It was lying on the floor in Risa Barsky's apartment the first time I went over there. The other half—the guy with the cigarette—he was gone."

"That's so strange," Julie mumbles. "It's beyond strange, in fact. I—I really don't know what to say."

"So you have no idea how it might have happened?"

She shakes her head emphatically. "I dunno. No idea, none. Maybe…maybe my dad gave her a copy." A frown. "But why on earth would he do that? That's the only thing I can think of."

"He gave her a lot of things, it's true."

She has no discernible reaction to this idea. She keeps her silence, like a fine diplomat, but still I'm sure her heart is quivering inside. *He gave her a lot of things.* Half the estate, for instance.

"You read your father's will, didn't you, Julie?"

"The will?" she says. "No, actually, I didn't. The lawyer, a man named Rupiper talked to my husband on the phone. He explained everything, what papers we had to sign. I didn't want to talk to him. I didn't care what happened. I guess I was too upset at the time. You understand."

So maybe she's telling me the truth. Or turn it on its head: Maybe Pinky kept this from her. If she never read his last will, how could she know about Risa? About the money that could have been hers? Should have been hers? Maybe she's much safer, much better off living in Santa Monica, away from her father and his crazy obsessions. My eyes scan the room beyond her shoulders. There's real art on the walls. Fresh-cut flowers in the vase. A child fast asleep upstairs. She has a sweet situation here. Nothing to complain about. And yet.

Chapter 20

TWO SEPARATE LETTERS from Risa Barsky are wedged in my mailbox at Park La Brea when I arrive home. The first one has just a check, no note or anything, but it's equal to the one Pincus Bleistiff sent me several days late. The second letter contains another check, this one twice as large. Also a note that apologizes for not knowing what my fee might be, but her sincere hope that this covers it. *I need your help, Mr. Parisman. The police are watching me. They follow me wherever I go and I'm innocent! Please.* At the bottom she signs her name R, the way characters used to do in old European novels. Very stylish, I think.

I fold the checks in half and tuck them into my wallet. Then I walk across the marble foyer and feel the evening breeze waft in from the parking lot through the open glass doors. By the time the elevator finally arrives, four people are standing there, waiting to pile in with me. A prim and proper Korean mother and her seven- or eight-year-old daughter, who's wearing tights and ballet slippers. A young skinny dirty-blond guy in a shiny gray suit. Sunglasses on his face, dreadlocks down his back. The last one to step inside I recognize, though we've never spoken. She lives a few floors above me, and I always think she must be some kind of nurse. The only times I've seen her, like now, she's wearing tennis shoes and those sloppy pink and blue scrubs. Comfortable, maybe, but I can't imagine any woman on the planet who'd leave home wearing something so ugly, not unless she had to. She must be coming off the day shift, I figure. Her hair is out of place. She seems particularly weary this evening. She asks me would I please push the button for twelve, and so I do.

It's getting on toward suppertime. Carmen will be anxious to go back to her husband and children. I unlock my door and there's my cousin Shelly in the living room holding forth.

"Amos!" he announces. "I've come for dinner. And more important, you'll be pleased to hear that I've brought you dinner." He has a big fat satisfied grin on his face. Loretta and Carmen are both seated on the couch staring up at him. Loretta is giggling. I can't tell if it's because Shelly has said something genuinely funny or that's just the effect he has on her. And what's it matter? If it makes her laugh, isn't that what the doctor ordered?

"That's great," I say. "Free food. Who doesn't love that?" I open up the closet and slip my jacket onto a hanger.

On the kitchen table are three large, white plastic sacks from Pacific Seafood on La Cienega. Loretta and I order takeout from them once in a while. It's good, but we usually buy too much, and then we spend forever figuring out how many more meals it can make. One Hanukkah, I'm not kidding, we had it for eight days in a row. A Chinese miracle.

"What's the occasion, Shel? Tell me. You getting hitched again? Or did the divorce come through?"

He clutches lightly at his heart, gives me a look mock of pain. How could I hurt his feelings? The answer is, I couldn't. Not in a million years. Not only that, he knows damn well I wouldn't. Shelly is flesh and blood. We go back to my nursery school days. He taught me how to ride a two-wheeler. Also how to smoke dope and what a naked girl really looks like, at least in the magazines. You don't throw someone like that under the bus.

He comes over and starts taking the warm paper containers out of the sacks and setting them down in a row on the counter. "Neither," he says. "You want to know the truth?"

"I always want the truth, cousin." I'm reaching into drawers and pulling out plates and forks and spoons and napkins. I glance back at Carmen to see if she might agree to join us, which would be a rarity. But she's already standing, wriggling into her sweater, hunting around for her purse.

"Well, yes," Shelly continues, unruffled by anything I say, "I am getting divorced, as you know. And yes, one day I'll probably be walking dear sweet Simone down the aisle. That's in the future. But it's not why I'm here."

"No?"

"No. I'm here, boychick, because I've found your missing crooner. And I thought you'd be pleased. I thought you'd want to celebrate."

"My crooner?"

"Risa Barsky? The klezmer lady? You're looking for her, aren't you?"

"I was. But she's not missing anymore."

"No," he says. "Because I found her." He starts spooning mounds of steamy white rice onto the plates.

"Did you now? And how's she doing? Did you talk with her?"

"Are you crazy?" he goes. "Talk with her? I wouldn't do that. I just, you know, followed her from a distance. And only once. I didn't want to interfere with anything. I was trying to be circumspect."

"Oh yeah? And where'd she go?"

Shelly has moved on to the Mongolian beef. "Go? Well, that day she drove to a supermarket. Bought some vegetables. Carrots. Cucumbers. And a pint of coconut ice cream. Maybe some other things, I didn't take good notes."

"Was she alone, Shelly?"

"She was alone, yes. But after a while I noticed a couple of other guys tailing her. They were in the next aisle over mostly. They might have been cops, I dunno. That was my first thought. But I could be wrong."

"They *were* cops, Shelly. The cops know where she is, too. And they're keeping an eye on her. They probably didn't notice the coconut ice cream, though. I'll let them know."

Shelly doesn't say anything more, but I know him well and he seems a little miffed at this. He goes on spooning the food onto our plates, but the childlike joy has left his eyes.

I put my arm around his shoulder. "Fact is, I found her a few weeks ago, Shelly. And it's not about a missing person anymore. Now it's more serious. Now it's murder. Two murders, really."

"You wanna tell me about it?" he asks.

"I'd like to," I say. "I would. But honestly, I'd rather you not get involved. It's dangerous." I give him a tight squeeze, kiss him on the cheek, and let him go. I love this guy, even though he acts like a blowhard and a jerk sometimes. "When was the last time you fired a gun?"

He shakes his head. "Never," he admits. "Never was the last time."

Van Nuys hasn't changed much. The same cars parked out front. The same spindly palms. Even the same burly policeman with his doughnut and paper cup in hand. I nod in his direction as I make my way down the stone path to the front of Risa's apartment.

A couple minutes later we're sitting at her kitchen table. This time there are no amenities. No coffee, no cookies. She's wearing jeans and a skimpy tan sweater, casual but revealing, and she's gone to the trouble of putting on makeup and lipstick and eye shadow. If she wanted to impress a wistful old guy like me, she's doing a fine job. "I'm so happy you're here, Mr. Parisman." For a moment she lets her hand rest tentatively on top of mine. "I just want this all to go away. Can you do that? Make it go away?"

I pull out my wallet and the two checks she sent me. I unfold them and lay them flat on the table. "These came yesterday in the mail, Risa. We maybe should talk about that."

"It's not enough?" she says, startled. "I didn't know what your fee might be. If it's not enough—"

"It's more than enough," I say. "That's not the problem. It's what it's for that I'm concerned about. The question is, what do you want from me?"

"I told you before. I'm innocent," she declares. "I want you to prove it, that's all." She frowns as though she's disappointed, as though I ought to know this is just another one of those immutable things in life, things everybody understands, like water always seeks its own level, or there'll always be an England.

"What you need is a decent lawyer," I tell her. "And not some loser like Melvin Rupiper. All I can do is come up with facts. And right now, I have to tell you, the facts don't exactly add up in your favor."

She lifts a Kleenex out of the powder-blue box in front of her and dabs her eyes. "I'm getting a lawyer. I—I'm talking to several lawyers. There's a firm in Beverly Hills—"

"You need a lawyer, Risa," I repeat, "and I'm sure you have enough money now to buy a good one. But if you want me—"

"I do," she says. "I do. And you know why? Because I trust you, Mr. Parisman. You're the only guy I've ever met who doesn't have an angle. You don't play games. You're not trying to rip me off or…or get into my pants or make me cry." She starts to tear up then and reaches for a second Kleenex. Then a third.

I wait for her to compose herself. Her eye shadow is beginning to bleed around the edges. "If you want me to help you," I say, "then it's not about the money. The money's fine. But there's one thing I do need from you."

"Just one thing?" she asks, perking up. "What's that?"

"The truth," I say. "You tell me the God's honest truth. I mean everything. And then I'll do what I can. I can't guarantee I'll get you off, either. All I can say is, if you trust me like you say you do, and you tell me the truth, well, you'll sleep better."

"Everything," she mumbles. She bites down on her lip. She seems like she's weighing it all out in her mind. It occurs to me that she may not be capable of telling the truth, not because she's evil but she may not know what it is. So many people have lied to her, after all, and how many lies has she told about herself? How many lies has she wrapped herself in, simply to feel safe? It's not hard to imagine. Who doesn't want to feel safe and warm and loved?

"Everything," I nod. "That's right, the whole truth. So, do we have a deal?"

She looks at me. "I guess," she says at last. "You'll have to help me, though. It won't be easy."

"All right," I say. "I can do that."

She laces her fingers tightly together. "Okay. Where shall we start?"

My eyes glance around at the kitchen and the living room. Everything is neat as a pin. "How about with the first day I walked into this apartment, Risa. Your friend, Lola, let me in. She was worried about you. Thought you might be dead. But you weren't here. You'd run off."

"Yeah."

"Somebody had come through before and trashed the place. Tore everything up. Tried to scare you."

"And they succeeded," she says. "That's when I decided I'd be safer with Pinky."

"We'll come back to him. But the day I came through, it was a mess, all right, but you know what I found?" I let the question hang there for a second. "There was this old black-and-white snapshot on the carpet, right near your bed. Half a photo, really. A good-looking woman in a sweater on the left, and—I'm guessing here—another person on the right who'd been ripped out completely. Does that ring a bell?"

She nods. "Those were my parents. At least, I think they were. I didn't ever get to know them."

"Because?"

She doesn't answer this, her face turns to stone, so I dredge up what Rupiper told me and try to fill in the blanks. "Because they died when you were a kid? Is that right?"

She looks away.

"I'm sorry."

"I didn't have any pictures," she says, "just that one. So it all came down to stories I heard growing up."

"Who told you stories, Risa?"

"Oh, people I knew. I had an aunt. At least I think she was my aunt. And there were people in the neighborhood. Teachers. People who took care of me later in foster homes. I moved around a lot."

"And what did they say?"

"Different things. The thing I remember most is that they said my parents were communists. Rich communists. That they lived on the Upper West Side. That was one story. I liked that story."

I stand up then to stretch my arms and walk around. "We need to unravel this business about your parents, Risa."

"Why?" she says, slowly growing angry. "Why? What does that have to do with Pinky's murder? That cop sitting across the street, he doesn't give two shits about my parents. He's after me!"

"It's all part of a piece," I tell her. "Who you are—where you came from—it means something."

"I don't know what you're talking about," she says. She folds her arms in front of her.

"All right, then," I say. "Let's talk about how you came to LA. That should be simple. Do you think it was just luck?"

"I don't know," she says. "Stuff happens like that now and then. I was a waitress. I was sharing a dump with two lesbians in the East Village. Singing three nights a week with a group in Soho. We had promise. I thought so, anyway. We were pretty good."

"Pretty good? You weren't making a living at it, were you?"

"No, but—"

"Don't you think it's kinda weird what happened to you? I mean, what are the odds of being discovered like that?"

"Stuff happens to me," she says again. "I don't think about odds."

"Yeah, well, maybe you don't. I do. Let's say there are a thousand girls in New York City like you trying to hit the jackpot. Does that sound about right? How many of you—"

"I don't know what you're talking about."

"I'm talking numbers, Risa. How many people are serious? How many are in a band? How many can even carry a goddamn tune? Any idea?"

"Like I say, I was in a band and—"

"It's a much smaller gene pool when you really dig down," I say. "But then, lo and behold, someone just walks in the door and plucks you—you, Risa Barsky—out of the blue. What were you thinking? That's what I wanna know. That you're Cinderella? That you won the lottery?"

"It was nothing like that," she says. "We were playing this club and an agent saw me one night. He was an older gentleman. Very polite. Very nicely dressed. His name was Zapruder and—"

"Yes," I say, "yes, I know all about Felix Zapruder. Did you know Zapruder was a close pal of Pinky's? Did he tell you that?"

"I don't—I don't understand."

"You understand a ton more than you're telling me, Risa. And I can't do my job if you're lying."

"I'm not lying!" Her voice is louder this time. "Felix told me he'd been to a bunch of clubs. I wasn't the first girl he'd considered."

"No, of course not."

"You're damn right, of course not!"

"And I'll bet he said you were just what they were looking for out in LA, didn't he?"

"As a matter of fact, he did."

"That must have been flattering."

She ignores that last little jab. "He had a line on a new band that was just getting together. He asked me if I'd ever been in a klezmer group. Was I familiar with that sort of thing? Could I sing in Yiddish?"

"And you said?"

"I said no, but I was a quick study. That's when he told me I was wasting my talent in New York. Said I could do better, so much better."

"And you believed him?"

"Not at first. But when he took out his wallet and started laying down hundred-dollar bills on my place mat, well, let's just say the conversation changed. It was more dough than I'd ever seen in my life. So you tell me, what's a working girl supposed to do?"

I don't say a word.

"I wasn't being naive, Mr. Parisman. I thought about it. I told him I needed some assurances. A contract, maybe."

"What did he say to that?"

"He said, we can do better than that. How about an apartment? How about we pay the first three months rent? I liked the sound of that."

"You liked the sound of your parents being communists on the Upper West Side, too. That doesn't mean it's true."

"What're you trying to say?"

"I'm not your therapist, Risa. A therapist might tell you how delusional you are. In my world you're just a liar."

She pounds her fist on the table. "I'm trying to be straight with you."

"No," I go. "You've been lying through your teeth all along. Just like everyone else. Pinky lied. Rupiper lied at first. You, too." I throw up my hands. "I can't help you if this is how it's gonna be."

We stare at each other for a long time. "Speak to me, please," she finally whispers. "This isn't easy for me. Please, I said I'd try to help you. I will. Just—just speak to me, okay? Go on."

I heave a sigh. "All right. Let's talk about something else, then. The gun, for instance."

"What about it?"

"You said the gun popped out of the glove compartment.

You hit a bump, remember? And the gun popped out."

"Yes. That's what I said. What's your problem with that?"

"Two problems, Risa. First, I don't believe you. Glove compartments don't usually fly open just because you hit a bump. Also, it makes no sense that you found a gun there."

"Why?"

"Because the car belonged to Pincus Bleistiff, and yeah, Pincus Bleistiff owned a gun, but he kept it tucked away in a kitchen drawer. I checked with the police. Did you know about the gun in the kitchen?"

She looks me over and shakes her head like I'm insane. "So that means what? He was killed with a knife?"

"No." I smile. "It means a gun appeared from somewhere. Maybe the kitchen drawer. Or maybe Ray Ballo had one and brought it along with him that night, but I somehow doubt it."

"He could have," she says, without much conviction. "He could have. I didn't see the glove compartment open. I was driving. It was dark. My eyes were on the road. Maybe he opened it and said, 'Hey look at this.'"

I cradle my chin in my hand. "The only trouble with that is there's no record of Ray Ballo owning a gun, either. And you said he was a sweet, gentle guy, right?"

She looks at me, then looks away. "So what are you suggesting?"

"I'm suggesting that what you said to me about how Pinky was murdered isn't true. Somebody killed him with a gun, I'll grant you that, and it might have been Ray, but the gun he used probably didn't come from the car." I turn my hands over and unfold them. A little imploring goes a long way, I figure. "So that's a question I'm hoping you can answer."

"Okay," she says, hanging her head. "Fine."

Chapter 21

IT'S A LITTLE LATE, but I often think I missed my calling in life. I should have been a teacher. Either that or a comedian, maybe. I know how to stand up straight and talk to people. I can grab their attention, make them forget their troubles and laugh. But when it comes right down to it, I'm not much good as a detective. Detectives—the best ones like Malloy—they're always holed up inside their heads. What they do is they think. I'm not saying I don't think. Sure, I do. Only with me, I think with my heart. There's never a road map to look at, no dictionary, nothing tried and true: I just wing it. That's the difference. You can think with your heart and go on to be a great poet or a fabulous teacher or even a stand-up comic. Not a detective, though. With me, it's personal, impulsive. Two and two don't always equal four, not the way I see it. I count my failures. What might have been. And for the most part, I've come to terms with them. Let's just say I'm no Stan Musial. I can't hit the ball out of the park anymore. Not like the early days. Now every night when I go home, I walk into my office and I stare at that picture of Enrique Avila. He's still standing in the dusty alley, grinning at me from forty years ago. I look at that toothy kid and what goes through my mind—through my heart—is that I've failed. I'll never find him.

Risa Barsky is looking at me intently now. She has taken meticulous care to dry her eyes and now she wants to help me get to the bottom of things. That's what she says, anyway. I'm here to help. So we go back to the business of the torn photo on the carpet next to her bed. Slowly the words form on her lips, and it starts to make sense. They were her parents. That much is true, and she knows more about them than the little song and dance she went through before.

"Helen Hartman," I say. "You recognize that name?"

She nods. "That was my grandmother," she says. "She was released from Theresienstadt in 1945, and a few months after that, that's when my mother was born."

"But Theresienstadt was a camp for children," I say.

"Oh, she was a child," Risa acknowledges. "She was thirteen, maybe fourteen when they let her go."

"And the baby?"

"A parting gift from one of the SS officers there. What I heard—it's just a story, maybe it's all a lie—but I heard he took pity on her when he learned that she was...you know. That's how she got out and survived."

"And she ended up in a displaced-persons facility in Bonn?"

"Along with my mother, Magda, yes."

"And you never met any of these people?"

She stands up, takes two steps toward the counter. "I'm going to make some toast now, Mr. Parisman. Would you like some? I like toast. It's the only thing that settles my stomach."

"No," I say, "you go ahead. But I want to hear more."

"Of course," she says. "Everyone does. It's a marvelous story." She drops a couple of pieces of sourdough in the toaster and pulls a stick of butter on a blue ceramic plate out of the fridge. "All of them are dead now. They came to New York in fifty-one. I think the Jewish Agency helped sponsor them, but that may or may not be true. I don't know that part. Anyway, they got here."

"And Magda, your mother? What became of her?"

Risa pauses for a moment, and when she speaks again, it's as if she's choosing each word that comes out of her mouth very carefully. "My mother had a normal childhood in Brooklyn," she says. "I mean, I suppose she did. More or less. As normal as you can have with a damaged parent like that."

"How do you know about this, Risa? Who told you?"

"No one ever accused me of being very logical," she says, dancing past that question. "And I could be wrong."

"But you don't think so, do you?"

"I've thought about it for years. Half my life. And when you do that—if you work at it and if you're lucky—there are these moments when you piece it all together. It's information you just pull out of thin air. That's what it seems like. Somebody says something casually to you in a bar, or you hear an old record, or you read an article in a magazine. By themselves, they're nothing, meaningless bits, but even so, you start piecing them compulsively together. That's when I get a picture of things. That's when you feel in your heart what it must have been like." She is deadly serious now. "I hope you don't think I'm delusional, Mr. Parisman. Do you understand what I'm saying?"

My mind is turning back to the cold case of Enrique Avila. To forty years of clues I'm sure I overlooked. "Yes." I nod quietly. "Yes, I do."

"Good," she says with satisfaction. "Because the last thing in the world I'd ever want is for you to think I'm crazy. I'm not, by the way."

"I don't believe that," I say. "But I'd like to know more."

The toast pops up and Risa pulls it out and spreads the butter. Takes a pinch of kosher salt out of a dish and sprinkles it evenly on both sides. "Okay," she says. "So I'll tell you what I know about Helen Hartman. We never met, but I do have a few facts." She makes quotation marks with her fingers around that last word. "My grandmother was a frugal person. A private person. She didn't talk about the war. She didn't like to watch television or listen to the radio. I doubt that she read very much. She didn't go out of her way to make friends. She was one of those people who just worked hard and kept her emotions buttoned up."

"Did your mother tell you this?"

"Maybe. I dunno. I was an infant when she died."

"But these are facts, you say?"

"Yes."

"And you picked them up early on, out of the ether?"

"No, not exactly. When I was nine or ten, one of my mom's old high school friends contacted me. She told me things. Her name was Dotty."

"Where was this?"

"That's when I was living with a foster family in Morningside Heights. It's a Dominican neighborhood. You know where the George Washington Bridge is? Everybody speaks Spanish. I met her on a playground there."

"Did this Dotty have a last name?"

"Probably. But she never told me. I never thought to ask."

"How did she find you? How did she even know who you were?"

Risa shrugs. "I can't help you with any of that. I'm sorry. Life doesn't always make sense, does it? Not my life, at least."

"Okay," I say. "So this total stranger shows up on the playground. What'd she have to say?"

"Now you're starting to sound like the police," she says guardedly. "Do you believe me or not? You have to believe me if you want me to continue."

"All right," I tell her. "Let's go on. I believe you."

In broken half-remembered anecdotes from decades ago, she opens up again, and now I see what she means about not being logical. "Whenever Dotty dropped by their apartment," she offers, "my grandmother would make excuses. She'd say she had a headache and lock herself in the bedroom. That's why I think things were only more or less normal."

She tells me how her mother grew from a shy child in hand-me-down clothes into a wild, unruly teenager. She tells me that Magda and Dotty started cutting classes and going to concerts and parties in the Village, that they would stay out until all hours. That they got into trouble sometimes with drugs and boys and alcohol.

"That was my experience, too," I say. "Your mom was no

different. Back then, if it didn't kill you," I say, "it made you stronger."

Risa shakes her head. "All that foolishness was killing her. That's what Dotty said. And I think just watching what my mom was doing probably killed my grandma, too. I can't be sure, of course, but—"

"No, you can't." I tilt my head to one side. "You don't know any of this for sure, do you? I mean, a stranger comes along and tells you stories about your mother, who you last saw when you were in diapers? Where am I supposed to go with that?"

"Nowhere, I suppose."

"So I'm guessing it's a lucky thing that Richard Barsky came along and married her in the nick of time, huh?"

"Maybe," she says. "Like I say, I never knew him. He was much older than she was. Had a real drinking problem, according to Dotty. He's the one who put me in foster care."

No matter how much we talk, and how much she reveals, it doesn't help; Risa can't seem to shake her nerves. But she keeps busy. She washes the dishes by hand, then shoves them all into the dishwasher for a second washing later. She lines up every knife and fork and spoon in the drawer just so. With her bare hand, she wipes off the crumbs from the counter that she made with her toast. Then she grabs a wet sponge and goes over the same spot again. And every ten minutes or so she sidles up to the window and peers through the Venetian blinds at the uniformed officer parked across the street. "They're never going to leave me alone," she says, tugging at her hair. "I just want them to leave me alone. Is that too much to ask?"

"It's their job," I tell her. "They probably don't like it, either. But you don't have to feel trapped here, Risa. Say, how about this. Why don't we go for a drive?"

Which is how we find ourselves in my Honda, tooling

cautiously along toward the freeway on-ramp. It's a sunny day in December, the kind Los Angeles is justly famous for. She rolls down the window, closes her eyes, and lets her hand drift carelessly in the breeze.

The cop from Van Nuys has not been caught napping. He wheels right around and follows us for a few miles, I see him in my rearview mirror, but as soon as we near the Golden State Freeway he suddenly drops out of the chase. That's when I'm tempted to open my big mouth and tell Risa to relax, that he's given up and gone home and she's free at last, but I can guess what's really going on. The Van Nuys police have surely alerted Malloy's office by now. Either he's put a plainclothes detail out to track us or, in light of our little chat yesterday at Du-par's, he's decided to trust me for now with his prime suspect.

Traffic is light. I have no idea at all where I'm going, but it doesn't take a genius to see that Risa is in a better frame of mind. On a whim, I take the Pasadena Freeway, which I've always had a secret fondness for, maybe because it's the oldest, or maybe because the lanes are more narrow and no one dreamed when they built it that cars would go ever so fast and you'd need to pay close attention to how it banks and curves. I point out the snow glinting off the top of Mount Baldy in the distance, which draws a faint smile from her. If I had enough gas in the tank, I think she'd be happy to just sit there in that seat forever. Instead we get off at Orange Grove and head up the slope past large genteel mansions with carefully coiffed lawns. As we approach Colorado Boulevard there is already heavy metal scaffolding in place for the Rose Parade.

"Where are you taking me?" she asks. There's no longer any fear in her voice; now it's just an innocent question.

"I won't know 'til we get there," I say. "To a place we can talk."

"What's that supposed to mean?"

"A place where you'll agree to tell me everything," I say.

I veer off a few blocks beyond the Gamble House, and we pass along through a venerable neighborhood with rows of mature oak trees on either side. Finally I pull the car onto the shoulder and park by the rim of the Rose Bowl itself. I crank down the window. There's a hawk circling overhead in the clear thin December sky. At that altitude he can't be hunting for rats or gophers; more like he's riding the updrafts to see where they take him next. Meanwhile down below, we're in a pretty posh part of town. No rats or gophers here. Just graceful old white palaces with Spanish tiles and thick walls and enormous arched bay windows that catch the sunshine. I don't know who can afford to live in these places, but whoever they are, I'm sure they sleep well at night.

"Here?" she asks.

I nod. We talk for a good hour. I don't try to consciously direct things. Even though I know that tomorrow morning Malloy's people are going to show up on her doorstep with a pair of handcuffs, I act like I have all the time in the world. The conversation ping-pongs every which way.

She admits that she gave some cash to Ray Ballo, not because she was still in love with him, she wasn't, but just to help him out. He was always finding himself in one jam or another, she says, and it was so unfair. Maybe he wasn't that bright. Maybe he was even kind of a putz when it came right down to it, but he was such a dear, sweet guy, she says. I gently remind her then that "was" is the correct tense when it comes to Ray, and she purses her lips and nods. Yes, she says. Ray's gone.

And at last, we come to Pinky.

I reach over and grip her hand briefly in mine. I'm not sure why, maybe to give her a tiny little jolt of confidence. "I know this is hard, Risa. But I need you to be absolutely straight with me. What went on between the two of you?"

"I'm not sure what you mean, Mr. Parisman. Are you some

kind of voyeur? You want to know about our love life? I told you
before."

"You told me a whole bunch of things. But I want to know
about Pinky. I've been turning it over in my mind for weeks
now. Kind of like you. I'm piecing it all together. All these dis-
parate pieces. He wasn't a total stranger, now was he?"

She looks at me. A vague smile of recognition passes across
her face. "No," she says. "No, actually, he was my second cousin.
He told me that night when I came to stay with him." To which
she adds—"at least he thought he was my cousin."

"Is that what you thought, too?"

"At first," she whispers. "I mean, it made sense. But then,
over time, I came to realize he was probably—possibly—more
than that."

"You want to explain? I need more than 'probably' or
'possibly.'"

She shakes her head, then shivers. "Whenever I was with
him it felt like—like I was always under this microscope. How
can I explain? And it wasn't even only me. That's the thing. It
was our whole family. He knew so much about me. It was amazing. He told me things about my mother, for instance. Things
that Dotty also told me. How she wore her hair, the kind of
music she liked. Even the food."

"The food?"

"She couldn't eat chili, any spicy food, really. That's what
Dotty said. It always gave her heartburn."

"Pinky knew that?"

"He seemed to. He said he did."

"What about your dad? What did he say about him?"

She scratches her head. "You know something? Not much.
Nothing, really. It's funny. I don't believe his name ever came
up."

An absolutely wild idea flies into my head then. I grab onto
the steering wheel with both hands and flex. My heart starts to
pound. So this is how you get exercise at your age, Parisman.

Subtle. Silent. Nobody gets hurt. Except you, maybe. And if you open your mouth now, the person right beside you.

"Tell me, Risa," I say as calmly as I can, "maybe I'm dead wrong here, maybe I'm going way out on a limb, but I'm gonna say it anyway, okay? Did you ever consider the possibility, did you ever think that Pinky might…that Pinky could…could be…your father?"

"My God!" she screams. Her face turns white and she twists away from my constant gaze. Her body lurches. She drops her head down between her knees like somebody hauled off and punched her in the gut, like he took her breath away, like she might puke. "My God!" Then all at once she jerks herself upright and she's rocking silently, shaking reluctantly from side to side. Cradling her stomach in her arms.

Back in high school I had an epileptic friend named Wally. I saw him lose it on a couple of occasions, and this is the closest I've come to that since then. Whatever it is, she stops talking. Shuts her eyes. Holds everything in check. Eventually, her voice—small, weak, and tentative—bubbles up to the surface. "I never had any proof," she says. "And he—he'd never admit it. Not in a million years. But that's the truth. That's what I came to believe. I mean, that's what I—what I felt."

I reach into my jacket pocket then and offer her my old beige handkerchief, the one with my initials on it that Loretta bought for me once in an attempt to make me look more professional. Risa accepts it, nods, dabs her eyes, presses it lightly to her nostrils. Neither one of us speaks.

I start the engine, let it idle for a minute, then turn it off.

"Are you taking me home?" she wants to know. Her voice sounds a bit more nervous now; maybe she's remembering the police presence at her apartment. Maybe this road trip into old Pasadena has lifted her spirits and she doesn't ever want it to end.

"Soon," I say, "but first we have to clear up this little quirky thing about Pinky."

"Quirky thing? What the fuck are you talking about? Why don't you just call it what it was?" she says angrily. "Why are we dancing around? Pincus Bleistiff was my father. You know it. I know it. My. Father. I slept with my father. It was an awful, sickening thing we did. There's no other explanation."

"And when you—when you knew—when you found out—"

"When I found out, the minute I found out, I left him."

"Okay, Risa, you left him. But the question I have—and it's the same one the police will have—is this: Did you leave him before or after you killed him?"

"I didn't kill him! I didn't kill him, I swear!"

"Right. But the cops are going to have a whole different take on this, don't you see? The DA's going to stand up in court and say that Pinky was a predator, that he knew your mother from years ago. That Pinky went back to New York to find Helen Hartman, but he found Magda instead and they had an affair right under Richard Barsky's nose. They're going to make Pinky into the creep he really was, but that won't let you off the hook. They're going to say he knew who you were and he paid for you to come out here. Even paid for your apartment and brought in a band to give you something to do. They'll say he was lonely after his wife died and maybe his memory was giving way and he conveniently forgot that you two were related somehow. And you know what else they'll say, Risa? They'll suggest what you just admitted. That you knew, too."

"Yes," she breathes. "I did."

"Yes. You knew. And that's the problem. It freaked you out. It made you want to jump out of your skin. Because you're a decent girl at heart. But you were disgusted. So maybe you didn't pull the trigger. Maybe you had Ray kill him after all. Maybe you told Ray what was going on and he got furious and—"

She shakes her head emphatically. "No, no, no! Ray didn't do it. I lied about that. I was confused. I thought I needed an excuse. But Ray—he would never do something like that. I'm sorry. I'm so sorry for everything!" Her eyes are bulging and she's screaming at me.

"Is that the truth?"

"The truth? About Ray? Yes. God, I wish he had, but poor Ray—he didn't have the balls to kill him."

"Okay," I tell her. "Let's just say I believe you. For once, anyway. You didn't kill him. And neither did Ray. So where do we go from here?"

She combs her fingers through her hair and lets her gaze turn toward the sky for a moment. The circling hawk has long since vanished, but a few wispy white clouds are forming in the hills over Glendale and La Cañada.

"You should talk to Javier," she whispers.

"Why?"

"Javier was there that night, that's why. He was in the kitchen. He heard everything."

Chapter 22

WE PULL UP in front of Risa's apartment later that afternoon, and I dash around to the passenger's side to open the door for her. There's a different officer now stationed in a black-and-white across the street. He's younger and taller and more athletic-looking than the morning cop, and I don't know why, but I get the distinct feeling he hasn't worn the uniform more than a week. Maybe it's because he seems so surprised to see us. Still, he's savvy enough to reach over to his radio and start making coded noises to his superiors. Good lad, I think. You'll go far in this business. I give him a neighborly wave and shepherd Risa up the stone walkway.

"You stay here inside, all right?" I tell her once we cross the threshold. I prowl around, poke my head cautiously into every closet and dark corner, then come back to where she's standing in the living room. "And after I leave, I want you to lock yourself in and prop a piece of furniture up against the door. Not just a folding chair, either. Something heavy, like that couch over there, or better yet, your piano. You understand?"

"No, I don't," she says. "What the hell's that going to do? That won't stop those fucking cops, will it?"

"I'm not worried about cops," I explain. "It's Javier you need to be concerned about."

"Javier?" She almost laughs. "Javier wouldn't hurt me. Javier's a gentleman."

"Oh yeah? Let me tell you something. Javier does what he's told. He's the guy who put your apartment through a blender."

"I don't believe you," she says. Then, in the same breath, "How do you know?"

"Simple deduction," I say. "You connect the dots. First off, it wasn't a break-in, what happened to you."

"Oh no?"

"No. Whoever broke in here, if that's the word you really wanna use, he had a key. Think about it. He just waltzed right in. And who had a key, tell me?"

She just stares.

"You. Lola. The manager. And Pinky. I'd say we can discount the first three. That leaves Pinky. Pinky's too old and decrepit to rip up a joint by himself. But he's good at hiring people. And he and Javier go way back."

"But why?" she asks. "Why would he do that?"

There's so much homespun sincerity welling up in her wide brown eyes, I don't know what to think. Well, actually, that's not true. What flashes through my mind is Judy Garland and Toto and *The Wizard of Oz*. That's what all this is, I think—a fantasy. Everyone's deluded. Everyone's lost in the Emerald City, and yeah, there's no place like home, but how the hell do you get there? "I dunno," I say. "Maybe he meant to scare you. Or maybe Pinky told him to scare you."

"Pinky? I—I still don't understand," she says. "What was the point?"

"Back up," I tell her. "Try to see it from his point of view. Let's say he's in love with you. Pinky brings you all the way out here from New York. He sets you up with a first-class band, even pays for your apartment. He's put out a lot of cash. He's a generous soul, sure, you told me that, but kindness only goes so far. In some ways, you're an investment."

"Investment?"

"Maybe he would never be so crass. But that's how his mind works. Everything's a transaction."

"So what if I am?" she says. She's on the defensive now. "Aren't I worth it?"

"Sure," I say, "you're worth every penny. But he was betting on you, Risa, and he was an old man and he was losing. He had to turn things around in a hurry. That's when he got his bright idea."

"And what could that have been?"

"Pinky's old-school. He liked to be in charge. He liked women who needed him, or at least relied on his judgment."

"And I wasn't like that? Is that what you're saying?"

"You didn't fit the bill, no. But he hoped you could be persuaded. So I'm guessing here, but maybe he got this bright idea. He put this question to himself: What if Risa Barsky comes home one night and sees that a stranger has broken in and turned her whole place upside down. Just ripped it apart. Who's the first person she's going to call for help?"

She doesn't answer me. But she's standing there, trembling, staring through me. The innocence is gone.

"And who came over right away to take you to Pinky's? Who rescued you?"

"Javier," she mumbles. "You know, it's funny. I wondered how he got here so fast."

"Pinky wanted you to love him, Risa. You knew that. You told me that yourself. And the first day I met him I thought he might be smitten with you. He didn't say it out loud, but he wasn't much good at keeping it secret, either. He loved you. He wanted you to return the favor. Desperate, in fact. And if that wasn't an option, well, at least he wanted you to need him."

She looks at me suddenly with admiration. Or I can't be sure, maybe it's more akin to shock.

"Really? You think so?"

"If you're telling me the truth now, Risa, then yeah. When you drove away with Ray that night, Pinky was still very much alive, wasn't he?"

"I don't know," she says. "Javier came out from the kitchen door. He heard us shouting. There was a lot of shouting, and after a while he came out. He had a gun, at least I think he did. There wasn't much light on that side of the house. Whatever he had in his hand he waved it at us, told us both to leave. Get out!

Get out! That's what he said. He screamed at us."

"So you never witnessed the murder, then."

"Ray and I were scared. He had a gun. We thought he had a gun. He was waving this thing in the air, and I was so scared I almost peed my pants. We jumped in the car. I had to fumble around for the key in the dark."

"Where were you when the shots were fired? Do you remember? Did you hear them?"

"I did. And they were just as loud as I told you before. But I didn't see anything, I swear. It was dark. I floored it and was heading for the main gate. That's all I cared about. I put my foot down on the gas and—"

"All right," I say. "You don't have to say another word. Just do what I tell you."

She nods. I press my cheek to her forehead, give her a little parting hug. Her hair smells like lavender. "Everything's going to be fine," I whisper. Then I'm out the door. I glance at my watch on my way down the hall. Unless I hurry, by this time tomorrow they'll be fitting Risa out in an orange jumpsuit, that's a fact. And if Javier's not around, it may be too late for her in any event. My pace quickens. I'm taking the stairs two at a time.

As soon as I reach my car, I punch up Omar's number. He sounds vaguely surprised to hear from me. There's some faint female giggling going on in the background and I wonder whether I called at the wrong time, not that that would stop me.

"Are you free?" is the first thing I ask him.

"Hey man, I'm always free," he says. He's speaking reasonably, but it's a lot slower than I'm used to. "This is the land of the free, right?"

"One other question. Have you been drinking?"

"Drinking? No, no. It's three in the afternoon. Lourdes and I just woke up from our little siesta on the couch, that's all. I'm sober as a judge."

"Good. In that case I need you to meet me at Javier Escovedo's house in Eagle Rock. Can you be there in an hour?"

"Javier? Who?"

"Javier. That fellow we visited before. He took care of Pinky's estate."

"You mean the one with the ripped screen door? That guy?"

"Exactly." I pull out my notepad and recite Javier's address. Not only that, I make sure he writes it down.

"Okay, man. I got it. One hour from now. Eagle Rock. I'll be there."

"Thanks, Omar. Oh," I say, "and one more thing."

"Yeah, what's that?"

"The gun."

"Gun? What gun?"

"The gun I gave you. My present to you. The Glock. You still have it?"

"Are we friends?" he says. "Of course I have it."

"Okay. Then bring it along. I don't have time to drive back to Park La Brea and pick up mine. See you in Eagle Rock."

I take the Hollywood Freeway south and angle my way into the proper lane for the cutoff to the Ventura. They call it the 134 now. The signs are everywhere, but I wish to hell they'd go back to real names. The Golden State. The Harbor. There was poetry then. Now all these numbers are just making people duller and more stupid than they already are, in my not-so-humble opinion. Before I went into the Marines, I used to drive out to Claremont every week to spend quality time with a girl named Ginger O'Neill who went to Scripps. Ginger had long red hair. She was raised Catholic, but she wasn't happy with that upbringing. She never said she loved me, but she hoped that by dutifully fulfilling my sexual needs that my Judaism would somehow rub off on her. Which, however you look at it, is a bargain. I had to go out on Foothill Boulevard. It wound through rolling orange and lemon groves. It also passed by vast tracts of rubble that would soon become tract homes that were indistinguishable from one another. The trip to Ginger's bed took forever. Then they put in the Foothill Freeway, which was faster, but it didn't feel like it, and anyway you missed all the exotic scenery. Then they renamed the Foothill Freeway the 210. Now it takes forever and there's still no scenery.

I call Carmen to let her know I may be late again for dinner. Maybe she can throw something together for Loretta? *Por favor?* In my mangled Spanish I tell her again how sorry I am. She's used to this kind of behavior when I'm on a case, but still I don't like to worry her. Or Loretta, for that matter. Though Loretta's not actually a problem anymore. In fact, sometimes in the morning when I shut the door to our apartment and take the twelve tired steps down the gray carpeted hall to the elevator, I'm really not sure Loretta knows I've gone. Or that I was ever alive. Carmen has learned how to satisfy her; Carmen is almost her whole world now. She doesn't say she misses me when I return, she knows who I am, I think, but she doesn't offer anything, not unless I ask her point-blank.

I arrive at Javier's long before Omar, which isn't so surprising. I pull over a few doors south of his house and park on the other side of the street, as though I'm visiting a neighbor of his. But now I have an unobstructed view from the driver's side. The first thing I notice is that he's fixed the slash in the screen door. In fact, it seems like he's replaced the old screen and put in a much more substantial metal door. Also he's home, I'm pretty certain. There's a speckled light coming from the kitchen window on the left. His dusty old white Toyota pickup has been parked at a slight angle in the driveway, and the front lawn looks like it's newly mowed. You can even see some of the grass clippings he left behind on the pavement.

Ten minutes later Omar arrives in his black Camaro. He

climbs out cautiously, shoves his gun into the small of his back, and covers it with his orange T-shirt. We look at each other and head slowly toward Javier's residence.

"Keep an eye on him," I whisper to Omar. "That's what I need you to do. I don't think he's dangerous, but I want to talk to him without worrying about any monkey business."

Omar has obviously been mulling over why we're here and the existential significance of the gun in his pants. I haven't discussed what Risa told me, but he's tense and ready. "That's why you had me bring the gun?" he asks, with a smirk. "Because you don't think he's dangerous?"

"I want to have a civilized chat. I want you," I say as I point to his chest, "to think he's dangerous."

"You saying he killed Pinky?"

"I know he killed Pinky. Well, wait a minute, I take that back. If Risa's telling the truth—if she's telling the truth, then Javier was the one holding the gun. And he was probably the last one to see Pinky alive that night. Now, does that make him a killer?"

"If she's telling the truth?" Omar frowns. "Shit, man, hasn't she told you twenty different stories already?"

"She has, she has. I agree. But this time I'm inclined to believe her."

"That's wonderful," Omar says. His lips curl into a perfect sneer. "That's marvelous. You believe her."

"I do. And if I'm right, it means she's only a witness to a murder. Which is not quite the same as someone who pulled the trigger, is it?"

"And Ray Ballo?"

I shrug. "Ray Ballo. I'm guessing Javier killed Ray, too. But that's just a wild guess."

"So tell me," Omar says, "is there any real difference between your belief and this wild guess of yours? You believe he killed Pinky, with no evidence. And you're guessing he killed Ray, again with no evidence. But we're just talking about two murders here. Two bodies."

"What do you mean?"

"I want you to be sure, that's what I mean. I mean, have you lost your fucking mind? I don't like charging into somebody's house with a loaded gun." He pulls the Glock out from under his shirt. "This is no joke."

"You're funny, Omar."

"Hilarious, man."

We stand silently then on either side of the screen door, and Omar holds his pistol at the ready flat against his thigh just in case Javier proves to be a psychopath. I knock three times.

Javier opens it and nods serenely at me. "Please," he says, "please, *señores*, come in."

Chapter 23

HE LEADS US into his living room, then turns and extends his hand for me to shake. His hand isn't nearly as rough as it was the first time. For some reason, I immediately credit this to the fact that he's come into more money than he's ever had before; maybe now in retirement he's started using lotion. But that's not the central thing. It's the way he looks. His black shoes gleam like he's just walked off a military parade ground, and he's wearing a solid blue tie over a tan dress shirt, which is passing strange, I think, since it's four in the afternoon and the middle of the week and he's home here alone. Who dresses like that in his own house? A sport coat is hung neatly over a nearby kitchen chair and he has undone the top button of his shirt and loosened the tie at the neck, something I also like to do as soon as I'm out of the limelight. This gives him the demeanor of an academic, or maybe an old-time newspaper reporter. Thoughtful. A little harried, but not unattractive.

"You're lucky," he says, suddenly mindful of how we're looking at him. "I just got home a few minutes ago. I was down at St. Dominic's. They're organizing a new group to help Latinos. Father Daniel said I'm a natural-born leader."

"What do they want you to do? You're starting a new job?"

His brow crinkles in consternation. "Oh, I wouldn't call it a real job, no."

"So what's that mean?"

"Just that there's no money to pay me. Not yet, at least." He shrugs his shoulders. "The church, after all."

He pauses. His dealings with the church seem like a private matter somehow. I'm thinking he wants to keep it that way, walled off, apart.

"I'm not sure," he says then. He licks his lips slightly. "I'm not sure where it will go, *señores*. Right now, they're having me talk to people in small groups, registering voters. That's a big problem. We have a lot of power, I tell them. It doesn't matter where you came from. If you're a citizen, you have the power. But only if you vote."

The interior of the house hasn't changed since we last were here. Except for one thing. On the same wall where the wide-screen television still sits, above it and to the right, in a corner niche all its own, there's a polished wooden replica of Jesus staring down at us in his final moments of agony. He's about ten inches tall. He's got sad green eyes and golden tresses. I stop to take it all in. The folk artist, whose name—Alarcon—is barely visible on the side of the cross, has gone to great lengths. You can see the anguish in the face, and while it's all in miniature, nothing has been overlooked—there are even a couple of red dots on his tiny outstretched palms.

"That didn't come from a flea market," I say with admiration. "You must have paid a pretty penny."

Javier shrugs. "I have an old friend in Guadalajara. He owns a gallery. I saw it in his catalog and decided I wasn't getting any younger. I called him up. Told him I had to have it."

"Sometimes you need to be impulsive in life," I say. "Otherwise, what's the point, right?"

"Exactly." He motions us to sit around his dining room table, which looks out onto his backyard. There's a formidable avocado tree at the center, and all along the white plaster wall behind are birds of paradise, succulents, and other plants I couldn't name if my life depended on it.

"I didn't know you were such a gardener, Javier."

"I did a lot of work outside for Señor Bleistiff." He wags his head. "It was easier, of course, when I was a younger man. I never got sick, you know, never took a day off." He waves vaguely at all the abundance. "But God has a way of wearing you down."

"Still, you have a fine garden out there. You should be proud. That took some doing."

"A couple of weeks ago I hired a fellow I met at the church. He's a tremendous worker, Raul. So strong. Never complains. Reminds me of myself thirty years ago."

Omar hasn't said a word yet. The minute Javier welcomed us at the door he shoved the gun back behind him before Javier could get a look at it, which was exactly the right thing to do, but now I think Omar has to be confused by all this parlor talk. I know how he feels: It's hard to just relax and chat, especially when a minute before you were standing outside in the shadows with your hand on the trigger.

Javier asks us if we'd like some refreshment. Coffee? Beer? I can see what's in the refrigerator? Omar shakes his head. "No, gracias."

"We don't want to take up too much of your time, Javier," I say. "But you're a smart man. You know how these things go. We're still on the job. And I still have a few unanswered questions."

"Questions, yes," he says, "I'm happy to help you, if I can." He looks down at his newly smooth hands and rubs them gently together and smiles. There's a nobility about him, I think, a way he carries himself that reminds me of my father. He's only a little bit younger than I am, but he has spent most of his life shoveling dirt in the sun, moving the physical universe from one place to another, and even though his body may be weathered, he still doesn't show it, not on the outside, at least. "I'm not sure you've come to the right person," he says. "And I don't understand. Señor Bleistiff is dead. He was the one who was paying you, yes?"

"Yes, but the good news is now I have a new client. Risa Barsky."

He nods. "Oh, I see. So Señorita Barsky wants you to find the murderer?"

"She's been very generous. It's hard to say no to what she's paying me."

We look at each other for a moment. I don't know what's going through his head.

I lay my hands down flat on the table. "Here's the basic problem," I begin. "The police have this idea that maybe she killed Pinky. I say they're wrong. It's a funny idea, don't you think?"

"Why do they think that?"

"Well," I say, "they've got a few things going, I'll admit. She was there at the scene the night Pinky died, right? You saw her there. That's what you told the cops."

"She was living there. She was sleeping with him, yes."

"And she drove away in a hurry. Stashed that fancy car of hers at LAX and disappeared for days. That's suspicious right there."

He makes a little face. "That's why they think she killed him? Because she ran off?"

"That, plus the fact that she inherited a big chunk of his money."

"I also received some money. Does that make me a criminal?"

"You worked for him for years, Javier. Also, there's a big difference between a hundred grand and a million or two, right? So I guess the way the cops look at it is, if you knew you'd get a million bucks, well, you might be tempted to do something rash."

"These may be facts," he says, "but surely they aren't good enough reasons to send her to prison." He doesn't like what he's hearing. His face is getting flushed and his voice is growing louder. "She didn't ask for his money. She had no control over what he put in his will."

"Damn straight," I say. "That's exactly what I told the cops. But you know how they are. They're a lazy bunch. Half the time they don't use their heads; they just look at what's in front of them."

"*De veras?*" he whispers.

I nod. I start talking with my hands then, pointing first to him, then at me, waving them around. Before long it turns into a rant. "And the thing is, nine times out of ten, they're right. Most crimes have simple explanations. I remember this case I had once in Pasadena. A wife kills her husband. Why? Because he's got a dead-end job selling shoes, he hates himself because he doesn't have the balls to quit, and because he hates himself he comes home drunk every Saturday night, beats her up for twenty years until finally, one day she looks in the mirror and says, enough." I wag my finger at him. "Or another one: A teenage kid in Arcadia—nice, but not so bright, you know what I mean?— he gets hooked on smack. Starts going into his mother's purse, lifting bills to feed his habit. That's okay at first. But pretty soon he needs more. He starts prowling around the neighborhood after dark, breaking into houses. One night he finds a gun in one of them. Then a few weeks later, he starts robbing liquor stores. Ends up shooting a clerk. It's not complicated, Javier. You just follow the breadcrumbs."

"I don't believe Señorita Barsky is the murderer," he announces in a quiet, measured tone. "They argued, of course. She screamed at him many times. But what does that mean? People in love do that. They get angry. That does not make her a murderer."

"No, it doesn't, you're right. But you saw her there on the night Pinky died. I need you to tell me what they said to each other."

He sighs, combs back his hair with his palm. "They weren't getting along. They wanted different things. He was talking to her, pleading with her. He wanted to be married again. He was no good alone. That's what he told her. It was no good. He needed a new wife."

"And that wasn't her vision of things, right?"

"No," he says, "not at all." He stands up from the table then and pushes his chair away with a jerk. "You will excuse me for a moment, gentlemen." He takes three steps toward the back door, which leads to a small tiled deck and down to the garden beyond. "Please, I need some air. I—I will be right back." He turns the knob and goes out, walks haltingly, like a man in a trance, across the lawn toward the sprawling avocado tree. He reaches out and touches the bark. Caresses it almost. His left hand slides upward above his head, and he presses his fingers onto one of the enormous overhanging limbs for support. Then all at once he stumbles and tilts forward as if he might faint. He starts to tremble. The tree is the only thing holding him upright. The tree gives him strength. He drops his head, and his tie dangles like a long blue tongue in front of him.

Omar gets up, too. "I'm going to go out and check on him," he says.

"No," I tell him, "don't. Let's wait. He's not jumping over the wall or anything. Just give him some space."

After a minute or two, whatever was bothering him passes. Javier eases up, relinquishes his grip of the tree. He brushes a speck out of his eye, straightens his shirt, climbs the steps, and returns to the dining room.

"Forgive me," he says to us as he resumes his seat. "I was just remembering that night. The things I heard. What I saw. It—it disturbed me more than I realized."

"Tell us about it, Javier. You do that, you'll feel better."

He leans over the table, takes a deep breath, the kind a doctor would ask of you if you were being examined. His hand makes a thoughtful cradle under his chin. "I am not a perfect man," he begins in a voice barely above a whisper. "I've done things, many things, I am not so proud of. But that will change, I swear."

"This isn't about you," Omar cuts in. "We want to know what Pinky and Risa talked about."

"You are wrong," he says then. "It starts with me. I was—I was his instrument. His hammer. That's what he called me once. I did whatever Señor Bleistiff wanted." He twists his head from side to side. "And what he wanted was wrong." There's a small ceramic pair of salt and pepper shakers in the center of the table. Javier takes one in his hand and shuffles it randomly around like a chess piece. Then he stops and looks up at me. "You remember how I told you I'd just come back home from St. Dominic's—from a political meeting?"

"You did."

"Well, that is true. But only partly. There *was* a meeting. And they did want me to help. To be the face of their efforts, they said. But afterward, I made confession. I stepped into a booth and closed the door and I told the priest—I told him everything I'd done. Everything."

"What are you saying, Javier?"

But he's not listening. "Everything," he repeats again. "And then I went back into the church and I waited for them to find me. I knew they'd come looking for me, and they did. It took them a few minutes, but then Father John spotted me. He put his arm around my shoulder and asked me if I wouldn't mind waiting for them in the conference room. They had some more questions, he said. No, I said, no, I wouldn't mind. But I already had an idea about what they were going to say. That something had come up. That they were not so interested in my leadership abilities. Not anymore. I sat there a long time. There's nothing in that conference room, you know, nothing to look at, just a long oak table and some metal folding chairs. Then Father Daniel came in with another priest. I didn't know his name. They told me they were sorry, very sorry, but that they were trying to think about the big picture. You understand this, Javier, don't you? That they had an obligation to take everything into account? They said they appreciated my talents, my enthusiasm, all of it, but for now, in view of certain facts, they felt it was their duty—their solemn duty, they said—to reconsider."

I try, but fail, to catch his eye. "What exactly did you tell them, Javier?"

He arches his fingertips together. Here is the church, I think, here is the steeple, open the doors and....

"The truth," he says. "I told them about all the years I worked for Señor Bleistiff. How sometimes he asked me to do things that made it very hard to sleep at night. In the beginning, maybe you could dismiss some of what I did. I was happy, you know, just to have a job. I had not lived in El Norte very long. My English was poor. And a young man is not always responsible. Isn't that what they say? I made mistakes as a young man. But the fact is, it never stopped. Even recently I did things. Even now that I'm older."

"Like what?" Omar asks.

He frowns, shakes his head. "He was jealous of Señorita Barsky's old boyfriend. He was worried she might move back in with him. That was unacceptable, he said. He gave me the key to her apartment, told me what evening she wouldn't be at home. Go in and destroy it. Those were his words."

"Is that all he said, Javier? Destroy it?"

"Yes. Why do you ask?"

"I dunno. Sure, he wanted you to trash the place, okay. Scare her good. I get that. But aren't you forgetting the rest of his instructions?"

My question momentarily startles him. "What? I told you. He asked me to destroy—"

"Yes, and while you were there, he also asked you to do something else, didn't he?"

"I don't know what you mean," he whispers.

"Yes, you do. He told you to find a certain photograph in Risa's album, isn't that right? A picture of a man in a polo shirt with a cigarette and a beautiful young woman in a sweater. You remember that, Javier? Is it coming back to you all of a sudden? What did he want you to do? That was part of the deal, wasn't it? Why don't you tell me about that."

"How do you know about the photograph?" he asks. His face has turned dark and suspicious.

"I talked my way into her apartment, that's how. After Risa disappeared from Pinky's and he hired me to track her down.

But I didn't find her in Van Nuys. What I found was the wreck you left behind and half an old snapshot lying on the carpet next to her bed. The rest of the album was intact. That was odd, I thought. Pinky asked you to tear that out, didn't he?"

"Yes," he says quietly, "he told me to break as much as I could, to make a giant mess. But you are correct about the other thing, too. He wanted the photograph, it's true."

"Did Pinky ever tell you who that guy was?"

"No. No, never. I didn't ask him, either. I have learned since, of course. But at the time it was just a job. He gave me her house key, told me what to do. It was not my business."

"His name was Richard Barsky," I say. "He was Risa's father."

"No, *señor*. No, he was not." Javier stares straight at me. "He took care of her until she was three. Until his drinking made him sick. He was a worthless individual, a poor excuse for a human being. He took care of her, perhaps, or he tried to, which is what a father—any father—is supposed to do."

"Who told you he was worthless?"

"Señor Bleistiff."

"But she *believed* he was her father, Javier." I shake my head. "She believed. Don't you think that's important?"

"I don't know," Javier says, shrugging.

"Maybe you're right," I say, "maybe he was worthless. And maybe because of him, because he couldn't stay sober, she ended up in foster care. She never saw him again. But still, he meant something to her. In her mind he was her father. And that photo was the only thing she had to remember him by. Don't you think it's important to remember your parents, Javier?"

"Yes. Of course."

"Me, too. Only Pinky couldn't tolerate that."

Javier takes another breath. If what I've said so far bothers him, he's not showing it. "Señor Bleistiff was a competitive man. He lived his life that way. Always clear about what he wanted. Always direct. He never hesitated. I admired that. The man had many admirable qualities. This is just my opinion."

I stand up, fold my arms in front of me. Most of the time when somebody says something stupid or crazy it's not my habit to get bent out of shape about it. Who cares? Stupid, crazy people are everywhere in this world. What I learned in the Marines. God made a shitload of mistakes; you just have to ignore them. Put your head down and keep moving forward. And I do. I do, except for those few times when I don't. Before long I'm carrying on, my voice is braying, and I can feel my cheeks turning red. "Let's not split hairs, amigo, it's too late in the day for that. Let's get real. You and I know the truth about Pinky. He was fast and loose with his money maybe, but he wasn't admirable, like you say. *Admirable.* What the hell kind of word is that, anyway? How the fuck could he be admirable? You know what he did. He was an animal! Jesus Christ, Javier, he was screwing his own goddamn daughter!"

My words ring out, and after I stop there's a long, awkward, hollow silence.

"It's true, *señor,*" he says. Javier's voice is calm and measured. "I know that now. I have learned. He was abusing the young woman. He knew who she was. He was living a lie. But for a long time, a very long time, it didn't seem that way. Not to me, at least."

"How do you figure?" asks Omar.

Javier makes a small begging gesture with his hands. "How do I know? I was there in the house almost every day. I was a witness. How kind he was. He bought her everything she ever wanted. He even gave her some of his wife's jewelry. Anything at all, just to keep her in his bed at night. He told me many times that he was in love. That she lifted his spirits." Javier studies my face intently, looking for any crack in the wall, any sign of doubt or compassion. "I ask you," he says now, "who doesn't want to believe in the power of love?"

"Is that what you think? That this was all about love?"

"I'm saying I believed him." He indicates the statue of Christ on the wall. "I believed him because all my life I was raised in the ways of Jesus. Jesus knows how sinful we are. How weak. How easily we turn away from the right road. Yes, Pinky asked me to do evil things; he asked me and I always complied and he always rewarded me. But I told myself, you are lucky to be working for this man, Javier. Lucky. Yes, he is not pure. Yes, he is complicated. But where would you be without him?"

"That's quite a bargain you made for yourself," I tell him.

"More like a trap," Omar chimes in.

"I lived with it for thirty years." Javier nods. "I was blind, I admit it. Up until that night, when I heard them fighting in the doorway."

"What did you do that night, Javier?"

He touches his forehead with his fingertips, then glances up at the ceiling as if for guidance. "I was in the kitchen cleaning up, putting away the dishes after his dinner. He always left his dirty dishes out for the housekeeper to do in the morning and I thought for once I would surprise her. I was going to go home, but then I heard shouting and screaming. It was coming from the front of the house. I knew Señorita Barsky had left an hour before and now it was late, after eleven, I suppose. I heard male voices shouting, and I thought perhaps Señor Bleistiff was being attacked. I rushed into his bedroom. He had a loaded pistol. He used to keep it in the kitchen, but when Risa came he moved it for her safety into the wall safe near his closet. I knew the combination. I opened it, ran around to the door by the kitchen, and slipped out."

"Who was doing the shouting?"

"Everyone. Señorita Barsky was standing there with a tall young man I did not recognize."

"And Pinky?"

"He was in the doorway. He was on his knees and his hands were raised like he was pleading for his life. I could see him clearly in the light, and I thought I recognized her voice, but not the other man. I was scared. I waved the gun at them. Maybe I shouted something, I don't know. It was late. Why would he be on his knees like that if he wasn't in trouble? I fired the pistol in the air. That was sufficient. Señorita Barsky and the man ran to their car and drove off."

Omar and I look at each other. My mouth is suddenly as dry as dust. I roll my tongue around in my cheeks. "That's why you're sure she didn't kill him? Because you watched them drive away?"

"Exactly," Javier says.

"But that leaves just the two of you," Omar says. "What happened next?"

"Next?" Javier shrugs. "He watched the car disappear down the driveway. There were tears in his eyes. Then he got to his feet and asked me to please give him back his pistol."

"And?"

"And I started to, but then I wondered why? Why do you need it? I asked. He said because he wanted to kill himself. Without her, there was no more reason to go on. He held out his hand. Give me the gun, he said."

"But you didn't, did you?" I say.

"No, I didn't. He tried to grab it away and we struggled for a minute, but I was much stronger. He ended up on the ground again. He picked himself up, but he was like a broken man. That's when he told me about who he was. Who Risa Barsky really was. Everything. I thought at first it was some kind of mistake, what he was telling me, a misunderstanding. It was too horrible to consider. You don't lie down with your own flesh and blood, I thought. You don't do that, it's wrong. I closed my eyes, and all the words I'd ever heard from the priests in my village came rushing back to me then, and all at once I knew what sin really meant. It was clear. He was sitting there, curled up in the doorway, and now all he wanted to do was to die. I raised the pistol. I pointed it at him. You know the rest."

Chapter 24

I PLACE THE CALL to Lieutenant Malloy and explain what's going on, then the three of us sit there at Javier's dining room table in the sweet fading afternoon light. There's nothing more to say, it seems; Javier looks rather relieved, in fact.

When the local constabulary pulls up a few minutes later in four squad cars, one right after another with their red and blue lights flashing, they don't ask him any questions. They don't even bother to draw their guns, which, for someone accused of a brutal murder, you'd imagine they would. But no. He opens his new screen door, they ask his name, and two seconds later they say he's under arrest. Now please turn around, they say, spread your arms and legs. One pats him down, another one reads him his Miranda warning, then they snap the cuffs on and take him away. It's all very cut-and-dried. No funny business whatsoever, no one gets hurt, which of course is how they like it. But on the lawn Javier suddenly stops shuffling dutifully forward. I'm right behind him staring at his back, but for some reason I glance across the street. A bunch of his neighbors have come pooling out of their houses to gawk at the show. He turns to me. His eyes meet mine. "Would you do me a great favor?" he asks. "Would you let Señorita Barsky know what happened?"

"Sure," I say. "Sure, no problem."

"Gracias." Then he moves on. They tuck him gently into the back seat and he's gone.

Afterward we stand around in the living room and chat with a flippant if somewhat pudgy sergeant named Picolini from the Glendale Police Department. Omar wants to know where Javier's headed, and the sergeant says probably just to a holding cell overnight until the Hollywood boys can bring him downtown for arraignment. I don't know what he means by "boys" exactly, but I figure I'm probably never going to see him again and so I keep my mouth shut. He takes our names and contact information, thanks us for all our help, and says we can go on our merry way, but he's got to hang around here and preserve the evidence, you understand. By which he means he's waiting for the professionals to show up.

I tell Omar he's free, this case is closed, then I climb in my car, pull out my phone, and punch in Malloy's number again. This time it takes him a few rings before he picks up.

"I think maybe you can cancel that arrest warrant for Risa Barsky," I say, "especially after what Javier had to say."

"We have," he says, "at least for now. But there's still a few loose threads. Pincus Bleistiff had a .38 registered in his name, and, yeah, the slugs match, but we still need to find the weapon and test it before we can go much further."

"Javier knows where it is, I'm pretty sure."

"You didn't ask?"

"No, Bill, I thought his confession was plenty."

"Well, unfortunately, it's not. I'm grateful, mind you. Problem is, any fool can confess to something, but unless there's corroborating evidence, it's just a lot of hot air. Hell, every time a movie star stops a bullet, I have six strangers coming out of the woodwork to confess. You know that."

"Yeah, of course, I know. But you're not completely in the dark with this. Javier was there that night on the premises. He had access to a gun. And he's got these deep, fundamental religious beliefs about who you can *shtup* and who you can't. I mean, he's crazy but—"

"Now, wait a second!" he says. "Are you saying you don't have an issue with incest, Amos?"

"No. I mean, yes. It's horrible, but it was what—two or three thousand years ago when they wrote all that stuff down, right? Did they even know what they were doing at the time?

And does that justify executing someone today? You ask me, that feels like another question."

"It's something we'll have to look at, though, if it goes to trial. What the Bible says." Malloy makes a sharp noise over the phone then, which I can't quite interpret. It's either a cough or a derisive snort.

"Javier," I say, "was pretty straightforward, you know."

"About the murder?"

"Yeah, sure, but more about what a sinner Pinky was. How he just couldn't take it anymore. How he snapped. That's the kind of thing could hang a jury. He'll probably say he did what he did because he was on a mission from God. He'll take the stand and quote chapter and verse from Exodus. All you need is one member of the jury to buy into that. On the other hand, it could be entertaining."

"I'm laughing already."

"Absolutely. But you can't leave this to a new hire. What you'll really need is a DA who has his Old Testament down pat. More than the California Penal Code, anyway. Somebody who can paint the big picture."

"I don't know what you're talking about, Amos."

"I'm talking about history, Bill."

"What's history got—"

"Look, it was scribbled down in the desert a long time ago. I know it. You know it. But that doesn't mean we have to tie ourselves up in knots over it today. That was a long time ago."

"So?"

"So you want a prosecutor who can speak to that. The Torah demanded the death penalty for incest, okay. He has to admit that up front. Get it out of the way."

"Why?"

"Why? To put it in perspective, that's why. Sure, he has to say, they frowned on incest back then. But not just incest. All kinds of things. If you got shit-faced after sundown on Friday night. If you slept with your best friend's husband. If you got mad at your mom and told her to go to hell. According to the Torah, you die. That's how Javier saw things. Go figure."

"I don't have to figure," Malloy says. "I just need to gather some hard facts, see where they take me. But for now, I agree with you, counselor. I'll hold off on Risa."

"Thanks, Lieutenant. I appreciate it."

When I get home that evening, there's hardly anything to eat in the refrigerator, so I end up taking Loretta out to dinner. There are a lot of new places around, and I used to want to try them out, but now with her condition, she can get finicky, so I stick with what's tried-and-true. It's a little family joint we go to on Beverly Boulevard, just east of La Cienega, called Mandarette. Not the most fabulous Chinese food I've ever had, but the owners are kindly, they work hard, and they always find a nice cozy corner table for us where we can watch the joggers and the cars go by. While you wait to be served you can stare up at the classy tin ceiling. And after you've cracked open your fortune cookie and read what's inside—"You will find success one day if you just keep at it"—no one minds if you sit there sipping tea for another hour, which we do. Loretta likes Chinese tea. She likes the whole tea experience, in fact. I tell her she must have been a Chinese princess in another life, and she likes that idea, too. Eventually, I look down at the remains of our meal. The rice has gone cold and the crispy sesame beef has begun to congeal on the plate. I signal for the check, and when the waiter comes, some cardboard take-out boxes. That's when all the events of the day start to tumble into place.

"How is your murder case?" Loretta asks suddenly, lowering her teacup. She used to quiz me a lot about what I was up to, but in the last couple years that has sort of petered out. I am surprised.

"Now, what brought that up?"

"Your case," she says again, more emphatically, "I want to know what you've done. I'm your wife." She says this last part almost like it's an ultimatum, like I should remember that, or else.

"Well, today," I say, "Omar and I went out to Eagle Rock and spoke to a man named Javier Escovedo. And by the time we were done, I'd gotten him to open up and explain why he killed Pinky."

"Who's Pinky?"

"The man Javier shot. He was my client for a while. Lived up on Mulholland Drive. You remember where that is, don't you?"

"You used to take me there to cuddle at night. We did things. I remember, yes."

"Those were the nights, huh?"

"Pinky was your client. You never told me that. Did he pay you?"

"Eventually," I say with a shrug. "It took him a while. But then he died. Not too many people write checks after that."

She gives me an odd look, squints her eyes, lifts her porcelain cup, and swallows the last of her tea.

I don't joke with her, not like I used to, because she's become very literal in the past year or so. When she talks, she only wants to talk about certain things. Food and Carmen and the many friends she thinks she has on television. Sometimes she asks about me, but I know I'm on the periphery. It's a kind of selfishness she practices. A selfishness born of necessity. I don't blame her. Words have specific meanings, and she seems to hold them more closely to her than ever before. She likes words that keep her safe. "Who do you work for now?" she asks. "Are you working now? Are you getting a paycheck? Tell me."

"I'm working for Pinky's daughter," I say. I reach across the table and cover her hand with my own, rub her fingers gently. I don't tell her that his daughter was also his mistress. That would ruin a perfectly good evening, I figure. She wouldn't understand, so I leave it alone.

"This time I'm buying you lunch, Amos, even though you're a royal pain in the butt sometimes and you talk too much and you don't deserve it." We're working our way through the menu at Musso & Frank on Hollywood Boulevard. I can tell by the sarcastic tone Malloy is taking that he really thinks I'm a great asset to the LAPD in particular and to law-abiding citizens in general.

"The word I like is *tuchus*, Lieutenant. I'm a pain in the *tuchus*, yes. Thank you very much."

Musso's is Bill's favorite restaurant, although he has a big soft spot for the Original Pantry on Figueroa. I get that. The Pantry is food for the working stiff. It's cash only but cheap, and the line to get in can be long. Some of the staff can also be a little hard-boiled; you look at them and you think maybe they're all fresh out of Folsom. But today we're sitting at Musso's, and Musso's is where he chooses to celebrate. It's old Hollywood, elegant in the manner of your late Aunt Dorothy, who drank bourbon and did the Charleston. It's got dark, cool, padded booths and waiters plodding around in red uniforms with towels draped over their arms. When you step through the door here, your first impulse is to order a martini. I never do, not at my age, but it's that kind of place. It's been around forever, and it still serves up giant platters of food from another era, when nothing was organic and they didn't skimp on butter. The last time we were here one of us (I forget who) had liver and bacon. You don't see that on menus anymore.

It's been unspeakably hot in LA, even though it's the week between Christmas and New Year's. Something to do with El Niño, they say. Or La Niña. One of those things. It's so hot, I'm wearing the vintage Hawaiian shirt I picked up at Jet Rag on La Brea. Loretta loves this *shmata*, says it makes me look like an old fading Jewish movie star. Well, I admit, I'm old, and I'm Jewish. When I win an Oscar, we can talk about the rest.

Malloy's got his tan summer suit on and he's lost the tie. Still a cop, though, no doubt about it. We order. He has the corned beef and cabbage; I have the oyster stew.

"I thought Jews don't eat oysters," he says quietly as the waiter walks away.

"Jews in Egypt didn't eat oysters," I tell him. "Jews in America? We eat whatever the hell we want. I do, anyway."

He nods, taps his spoon down rhythmically on the white linen tablecloth. It's been three days since they brought Javier Escovedo in for questioning. Three whole days, and I haven't heard a word. Not that I'm entitled, but I'm interested. Let's just say that up front.

"This case hasn't panned out the way we expected," he begins. "Not nearly."

I look at him. "You got your man, didn't you?"

"Yes," he says. "Yes and no."

The waiter sets a basket of warm sliced bread and a dish of butter before us. Malloy reaches over, takes a piece, then puts it back down.

"We can't charge Javier with killing Pinky."

"How come?"

"Well, he admitted it—to you. But he hasn't said a word to us. In fact, now he's not offering any help at all."

"I don't understand, Bill. He was glad to get it off his chest when we talked to him."

"Yeah, well, that was then."

"You asked him about the gun?"

"Of course. He says he doesn't know what happened to it."

"So is he still in custody? You can't keep him indefinitely without a charge, can you?"

"Oh, well, we're charging him. That's not a problem. Not for Pinky, though. Turns out Javier murdered Ray Ballo."

"He admitted to that?"

"No," Malloy says. "Not exactly. But we have surveillance video of him outside Ballo's apartment before and after the time of death. And there are a few partial prints in the apartment that match. Javier hemmed and hawed, even after we showed him the video, then he said he went there to pay Ray Ballo off and that things got out of hand. Self-defense is what he said. We're not buying it, but it doesn't matter."

"Pay him off? I'm not following you."

"I don't know what's true, Amos. Everybody's pointing fingers at everybody else. If you listen to how Javier tells it, Risa was the one who killed Pinky."

"Javier saw her do it?"

"No, he says that he and Pinky struggled over the gun, it landed in the grass, and Risa picked it up. That's when Javier claims he got in his car and left."

"Okay," I say, "I guess that's possible."

"And if you believe Javier," Malloy continues, "then that means Ray saw her kill him. He was probably the one eyewitness we could have used."

"If he'd lived long enough."

"Right. If he'd lived. And if he testified. According to Javier," Malloy says, "Ray realized early on that his silence was worth something. That's when he started blackmailing Risa."

"I thought he loved her."

"I think he probably did, at some level. Pinky loved her, too. But what does that prove? People are fucked up," Malloy says. "He was blackmailing her, though. There's no question. I sent Jason and Remo out to talk to that singer in his country band, Phoebe? Maybe you remember her? Cute little thing."

"I do."

"She told us the night before he died, Ray got seriously drunk. Started mumbling all kinds of strange stuff. How he'd landed himself a new career. How he needed a lot more money from Risa, said she owed him now—big time."

"Okay," I say. "But why did Javier have to pay Ballo?"

"I thought about that," Malloy says. "My opinion? Risa was terrified of leaving her apartment in Van Nuys. We were watching her day and night. She couldn't move, not without some cover. Thought she'd get arrested. So she wired money into Javier's account, asked him to break it down into small bills and bring it in a bag to Ray's. That's when things went south."

"How much?"

"Twenty grand. And that may have just been the first installment, who knows."

"You ever find it?"

"We did, yes. It was sealed in black plastic in the back of Javier's freezer, behind a couple pints of ice cream. He probably should have left it at Ray's. That would have been a lot smarter. Then maybe the Burbank cops would have gone on thinking it was just a drug deal gone bad."

"So now what? Where does that leave us, Bill?"

He purses his lips. I can almost see the wheels spinning inside his head. He is a consummate professional. He'd like nothing better than a clean outcome for all this tumult. A moral ending. We all would. "I don't know," he says, shaking his head. "Right now Javier's being charged with second degree murder. Ray Ballo's a failed extortionist, in every sense of the word. And Risa Barsky? She's an incest victim. I can't imagine what special kind of hell that is. She'll be haunted forever. And the thing is, she may very likely be our killer."

"You think?"

He nods. "A killer who's gonna go scot-free. It's bad luck, is all. I'm not the DA, of course, but I don't see how we can touch her with what little we've got. The optics would be terrible. How's that for a scorecard? You tell me."

The food arrives then, the steam rises, and for a few minutes we stop talking to pay attention to why we came here in the first place. The oyster stew is good, but what Bill's recounted has left me sad and slightly sick in my stomach. Where did I go wrong? How could I have put even an ounce of trust in any of these people? I drink all the ice water in my glass tumbler. A waiter steps up and pours me another, and I drink that down, too. Even though it's cool in here, I'm feeling off-balance. I'm starting to sweat. I'd ask for a martini about now if I thought it would do any good.

"Sometimes you have to take what you get," Malloy says. "I'm not happy myself. But I figured you'd want to know, right? It's just what it is."

Chapter 25

FOR TWO WEEKS I sit around my apartment and mope. Omar calls me once, says he's in the neighborhood and do I want to meet him at Molly Malone's to talk and grab a beer? I think about it for a second or so, then realize I'd be lousy company and turn him down. Hey, maybe another time, all right? That's what I tell him. Sure, he says, sure, you bet. And after we get off the phone, right away my ears begin to burn and the voices start cranking away in my head. I never used to listen to critics, but now they're at my throat, all ganging up on me. I feel ashamed of myself. I pace the living room and stare at the wine spots on the carpet, and I imagine I hurt his feelings. That's what I think, even though I know it's crazy. It's just a beer, he'll get over it. He's young and tough, and no matter what I said, we go back a long way, he'll still love me in the end, I'm sure of that. But now? Now I'm letting him down, and a voice inside is telling me it's too damn late.

As a kind of atonement, I play checkers all afternoon with Loretta. I always let her win. She likes that. Years ago we used to play chess, and back then she would beat me on a regular basis. Now we're down to checkers. It's okay, though. Dr. Ali says what really matters most is keeping her mind occupied. You don't want her drifting off, he cautions. As if drifting off was something I could somehow prevent.

What I notice is that he never talks about me and my mind. That's because I'm not his patient. I get that, all right. Thing is, Loretta's not the only one here. Both of us live in this fucking apartment. We breathe the same air. That's what I should say to the doctor. What about me? I might drift off, too, I want to tell him. Did you ever consider that? I might drift off. But in the end I keep my mouth shut. He's only doing his best, after all, what they trained him to do in med school. He separates us, draws distinctions, one from the other. It's not his fault.

New Year's Eve comes and goes. The city puts on a massive spectacular fireworks display. From my ninth-floor bay window I also catch dozens of other homemade demonstrations. There's green and red and golden joy sparking up over Echo Park and East LA, and in the back alleys of Hollywood, young men, imbued with a wild spirit of optimism, are running around and laughing and sipping beer; they're playing with matches and sending cheap Mexican ordnance as far as possible into the night sky. This is anarchy, that's what I whisper to Loretta, who's still lingering over her ravioli. She looks up from her plate, asks me what that means, anarchy. I smile, shake my head. Nothing, I say. Nothing, forget about it. I stare back down into the streets below. Just a few miles away, maybe around Melrose and Normandie, another red flare goes up. It's a war zone. All these pops and screams and whistles, I'm sure they drive the fire department mad.

I read the story in the *Times* about Javier Escovedo. It's buried in the back pages, just below the fold, and right next to a piece about climate change. His trial for second degree murder is set to start next month in Burbank. Meanwhile he's out on bail. He's found himself a high-profile lawyer from Beverly Hills—Meredith Lincoln—to represent him, and from the little I can glean, it looks like they're pinning everything on the self-defense idea. The reporter cites an alleged dispute between the two men, that's all. There's a startling picture of Javier standing there with his lawyer on the courthouse steps sparring with the press. Javier's in a dark sport coat that's entirely too big for his frame, like something he just pulled off a sales rack at J.C. Penny. Also, his hair is out of place and his face is worn. Ms. Lincoln, on the other hand, is dressed to the nines. Red pantsuit, high heels, gold earrings. I've seen her on television before, and I thought she mostly handled celebrity divorces and such, but what do I know? Maybe she's branching out. She chooses her words surgically. No mention of the Pincus Bleistiff affair, except to say that her client, Mr. Escovedo, had worked for him for many years, a devoted servant and all that. No mention of why Javier decided to knock on Ray Ballo's door in the first place, no talk of the bag filled with cash. And not one syllable about Risa Barsky, either.

I read through the piece a second time, slowly, just to see if I missed anything, and when I come to the end, it strikes me that in the big scheme of things, a murder trial in Burbank is really pretty small beer; maybe the only reason it landed in the *LA Times* is because Meredith Lincoln wanted it there to pad her résumé. Then I fold the paper over and lay it down on the coffee table. Loretta is calling me from the kitchen. Do I want to play another game of checkers?

"Is that what you want?" I ask.

"That's what I want."

The studio at Sunset and Doheny is modern, I guess you'd say, like a lot of buildings in LA. A soft-white, stucco two-story affair that started out as one thing and turned into something else. I can't quite figure it out. It's very roomy, maybe too roomy, in fact, for what they really needed. It also feels vague and unloved, like a work in progress, like some decorator put stuff in on a whim to see if he liked it or not. Sure, right now it's a recording studio, but it could be anything from a dental office to a car dealership. The minute you step inside, you feel the air-conditioning hard at work and Johann Sebastian Bach filtering peacefully down through the fifteen-foot ceiling. Downstairs is the reception and office area. Three young women with short, mannish haircuts are tapping away at computers behind a raised, polished black-slate countertop. I don't know why the countertop is there, except as a barrier. I look hopefully over at the typing pool. My presence doesn't seem to affect them one iota; or maybe it does, but still they don't glance up from whatever it is they're doing. There's an art exhibit on the wall—delicate, whimsical sketches of musicians with their instruments—and through the large sunlit windows just above the file cabinets, the architect added a private patio beyond, a green, leafy sanctuary complete with outdoor tables and chairs. I let my mind wander; I picture myself opening a paper sack with my peanut butter sandwich inside at one of those tables and I think, *Okay, Parisman, this might not be such a bad place to work. I could probably get used to this.*

That's downstairs. Upstairs is where the music is made. There's a wide staircase, but if you've got heavy equipment to lug around—drums, say, or a stand-up bass, you take the elevator. I don't have anything to carry, but my knees are acting up today, so I step into the elevator and press number two.

Seems like they're not planning to decorate much on the second floor. Either that or they haven't given it any thought so far. Here it's all about functionality, a word I've never embraced, but it fits in this instance. The walls are bare, cement and rebar; the carpet is old; and the bank of mixing machinery is tucked away behind a thick glass barrier. On the other side, five male musicians are seated on metal folding chairs. They're wearing blue jeans and short-sleeve shirts, and they're huddled together in a semicircle listening to the engineer explain things.

He's a lanky young man with some stubble around his chin and a long, droopy red ponytail. His name tag says Randy. Actually, it says "Hi, I'm Randy," which anyone in their right mind would be embarrassed to wear, but not him, apparently.

"Don't worry about mistakes," he's saying as I walk in. "You're going to make them, everyone does, that's just how it is. Let it be, okay? This doesn't have to be perfect. Just relax. If I need to, I can go back later on and correct each tune, note by note. Leave it to me."

The musicians nod and start to whisper among themselves. One takes a long, thoughtful swig from a plastic bottle of mineral water by his feet. The trumpet player makes a few rude noises on his axe, then sets it down. It's not all the same guys from the Simchat Torah party, but I recognize two of them from the old Dark Dreidel band. "These machines are kind of magic that way," Randy continues. He looks down at his wristwatch. "As soon as Ms. Barsky gets here, we'll get started, okay?"

He turns away. That's when he notices me standing at the doorway. "And your name?"

"Parisman," I say. "Amos Parisman. Ms. Barsky said she'd be willing to meet with me here for a few minutes. But don't worry. I won't take up much of your time."

"Hey, it's not my time, man. It's her time. She's paying for it." Then he raises his eyebrow and cocks his head, still unsure. "So you're not with the band?"

"Do I look like I'm with the band?"

"Not exactly."

I hand him my business card, which he glances at, grimaces, and gives back to me. Now he has adopted a blank expression. "Investigator, huh? What's she done wrong?"

"It's a long story, Randy. I'm not gonna bore you with it. She and I just need to talk a bit. Clear up a few things. In private, if you know what I mean."

He shrugs, points a lazy finger toward another room at the end of the landing. "I guess you can use that space if you want to be alone together. That's the boss's office. He's in Hawai'i 'til next Friday."

"Lucky man."

"Newly married man," Randy says. His voice is flat. I can't quite tell what he means by that, whether he's pessimistic about the marriage his boss has just made or whether he's dismissive of marriage in general.

The elevator doors open then, and Risa Barsky steps out. She has a sheaf of music under her arm, and she's wearing a dark gray tracksuit and white tennis shoes. It looks like she's lost weight since we last spoke. Her face is gaunt and her hair seems thinner than I remember.

"Hi," I say.

"Oh," she says. "You came. I wasn't sure you'd show up."

"Well, like I told you on the phone, there are just a few things—"

"Yes, of course," she says matter-of-factly. "We should settle this once and for all. I'd like to move on." Then she says hello to the band, hugs two of them, and shakes hands with everyone else as she passes out the sheet music.

Randy points again to the boss's office. "If you need to talk, that's about as private as it gets around here. Unless you want to go out to the patio."

"No, no," she says, "that works." She turns back to the band. "This won't take very long. Why don't you run through some of this without me?"

I lead her into the office and click the door closed behind her. It's not a huge room we're in, little more than a glorified closet, really, and nothing at all suggests that it belongs to an important person. There's the usual oak desk and chairs. It's got a nice arched window that faces out onto the street, but you can't see any traffic from here, just the tops of a couple of palm trees. Across the street below is a Wells Fargo bank and a beauty salon with Vietnamese writing over the doorway. I take the padded chair behind the desk, and she settles into a comparable one on the other side and crosses her legs. I'm staring at a classic poster of Jimi Hendrix on the far wall, the one we're all familiar with, the one where he seems to be bent over in a frenzy, pushing and pulling impossible notes out of his guitar, notes you can barely hear, notes that simply don't exist in the universe. In front of me there's a push-button telephone plugged into the wall, an old framed snapshot of an anonymous man—the boss?—and two little girls in braces at the beach, a Starbucks coffee mug filled with pens and pencils, a yellow legal pad, a stapler, and a laptop computer, but it's been turned off. There are also three manila folders stacked up neatly on the right-hand corner and what looks like two weeks' worth of unopened mail in a blue metal holding bin.

I throw up my hands. "Guess these are the perks of being an executive," I say. There's derision in my voice, which she gets immediately.

"They're new," she says. "Still moving in, really. I think that's the reason they're letting me record here. Not that many bookings, I mean. Not yet."

I nod. "You know why I wanted to come down and talk with you in person, Risa?"

"No," she says, "not really. I was surprised when you called. I mean, I thought everything had been worked out. The police told me they weren't going to press charges, which, I have to tell you, was a huge weight lifted off of me."

"No, you're right," I say. "The DA's a good guy. He's not going to charge you with anything." I prop my fist just under my chin. "But that doesn't mean you're innocent."

"What do you mean by that?" She's gone on alert. The room is suddenly an echo chamber. Her face is taut and she's leaning forward now, trying to catch every syllable.

"It means," I say slowly, "that they think you've pulled off the perfect crime. Which is a compliment in their world. You don't see it very often. You killed somebody, Risa. You know it, and they know it, but nothing's going to happen. Pretty amazing, huh?"

"They think I killed Pinky? I didn't! I. Did. Not. I already told you, Ray Ballo killed him."

"Right. He was more likely than you to shoot him, I'll give you that. But unfortunately, Ray's dead, so we can't turn around and ask him to back you up, now can we?"

She doesn't speak for a moment, but she's staring straight at me. She purses her lips. "No," she whispers. "It's sad. Ray's gone, too."

"Of course," I go on, "you could maybe get Javier to speak up for you. He heard the argument, right? He's the one who came out with Pinky's gun. That's what he told the police, anyway. If the gun hadn't ended up on the grass, well then, Ray wouldn't have picked it up, would he?"

"Javier brought out the gun, it's true."

"Exactly. But that's not what you told me. You told me Ray found the gun in the glove compartment. You hit a bump, remember? That was one story."

"Yes," she admits. "I told you that. Only it wasn't true."

"No, it couldn't have been true. Glove compartments just don't pop open like that, and even if they did, Pinky'd be unlikely to keep his gun there, let alone a loaded gun. He had a gun because he was scared to death of burglars. That's why he bought it in the first place."

"All right," she says. "I lied. Now let it go."

"That was the first story," I say. "Then you told me that business about Javier coming out of the kitchen waving a gun and scaring you and Ray off. How you heard gunshots as you were leaving. Which would seem to pin the blame on poor old Javier. Any truth to that?"

"Yes," she says almost before I can finish the sentence, "that's what happened, I swear."

I shake my head. "I don't buy that either, Risa. You wanna know why? Because the minute Pinky died, you started funneling cash to Ray. Large amounts. Plastic bags full of cash. And Javier was your go-between. What a guy, huh? Now, if it was me, you see, I'd steer clear of Javier. After all, he just killed someone in cold blood. And you were around that night. Which makes you a possible witness. Me, I'd be afraid of what he might do next. But you didn't do that, did you? No, you called him up, you said you wanted him to deliver cash to your ex-boyfriend. Now that takes chutzpah, Risa."

Through the glass panel I can hear the band practicing, faintly, the same musical phrase again and again.

"I wanted to help him out," she says finally.

"Help him out, right. He was in a tight spot. That's what you said."

"It's what I said. Word for word."

"The trouble is, Risa, it doesn't square with the truth. Ray Ballo had a steady gig. He was a working musician. He wasn't rich, but he was making the rent. He didn't need your money to get by. Not really."

She sighs. "No, no, it was true. Up to a point, I mean. He was a decent human being and he was just living hand-to-mouth. That crummy old apartment he had before. It gave me the creeps just to walk in the door. I wanted to help him out if I could. Nothing wrong with that, is there?"

"Not a thing," I say. "But I think I have to disagree with you. Ray might have been a nice guy—once upon a time, at least."

"He was always a gentleman."

"Of course," I say, "but when Pinky died that night…gosh, I don't know, Risa. It was so violent. It had to have been a shock. And you must have noticed. Didn't it seem to you like it did something to Ray? Like all of a sudden, he got these strange new ideas?"

"What are you talking about?" she says.

"The latest lie, Risa. That's what I'm talking about. Javier's already told the cops about how you were being blackmailed. And Ray wasn't too good at keeping it a secret, either. Half his band knew something was up. What I'm saying is, you don't have to lie anymore."

"He wanted money," she mumbles under her breath. "More and more money." She bites her lower lip, tugs compulsively at the ends of her hair. "I tried to help, but—"

"Now, that's the part I don't get," I tell her. "If Javier waved his pistol around and scared both of you off, if it's like you say, that Javier killed Pinky, then what kind of hold could Ray Ballo possibly have on you? Just tell me. Because so far as I know, an innocent person can't be blackmailed."

She goes silent then, tense. I see her eyes darting back and forth.

"Don't you see, Risa? You can't have it both ways."

"They were wrestling," she says quietly. "They were wrestling, and the gun slipped out of Javier's hand. It fell on the ground. I—I picked it up and pointed it. I shouted at them to stop. Stop, I said. Please stop. I begged them. They wouldn't. That's—that's when it went off." She bites her lower lip again. Tears are welling up in her eyes, tumbling down. "I don't know what you want from me," she mumbles. "All I want is to push this thing—this awful, disgusting thing—as far away as possible. I just want to go on with my life. I'm a simple person, really. I just want to sing, that's all. Have you ever heard me sing, Mr. Parisman? I think I have a good voice. A special voice. I think I can bring something true and wonderful to life. That's—that's worth doing, right?"

"It's worth doing, Risa. You bet it is. And as I said before, the good news is that no one's going to charge you with murder. There's no evidence. That's the whole thing. In the end it's just talk. I'm glad you told me, though. I am. You may have pulled the trigger—"

"I did," she says. "Once."

"Once? Did you hit him?"

She winces. "I don't know. Maybe. It was dark. He was on his knees. Does it matter?"

"Probably not," I say. "You tried. The other shots finished him off, for sure. But who—?"

"Javier grabbed it away from me then. That's when Ray and I ran back to the car. I heard him firing as we were driving off. I don't know how many."

"But don't you see? All that stays in here, between us. It doesn't count as evidence. I can't take it into a courtroom. And you want to know something else? I'm not about to. Not today. Not ever. Why would I? Pinky was hardly a perfect human being. What he did to you was—was unforgivable." I reach across and cover her hand with my own. "This has to end. Right now you're free to move on with your life. No matter what happened. That's the good news."

"I guess that's true," she says, brushing back a tear and forcing up a smile. "I'm free."

Chapter 26

THE WORLD DOESN'T CHANGE when you solve a case, or even when you don't solve it, for that matter, and the killer goes free. You feel like a failure for a while, and that's a crummy sensation, but life is full of failures, isn't it? Wrong turns. Dead ends. Shutouts. Sometimes you just don't have the evidence to give to a jury. Sometimes a case will send you scampering down five different alleys, every one of them blind. And sometimes, like this time, justice simply eludes you. The fog never lifts. A man is dead, and all you can do is make a guess—and it's not even an educated guess—at what really happened that night on Mulholland Drive. You give it the old college try. Then you leave it the hell alone.

It's a Saturday morning, a little after 11. Valentine's Day is weeks away, but on television it's like someone's fired a starting pistol; they're already off to the races. They're talking about chocolates and sports cars and panties and diamonds. Diamonds for the woman in your life. I see it plastered on the rear ends of buses and inside magazines I pick up at the doctor's office. This time don't hold back. Give her what she's always wanted. That's a helluva message.

The light changes then, and I cross Hauser heading west. There's a skinny teenage girl planted on the bench at the bus stop. Her legs are crossed. Her jeans are torn. Her hair is short and blond and needs a brush. Also something about her tells me she hasn't had a shower in a while. A runaway? Maybe. She's working on a cigarette with one hand and manipulating her cell phone with the other. I pause for a split second, then I walk on. There's probably a story there, okay, and I'll bet you a nickel it's sad, but she didn't ask me to help, now did she.

Loretta and me, we don't do presents anymore; we're too old and practical for that kind of *mishigas*. But if I were God, you know, if I could give her anything in the universe, it sure wouldn't be diamonds. No, not at all. I'd give her back her mind. Fuck diamonds.

The sun is shining relentlessly. Omar meets me on the corner of Gardner and Third, next to the bronze statue of Haym Salomon. "One of my people," I tell him. "He put up a lot of money for George Washington during the Revolutionary War. Kept him afloat."

"Why'd he do that?"

"I dunno, I guess he was a true believer. Some people fight with guns. That's all they have. Haym had cash. Turns out you can't fight a war without money, not for long, anyway, not really. That's what bankers are for."

"Yeah, but it was a loan," Omar says derisively.

"A loan that was never repaid," I say.

We walk together under the jacaranda trees, past a sleeping homeless couple and down the dirt path that leads to a softball diamond. There's a pickup game going on. A bunch of stocky, middle-aged guys in T-shirts and shorts and caps, running around, shouting encouragement in English and Spanish, trying to stay forever young. I can sympathize. We plop ourselves down in the grass near the first base line to watch.

I tell him I'm sorry for not showing up for a beer when he asked me the other night, that I was worn out and just plain overwhelmed by the whole Pinky Bleistiff matter. "You wouldn't have wanted to be within three feet of me," I say. "You didn't miss much."

"Yeah," he says. "But you did." Then he tells me he heard from a Latino lawyer friend of his downtown that they're not going to press charges against Risa. That's the word, at least.

"The lieutenant told me that, too. Can't say I'm surprised. I'm sure the DA was always reluctant to put her on the stand.

Who'd want to open up that whole can of worms about incest? Can you imagine how that would look?"

"Exactly," Omar says. He pulls a toothpick out of his shirt pocket and starts working it idly around in his mouth.

"On the other hand," I say, "they still have the Ballo case. It shouldn't be a total loss, if you know what I mean."

"The Burbank cops are handling that," says Omar. "And don't quote me, but they seem to like things simple in Burbank. What I heard. My friend thought they're going to try to put it all on Javier."

"Both murders?"

Omar shrugs his shoulders. "Ballo's for sure," he says. "They've got surveillance video, fingerprints, the whole enchilada, really. And it would be nice—convenient for everyone—if he copped to both of them."

"Not for him," I say. "Not if his attorney has anything to say about it. She's sharp."

"Of course," Omar says. "But you can see how they'd lay it out, can't you? Risa goes to get her things out of Pinky's house. She brings Ray along because she's scared. She and Pinky get into a shouting match at the door. Javier comes running out with the gun. He doesn't know what's going on. There's a struggle. Words go back and forth. Everybody's emotions are revved up. Maybe that's when Pinky opens his big mouth, admits that Risa's really his daughter. His flesh and blood. Maybe it's all too much for Javier and he snaps. Bang, bang. Adios, Pinky."

"Maybe," I say. "Although right now Javier's still not talking about that part. He told us, and okay, he said he told it to his priest, but more than that, it gets pretty murky."

"Murky's the word," Omar says. He extracts the toothpick from his mouth and holds it in his two fingers like a tiny baton, like he's a teacher up at the blackboard making a point. "I don't know what they do with it, man. All I know is if they wanted to, they could probably tell a damn good story that he killed both of them. He had reason to kill, you know what I mean? And I tell you what, man, if I was on that jury, I'd believe it."

The guy at bat, a short, heavyset, unshaven fellow in an old tattered Dodger blue jersey with VALENZUELA printed on the back, whacks the ball far into the left field corner. The man on third scores. The ball winds up in the bushes, and the batter, who was running at top speed, turns at first. He sees it's going to be lost for a good long while, so he slows down and trots around the bases, beaming, clapping his hands over his head in triumph.

"Wow," I say. "He put that one away, didn't he?"

Omar nods.

I nod, too. I don't tell him what I know. That Risa fired the first shot. That as he lay on the ground, Javier grabbed the gun and she ran back to the car. That it was Javier who finished him off. I could tell him, but he's put together a wonderful scenario of his own. What good would it do?

And as it turns out, Omar's dead right about the eventual trial, which is not a trial but a meeting, a negotiation, a compromise worked out by both sides. In court for slightly more than an hour, Javier raises his right hand and pleads guilty, not just to killing Ray Ballo, but also to the murder of Pincus Bleistiff.

I managed to get ahold of the transcript. On the witness stand Javier states that he felt he was commanded by God to put an end to the pestilence that Mr. Bleistiff represented. That while he feels deep remorse for his action in the heat of the moment, he believes that his reading of the Bible required him to do this. He also states that subsequent to Mr. Bleistiff's death, Ray Ballo was extorting money from Risa Barsky, threatening to claim that she was responsible for Bleistiff's murder. That he had gone over to Mr. Ballo's apartment intending to pay him money on Ms. Barsky's behalf but that Ballo had insisted it wasn't enough, that he was going to take the money and expose Ms. Barsky anyway. Escovedo claims he tried to leave and that unfortunately a fight had ensued, which resulted in Ballo's death.

Does the prosecution dispute any of this? the judge asks. No, Your Honor, we do not.

The defense attorney, Ms. Lincoln, then makes a short eloquent explication that Javier Escovedo, a loyal servant and a good Catholic who has lived an entirely moral life, was devastated when he learned about his employer's abuse of Risa Barsky. Since the events of November he has been seeing a therapist twice a week and has spent the past several months attending church every day. He has also been actively working at the local food bank in his home community of Eagle Rock.

Her speech concludes with a fervent plea that the court take all of this information into consideration when making its final decision regarding Javier Escovedo, to see him not as a craven killer but as someone torn between his fixed religious beliefs and his sense of duty. There has been much retribution in this matter, Your Honor, but little or no justice here for anyone. No justice for Raymond Ballo, who was drawn in as an innocent but wound up trying to blackmail his lover; no justice for Risa Barsky, a footloose foster child who was lured to Hollywood and methodically abused by her father; no justice for Pincus Bleistiff, who fell in love with his own flesh and blood, who manipulated her for his own purposes and paid the ultimate price; and finally, no justice for my client, Javier Escovedo, a principled man, a God-fearing Catholic, who worked all his life for a depraved individual and simply could not abide it any longer.

These are the facts that need to be weighed, Your Honor, before you can come to a fair and compassionate understanding of this matter. Thank you for your time.

Risa Barsky's album is called *Hum a Few Bars*. It's a mix of sultry jazz standards and Yiddish love songs resurrected from the Depression era and before. It's got a photo of her in a low-cut black evening dress, leaning seductively against a grand piano. There's a debonair young man in a white tuxedo seated on the bench behind her, presumably making music. And on top of the piano itself there's a pair of glasses, each holding something attractive and alcoholic. One looks like scotch on the rocks, the other could be a martini. They're untouched. You can't help but notice the cocktails because they're perfectly lit by a shaft of golden light.

I buy three copies at Amoeba Records and drive over to my local post office at Beverly and Curson. One CD I drop in the mail for Lieutenant Malloy. He probably won't care for her music, I figure, though the band is pretty tight, and there's one standard tune at the end I want him to hear: "Bei Mir Bistu Sheyn" ("To Me You Are Beautiful"). Every Jew over a certain age has heard that. But even if he doesn't exactly approve, I want him to have it just so he'll know that life goes on, that something good can happen, even after a frustrating case like this.

The second one I send with a note to my cousin Shelly. I tell myself he'll appreciate it, because we grew up listening to this stuff in my parents' house, and because even though he acts like a tough, ballsy, know-it-all, when it comes right down to it Shelly's like a balloon: He has nothing inside. Just a lonely old schlub with three ex-wives, all of whom he still secretly pines for. This will crack open his heart, I think, maybe give him back some memories. Good ones, I hope.

The third copy is for me. I bring it back to Park La Brea.

Loretta is giggling in the kitchen with Carmen; they're finishing up a strange new form of dominoes when I come in. This game has no rules, as far as I can tell, and no one's keeping score. I scratch my head: Loretta used to be a whiz at dominoes; she could count and calculate, far better than me. Now, she's laying them down, one by one, even though they don't match. And

Carmen thinks it's just fine.

A minute later, when Carmen says goodbye and closes the door behind her, I head for the living room. I drop my jacket on the couch, turn down the lights, and put Risa's music on.

"What are you doing?" Loretta calls out from the kitchen. "I like the lights on."

"Come over here," I say. "I'll show you."

She pushes her chair away and edges toward me. There's a shyness in her step. Carmen must have spent time with her this afternoon combing out her hair. Now I see it's hanging in ringlets around her shoulders, the way it did when we were first together. Night is falling outside the window.

"Listen," I tell her. "Listen, do you remember this tune?" Then I take her hand, squeeze it gently, lean my tired old cheek against hers. We lapse, like the couple we've always been, into a slow, spontaneous waltz. I can feel her heart beating inside her chest. It's been years, but she hasn't forgotten how to move. No, she has never forgotten. Light and effortless, like a carousel. One, two, three. One, two, three. Round and round. The memory is still there in her feet. "Close your eyes," I whisper. "Close your eyes. Think about the day we met. Let's pretend we're in love."

"Why pretend?" she whispers.

I kiss her then and she responds eagerly. And I close my eyes and smile. And even after the melody ends, we stand there clinging to each other for a long, long time. This is who we are. I breathe her in. It doesn't get any sweeter than this.

A Few Words You Might Be Wondering About

alav hashalom - Hebrew, may he/she rest in peace

alte katchke - an old duck

beshert - fated, destined

bissel - a little bit

boychik - little boy

bubkes - nothing, or a very small amount

chutzpah - nerve, gall, impudence

daven - to recite prayers in Jewish liturgy

farblunget - broken down, wasted

farkachte - addled, confused, mixed up

goyim - non-Jews, gentiles

Kaddish - tradition Jewish prayer for the dead

kasha varnishkes - a cooked dish of bulgur wheat and bow-tie noodles

klezmer - a musical tradition blended from Eastern Europe; Jewish party and folk music

L'chayim - To life! Cheers! Traditional Jewish toast

landsman - a countryman, a fellow Jew

le sholem - (Hebrew) May he/she rest in peace, term invoked after the name of a deceased person

luftmenschen - dreamers, literally, "cloud persons"

macher - big shot, wheeler dealer

mamzer - bastard

megillah - a long involved story, or account, usually stated as "the whole megilah"

mensch - a man, in usage, a principled, decent man

meshugenah - nonsense, silliness

mishigas - craziness

mishpuchah - family, could be extended family

mitzvah - (Hebrew) a good deed

nebich - so what, whatever, big deal, who cares

nu - so, well

nudnik - a pest

oneg - a Jewish social gathering held on Saturday afternoon
   or Friday evening

rebbe - rabbi

schlub - stupid, clumy, oafish person

schmata - literally "rags," but generally understood as
   clothes

shicker - a drunk

shmutz - dirt, filth, grime

shpilkes - pins and needles, connoting anxiety, tension

shtup - sexual intercourse (vulgar)

sufganiyah - (Hebrew) Israeli jelly donuts

tallis - prayer shawl

tchotchkes - knickknacks, little things

tikkun olam - Hebrew, the mystical concept of repairing or
   mending the universe; justice

tsimmis - literally, a Jewish stew, but more usually, a
   commotion, an upset or turmoil

tsuris - hurt, trouble, woes

tuchus - a person's behind, rear end

Acknowledgments

We think of writers as loners, but nothing could be further from the truth. Yes, I often work in solitude at my kitchen table, but God knows I have help. I rely on a small cadre of far-flung fellow writers who read what I'm doing in its various stages. Their criticisms and thoughtful directions have shaped this novel, and I am in their debt.

In particular, I have to mention my writers group friends in Pasadena: Michael Farquhar, Ned Racine, Emily Adelsohn Corngold, and Melina Price. Also Ron Raley in Hollywood, whose screenwriting expertise was instrumental in helping me with plot twists I would not have otherwise thought about. Gracias siempre to Cheryl Howard in New Mexico, whose poetic sensibilities and knowledge of colloquial Spanish make me seem hip. On the legal side, my thanks to attorney Richard Conn and retired judge Ann Dobbs, who not only put up with all my questions, but actually answered them.

My family has been a great source of support. Sons Gideon and Tobias and their respective spouses and children have been there in good times and bad to cheer me on. Also, I should say a word about my brother, Jonathon, who is a veritable fountain of wild ideas when it comes to fiction. I don't often use them, but they let me dare to think outside the box.

As always, I could not have managed without the tender care and nurturing of my staff at Readers' Books in Sonoma: Jude Sales, Thea Reynolds, Rosie Lee-Parks, Brian Massey-Todd, and Barbara Hall. And in terms of its physical creation, I could not have done this without either the eagle-eye proofreading of Monica McKey, or the tutelage of Colleen Dunn Bates and her fearless crew at Prospect Park Books.

Oh, and thanks once again to Lise Solomon of Consortium for first connecting me with Prospect Park. It's that kind of serendipity that makes this world so sweet.

Finally, inspiration for this book comes from many people I love. From my parents, Arthur and Moosie, whose New York working-class lives are partly mirrored in my characters, to my good friend Beth Hanson, who has taught me the value of kindness and patience, to, of course, my late wife, Lilla, whose spirit I hope lives on forever in everything I write.

About the Author

ANDY WEINBERGER is the author of *An Old Man's Game* and a bookseller who opened Readers' Books in Sonoma, California, with his late wife, Lilla Weinberger, in 1991. Born in New York, he grew up in the Los Angeles area and studied poetry and Chinese history at the University of New Mexico. He lives in Sonoma, where Readers' Books continues to thrive.